WOLFHEAD

RORY HEADREN

Typeset in Sabon

Cover design: Kobir Miah
kobir_miah@live.co.uk

Design Consultant: Robyn Ricci
RobynRicci@yahoo.co.uk

Typesetting and publishing by UK Book Publishing
www.ukbookpublishing.com

978-1-916572-10-2

WOLFHEAD

PROLOGUE

It is said that the great rebellion against Rome,
undertaken by British Celts in first century AD,
began with Boudiga. No, it ended with her.

THE NORTHERN FRONTIER, 61 AD

HIS NAME WAS BRENNUS, chieftain of the Abrentii, a sub-tribe of the mighty Brigante nation ruled over by his half- sister, the beautiful yet treacherous, queen Cartimandua. The praise name for Brennus was 'Bear'. To the fighting men of the Abrentii the honoured title of 'Ring-Giver' was also commonly recognised, both forms of address being deemed appropriate.

Toward dawn they approached the unseen river with caution. In this calm spot it seemed impossible that upon the far bank the largest concentration of military might yet witnessed in the land of the Britons, lay out of sight beside the colonia of Lindum on 'The Hill'. The Abrentii knew it only too well. Tough shaggy ponies carried them there, as close to the enemy as their riders deemed safe. Sure footed, bred for speed and endurance, they'd taken a full part in this bloody act of defiance.

The previous day, the Abrentii had launched an all-out assault against an auxiliary turma, a cavalry unit consisting of thirty green-cloaked riders belonging to the elite Petra's Horse, at this time on attachment to legate Balbilus' 20th legion, Valeria. It turned out to be an attack from which few escaped, certainly not Lucidius Salva, who, as Rome's skilled arbiter with the growing client nations of the region, was detailed to arrange certain goods and provisions from the neighbouring king, Tadoc of the Cornovii, regarding the coming campaign against the Drus-Wyd. This was an agreement that Tadoc, aware of its edgy religious implications, was cautious about. So, armed with advice given by his old friend, Volisios of the Coritani, he felt obligated to go along with Rome's plans, at least for now.

This gave an opportunist such as Brennus, the once in a lifetime chance he'd been looking for. A show of solid Abrentii defiance might give him the chance he long awaited, a warning delivered to the oppressor, perhaps even halting its intention to destroy Mona's sacred oak groves and temples standing defiantly upon the far side of the Menai Straits.

A price had been paid for this ambush on Petra, a quarter of the warband being diminished in the bloody business of killing. Taghe and Varan, Brennus' sons, considered it worth the cost, viewing the assault as a wake-up call to all waverers and doubters who feared the awesome, ubiquitous power of Rome.

Daylight began to break as the remaining horsemen silently fanned-out over the slob land. Some of the riders carried severed heads, grisly trophies of war-spoil tied to horse trappings or struck on the upraised spearheads of lances, gory tokens of victory. A fetid smell of dried blood extended equine nostrils and despite the chill air, rivulets of sweat sheened down their flanks.

Taghe, leader of this battle-scarred group, quietly approached the riverbank as a pallid light filtered from above. His trained ear listened carefully for sounds. There were few, save for a soft rattle of harness that accompanied the occasional kiss of metal on metal. Nought else broke the silence, when like a stalking wolf seeking its prey, he sniffed the damp air, recalling that his father oft boasted that his nose could smell out the presence of Rome long before it could be seen. The tale held some worth, Brennus having criss-crossed the deadly flightpath of the eagles on more than one occasion.

It was a pity that the wily old chieftain, owing to age and infirmity, was absent, the final act being left to Taghe who, after briefly exchanging a determined glance with brother Varan, eased his pony quietly forward. A thought that it wasn't just the legions which had to be feared, entered Taghe's mind. The land upon which they now trespassed so boldly also belonged to Volisios of the Coritani nation, a devout hater of Brennus and his troublesome brood, who during one of their many night-time raids, raped and murdered the king's wife and fair young daughter, Alorad. That was a decade ago. During the attack, Volisios, to add to the tragedy, took a crippling wound that would inhibit him from ever again leading a Coritani war-host, this duty passing to his eldest son, the respected prince Armet.

Attempts to hunt down the elusive Abrentii in the wild western regions of Brigantia had so far proved futile for both Armet and his younger brother, Gort. Several times over the years they'd almost snared their hated enemy and several times again found him to be cunningly elusive. Nevertheless, both peoples remained sworn enemies, waging a no-holds barred vendetta, a struggle contested long before the arrival of Rome.

Seconds passed and Taghe scanned the watery scape once again, his taut fingers finding the rich ivory pommel of the sword. The familiar coldness of the hilt gave comfort in the same way as the shield strapped to his muscled arm gave comfort. Such objects were tangible realisations of the warmth of life and death's iciness. A fighting man's things..

From the reedy marsh-bed a bittern's foghorn boom broadcast displeasure at the approach of strangers, startling a family of coots from their haven before vanishing into the mist. A third rider leaving the group came abreast of Taghe and Varan. His name was Stegae Hud. The wooden stave he carried showed a mounted image of the Celtic war god Taranis, bringer of thunder, who cast lightning bolts from his crown. This insignia marked Stegae out to be a secret warrior member of the 'Druse', a name the legionaries gave to Stegae's branch of warrior priests. Like so many practitioners of Druidical teaching he was a wanted fugitive, outlawed by decree of the late emperor Claudius three years previously.

Defiantly he nudged the pony with its burden several paces ahead while a second horseman from the war party came abreast. Dismounting, he dragged the weighty sack to the ground, deftly incising the coarse cloth with a slash of a knife to shake forth the bloody contents. Half a dozen human heads tumbled into the shallows. Moments later, impaled on spear shafts, five were decorating one of the bridges of the two pontoons spanning the river. The sixth, that of the luckless Lucidius Salva, his eyes still appearing to register puzzled astonishment, would serve some other purpose. Taghe received it with a brief nod.

As if on cue, from the river's still unseen far bank, invading the rising mist like the angry bellowing of a bull, came the unmistakable groan of a cornu. Taghe nudged his horse forward a pace, the harsh note of the Roman battle-horn suddenly urging him into action. As the deep throated instrument growled mournfully yet again, the warrior, holding the pale head of the unfortunate arbiter by the hair, swung it above him several times, prior to tossing it onto the bridge. For a space he and the others watched it spiral almost gracefully on the chill air as a weak morning sun finally pierced their cover. The dull thud that followed proved it had been well aimed, gaining a low murmur of approval for Taghe's accuracy from the watching riders at his back.

Later, others would find the blood splattered heads and earnestly seek to punish the Abrentii for what they'd perpetrated. This was inevitable, it would happen. Indeed, Brennus and his brood counted on it.

ONE

A S IF IN A DREAM Gela stood beside a river, its banks thick lined with twisted osier and coarse hawthorn, a place where time stood still.

A remembrance of ancient tales and myths sharpened her senses, drawing from her all that seemed mundane and ordinary. Yet she felt no fear as her eyes focussed on the dark running waters, seeking not to wonder how if time were frozen, the river still ran fast beneath her feet.

A myriad of flickering shapes danced across the surface like fey stars in a doom-laden sky and when she felt compelled to peer closer, the shallows appeared to erupt into a terrifying scene of burning flame, while in the inferno, horses and men screamed in terror before the image slowly dissolved, leaving an icy chill in the air.

While she contemplated these fearful imaginings a dark figure manifested itself at her side, its countenance hidden by a heavy cowled cloak. She felt a calloused hand resting on her milk-white shoulder, a hand with fingers hard as goat horn. The creature stood silent for several seconds before vanishing as suddenly as it came, transferring an inner pain which burrowed deep within her, gripping tightly at the young girl's heart.

When a child, her father Tadoc weaved stories of gods and goddesses hailing from a far-off land, tales where a fearsome giant, with one blazing jewel for an eye, rowed a grey boat which carried into limbo the souls of the dead. At first these narratives frightened her as scary tales for children, like that of the crone Morrigan, decked in her raven black war-robes, goddess of famine and death, but as she grew, she understood their purpose, an attempt to bring order to chaos.

Was this the same figure which violated her thoughts so abruptly?

In the silence, her body shivering beneath her robe, reality brought Gela back into her own world with a jolt, and the river was just a river, one she'd often swam in with her older brother, Fomah. A flash of silver sparkled in the air before her, as a fish flip-flopped back beneath a spreading ripple of water.

She hoped that in time the vision would fade naturally, as others had, yet something warned her that this fleeting glimpse of the otherworld, embodied by the sudden appearance of this cowled apparition, could return to haunt her yet again.

Later she confided her imaginings to Fomah, who was typically dismissive.

'It's that ogre of a man, Brennus the Bear, and his murdering brood that bring forth these idiocies, either that or the teachings of your servant, the old witch, Ulvina.'

'Armet at least is somebody who treats me seriously,' retorted Gela, switching to the defensive.

'Prince Armet is nothing less than a traitor to the Coritani and ourselves!' said Fomah with scorn. 'Son of an ailing king, fast becoming a true slave of Rome. Best beware of him little sister or start making eyes at his brother Gort....... if anyone can find him!' Fomah the warrior, only son of Tadoc, king of the Cornovii, and once Armet's close friend, then walked away, leaving the girl to her private thoughts and what he so scornfully termed her 'infantile fancies'.

Her brother's criticism of the Coritani prince had, though she'd never admit it, cut her to the quick. Once close friends, the present fraught relationship between Fomah and Armet was regrettable. Yet the gulf created by recent events seemed unbridgeable now, and Gela's mind drifted to better days, to a simpler world, before the legions reached their territory.

It was a time of abundance during the feast of Beltane when the young daughter of Tadoc first encountered the prince, a few weeks before her fourteenth birthday, when the hurtling chariot unwittingly showered her with mud. Whilst happily skipping along the path with others of like age, gathering bunches of wildflowers, making her way homeward to arrive in good time for the fire festival, the light-weight vehicle, carrying its three incumbents, swept on past the group of maidens at a dangerous rate, covering the giggling group in a shower of cloying debris.

Amid their boisterous protests, Gela briefly glimpsed the car's driver, a dark-haired, sullen youth, lips set in concentration while gripping tight to the reins of a brace of spirited, grey-dappled ponies. Later she would learn his name was Gort, king Volisios' second son. Yet he wasn't the person who caught her main attention. Instead, her gaze took note of the car's taller male occupant, Volisios' first born, prince Armet.

During the height of the celebrations, Gela joined with the host-dancers to honour her father's guests, giving her an opportunity to observe the prince at closer range. At first, she confessed, she thought his nose a little overlarge and his eyes too brooding, as though his mind harboured graver thoughts. Then she recalled being mesmerised by the chariot's third occupant, Armet's wife, the beautiful fair-haired Tae. Less than a year later she would be dead, cruelly taken by an unknown malady while pregnant with her first child. A devastated Armet, this being an obvious love match was for a long time, inconsolable. Little did Gela know that within another six years she herself would be betrothed to the prince.

TWO

THE EDGE OF THE WORLD they called this part of the misty islands, a strange place. Across the river where their forest world began, foul furies and a host of unknown terrors might well disturb the superstitious. North and west of the recently established Limes, behind the barriers of Humber and Severn, ancient roads overlaid by Rome's pioneers came abruptly to a halt. No other town or settlement worthy of the name, unless one counted the newly created outpost of Deva, half built, undermanned and isolated, yet truly existed. The proverbial sore thumb, one hundred and thirty marching miles from Lindum, it remained the only real military presence guarding the western edge of Rome's long frontier with the warlike Brigante nation.

Further south at Glevum, 2nd legion Augusta, square-on, faced the wild borderlands guarding Wales. Like Lindum she was a sprawling construction, slow in progress, a prime example of Rome's knee-jerk reaction to consolidate a permanent presence along Britannia's restless frontiers, a menace which Augusta was compelled to confront, given the resurgence of hostility offered by the itinerant Silurians. Dedicated guerrilla fighters, using the well-rehearsed tactics of hit and run, a strategy perfected by their betrayed leader, Caractacus, with no small success, their presence remained unnervingly effective. Worn down and dogged by almost continual assault, the dominance of Augusta's cohorts as a capable fighting unit in the region proved severely handicapped.

To the north-east, the Roman colonia of Lindum had problems of its own, things there being only a fraction less fraught than at Glevum. In the territory of their king, Volisios of the Coritani, Huns from the Rhine, horse archers from Syria, Thracian light cavalry, Tungrian lancers and stone-slingers recruited from the sun kissed Adriatic kept vigil, adding to the motley assortment of humanity squatting below 'The Hill.' as many in the army had learned to curse the sprawl of humankind presently dominating the area.

Beneath eyeless sockets of a dozen assembled catapults and ballistae, machines sited more to impress an outsider rather than possessing any defensive value, they stood witness to an alien power. Overshadowed by these monsters stood a file of ten scorpions, smaller weapons which had the capacity to launch their deadly missiles a distance of three-hundred yards or more. Mounted on wheeled carriages for speedy manoeuvrability they could prove fearsome adversaries. 'My babies,' legate Julius Balbilus of Valeria fondly drooled. Only one conclusion could be drawn from such an outward show. It was manifestly clear this was an army of occupation, here to stay.

Around these children of war stood Lindum's outer defences, protected on three sides by a stone-based timber stockade, the river itself being the colonia's fourth deterrent. Within this perimeter lay the disciplined lines of 14th and 20th legions, Gemina and Valeria, those destined to play a major role in governor Paulinus long awaited' 'big push' against the apparent Druid threat based in western Anglesey, a hundred and sixty miles distant.

Beyond and below the stockade and towers, pushing away and drawn toward The Hill, the promise of gain to be had from twenty-five thousand soldiers assembling there, drew large numbers of itinerate traders to daily ply their wares amid a growing jumble of huts, tented dwellings and popular makeshift bordellos, the latter a constant headache occupying the colonia's overworked medics. Further away, two measured Roman miles upstream, camped the bulk of the auxiliaries, both cavalry and infantry, on permanent attachment to all three legions.

Notable absentees from this throng of humanity were three squadrons of Coritani, four hundred chosen horsemen under the leadership of Volisios' eldest son, prince Armet, part of Cerialis' intention to enlist the very first unit of Britons into a legion. Now they shared the nearby holding station of Crococalana along with several other cavalry units, a base garrisoned by an obligatory but not quite trusting century of wary legionaries.

Standing ominously at the colonia's northern outer limit, in a carefully chosen area, stood a row of tall timber crosses. Only one of the six claimed a victim, its timbers bearing the sagging remains of a runaway slave whose luck had finally run out. Left hanging limp in death, his body served warning to any fool choosing to flout Roman law. It was a place most superstitious people sought to avoid, men like optio Priscus and his team for instance, whose task it was to collect the discarded heads from the river pontoon.

Seasoned troops, although trained to observe death in a host of violent ways, they might well have objected to having such a naked form of rough justice displayed at close quarters, with the maxim that there was a time and place for everything. Others had no such luxury of choice. Here, when the wind wafted in the wrong direction, the stench could be overpowering, a stark reminder to anyone who might think of absconding, salt being added to the occasion in the form of a rotting corpse that might be left to hang for days until removed.

Another night would in a few hours' envelope this growing colossus. Rush-brands would spring to life in a recurring ritual, helping to hold back the dark as the army settled down to more hours of boredom mixed with nagging unease. Something had changed since the discovery on the bridge.

Petra's Horse!

Some had already fashioned a feeble joke. A goat butting the arse of a lion, went the jest. Yet the happening couldn't be shaken off lightly. There were few mounted units better than Petra, and their loss was an unsettling event not to be ignored. As far as Cerialis, legate of legion Hispania and overall commander of the colonia was concerned, this ill-timed upset was the last thing his men needed to enhance their morale.

In the land of the Brigante, news that its unpredictable queen had finally ended a tempestuous on-off relationship with Venutius, erstwhile friend of his betrayed hero, Caractacus, was another worry for the legate. That the woman was untrustworthy, was no secret. Despite casting aside her husband, risking the threat of possible civil war, such events did little to weaken her desires, and perhaps even added to her strength. Coupled to this, perhaps even more threatening, the queen commanded the largest army of

Britons outside Rome's new province, her borders a mere javelin's throw from Lindum.

If these certainties weren't bad enough, the legate also feared that her vengeful ex-husband was never going to allow Cartimandua to live in peace. Still chaffing to get even with her for her callousness regarding the trusting Silurian king, Venutius broke from the queen's clutches, gathering to him an unknown number of warriors, fine ingredients for making trouble not only for her, but for Rome itself. To make matters worse, if the latest report proved true, it looked as though this hater of imperialism was set to join forces with Brennus and the Abrentii, the suspected slayers of Petra's Horse. This growing threat to Paulinus' plan to wipe the land clean of the Druse, Rome's name for the rulers of the heathen cult, or the 'wooden heads', as they often contemptuously called them, was to say the least, a worrying possibility.

On another level Cerialis wondered where things stood personally between him and the 'she-wolf,' it being several months since their last encounter. Her armourer, Vellocatus, was said now to be enjoying her bed, a situation that gave the legate the impression that he no longer enjoyed the fickle queen's attention.

Overall, an intangible mood prevailed at the heart of the assembling trio of legions in and around Lindum. The legate, in full charge until governor Paulinus' long-awaited arrival, sensed the presence of legions Gemina and Valeria strongly. This strained atmosphere might well go unnoticed by the passing observer, for all the normal sounds of an encamped army were unmistakeable, the whinnying of a restless mount in the horse-lines, a lesser sound below the loud clatter of cooking pots coming from many kitchens to mix with a bout of sudden laughter over some ribald joke emerging from the tents. All the usual accompaniments that travelled with an army prevailed about The Hill. Yet, as history so often shows, in the short life of man things can go belly-up with unexpected speed.

Cerialis and the presiding Hispanics would be mightily glad to see Paulinus take himself and his army west, their presence continuing to lay a heavy burden on Hispania's local resources, including necessary amenities and hygiene, the latter obviously heightened by growing cases of a sexual nature. This meant that every being on and around the colonia was vulnerable, a subject that the legate would raise at the weekly briefing. Hopefully then things would fall into place, returning Lindum to something akin to normality.

Sitting alone in the praetorium the legate studied the list Straba, his Greek scribe, had earlier dropped on the desk. A copy of the regular army list put the strength of legions in Britannia, including auxiliaries, at around thirty-five thousand men. This seemed a major exaggeration against which a group of senior officers offered their own take on things. There were also other questions circulating of late, a common one being, *why four damn bloody legions?* An astonishing count when it was common coin that a province such as Gaul, twice the area of Britannia, seemed to manage its affairs with only two!

'With this number of legions, we should be nothing short of invincible!' Cerialis complained more than once to friend and secondus, Aquilla. Why did he get the feeling that unconsciously, mighty Rome was gradually moving toward the defensive?

Truth was, no single legion was ever happily up to scratch. As for the hostiles that opposed Rome, their fighting strength would always be hard to calculate. Sometime in the future there would be men who'd think it strange that a ruling power such as theirs, an armour-segmented dinosaur whose soldiers patrolled the frontiers of Germania, challenged the deserts of Africa and the wild hills of the Britons, should have carelessly overlooked one simple weakness.

They'd perhaps become too much accustomed to their own success.

THREE

THE GREATEST EMPIRE ON EARTH had a major problem. Britannia! After eighteen years it had become obvious even to the most casual of onlookers that a guaranteed promise of various precious metals, apparently abundant in the province, looked like a bad case of wishful thinking. Yields of the usual metals, gold, silver, copper, iron and tin, when weighed against the massive expenditure needed to provision four combat-ready legions and their accompanying auxiliaries, had still to materialise. The situation lately led to a bitter exchange of views among the army's senior commanders, with some defeatists bent on persuading their emperor that Rome might have to consider the unthinkable, vacate the island completely and return to Gaul, thereby cutting their losses. What happened at Lindum would only add more water to a stream that was fast beginning to flow, implicating all men gathering in and around the colonia, including those of 9th legion. Hispania.

Half of the contubernium of six that morning, was detailed to clear the bridge of the served heads untidily left by Brennus' Abrentii. The three men should have been four of eight, the designated number, but like the rest of the legion, 8th cohort was seriously under strength, which meant there'd be no more replacements for the foreseeable future.

'I knew it, I bloody knew it!' moaned Philo for the third time, throwing a head carelessly onto the back of the cart pulled by a reluctant mule, both items indented from Hispanic's irritable quartermaster up on The Hill.

'What are you griping about?' said Priscus, senior member of the group. 'It gets us off worse fatigues, so be grateful.'

'Yeh, thanks for nothing! I'll remember that benifit,' Philo muttered.

'It's odd though how we get all the shitty jobs?' remarked Verra, trying to wrestle a stubborn head from the sharp tip of the stave.

'Nothing funny, there,' said Priscus, flatly.' It's Iber. The sodding knob-head hates us, or didn't you know?'

'One fine day someone will stick a dart up his shitty arse,' Verra spat with feeling.

'You'll have to get in line, then,' Optio Priscus joked. 'It's a bloody long list.'

The three legionaries took their time doing the job allocated by centurion Iber, it being less exacting than many of the other tasks that could be theirs during the rest of the morning. Therein lay a question, what to do with fighting men when they weren't engaged in battle?

Thus lay the reason why the arrival of supreme legate Paulinus was awaited with mounting expectation. His presence meant war, the one thing that would put an end to Lindum's destructive lethargy.

The legions had prayed desperately for action! They wanted to kill while at the same time, exacting revenge for Petra. The future in the form of Suetonius Paulinus, would give them that.

The three men, the mule and the cart containing the half-dozen severed heads, slowly made their way along the riverbank to an open area up-stream, some way from the main camp's sprawl. Here the bodily remains including the head of the luckless emissary, Salva, would be cremated. This open area, the place close to where condemned offenders met their end, was a haunted spot that suddenly urged the trio to complete their unenviable task with haste.

FOUR

SOME SICK COMEDIAN had nicknamed it 'the sweathouse', as it was the place where men were sent to suffer or die. Certainly, the surviving pair of Petra's Horse would have preferred to do neither. A disconcertingly youthful looking medic drew back the blood-soaked linen covering the optio's wound and set his lips while he probed. A second, even younger looking orderly, hovering at the medic's elbow, watched the proceedings with feigned interest.

With the steady procession of visitors to the temporary hospital that might have filled an arena, he could have sold tickets, the young medic told himself. *'Temporary* 'suggested that a more permanent structure, like one third of Lindum colonia, remained irritatingly incomplete, meaning the surgeons were obliged to work mostly under canvas, with all the accompanying drawbacks.

'This won't be pleasant,' he said pointlessly to the sedated cavalryman as, with the help of his assistant, he started to unwind soiled rags from the shattered thigh. 'I'm telling you this, so you won't curse me for it later if you ever reach the afterlife, understand?' He continued to speak to the patient as if the man were aware of his presence, more to calm himself than anything else, having only recently been assigned to these more urgent needs in a matter of hours, the legion's senior surgeon having chosen to be suspiciously absent elsewhere. The phrase *'ducking the issue'* came to mind. Being thrown in at the deep end with scant warning, unprepared, he was doing his best to cope with what little he had to hand. Thankfully, help was on its way. It couldn't come fast enough, two further members of Petra having already died this morning under his watch, a fact which prompted the overworked youth's determination not to make this one a third.

He saw the problem. The blood congealed inner wadding to the thigh, a botched job administered in haste during the retreat and now pressing into the vein. With trembling hands, he peeled aside the bandage to uncover a wide gash that the temporary treatment had caused. Earlier, when the trooper was half-awake, a tiny shard of metal was retrieved emitting, despite sedation, a sharp whimper of pain as the second medic applied a liquid concoction into the open cavity. After, he lay still, the penultimate survivor of the turma, his once laboured breath becoming gradually less erratic. The medic carried out his task with as much care as he could muster, knowing he'd managed it in time, experiencing relief that

14

this was a clean wound which would give the trooper a more than fifty-fifty chance of recovery. Finishing up, he indicated the obvious final procedure to a third hovering assistant who began a hasty cleaning of the wound before applying necessary stitches. When completed the wound was salved with healing ointments before bandaging with fresh linen.

A face well recognised round the colonia ducked his head under the tarp and slowly appeared from behind the flicker from half a dozen oil- lamps. Although almost noon, the late-spring day was heavy with cloud and the medic still needed light, the heavy material of the marquee allowing little in terms of vision. 'What brings you here, scribe?' his question identified. 'I thought you of all men might have found something better to do.'

The slim frame of Straba the Greek, secretary to legate Quintus Cerialis, commander of Hispanics, a russet cloak covering his frail figure, produced a nervous smile. 'Take my word for it. I'm not here voluntarily. I've been sent on behalf of the legate to learn more of what happened yesterday, out there,' he jerked his tousled head with visible reluctance in the rough direction of the river pontoons.

The medic spoke, wiping his blooded hands, vigorously. 'A few minutes earlier and your visit would have been noted as an example of very bad timing. This wretch was no easy patient, the drugs taking more time to work than is usual.'

'Will the fellow live?' Straba asked hopefully, his smooth face pale and voice, unsteady. The question sounded like a poor joke, a doubtful assumption coming from a young man not largely known to possess a sense of humour.

'What do you think?' answered the medic, wearily. 'If he does, he'll have to bid farewell to any form of military service in future, unless he's given a desk job, unlikely, I'll grant you. If he's lucky, the wound will heal, but the muscle has been sliced through,' he waved a shard of blood-covered metal under Straba's reluctant nose.

The scribe blanched. 'It seems I've been told the wrong story, that this man had a fair chance of survival,' he gulped, feeling a familiar invasion of sickness in his delicate gut.

'As others were also told,' complained the medic. 'They've been barging in here all morning, getting under my feet, from that damn legate Balbilus to every other rank down to centurion, trying to draw out any information they can get.' He sniffed, plunging his arms up to the elbow in a vessel of warmed water. 'All for nothing, just look at them,' he jerked his head in direction of the survivors. 'I doubt the poor buggers would recognise their own mothers right now, let alone stand up to questioning from half the army.'

Straba, biting his lower lip, took a quick glance at the men lying on the pallets. 'Confidentially speaking, between you and me, I'd shun this place like the plague, had I but the choice,' he muttered, supressing a shudder.

'Pardon my bluntness, scribe. It's been a long session,' observed the medic, drying his fingers with a soiled towel. 'These poor fellows served under Balbilus. You know how that awkward bastard feels about Hispania's legate. His dignity will be mightily pricked had he the slightest suspicion that Cerialis had shown up here to perform what is, in effect, legion Valeria's responsibility. No doubt the old shit will be back, but I'll tell him the same as I'm telling you. Four came in, two will go out, if the gods allow,' he added finally.

As for Straba, the stomach upset he'd suffered after visiting the medical ward reminded him of an old complaint, a curse of a delicate nature not helped by some of the unpleasant sights he was duty bound from time to time forced to witness within the colonia's confines. Indeed, there were moments when he asked himself why he was where he was?

Sadly, the answer to the question was all too clear. An educated youth, going on twenty, fully conversant with the power of nature and the wonders of the cosmos, along with an assortment of other talents, nevertheless remained a slave.

FIVE

L ESS THAN AN HOUR after his hasty departure from the medical tent, Straba would be throwing up the contents of his meagre breakfast outside the praetorium over the booted foot of an unsympathetic sentry who reacted with a heavy cuff to the scribe's head. Often the butt of amusement amongst the Hispanics, even a reason for his precarious existence in some ways, one might say, news of his latest unfortunate mishap would soon spread through many in 9th legion's idle ranks, their knowing his delicate condition was always good for a laugh.

Laughter was the last thing on the mind of Julius Balbilus though, as he revisited the surgeon's tent, as predicted. Accompanied by Gallinus, a muscular multi-scarred ex-gladiator with over seventy kills to his credit, the legate of 20th legion Valeria, wrapped in a fur-lined cloak hiding his armour, fought his way between the tented lines in the face of a sudden squall. He was in bad humour; not that unusual for him, and even the tale of Cerialis' scribe throwing up failed to dent the mood when it later came to his ear. That was the trouble with Greeks, he thought. Capable as they were, when it came to the bloody crunch, no sodding guts. He allowed himself a smile, vaguely amused at the crudity.

Who was it said, bad news travels faster than fair? There had been unnecessary delays, partly due to what Balbilus, seeing himself as a man of action, viewed as governor Paulinus' 'dithering about' in the south. The legate desired the immediate rounding-up of the renegades who'd jumped on Lucidius Salva and his escort. Retaliate while the iron's hot, was his advice, a suggestion soon overruled by an upstart Cerialis who, on being appointed commander of all military movement in the area was, at least until Paulinus' belatedly appeared, the army's official senior legate, like it or no.

This unpalatable situation did little to dampen Balbilus' present ire. Disgust at the lack of movement and a seeming absence of any sense of urgency had unsettled him. The cold fact that Paulinus had gone over his head, giving the younger less experienced man overall authority, deeply rankled. He felt both underestimated and slighted, bitter pills for a stoical old soldier to swallow. If there was any justice left in this damn world, the position that Quintus Cerialis presently held, should be his by right.

A stickler for discipline, Balbilus had done all that was militarily possible to minimise boredom among his own command. Never an idler, he was fully aware of the advantages in keeping large bodies of men fully occupied. To him the legion must be a well-oiled fighting machine, ready for action in the field, not some soft garrison posting, and his Valerian's hadn't been dumped on the edge of empire merely to rust beside the muddy edge of some filthy river.

There had been moments lately when Balbilus thought Paulinus, the honoured general and famed victor over the Mauritanians, a fellow and intimate companion he'd once admired, to now be fast losing his wits. Maybe at fifty-eight, the supreme legate of Britannia was growing a little crazed in the mind, taking more interest in the youth Auspex, his current boy lover, than more urgent affairs.

When he walked, Balbilus moved rapidly for a small man. Speed was ever important to him, as those who'd once marched with him could well testify. He also had an unnerving habit of showing up when least expected. Two more of the wounded had died and their bodies removed for cremation since the legate's early morning check-up. In the surgeon's tent he came once more to check on the supine form of the wounded optio, his dignity still smarting over the preening upstart Cerialis.

Julius looked down upon the recumbent form and thought of Lucidius Salva without any outward show of sentiment. Salva was once a serving officer and as such, knew the score. As he himself was often heard to say, it went with the job.

A surprised sentry, out on the usual patrol, had discovered the six bruised and blooded heads that misted morning on the pontoon. Later when it became obvious as to what had occurred,

Balbilus reflected that it said much for the toughness of Petra's men that any of them had made it back to Lindum at all! There came a few garbled words before the optio again lost consciousness. From what he'd gleaned so far, it appeared that a bunch of murderous Brigs had launched a ruthless ambush sometime during the third watch, a time when vigilance is usually at a low point. The surprised turma thus had little time to arm, being completely overwhelmed by the savagery of the assault. The legate of Valeria simmered with anger, imagining the rest, the barbarity of these heathens, the rampant killing. Someone will be made to pay eventually, he vowed.

But that's the problem, he thought bitterly. Eventually was too long a wait for the punishment he'd got in mind. Later, after further unconvincing reassurances from the tired medic that the optio was slowly on the mend, he left the cloying atmosphere of death, his dark mood unabated.

An old school no-nonsense soldier, with twenty-one years of service under his belt and riser from the ranks, he chose to continue leading from the front. Lack of respect for favoured men like Cerialis was perhaps understandable. Be that as it may, he would seek explanation as to why Cerialis went over his head. Later there would be other vital questions seeking further answers.

Ducking his balding head under the tarp later, he paused to breath clean air. Broken clouds scurried overhead as he made his way to the temporary quarters allotted him in the 'no frills' annex of Cerialis' praetorium on The Hill. There, he cursed again over Paulinus's latest order just received. It contained the same instructions as that given two days earlier. No action to be taken over the problem regarding the hostiles until he, as supreme legate, took up personal command!

And so on. Blah blah blah.....................................

Puffed up little prick!' Balbilus swore. Why, by the gods, was he not already here so that we could get the damned job finished? He beckoned for the hovering figure of Gallinus to pour wine. The once champion gladiator, he noticed, was putting on a little too much weight, just like the rest of the damn army. When the long-promised arena was built he would, as an over-cheerful Cerialis had casually suggested, install Gallinus as games master. That would make 'em jump.

It would be the one thing to celebrate, an instant when both legates agreed over something, a fact which perhaps showed the state of boredom to which the colonia had gradually sunk. As it was, the legions in Balbilus' judgement were now decidedly hamstrung. What vexed him equally was how murdering bands of cut-throats, the Abrentii for example, seemed always to be one jump ahead of the game?

Some days later, when the second survivor of Petra's Horse finally regained consciousness, he immediately began to complain. 'What are you telling me?' he gasped, obviously still in pain, 'that you've managed to make me a bloody cripple?'

The dour senior surgeon who'd missed the previous events, was near to retirement and, having seen much worse in his years of service, merely offered a slight shrug. 'You still have most of your vital parts, optio, have you not?' he said with mild irritation. 'Think yourself lucky to be alive, is my advice.'

'Lucky!' the recovering patient echoed, angrily. 'A useless cripple reduced to begging alms on the shitty streets of Narbone, when they ship me back! You call that lucky?'

'You'll get a well-deserved pension,' answered the medic, lightly. 'Then there's your nine-year service to be taken into account. Think about it, man. You'll be the local hero.'

'How long will it be before it mends?' the survivor asked with resignation, lifting himself, gingerly.

'Perhaps a month or two.'

'Well, thanks for nothing, you unfeeling old bugger,' the optio swore quietly, falling back on the pallet.

'Who knows, you may even get some kind of award,' remarked the surgeon, almost cheerfully.

The unnamed survivor of Petra silently glared at the figure of the departing medic, thinking bitterly as to where he'd like to shove it.

SIX

'**Y**OU LOOK PALE, Straba,' Cerialis remarked, later that evening, while indicating a seat with a casual sideways glance.

'It was the visit to the surgeon's tent, legate. Not a wise move, as I learned nothing.'

Cerialis, straightening up, turned away from scrutiny of the unrolled map on the desk, looking the dark-eyed Greek up and down as if carrying out a parade inspection.

'Indeed!' he smiled with amusement. 'You too? They must be selling tickets down there.' Straba pretended to be unfazed. The joke was gaining ground rapidly in this part of the colonia, but Straba failed to see the humour in it. 'Old bugger Balbilus paid a visit earlier,' Cerialis offered by way of explanation, 'along with his minder, that damn one-eyed colossus from Crete, the secutor who seems to accompany the legate practically everywhere.'

Cerialis threw an open-ended glance at the scribe in case he asked, just what *was* a secutor? When he failed to oblige, Cerialis sipped wine and continued. 'Even our friend prince Armet looked in. I must say that the medics tent seems to be a most popular place.' Cerialis stretched his legs. 'It's getting late Straba, and you should rest. A full day of discussion looms.'

Straba sat on the hard bench, easing his spine gingerly against the plastered wall, closing bloodshot eyes to obscure the light of the lamps, blocking for a welcome moment the inward dread that had lately overtaken him.

Outside, beyond the half open shutters of the praetorium, thunder rumbled over the hilltop colonia, swamping the rhythmic tramp of nailed sandals on the paved yard outside, as the relief guard took over second watch. Straba waited as the final crack rolled away before replying. 'That is so, sir,' said the Greek, wearily. 'Don't you too, find sleep difficult?'

'Tedious rather than difficult, scribe,' the legate indicated a cluttered table strewn with sheets of papyri. 'There is much to be gone over, before our revered governor gets here.' He allowed the flicker of a smile to part his lips. 'As long as I'm saddled with such responsibility, sleep remains a luxury I can't afford.'

The Greek found himself staring at this young man, so full of confidence and ambition, assessing him yet again. Thirty-two years of age, P. Quintus Cerialis had to live with the distinction of being the youngest senior officer to lead a legion in the entire empire. Straba wondered at this yet was sensible enough to realise that such a distinction had been earned the hard way.

Sometimes success cultivates envy, especially when it's achieved so rapidly. Yet in the two years that Straba had served as personal secretary he had been given advantages that allowed him further scrutiny. There was little he could find to be adversely critical in his master. A good soldier despite his cool disregard for the rule-book – or because of it – he obviously found the commanding of a shield-wall in the heat of battle preferable to sitting behind an administrative desk, the present position he reluctantly held.

Straba had known Cerialis long enough to discover that his outwardly laid-back manner and personal pleasantness hid an iron hand. How else could he have moulded his Hispanics into a fully functioning and disciplined armoured machine which many believed the best of the best, the toughest group of legionaries in the army, who would follow him into the jaws of death if so required? At least, that was the story.

'Well?' he heard Cerialis say, interrupting the scribe's thoughts as if from a distance. 'I presume you're here for some bloody reason?'

'I came to talk, only to talk.'

Cerialis yawned, stretching out his legs once more, placing one across the other. 'You are a bad chooser of time, scribe.'

Then blame the poets! Straba's aching head silently advised.

'Down there with the medics,' he then continued, 'I've not often been as close to horror as I've been today, seeing the mangled bodies of those two men and others.'

'Those two men as you call them are soldiers of Rome,' Cerialis intoned casually. 'They fight for the empire, as we all must on occasion. It is extra fortunate for you that you don't have to share the experience.' The legate paused. 'What have others been saying around The Hill, about what happened?' The question came abruptly in its delivery and startled Straba by its directness.

'To be honest, I think there are those who have been deeply shaken by the tragedy undergone by Petra,' the Greek answered.

Cerialis stared down at his feet, contemplatively. 'And?'

Straba hesitated before he gave answer, not quite sure as to his master's reaction.' Men are taking bets as to,' he paused nervously, 'how you will handle things.'

'Are they, by Jupiter?' Cerialis cursed quietly. 'Am I about to tread upon a few sacred corns? Is that it?'

Straba gave a helpless shrug. The scribe had Julius Balbilus, the old warhorse and commander of the Valerians, in mind, though he dared not say so. After all, Petra's Horse made up a vital part of the 20th and out of respect he should have been the first to have been informed of the disaster, rather than the younger Cerialis, as others thought.

'Overriding legate Balbilus might cause a few problems, sir.'

Cerialis sniffed, a contemptuous sound in the near silence. 'Everything concerning that old warhorse causes problems. But I have others, including the construction of a gladiatorial arena for the colonia. A chance for you to shine, Straba, eh? Get some exercise, put meat on those bones. I've suggested Gallinus as trainer, Balbilus' minder, what do you think?'

Straba, ignoring the jest, or was it? shrugged once more. 'I've heard that the legate is saying you might overstep your authority, and, as you say, stamp on sacred corns if you go against these Abrentii, without the governor's permission.'

'Believe me, Straba,' Cerialis said with a curse, slapping his hand on the table. 'I've bloody well thought about it. I'm with Julius on that one, a fast pursuit, catch them on the run, with their breeches down. But, had I done that I reckon I'd be packed off to Rome with a flea in my ear. You understand me?'

Outside the praetorium, thunder, more distant now, rolled away. Cerialis rose from his seat followed by the dark eyes of the

Greek as the legate moved across the room to the window. Before closing the shutters, he stared long and hard at the encroaching night. Because of the rain he knew that the campfires would be few now and feeble. Soon the vast army surrounding the colonia would sleep. Only here, in the legate's quarters, was there some meagre light. A half-dozen pitched-soaked torches would, until dawn, hold darkness at bay.

'How do you judge me?' the legate asked.

'I am a slave sir. I don't judge.'

'Come on, Greek? After two years working for me, is that all you can say?'

The sudden question, again coming out of the blue, alerted Straba because it was unexpected and overly blunt. It then became obvious that the legate had drunk a little too much of the content of the jug. For a moment he was stuck for an answer. 'I respect that you have given me a place here. I have food and warmth for which I thank you.'

'And Rome? Do you respect her too?'

Of a sudden, Straba feared that this was turning into a late-night interrogation rather than a two-way chat. 'I serve you, therefore, her?' he countered, warily.

Cerialis turned inward, away from the torches and the rain. 'Why are you Greeks so masterly when it comes to words?' The room was dimmed, though not enough for Straba not to notice the smile upon the legate's face.

'Maybe because we need them to get ourselves out of awkward situations, sir.'

'Like now, eh?'

Cerialis reached again for the jug, pouring the rest of the wine into a pair of beakers. He offered one to the seated scribe, who accepted it hesitantly. 'You Greeks,' he said, with undisguised cynicism. 'I know you, what you think, feel. Masters of the world when Rome was a dirty bitching village on the Tiber. Am I correct?'

'That's history, if you'll pardon me,' Straba replied, wondering where this was leading.

'And your subject, I think.' Cerialis triumphantly paused. 'What will you say about us, when you come to write your great history of these islands?'

'I shall say that Rome brought peace of a sort, legate.'

'Another diplomatic reply. Pax, a noble aim in a corrupt world, wouldn't you agree? Yet it has its price. You cannot have that without protection, and you cannot have protection without payment, nor payment without taxes.'

Straba sipped from the wine-cup. 'As you say. A corrupt world.'

'Yet you would concur that conquest is necessary?'

Thought lines drove furrows onto Straba's forehead. 'It depends on how one goes about it,' he said, thinking he might be painting himself into a corner, still trying to discover just what the legate was getting at.

'We have done it better than most empires, this conquest, don't you agree? Taking people out of their miserable hovels and giving them something more tangible to aspire to, exchanging breeches for togas, protecting wives, children, families. Many an invader has done less.'

'Yet in exchange I believe you rob people of their pride and heritage,' sighed Straba. 'Life is really quite unimportant when you stifle the joy of it.'

Cerialis poured more wine into his cup. 'Your life, Straba, has Rome taken it from you?'

'No legate, thankfully my life still has purpose,' said the Greek, softly, 'yet I fail to understand this need to kill, a compulsion from which Rome appears to get an inordinate amount of satisfaction.'

The oil lamps were fading and the air in the room felt suddenly chilled. 'We are soldiers, that's what we do. More to the point, we kill because there is a need for an army to kill. That's why we pay a legionary two-hundred and twenty-five denarii a year, to kill. You see what took place this morning as a disaster while I see it as a spur, a cause that will shake this army out of the sloth and stop the rot. I'm with Balbilus on that. As soon as prince Armet brings me word as to the identity of the culprits, I'll know what to do.'

'And then?' Straba prompted.

25

'Then my dear scribe, some action will take place and you can set about writing it in your history.' Cerialis replied, sitting comfortably, resting his back against the leather chair. 'But now, seeing as you're here, you can take this down.'

Straba hesitated, carefully choosing his words 'I would like your permission to be a part of the task force, sir!'

Cerialis looked at the slave as if he'd suddenly lost all reason. 'Permission refused,' he answered bluntly. 'I need you here.'

'You have other scribes,' Straba protested. 'My request is not made lightly. I must be part of this.'

'Why, by Serapis? Are you so sympathetic to these wayward priests, that you want to write about them?'

'My sympathies are neither here nor there, legate. I wish to study war at close hand, that's all,' he replied, puzzled momentarily as to why his legate swore by a Grecian god.

'Take a good look at yourself, Straba, you're an educated chap. But a worse object for a soldier I've yet to see,' jibed Cerialis, wiping his lips. 'Best bugger off and read the works of fellow Greeks, Herodotus, Thucydides, along with the rest. Believe me, it'll be safer.'

Straba, plucked up what little courage remained. 'With respect, legate, my conscience, not theirs, is my guide in this.'

'Slaves aren't supposed to have a conscience,' Cerialis said dismissively. 'Do you really expect me to grant you a privilege I cannot allow to myself? Speak more of this nonsense and I'll have you clapped in chains quicker than you can say, Aeschylus!' Cerialis drained the rest of the cup's contents. 'Your request is denied,' he said finally. 'I've various reports that must be promptly sent abroad.'

Straba, damping down his frustration, suppressed a smile on hearing his master's reference to the Greek tragedian, knowing it was to impress, and dutifully drew tablet and stylus from the satchel. 'Most noble, Supreme Governor, Paulinus,' the legate began to dictate under the half-light. The scribe, as he took dictation would soon learn much from this night's correspondence.

He knew of Brennus, who around the camp did not? But just who was the man Venutius, mentioned by Cerialis during his dictation?

Straba worried that, as a slave, he may have opened too much of himself to his master's scrutiny, and his unease grew so much that night that he found it even more difficult to sleep. It was then, at a late hour, that he made perhaps the biggest decision of his young life. Cerialis had been right in challenging him about his lack of military prowess. Yet how could he possibly write the history of Britannia's conquest without first-hand experience? It was a long time since he'd carried a sword and he had once sworn never again to use a weapon in anger.........

He should have known, fool that he was, that obtaining the legate's blessing was something that would never be granted. More than that, he could have been severely punished for his stupid insubordination. Be that as it may, he already knew that fate would compel him to follow the army west and to trust in his own ability, a not reassuring thought.

Some hours later a grey dawn began to pierce the river mist when a sentry discovered the dead body of the eagle. It lay in thick mud at the foot of the north gate where the unpaved road led in the direction of the territory of queen Cartimandua and her Brigante. With its feathers and plumage marred in blood, its breast violently torn open, it appeared to have been savaged by a fox, or some other denizen. The sentry who found the carcass kicked it into the river with a booted foot, dismissing it without a thought as to its significance, the one thing on his mind being the end of a two-hour stint of guard duty, and how he might best fill in the remaining time. If he were one of those who'd heard of the latest prophesy gaining ground, concerning a wild animal and a dead bird, he had forgotten it by now.

SEVEN

QUEEN CARTIMANDUA received the news of the attack on Petra's Horse with mounting anger. Her stupid fool of a half-brother, Brennus, by his rash actions had at once placed her in a dangerous and extremely awkward position. Ruler over the most powerful people north of Lindum, or any part of Britannia for that matter, she'd long played a cautious cat and mouse game with the presence of Rome's 9th legion squatting on her borders. The ever-present problem needed all her powers of concentration when seeking to adopt a lasting agreement with the greater power. Desperate to control Brennus and the troublesome Abrentii from stirring-up the pot, she'd have to resort to far firmer measures in order to blunt the Bear's future ambitions, as her own future might depend upon it.

Pro-Roman, at least for the time being, Cartimandua rightly calculated it wise to take some sort of redeeming action of her own, dispatching a peace seeking delegation to supreme legate Suetonius Paulinus while on his way north. At the same time, she'd apprehend her feckless brother and hand him over for Rome to deal with. The business was easier said than done, and she knew it. Yet in order to remain on speaking terms, decisive action must at least be tried.

Cartimandua, her name translated as 'sleek pony,' was still seductively beautiful, an asset she found useful to exploit when needing to get her own way. Her estranged husband, Venutius, consort for a decade now, had once been like herself, diplomatic in his approach to a hovering Rome. Change of mind came quickly though, when he saw how Rome dealt with those who dared to oppose them.

Venutius was not the usual idea of a man of his nation. He belonged to the wild and volatile Carvetii, an ancient part of the Brigante federation lying far to the north, bordering territory inhabited by Picts, a strange and almost mystic cult whose warrior people still held to the dying practise of smearing their half-naked bodies with woad before battle, a warlike stock, feared even by the Brigante. With one eye warily cast on them, Venutius opposed his former wife to follow his ambitious claim to half of Brigantia.

Cartimandua however, was quick to pursue the war lord's change of mind. Arresting close members of his family, including his only son, she decked them in chains then immediately divorced him. Somewhere they still languished in captivity. This was not Venutius' only grievance, there was a further reason for his mounting rage. Caractacus, a famed guerrilla fighter and close friend who'd resisted the ongoing Roman encroachment of western Britannia for years; leader of the stubborn Silures, received the same harsh treatment dealt out to Venutius' kin. After a reversal of fortune, to avoid being captured by his Roman adversary, Ostorius Scapula, Caractacus trustingly accepted sanctuary from someone he thought to be a staunch ally. Bad decision, as callously the she-wolf shamelessly handed him back to Rome. Later, the dogged leader was presented to the then emperor, Claudius, as a gift from the loyal queen. Held captive for years it was said that he was secretly garrotted by his captors in the basement of a squalid tenement in Rome's city slums. Others spoke to the contrary of a not too stressful relationship with the emperor, which allowed him to see out his days in a modest villa on the Palatine. Whatever the story, Caractacus would never again return to the land of his birth.

The betrayal only added more fuel to the fire that inevitably led to a growing struggle for power between the two fractious groups. Quick to recognise her precarious position, Cartimandua found herself perching on a cliff edge from which she might at any time be toppled. What had happened with Petra's Horse was by no means helping. Bowed by the fates, the episode gave her enough reason to seek a tighter relationship with Rome.

She was correct in fearing for her future. There were already signs that Rome in the guise of Quintus Cerialis, was shifting its support away from her, giving instead visible support to king Volisios, client king of the Coritani nation. To its young upstart prince, Armet, a place of new-found importance was gifted in the shape of the formation of a special unit of four-hundred cavalry scouts aptly named, 'Exploratores'. The act bore the stamp of legate Cerialis, a typical rashness of a man going places, though in using the Coritani in his plans he was close to breaking the rules. Safer to have men like that on her side, she mused. The best horsemen in the world, the four hundred scouts.........

A keen rider herself, the queen appraised the expert way in which they handled their mounts, the manoeuvres, the uncanny ability to train horse and man as one. It was rumoured that they originally imported their mounts from southern Gaul, an area famed for good equine stock, which meant they didn't come cheap. Reluctantly, she was inclined to agree with Caesar's boast. If only she'd such a force to bend to her will, instead of the many doltish cretins she commanded. She alas, was not the first to appreciate this elite group.

Any necessary diplomatic encounters between legate and queen had been brisk and flat, seriously following official protocols. They conferred mostly at some isolated spot along the invisible frontier, with few witnesses. They were almost never alone, yet several subtle looks exchanged between the two were telling, or at least they were to an observant Straba the scribe, present in an official capacity to take note of proceedings, while secretly hiding those few items he'd added to his own take on history, all the time thinking what a jealous Julius Balbilus of legion Valeria would make of it, were he ever a witness.

She'd more than once thought of taking Cerialis as a permanent lover. With his growing reputation it would have been, to say the least, interesting. Seriously seducing the most influential personage in her world would be easy enough, as had become clear during their first meeting. Beyond that, for once being any way honest, it appeared that she might have need of him yet again, in the seemingly constant battle with her enemies.

Now the queen, gaining further tidings, seemed threatened twice more, from other directions. It was put out that Venutius had drawn others to him lately, unknown men dwelling north of the Carvetii, men clothed in fur who'd hardly heard of Rome.

There was talk too, of Venutius including her near neighbour, Mogonus, king of the chariot people, the eastern Parisi, in his plans. What words spoken between him and her rival for power, could only be guessed at. All reports received, spoke of a hostile war-host at large, stronger than seen before, strong enough to not only challenge her, but also cast an eye over Rome's presence itself.

EIGHT

A STRONG WIND strengthened as Gaius Aquilla, accompanied by several legionaries bearing lighted brands, joined their commander on the catwalk. It was time for the ritual guard-mounting as the group made their way down through the barbican gate to a temporary parade ground lying at the foot of The Hill. That night, half a cohort of the 9th, doubled in strength, paraded for inspection. It was certain that the shock of the bloodied heads staked out on the bridge the day before, had made Cerialis decide to oversee the familiar evening inspection in person, as if he himself were taking responsibility for the unfortunate demise of Petra.

The contingent forming up were fully armed, each man carrying the normal daunting weapons of javelin, gladius and shield. Russet cloaks hid their lorica segmentata, a largely untried form of protection recently introduced to Cerialis' legion exclusively, guinea-pig fashion - at least until proven seriously successful. Of lighter weight, twice as flexible as any previous armour, it would later be accepted by all twenty-eight legions of the empire.

The ranks of Hispanics stiffened visibly at the legate's approach. The centurion carrying another lighted brand saluted, a mark of respect that Cerialis briefly acknowledged.

Quintus Petillius Cerialis Caesius Rufus, legatus legionis, to give him his full title, wore no helm. A mop of dark hair, although expertly trimmed, failed to hide the jagged scar where a Cherusi sword left its jagged mark below his right ear, a wound taken during one of many skirmishes in Germania some years before. Because of Cerialis' rapid rise in rank, much talk circulated within the army over his success, Julius Balbilus naturally being one of the most vocal.

If animosity kept the younger legate awake nights, it didn't show. Son of a moderately wealthy family, Cerialis entered military service as a junior officer on short time. Within the space of nine years, through various promotions, from quaestor to tribune of the plebs, plus service with the Rhine legions, he'd charmed his way up with people that mattered, in order to enjoy the highest of positions he now held. Inevitably, such an outgoing and popular personality could hardly fail to attract its share of envy.

Unlike some of his peers, the impetuous legate never underestimated the power of the cavalry arm which on occasion had rescued him from more than one tight spot. Just such an incident occurred during time spent as a captain of equites.

In territory east of the rivers Meuse and Moselle, land then inhabited by the Treveri, an unpredictable tribe who were in revolt in an unpredictable land, he was to quickly learn the danger of overconfidence and the frightening helplessness of a small unit of footsloggers threatened by fast moving horsemen. As a roll-up plan, brilliantly conceived by the opposing Treveri commander, it proved to be a classic example of a surprise assault by cavalry, carried out with the kind of dash and impudence such a man as the youthful Cerialis quickly learned to appreciate. In short, it was a day he never forgot. Rather, he chose to stuff the occasion in his mental pouch for future use.

It might well have been the end for him and the small unit of Thracian auxiliaries. Had the Treveri leader thought otherwise, he could have massacred Cerialis' small force on the spot, being many miles from home-base with nobody the wiser. Trapped on all sides he had two choices. Fight a way out or negotiate. With an uneasy mind he opted for the latter, laying it on with the one thing left to him, an outgoing personality. Making promises that were not in his power to grant, knowing that the Treveri had long been discontented over certain unfulfilled agreements concerning tribal rights in the past, Cerialis convinced his captors that he'd indeed been on his way with generous offers of peace and reconciliation.

An unadvisable approach, but it worked!

Julius Civilis, his immediate superior, though not exactly pleased had to grudgingly acknowledge that in a bold move Cerialis had not only saved his men from certain death but inadvertently managed a diplomatic coup that senatorial authority itself had failed to accomplish. It followed that the Treveti shortly became a valued ally in the governing of the now settled territory. It was a typical example of the legate's rising fame, a reason why he aroused grudging envy in men such as Balbilus. Cerialis' easy manner, coupled with genuine concern for those who served with him, gained an early respect among the tough veterans of the Hispanics. All he demanded from them was unbridled loyalty, promising in return the privilege of serving in *'the best bloody legion in the whole damned army!'*

Not much of an exchange, but again it worked.

His valuable insight into how to cope with the boredom and isolation of frontier life, such as experienced earlier with Rhine Army, was enough to lead him by various roads to the position he now held as legate of the Hispanics.

Cerialis' prime weakness, if it were such, was a not infrequent desire for sexual dalliance, not in itself a rarity when one considered the sheer tediousness of manning an untamed frontier post. In the rank and file of his men the legate's open pursuit of the opposite sex had become almost legendary and those in the legion, possessed of a more inquisitive nature, followed his progress with unbridled interest, taking bets as to just how long the latest coupling would last. Late attention now fell upon the she-wolf of Brigantia, no less. Rumour already suggested that meetings between the legate and Cartimandua were more than diplomatic, and true or not, such stories abounded and were never denied.

NINE

'QUINTUS!' Aquilla, the legion's secondus and friend, spoke with concern as they turned away from the separate columns marching to their points of duty around and atop The Hill. 'What does it all mean? Where does the infernal Brennus figure with Venutius?'

'Venutius is a king in his own right, ruling over men from the far north, the Carvetii; Brigante in all but name. I believe he has a strong talent for war, a dark horse who I'd gladly have on our side. It appears that he's giving aid to Brennus' Abrentii, yet I suspect deep down he has bigger plans,' Cerialis answered.

'Forgive me, Quintus, but you appear to know a hell of a lot about this renegade.'

Cerialis nodded. 'I've had help,' he grinned in the shadows. 'Some while back, before your time Quintus, the man challenged us and at the request of Cartimandua, we sent him packing. His presence tells me now that he's building up to something on a larger scale.' Cerialis loosened the saffron coloured scarf around his neck. 'Characters like him never give up.'

'The Brigante queen, she'll be wanting help from this quarter again?' Aquilla speculated as well as probed.

Cerialis grunted agreement, running a hand over his dark crop of hair. 'Thank the gods it's not up to us this time, though. A matter of a couple more days, with exchange of mounts along the way, the Fates will give us Paulinus. When they do, he can have the privilege of making his own bloody choices.'

'Well, he can't come soon enough for me.' Aquilla interrupted, with a curse. 'I hear he's giving old Balbilus charge of the advance guard.'

Cerialis shook his head. 'Not yet decided.'

'Within weeks the army should be heading west,' Aquilla spoke with scant optimism, 'which will give us more space in which to stretch our legs.'

'You surprise me, Aquilla,' remarked Cerialis with a chuckle, while staring into the darkness enveloping the river below. 'I thought you might enjoy the extra company.'

'With that sly old fox Balbilus watching over our shoulder day and night?' the secondus swore. 'No bloody thanks.'

'You don't appear very happy,' Cerialis observed. 'Anything on your mind?'

'I hear Poenius of Augusta thinks Balbilus should chuck it in, retire,' Aquilla mused. 'Praise me, he's the very last person I would be easy with, in the matter of things as they are.'

'And just how are things then, secondus?'

'This business with the Druse,' Aquilla confided with open concern. 'These Britons regard their Celtic wise men most seriously, I'm told.'

'There will be trouble from that direction, we expect it,' spoke Cerialis bluntly. 'Whatever, it can be handled. The camp prefect of Augusta is *wrong*, I venture. Julius Balbilus is a brave Roman, a man who took the hard road and fought his way up through the tight closed ranks of privilege and birth. You must respect a character like him, whatever his other defects.'

'I can't argue with that,' the secondus grudgingly agreed. 'Perhaps that's why he envies you so much.'

'Aquilla is right,' echoed a familiar voice behind them as they turned to enter the praetorium. 'Balbilus bears you little regard.'

Cerialis briefly acknowledged the newcomer. He didn't bother to ask how Armet had arrived unchallenged by the guards, the busy praetorium being well used to the presence of the Coritani prince, who came and went, such was the trust, with the minimum of challenge. His presence seemed to be based on the level that if it was alright with the legate, it was equally alright with the men that obeyed him, the very opposite of what a strict disciplinarian like Julius Balbilus might have sanctioned.

'The governor has put Julius' nose out with giving me control overall, at least until he arrives, prince. By right he is senior in rank, it must naturally plague him.'

'Perhaps he's more upset over your new powers than you think,' The first son of Volisios smiled against the wavering flutter of a brace of wall brands. Beneath a fur lined cloak his muscled body was hidden by a tunic of leather bearing the horse insignia of the goddess Epona on its breast, a gift from Tadoc's daughter, Gela, his betrothed. In stature the prince stood slightly higher than Hispania's legate. Brown-eyed and, like Cerialis, dark of hair, even under the cloak partly hiding his face, one could see enough to dub him ruggedly handsome. A wide belt encircled his waist from which the jewelled hilt of a dagger was visible. As a trusted ally of Rome and eldest son of a near client king, positioned north of the Trent, he and the Coritani had never been party to Scapula's now redundant and unworkable law regarding the carrying of arms.

'As I said, Balbilus is an honourable man,' Cerialis spoke, regarding Armet closely under the lighted brand. 'But what brings you here so late, not another bloody report of unrest, I trust?'

'I hear legate Balbilus is to command the advance guard against the Druids on Mona,' Armet said directly.

'Not you too? sighed the legate. 'You're as tedious as Aquilla. Why do you ask?'

'Because I and the scouts wish to be part of it.'

Cerialis slumped onto a chair, stretching his legs, indicating another cushioned seat. 'Are you volunteering for Rome's sake, or for your own?'

'Both,' Armet replied with frankness, preferring to stand. 'I won't be thwarted. He didn't add that it would be a front row seat, like sitting in the arena, a good opportunity to study an aggressive Rome. The prince was suffering no illusion here, as the day might well arrive when a man's loyalty could be tested. Just now, he knew how far to push himself, as Cerialis no doubt, had long considered much the same thing.

After a pregnant few seconds of silence Cerialis chose to dismiss an over curious Aquilla.

Within the confines of the dimly lit praetorium, Cerialis stared intently. 'You told me once, you'd risk *all* to get at The Bear,' the legate calculated. 'I only half believed it then.'

'And now?'

'I know well what it means to you. But it's a hopeless request to be allowed a place in Paulinus' big push., especially given the religious element. You know it. So why risk the chance of being refused?' Cerialis sighed. 'I suspect you have another reason for such zeal?'

It was a strange and uneasy bond shared by both men, first forged from the period of Armet's earlier period in Rome. The son of Volisios had quickly been introduced to bewildering experiences, some good, others not so. There was his brief introduction to the current emperor, Nero, wherein lay the future of the deal. When a people such as the Coritani were about to approach a new status of client kingship, it was customary for Rome to foster a closer relationship with the person who would one day rule over many people in a Roman controlled new world. In this case, Armet had to be that man.

Cerialis pulled his cloak tighter about him, for the night grew chill even now, within the confines of the praetorium. 'Volisios, he thrives?' he enquired, abruptly changing the subject.

'As well as can be hoped for,' the prince replied. 'Yet I fear I don't always please him.'

Cerialis chuckled. 'I guess the same might be said of any father if sometimes, one doesn't see eye to eye.'

'We understand each other enough,' Armet acknowledged in a clipped tone, a hint of surprise and puzzlement in his voice.

'A cup of wine?'

The Coritani prince declined. Cerialis poured from a beaker.

'Well, Armet, you did well. Paulinus will be reassured of Tadoc's support, thank the gods. A trusted line of supply will be essential for the success or failure of this campaign,' the legate paused and stared earnestly at the prince. 'There can be no place for error.'

'I have made my report and we have Tadoc's promise of help. For me that is enough.'

For a moment there was a silence between them. 'We won't have long to wait,' Cerialis pondered, satisfaction in his voice. 'The latest report puts Paulinus here,' he stabbed at the chart on his desk. 'Two days ago, he left Camulodunum with his own company of equites. Today he should be well along the way.'

'A taxing journey for an older man,' Armet observed.

Cerialis shrugged casually. 'Not at all Armet, he's an old warhorse.' The legate rose. 'Tomorrow, take some of your scouts and try to locate the actual place of Petra's massacre,' he spoke seriously. 'Paulinus will want details, facts, figures. After that, I suggest we take it on from there.'

'You'll speak to Paulinus of my request for inclusion in his plan?'

Cerialis nodded an affirmative. 'Yet I doubt he'll allow you anywhere near Mona.'

Later, when Armet had left the praetorium, he reached for the hilt of his dagger as Aquilla, exiting from an unlit side room from which he'd quite obviously been waiting, fell in beside the prince. Even here, especially here, Armet had trained himself to be ever on the alert. Aquilla spoke in a conspiratorial whisper. 'I pray you are right about Tadoc, my friend, for much depends on it.'

'The old man has been my father's close friend for many a year, Aquilla,' Armet answered. 'As I said to Quintus, I've vouched for Tadoc, enough to marry his daughter, anyway.'

'And that suffices?'

'It suffices for me,' answered the prince. 'You worry too much, secundus,' he added, familiarly.

'I have cause, prince,' Aquilla continued. 'I hope, despite the contrary that the Brigante have learned little of our designs. You seem unconcerned, yet I'm uneasy with it.'

Armet didn't have the heart to tell the secundus, a man he held in some regard, that the enemy were probably completely aware of the situation concerning Rome's movements against them. Instead, he steered talk away in another direction.

'Cartimandua should have docked Venutius' tail long since, when she had the chance,' he said as they walked down toward the barbican's well-guarded gate, allaying his concern while thinking of the queen's heartless betrayal of the great rebel leader Caractacus, a terrible act that much disturbed Armet, despite a promise to his father to cooperate whole heartedly with the invader. The promise that had already cost his conscience dear as well as estranging his younger brother Gort who, after a final conflict of views concerning Volosios' new alliance with Rome, was now lost to him, possibly forever.

Reports coming in of Gort being seen in random places were many and inconclusive. So far Cerialis, in essence Armet's commander, had not questioned him on the subject, but inevitably it would arise sometime or other. This was the prime fear! Gort was playing a dangerously open game, and Rome's patience was hardly inexhaustible. Whatever Armet's volatile brother might bring about could likely focus unwanted attention upon Volisios and himself.

Then there was the danger posed by Brennus!

Whenever the name was mentioned, the past, like water from a breached dam, came flooding in, many years encapsulated in a frozen moment. The sudden attack on their capital, Rina, one of several carried out by the troublesome Abrentii, the savage violation and death of his little sister Alorad, along with his mother at the hands of Taghe and Varan, murderous cubs of The Bear. Volisios too suffered severe injuries which had long left the king in constant discomfort.

Armet remembered every minute of what happened on that fatal day, the burning huts, the casual slaughter. Ever after he recalled these times with acute sharpness. Then he'd sworn, while lying for dead in his own blood, that one day he'd confront the guilty and so redress the balance, even if he had to use both the power of an unpopular Rome and an untrustworthy queen to help him do so. That was the cold way things now stood. The position of the Coritani being a future client fiefdom was Armet's fate, and he wanted vengeance, but gaining the trust of Rome was equally of import, for such was the wish of Volisios. Though this didn't fit in with his own personal strategy, the stakes had never been higher.

With his face hidden from Aquilla under cover of his hood, the Coritani prince set his lips. 'It matters not,' he answered the secondus at last, 'whether our enemy knows of Paulinus' future intentions. What *really* matters, is do we know anything at all about what's going on in the head of warlord, Venutius?'

Leaving the secondus, he made his way through an ill-lit corridor to the stables, where the mare, Flavia, stood waiting patiently. Crossing paths, he almost collided with the tall figure of Nardon, captain of loyal Batavians, Paulinus' favourite unit among the ranks of the auxilia, and his most trusted of soldiers. With two-thousand seasoned fighters under his command, Nardon served at present with Tullius Roscius' legion Gemina, who, like the supreme legate, also spoke glowingly of the man's proven unquestioned dedication to Rome. Possessed of a reticent demeanour, he barely acknowledged the prince, save for a sharp nod followed by an inaudible grunt as they passed each other.

Although Armet prided himself with a certain talent for knowing the worth of a man, he was forced to admit that Nardon left him stumped. At one moment affably approachable, an abrupt change of mood could sometimes turn him into a very different being. That the prince's feelings seemed greatly at odds with Paulinus' and Roscius' judgement, wasn't that unusual, for he rarely saw eye to eye with the self-satisfied arrogant beast that was Rome. To the son of Volisios, it mattered little that Nardon and his fellow Batavians had once shared with Ofonius Tigellinus' praetorian guard the distinction of being part of emperor Nero's personal retinue. Armet already held one definite summing- up of Nardon of the Batavi, a creature whose outward show denied a glimpse of something not yet defined. Until such a time, Armet could only speculate.

TEN

W HEN THE UNMISTAKABLE SCENT settled over them, Armet knew that this was the place he sought.

Earlier that day the prince of the Coritani, eldest son of Volisios, clattered noisily out of Lindum over one of two pontoons, accompanied by a loud chorus of well-directed curses and insults from a sweating gang of Roman sappers busy constructing yet a third. Earlier, leaving Crococalana for Lindum, after a brief exchange and an even briefer cup of wine in legate Cerialis' quarters, he vacated the busy colonia under a threatening cover of cloud. Accompanying him went his uncle, Culchul Hud, plus a small retinue of thirty riders. It was a decision not entirely sitting at ease on the shoulders of Paulinus when he'd bowed, only half convinced, to Cerialis' provisional request for their being accepted into the ranks of Rome's auxiliaries. They were still waiting for his final approval.

Some of these horsemen were abroad, scouring the undulating middle land betwixt Lindum and the Trisantona, now part of king Tadoc's territory. Apart from the prince, his followers didn't look much like imperial auxiliaries supposedly ought to look, shunning the cumbersome weight of regular chain mail, they opted instead for flexible tunics of plain leather which contrasted with motley-coloured breeches of checked tartan. Their arms were bare save for coverings, wrist to shoulder, of swirly shapes of intricate tattoos and bronze wrist bracelets. Excluding their leader, none wore a protective helm, allowing their long hair, carefully woven into plaits for some, to fall free below the shoulder.

Their weaponry was mixed, but all carried the cavalry sword – the spatha – a tool that sought final decisions, cleaving a man from head to foot with one well-directed blow. The rest of their war-gear ran to personal taste, a conglomerate of small dagger, hand-axe and spear. To complete the display, a defensive circular-shield of wood, strengthened with a rim of iron and strapped firmly to the arm, was carried by almost every man. One rider, a young warrior named Patux, in rank the equivalent of a Roman signifer, carried a long wood-stave instead of a spear. Mounted atop the stave, a whitened skull of a wolf gazed down from eyeless sockets above the crossbar, itself decorated with a half-dozen drooping tails from the same canine predators, each appendage bedecked with coloured ribbon.

Armet preceded the signifer along a familiar route. Somewhere ahead he hoped to confirm suspicions concerning Brennus the warlord as the culprit most likely guilty for the destruction of Julius Balbilus' squadron of riders. Then, to complete the task given to the luckless Lucidius Salva, he would travel on to Tadoc's settlement where agreements over vital supplies destined for Suetonius Paulinus' 'great push,' needed finalisation.

The distance from Lindum to the Great River was less than a day's ride, a short excursion that Armet had taken many times to his father's old rival, now friend, king Tadoc of the Cornovii. There was also a third reason, not officially a part of the briefing, a more pleasant prospect involving another occasion to see Gela, his betrothed, a meeting far too-long delayed.

The prince had been married once before, six years previously, when barely seventeen. Her name was Tae, a girl even younger than himself, and the arrangement might have yielded much had she not caught an incurable fever and been taken tragically from him, all within that first short year. Now, unexpectedly, he had discovered a new love in Gela, whom he'd met soon after his return from Rome.

The journey west being largely routine, Armet followed a familiar route before arriving at the forest edge under a second shower of rain. Wading their horses across a wide running stream that men, trained for war, ironically called 'Tarm,' meaning 'Healer', they crossed into the territory of the Cornovii. It was there that they confronted the evidence.

'Wolf and crow both, would have thought their lives blessed over this banquet for buzzards,' swore Esico, one of the younger scouts surveying the carnage.

Scattered shapes bearing little resemblance to men lay all around, remains of Petra's Horse and other random corpses. Most of the dead told their own story. Many were headless, laid and stripped bare of armour along with any personal items they may have possessed. There was a suspiciously small number of stricken horses lying amongst the wreckage of shards of broken detritus and weaponry, a sure sign that most of the surviving beasts had been rounded up and driven off to be augmented into the ranks of the Abrentii's, dwindling stock. Most of the unfortunates of Petra's Horse were just mangled shapes. Bound with coarse rope to several trees, eyes gouged out and minus their genitalia, they'd suffered all the agonies of a slowly drawn-out death.

'This is the place, Armet,' Culchul Hud confirmed, removing his helm to reveal an abundance of greying hair falling over broad shoulders. He wiped his brow and spat.

'The old enemy,' Armet agreed with resignation.

'These buggers wouldn't have stood a chance,' Culchul muttered, glancing about. 'It's a timely reminder of what men will do in the name of their fire-eating god, eh cub. Anyway, to which foe do you refer, Abrentii or Roman?'

Armet smiled briefly and ignored the question. 'This time let's pray to *our own* gods that they prove less unkind. With Paulinus and his legions we may at least bring The Bear to heel, make him and that murdering scum of his go a little way to repaying the debt,' Armet spoke with studded determination.

'It's a great pity having to use Rome though, to watch them triumph where we ourselves failed,' Culchul Hud quietly cursed. 'It's been a hard time, eh? Revenge should never take this long.'

Culchul's appendage 'Hud' was the accepted title given to a dwindling group of warrior Druids, a band of isolated and maverick priests who, like most of their kind, stayed hostile to the Roman overlords. Viewed as dangerous and devious troublemakers, they were outlawed by decree and, as such, known only to a few trusted friends.

Under cover, they ran a very real risk of capture and death if betrayed, as did those knowingly harbouring them, a reason why

Culchul met with Armet only occasionally, at times like now, not joining up with the prince's party until well away from Lindum's baleful eye. Armet and Volisios, Culchul's older brother, kept the secret out of family loyalty, mindful of the fate they could expect if discovered. It was a firm relationship, unsullied and unquestioned. Too dangerous to linger long in one place, his presence among Armet's followers would be a brief one.

Nevertheless, as a respected member of a particular branch of wise men, he chose to tread a fine line indeed, especially since his orders originated from a higher level of authority coming from mistic Mona.

The horse, Flavia, Armet's spirited black mare, an unexpected gift from legate Cerialis, a premature offering anticipating the founding of the Exploratores, flattened her ears, shying side-on to tremble while eying the pack of hovering wolves nearby who, disturbed in their feasting, cautiously backed off. Disciplined to unswervingly obey from birth, the beasts remained completely still, ready to pounce, given an opportunity. Conna, the youngest rider in the group, uselessly hurled a spear in the direction of the predators, and they sensibly drew a little further into the dense haven of bracken.

The prince, calming the mare with a soft stroke of the hand, dismounted, where the edge of woodland protected them from the elements, and under cover of overhanging branches that served to shelter dryer ground of toughened grass and bramble, Armet bent over one of the dead.

Culchul, sliding from his horse, joined his nephew, crouching above several warrior cadavers separated from the rest of the fallen. The fact that their heads were still attached to their torsos marked them out to be the few unlucky recipients of the desperate fight for life by Petra's Horse. It was obvious why these men had been abandoned after the attack as the visible severity of their fatal wounds said it all. They had callously been left to die, according to the Abrentii creed, not being worth the time and effort of saving. Other shapes lay face-down. The Hud casually turned one over, his sword-tip, probing. A tattoo of what appeared to be the antlered head of a stag decorated his upper arm and instantly caught his interest. 'Only men of the Dobunni wear a mark akin to this,' he growled while his hands searched a second body.

It was rumoured that Culchul could identify the warriors of most of the neighbouring British nations by the intricate body marks many displayed. 'And this,' he added triumphantly, holding aloft a blooded severed arm, a falcon in flight depicted on the wrist. 'Again, not Abrentii, for they use none of these signs.'

'This fellow isn't one of them either, prince. Closer to home, Deceangli most likely,' spoke Esico excitedly, not to be outdone, twirling a crudely fashioned disc on a copper chain playfully, the only bit of decoration so far gathered from any of the looted dead.

'I had such a trinket myself, taken during the days when Volisios fought against the Vetae twenty years since,' said Patux, 'he *too* rode with the Dobunni.'

'Then lad, he travelled a fair distance just to find death this far from home,' growled Culchul in disdain.

Armet nodded, slowly easing himself back into the saddle. Unlike his motley dressed followers, with their plaited hair and loose tartan clothes, the prince of the Coritani wore the latest Roman cavalry gear, complete with cuirass and helm. The latter he removed as his eyes scanned the scene. Minutes later, identities of the slain were completed.

'I half expected the day would come,' he addressed his uncle. 'Though when I dreamed of such a possibility, I thought it merely a vision that could be shrugged away, with the dawn. Now it seems rumour had become reality, like a child stillborn.' He rubbed a hand over his brow. 'It was as I thought. I fear the Abrentii haven't struck this blow alone. It seems the Bear has allies.

'It makes sense though, doesn't it?' Culchul growled, remounting. 'Brennus wouldn't have dared risk himself, had he not gained support from others of like mind. Reckless bastard he may be, but he never was a fool, damn his eyes.' He cast a glance over the scattered corpses, his face solemn. 'He must have known such a deed would bring a heavy reckoning,' He wiped a soiled hand on his tartan breeches, 'Yet he's done it, anyway.'

45

'But it all fits', a balding Gralos, old friend to Culchul, joined in. 'If one believes the wild boasts made by Brennus, that one day the western nations will gather their might under one leader and bring about a reckoning?'

'Such a thing would indeed be odd news, Gralos,' Titocuna, a brazen youth smirked behind his shoulder, ever looking for confrontation.

Culchul stared upon the carnage about him with a cold eye, shaking his head. at this voicing of the unimaginable. 'No,' the older man replied. 'If that old boast were true, I pray that the Bear is no major contender in such a gathering, the murderous scum.' He then shook his head vigorously, 'there has to be another's hand in this.'

'Venutius?' Armet voiced.

Culchul nodded. 'He left Cartimandua's land with an unknown number of fighting men a few days ago. With the Roman offensive looming over Mona being common knowledge, my gut informs me that he may be joining up with the Bear to maybe halt Paulinus' advance, and there's only one place that comes to mind.'

'Dorona,' agreed Armet, deep in thought. 'A point directly in the path of Paulinus' line of march. If strongly defended it might delay the planned assault on Mona by many days, if not deter it altogether.'

Culchul smoothed his beard in thought and eyed the prince. 'They mean to stop Rome in its tracks at the settlement!' Bending in the saddle he spat with open contempt. 'As a 'Hud' he spoke to Armet, so as not to be heard, 'A part of me must be pleased at that, the sparing of the sacred oaks, should Paulinus be thwarted. Pity that it's our mortal enemy who might well bring that about.'

This was the great dilemma for people such as the Coritani. Living under the imperial gaze of Rome took great skill when pressed. Using one foe to eliminate another might be advantageous in the short term, but what could come after?

The prince set his lips. If it were true, it might account for the Abrentii decimation of Petra's Horse! A dangerously flagrant snub to Rome, or a cunning ruse? Was Brennus, with the help

46

of Venutius, luring Rome out? It would seem so. Not that their army, kicking its heels in Lindum, needed any lure. Nigh on three restless legions, inactive within the limited confines of the colonia for weeks on end, would follow anyone who gave them an excuse to vacate their confinement.

As far as it concerned Armet, he'd long seen the possibilities in the situation unfolding. If Rome were going into The Bear's den, then he felt duty bound to make certain that his people should be hard on their heels whatever Cerialis implied! The prospect was inviting. After years of enmity, following the deaths of mother, sister, and others of his kin during raids, skirmishes and other similar confrontations, an end to his enemy might possibly be in sight?

His dark eyes focussing, he took a final look at the dead. Volisios' second son should have been here to see this, he thought. Not that the headstrong Gort, having little love for Rome, would have shed one salty tear at the loss of Petra's Horse. But the man who did this work in the land of king Tadoc, was the same merciless enemy who before the legions came, descended on Rina's capital, a place the Romans had renamed Ratae, to carry out the worst of outrages on the Coritani.

As a boy of twelve the prince remembered the pain and grief inflicted by the Abrentii on his people, acts that would never be forgotten. Ten years was a long time to harbour such thoughts with a foe like the Abrentii, who proved to be elusive and slippery, meaning any attempt to defeat them had always ended in maddening frustration.

The absence of his younger brother was, since their final violent disagreement, most worrying. He had been missing from both Lindum and Rina for two months now, along with Dasal Hud, another renegade and distant cousin of his uncle, together with a close companion Tove, plus several score of like-minded Coritani supporters. They could be anywhere. At another time Gort's conduct would have been of little concern, he was his own master. But rumour was growing fast in a time unsettled, news of unrest in the territory of the Iceni and their neighbour, the

Trinovante. On a like note, the passing of new people through Volisios' realm became more frequent. Groups were limited in number and moved through the land in peace. Yet there were others from places far distant, strange looking folk with whom the Coritani had scant contact. Also, men from wild and lawless lands to the north, beyond the grip of Rome, passed through the land unchallenged.

More uneasily, the Coritani noticed people closer to home encroaching on their borders, men like those of the Parisi, keepers of the golden chariot, long-time enemy of queen Cartimandua, ruled over by their king, Mogonus the Sly, from whom Armet's younger brother had learned to master this mobile instrument of war.

All the above were permitted to pass, a recent concession granted hesitantly by Volisios. Hesitantly, because any one of these dangerous movements might come to the attention of traitorous informers and their Roman paymasters squatting on The Hill, and being a king didn't necessarily lift him above suspicion.

With his mind dwelling on many of these things, Armet finally tugged hard on restless Freya's reins to wheel about, taking off in the direction that led to king Tadoc's settlement. Yes, he thought bitterly as he put heel to horse, Gort should have been here!

ELEVEN

IT WAS A BITTER TRUTH and should never have happened. Armet missed his younger brother every passing moment and, hoping against hope, looked for reconciliation. The unwanted situation couldn't be hidden, though there was much to conceal. Things hadn't always been so, but the arrival of Rome, bringing with it a generous offer of a possible client kingship for Volisios, changed the nature of many old and tried traditions.

CHAPTER ELEVEN

At this stage the Coritani, for their sins, were bordered by the Brigante in the north, the Iceni in the east, the Catuvellauni to the south and the Cornovii in the west, all four nations hereditary contenders for power. Once, Armet's people were known as the Corieltavi, and a few still held to the old name. After Cartimandua's Brigante, they were acknowledged to be the largest holders of manpower in Britain, possessors of, according to Julius Caesar, the finest light cavalry in the empire, a fine coup for Rome if negotiations went their way. Rumour abounded that legate Cerialis was already working on the advantages.

Whatever might befall, the Coritani possessed a strong and proud heritage, minting their own coinage and adhering to ancient law under their leader, Volisios, a man who for thirty years ruled with an even-tempered hand. It was only when he agreed to confer with Rome in earnest, regarding terms of mutual favour to be had under client membership, that the bench of elders went against their king in open conflict. Volisios, stubbornly defending his ground, spoke of several promising trade benefits to be derived from aiding the invader, plus the possibility of helpful grants that might greatly benefit the nation. A schism between doubter and believer instantly became evident and Armet, the king's first-born, felt duty-bound to support his father.

Gort, younger than his brother by two years, not burdened with such a filial responsibility, like many of the elders, thought otherwise, expressing his distrust of Rome while citing the southern Trinovante as a vivid example of imperial treachery where its king, Obrig, rotting in prison, was made fully aware during the mental part of his torture of the ongoing hunt for his fugitive son, Adomarus, thought to be attempting an escape to Iceni territory from where he would continue to carry on his resistance.

A day inevitably came when the two-way tug of opinion finally broke and, after one last bitter argument Gort became, like Adomarus, a wandering maverick. However, Volosios' feisty son had only one real ambition. Persuading others to join him he'd boldly seek, with the aid of an increasing number of like-minded among the nations, to throw Rome's unwanted legions back across the narrow divide separating the Britons from Gaul. A lofty ambition. A worried prince Armet, expecting as much, fell to tracking Gort's movements among many peoples, so far with little success.

Truth was, this uncertainty over Gort muddied the waters with Rome's negotiators, making the present situation difficult for the prince, especially with Paulinus' pending assault against the sacred stronghold of Mona looming. Whether this wary atmosphere would have lasting effect on the future, remained to be seen, and Armet's loyalty to Rome was being tested, not too subtly, by this visit to Tadoc.

TWELVE

W HEN GORT WAS LESS than a man yet something more than a child, life was a time of wonder and experiment. From early on his enthusiasm seemed beyond boundless. Since a time when his height reached only as far as his father's belt, his bouncing energy appeared limitless. Unfazed, he would rise against those that sought to scar his pride while excelling in all things that employed daring. Quick to challenge any supposed form of insult, too quick some might say, he always stood his ground. With reasons difficult for lesser mortals to calculate he viewed any opposition that went against his character as nothing less than a slur, challenging anyone who dared question it.

Gort!!!

The recalling of the name drummed away in Armet's head, pushing back the years as he rode toward Tadoc. On that faraway day the laughter and jibes of Gort's peers must have buzzed in the boy's ears like an angry swarm of bees. The lad expected gentle mockery, even though he had acquitted himself well with all manner of tests in last year's athletic games. Good-natured ribbing, he would accept, to a point. But that day his tormentors made the grossest error in opting to impishly humiliate him in front of his young sister Alorad who, it was obvious to all, worshiped him like a minor god.

'What deed would you fools have me undertake to still your stupid mouths?' he'd yelled dramatically, challenging the small group gathering to enjoy the entertainment. Apart from several catcalls and name-calling, only one answer came. 'Challenge the priests who have gathered in the circle of stones,' a voice cried. 'Show us just how brave you *really* are, wonder boy!' There was no hesitation. In his rage he leapt angrily onto the back of his pony, pulling Alorad up behind him, grabbing at the pony's flowing mane while, at the same time, heel-kicking the startled animal angrily into motion.

Perhaps it was the quantity of forbidden ale that he'd foolishly consumed that finally prompted him to show boldness, that and perhaps an overconfidence which would inevitably lead him face-on, into trouble. Even now Armet could recall with an inward smile how his little brother chose to favour ale rather than wine, reasoning the latter a prime symbol of Roman dominance. Yes, Armet mused, it had really gone that far. Now, with the japes and jeers of the group of youths fading as the animal under them gathered pace, the pair hurtled downhill at breakneck speed, Alorad seated precariously behind him, legs astride, arms encircling her brother's naked chest, tightly holding on for dear life. Thus together, they raced toward the waiting ring of standing stones.

Several grey-robed figures occupied the centre of the hallowed grove, one still probing with blood covered fingers the gory entrails of a newly sacrificed bird. All three glanced up at the sound of approaching hooves. One of them, the bearded elder, eyes glaring with rage beneath his cowl, dropped the curved blade and stepped forward. He clutched the wooden staff of office, with its image of Astarte on the crown, tightly in his hand, as though expecting violence. When the priest identified the rider and passenger, he lowered the staff a little, still not sure as to what these unexpected visitors had in mind.

The old priest shouting angrily, approached. 'What is the meaning of such reckless stupidity?!'

The youth reined-in and slid from the pony's back, conscious of the disappearance of his detractors who'd beaten a hasty retirement, not stopping until they'd reached the cover of the nearest trees from which they'd watch the unfolding drama in relative safety. This was the moment where Gort might have paused had he been possessed of a modicum of sense, returning instead to his tormentors, soundly to beat their cowardly hides. But having already done enough to prove his courage as he saw it, just by being there in the sacred domain and facing up to a grey-bearded Druid, reason should have urged him to grab Alorad and run.

Yet flight, still in full view of his tormentors was unthinkable. He knew he'd overstepped the mark, and a whipping from the hand of his uncle, Culchul, would certainly be the most likely outcome. He also knew he'd no option but to stand his ground and face it out. Alorad, displaying a small touch of Gort's zeal, leaped from the pony and stood beside her brother in confrontation with the terrifying shapes dominating the sacred circle. Hesitation may well have gripped her, yet she would not leave her brother to face the priests alone.

'What is your reason for invading our ritual in such a wild manner?' the youngest of them, whom Gort instantly recognised as Dasal, demanded, throwing back his cowl. 'This is hallowed ground, dolt that you are. Has the good Volisios taught you nothing?' The flushed faces of the older priests looked at Alorad whose heart was now racing to bursting point. 'Take this mindless clod away little one, before I get *really* angry and batter his empty head,' spoke the second elder.

Gort hesitated, glanced up at the azure sky, dazzled by a brilliant orb of the sun which temporarily blinded vision. There seemed no way out. It was as if a far greater power than this trio of priests controlled his every move. Some years later, as Armet vividly remembered, Gort would confess to him that he'd have given much for his brother to have been near him that moment when he stood with Alorad, face to face against Dasal, a man later to figure somewhat in Gort's affairs. A forlorn wish on Gort's part, as Armet had long been sent to Rome at the time, a customary procedure for those who might one day inherit power. Instruction in the ways and manners of this new world of imperialism, that was the deal. Therein lay the great gulf that divided the brothers to this day, with the gap widening.

The figure of Dasal came to tower menacingly over Gort. 'You're not clever enough to be so glib, whatever your feeble brain may tell you. And what great honour are you granting the gods, by bringing yourself before them in such a sorry state, idiot fool that you are?'

Gort walked further into the ring of standing stones, making no reply to Dasal while ignoring the others. Placing his hands flat on the central altar, the slab turning icy under his touch, he nervously offered himself up to sun and moon, the wisdom of Andraste, the mightiness of Macha and the generosity of Epona, who rode the best of horses and held sway over a timeless and mystical realm. The oaths were swiftly followed by as many other deities as his racing brain could recall within the sacred circle. Whatever it was, it worked as in silence, the priests drew aside, not choosing further to bar his way. Rather they marvelled at the boy's bold audacity, Dasal confessing later to Volisios that he'd felt inclined to belabour the boy mightily with his staff. What then had stopped him? An odd premonition, remarked Dasal, some unchartered part of Gort conveying a power far and away older than his tenderness of age, this somehow stayed his hand.

Volisios' second son put out his palms, raising them high. 'Give me your promise that, one day, I shall be a wiser ruler than either brother or father, so that no one shall ever doubt me after. In return, I, second son of Volisios, vow to one day drive Rome from hence. This I offer as a fervent promise, sealed in blood.' He retrieved the dagger that the priest had dropped, In raising it he felt a sudden warning tremor grabbing a tight hold on his limbs.

'No! Not here, not now! I beg you,' he cursed softly.

The occasional seizures that had plagued him since birth would now and then force him to collapse, his body convulsing rapidly. Though short in duration, these violent attacks would sometimes leave him confused and helplessly disorientated for a spell. But mercifully this one relented, and he breathed an inward sigh of relief as the knife seared his palm.

Behind him, Alorad failed to see any sign of Gort's discomfort. Instead, she giggled at his boldness in challenging a high priest so tempestuously on his own ground within the sacred circle. Later that night she'd swear she heard the howl of a distant wolf complimenting such affrontery.

When Gort, recovering from his momentary spasm, finally departed the ring, the priests shook their heads in mock dismay, for never had they seen such playacting. Sadly, less than a month later, Alorad and her mother, Carala, were dead, ravaged and slaughtered by Brennus and his warrior sons. As Armet later bitterly recalled, Gort was at the time, barely ten years old.

THIRTEEN

THE FORMING OF THE EXPLORATORES had for a long time been Cerialis' growing passion. As an idea it wasn't entirely unique, having been tried once before in the province with the then cooperative Atribates, to no great effect. The legate thought he saw why, their efforts having lacked a full grasp of the advantages, meaning those charged with the project hadn't seriously got the subject up and running so, thereafter, the idea dwindled.

Never let it be said that Rome's auxiliary mounted units, such as Petra's Horse, lacked excellent support when pitted against the enemy, but her military power at this time never rated cavalry highly, preferring instead to put most of their reliance on the might of her legions, boots on the ground, in effect. To Cerialis, ever an avid supporter of the mobile arm, this was disappointing, his argument being that mobile squadrons of horse should have been employed to much greater effect in the past. In the legate's mind there was a promising vision. Groups of expert riders, lightly armed for speed, ready to move well ahead of an advancing army, was his desire. Above all, itinerate horsemen who were familiar with the terrain and its hidden dangers were the perfect choice, provided they were correctly led by a soldier such as Armet. Like Balbilus with his 'killer babies', Cerialis strove hard to realise the creation of these modern skirmishers.

Surprisingly, when he first put the idea to Paulinus it wasn't immediately dismissed out of hand, though there was a characteristic deal of caution. 'The men you propose to enrol, they are untried barbarians, people we haven't taken full measure of,' he conjectured. 'Now I understand you wish to recruit these untried heathens, placing them at the cutting edge against similar savages who insist on making human sacrifice on their cursed altars, a cult which mistakenly reveres their atrocities as a golden key to their idea of paradise.' Paulinus raised both hands in mock horror. 'What's the difference between confounded Druse worshippers and your precious Coritani? As for them being better horsemen than our own equites, I can easily imagine what men like friend Balbilus will say, after the debacle with Petra.' The supreme legate drummed his fingers on the desk, a frequent as well as an annoying habit. 'I trust you already have in mind the leader of these damn scouts?'

Cerialis nodded. 'The Coritani are said to be the finest light cavalry in the province, perhaps the empire, eminence, despite your doubts. The four hundred proposed will be chosen from their best. Prince Armet is a loyal friend of Rome, having proven his loyalty more than once. I hardly need remind you of our problem with queen Cartimandua, regarding her conflict with Venutius, and how we restored her to power again. Armet was no small player on that notable occasion, eminence.'

An instant picture of the prince leading the Coritani horsemen to cut a bloody path through massed ranks of Carveti wild men in a second struggle to reinstate the Brigante queen, came instantly to the legate's mind, a brilliant vision in which he would seek future credit.

'I think you over romanticise, Quintus. I'm aware of your very-public displays,' Paulinus added, icily, 'along with several other acts of insubordination. It's well that I wasn't governor then, or I'd have seen you disciplined, quick time.' He fell to shuffling the pile of papyri on the cluttered desk, then shoved it irritably aside 'But she's a lesson, the she-wolf,' he fell to drumming fingers again, staring intently at the table. 'A good example of what happens when a woman is handed a nation, especially a shameless whore like her,' Paulinus added. 'No diplomacy when it's really needed, no real idea of how to govern. That's no way to rule!'

Cerialis raised an eyebrow in surprise, knowing Paulinus to be a man of few words, perhaps the man's best attribute, brevity being all. Yet a put-down of the Brigante queen, especially after his earlier rant, came as close to a speech as Cerialis had yet heard from his superior. Was he really referring to Cartimandua? Obviously, the man had never met the woman. The legate had to silently disagree that such casual disdain for the she-wolf who, whatever her character, happened to keep control of a large swathe of Britannia, a woman with a known reputation for getting things done, seemed hardly deserving of such dismissive comment. Then again on second thoughts, Cerialis had to admit that he was perhaps more than a little biased.

The supreme legate had also displayed an equal bias on the subject of the Coritani in general, remarking on their distasteful habit of collecting human heads which they sometimes hung from their saddles as battle trophies, no uncommon ritual among the nations of the Britons. He also took a dislike to the wolf-head skull nailed firmly to their battle-stave's central crossbar, carried proudly by its signifer, Patox. Upon either side of the animal's skull, to compliment the image, three wolf-tails hung limp. This last example of Coritani disregard appeared to annoy Paulinus even more than the business of the heads, believing it to be a blatant mockery of their eagle standards, a direct insult to Roman history, the wolf having been instrumental in the founding of Rome itself.

That aside, the determined persistence of the legate seemed to have won the first round with his project, at least for the present. Now he'd have to fight a second, an understandable reluctance hailing from the opposite direction.

'Four hundred chosen riders,' mused Armet, later. 'A tall order, Quintus.'

'You think king Volisios will agree?'

The prince shrugged. 'I'll put it to him and the elders. But I think you push things a mite too far, too soon,' he cautioned. 'We're a free people in our own right who find it hard enough to fall in with your ways of doing things. Doubtless the question of what's in it for you will be vigorously debated,' he added lightly while accepting an overspilling goblet of Falernian.

'Co-operation,' the legate replied firmly. 'With you at their head your Exploratores will become a vital arm of the legion.'

'By 'legion' I assume you mean, Hispanics?'

Cerialis chuckled. 'You really are a damnably suspicious bastard, Armet.'

'And you're a damned self-centred one.' Armet countered with a tightening of his forehead. 'Yet Rome always has an eye on the first sesterce, does she not? The main chance, a lucky throw of the dice.' Armet drank the vessel dry and wiped his lips with the back of a hand. 'Rome, if it be anything at all, is a nest of gamblers.'

Cerialis smiled. 'Gamblers maybe. But you'll follow her, providing Rome is prepared to pay enough for your services. You've already gone far, citizen of Rome, conferred by Nero himself. The empire is everything or its nothing, remember that. You're either a part of its future, or you're not.'

'Everything comes to nothing in the end, even Rome,' Armet spoke finally with unguarded cynicism, aiming a parting shot at the bemused legate as he left the room.

FOURTEEN

THE BOYISH RECRUIT, Servilus, paused to pick hold of the four skins of wine as he watched the departure of Armet and his tough looking band of Exploratores ride out of Lindum that morning. The horse the prince rode he picked out immediately. Sheened like the dark hue of midnight she was, so Servilus had been informed by his comrade Philo, who knew everything, or thought he did; that the horse was named, Flavia, personal gift from legate Cerialis. Nice for some people, Servilus thought. A few minutes later, with weary resignation, he again hefted the load over his shoulder and began the long walk uphill to 9th legion's praetorium. It was hot work, because The Hill was permanently steep and the skins heavy.

For reasons of youth, he was barely nineteen, comrades in the contubernium still called Servilus, 'our recruit,' although he'd been a legionary for over a year. Their humour was a rough form of barrack-room mockery, largely well-meaning and easily accepted because, for the first time in his young life he really felt, having been born an orphan, that at last he belonged to something.

Half a century ago young men like Servilus would never have been allowed within the ranks of the army, but after the disastrous loss of three crack legions along with their commander, the out of luck Quinctilius Varus, in Germania, half a century ago, Rome was required to change the rulebook with regards to recruitment, and future levies were mustered from the chosen, non-citizen, peoples of an expanding empire. This didn't mean a recruit like Servilus would instantly be entitled to Roman citizenship. Although he was a free man, one of the peregrini, he'd still be required to serve a full term of service before *that* privilege might be obtained.

The morning, though the clouds promised showers to come, was brighter than the previous few days and later a clear sky, pale blue and clean, would remind him of his distant homeland. But musing was a luxury he found difficult to nurture, serving under such a harsh regime. Beneath his unlaced tunic he sweated heavily and began the third ascent with the satisfying thought that this was his last trip. The local weather could change with surprising speed, he'd soon discovered. The day before he'd been glad to wear his leather jerkin, while carrying out the same task, it had been so damned cold, what with the ill-wind and intermittent rain, but that morning, even with a lack of direct sunlight, he perspired like some hard-pressed gladiator while struggling the quarter mile separating the legionary quartermaster's stores from the legate's H.Q.

There had been a brief time at the start of his life in Lindum when he'd toyed with the idea of getting out, thoughts that very soon left him when he reminded himself of the crosses erected up-river. All six, thankfully for the recruit's sake, stood unoccupied when he'd passed the spot earlier in the day, while engaged on other fatigues ordered by his hated centurion, Iber.

As the recruit saw it, a combination of circumstances found him on fatigues that week, with Iber being reason numero uno. His current punishment was a lesser one, when chancing his arm, he'd been absent from a parade line-up. Luckily for him the centurion wasn't around. 'You were dead fortunate, there,' Lentilus remarked, afterward. A veteran of nine years with Rhine Army, Lentilus was one of the men with whom Servilus shared a tent. 'Last time I made that mistake I got a right flogging!'

Almost at the end of his climb with sweat damping his body, he cursed again. One of the skins slipped a little and the leather strap grazed his already sore shoulder. Only one consoling thought crossed his mind. For a while he was free of Iber's hysterical outbursts and the sly references as to his birth, amid the monotony of parade ground drill. Lately there'd been plenty of both. Weapon training, battle tactics, defensive deployment, formations of attack and the like, and always the grating yell of the centurion's lashing tongue.

'Thrust! Parry! Maim! Kill! Fuck the bleedin' sod up before he damn well gets you, son of a whore!'

When Pug Face, one of the more polite descriptions by which Iber was called, issued an order he didn't exactly shout, he erupted like magma from a volcano, all a part of the constant bullying.' What are you doing with that fucking pilum, soldier, taking it for a walk or shagging it?!' Servilus began to wonder if the bastard had ever spoken in anything like a normal tone. There was also something else he was learning about the man. Iber had a predilection for good looking youths like himself, and a groping hand often landed on the young man's upper thigh, more times than could be accidental.

In his dreams a rosy prospect beckoned. If he were really to give way to Iber's desires, less guard duty and fatigues maybe, or more leisure time would perhaps, come his way. It might well work, save for *one* obvious reason. Servilius, like most of his comrades, loathed Iber's guts. The recruit was under no illusion, his future could well be on the line. He could take the problem to a higher level, that much was open to him. Aubanus, primus pilus of the legion, for example. Meritorious if he won his case, crap if he lost it............

Everyone was aware of Iber's persuasion. After fifteen years of service, he was under the impression that perhaps he'd be one of the next in line for the lofty position of senior centurion, prompting him to think that making life uncomfortably tough for lesser beings, was a key step toward achieving that goal.

Optio Priscus was certainly convinced, when engaged in sex, the centurion probably shagged by numbers. When Servilus told him of his suspicions, Priscus chuckled. 'Coming that old trick, is he? One good tip, boy, if the swine tries to feel you up again, plead the clap, or tell him you've got piles.'

Few men grew fat in the legion. Expected to carry fifty pounds of equipment on their backs in the field, there was little place for anything but muscle. Iron muscle, muscle as tough as the cooking pots which served up their version of barley soup every twenty-four hours. A legionary was trained to march twenty-five miles a day on campaign, sometimes extra. He probably did more marching than any soldier in the world, that's why boots were important to him, boots made of pliable leather strapped half-way up the calf. Servilus paused, looked down at his own. He again noted with disdain that the left boot had split half-way. He remembered the edge of his sword had caught it during one of the interminable drills, and he made a mental note to get it repaired before Iber plagued him over that too.

Servilus passed through the open gate that led to the praetorium, giving a third familiar nod to the legionary guarding it. It was a small courtyard encircled by a wall, stone at the base, timbered above. 'Put them in there with the others,' the decurion instructed. A grateful Servilus entered the kitchens and laid his burden on the bench. Flexing his arms and shoulders he fell back against the wall, glad of the rest. Several house slaves, silent and anonymous, appeared and disappeared with the skins. The decurion belonged to legate Cerialis' staff, a middle-aged, greying figure with a pronounced limp. He came forward to lean against the bench. 'Servilus, right?'

The recruit nodded, helping himself to a beaker of water. 'Daily fatigues?' asked the decurion, poised with a stylus and slate in his hands.

'Weekly, more like.'

'Who's century?'

Servilus wiped a sweaty palm on his tunic. '8th, 2nd cohort.'

'Iber's fuckin' mob,' the decurion stated, glancing at the recruit and grinning knowingly. 'Well, sod your horrible luck, soldier,' he grinned. 'Never mind, action at last, eh?'

Servilus looked at the decurion in puzzlement, sure what he was about to hear wouldn't be pleasant. 'Go on,' he prompted with reluctance.

'You'll be glad to know your shipping out, you and two brother cohorts, one from each legion. Your part of the long-awaited advance guard to Dorona, Suetonius' big bloody push. You'll probably be leaving in a day or two, so if you're shagging some whore down below, give her a farewell poke from me, who knows, it might well be your last.'

'Bugger!' was all that the recruit could manage. 'Who said?'

'Someone heard the legate's secondus and a senior officer from Gemina discussing it a couple of hours ago. Maybe just a rumour, you know how these barrack room stories get about,' said the decurion dismissively. 'Anyway, it would countermand Paulinus' orders about us lot doing nothing till he arrived. Then again though, the governor has a habit of using fast gallopers, hasn't he?'

Servilus wiped his brow, shifting his weight from one foot to the other while absorbing the news. One tale, on top of several, he thought, dismissively. This one might go the way of the others and he decided, to avoid disappointment not to mention this unconfirmed information to his comrades.

'Right, that's enough hanging about,' the decurion said finally, with a viciously efficient stab at the slate. 'Twelve goat skins of Falernian. That should keep our betters happy, at least for a couple of days, boozy bastards. Oh, to be an officer.' He put the slate under his arm, looking Servilus in the eye. 'Feeling thirsty?'

Servilus nodded. 'Sore throat,' he said, glumly. 'Feels as if I've swallowed a mouthful of sand.'

'Better see the cook. Tell him Telachies sent you along to give him a hand. He'll see you alright.'

The kitchens proper, a low roofed set of rooms at the rear of the building looked out at another yard, in which Servilus guessed, stood the cavalry stables serving the equites, the aristocratic turmae. The recruit sipping at a cup of indifferent wine given him by the cook, eyed the attendant groom leading out one of the finest looking stallions that Servilus had ever clapped eyes on. The mount was completely white, the opposite to the night-coloured sheen of her twin. In naked sunlight, this one's flanks shone like polished marble, and it tossed its silken mane proudly, as if slightly contemptuous of the humble surroundings of the compound, presenting a sight the farm boy from Tarraco scarce expected to see in such an unforgiving place.

Servilus, before joining the legion, had been brought up around horses, pleasant memories that would never be extinguished. He didn't know the reasons, he just felt at one with them. The cook was of course, correct. The animal was worth far more than he could ever earn on his meagre pay.

When his elderly benefactor suddenly upped and died, Servilus was forced to seek other employment. After a disastrous winter blighting the land, he found himself without work or any means of making a living, hence his present situation. With lofty ambition and knowledge of horses, he would have liked to join the cavalry. But that took money, meaning the purchase of a horse and the necessary gear was way out of reach for a creature of his meagre means.

'Right, holiday over, soldier.' The cook broke the recruit's reverie. 'Start making yourself useful for a bloody change.'

Servilus turned. The man faced him, holding a wooden tray on which stood a large jug, filled almost to the brim with wine. The jug was accompanied by six beakers which he placed on the bench.

'Who owns the horse?' the recruit indicated as she was trotted by her groom in a wide circle.

'The legate, who'd you bloody think?' The cook showed broken stumps of teeth in what Servilus took for a smile. He stared hard in envy. 'I'd give a lot to have a shot at that one.'

'I bet you bloody would,' chuckled the cook, 'but your total period of service wouldn't get you anywhere close to making an offer.' The man turned, silently indicating the bench with his eyes.

'That's slaves work,' Servilus protested sulkily. 'Let them do it!'

The cook, with some roughness, forced the object on the recruit. 'Slaves have more important tasks to do, heavier loads to carry. Think yourself damn lucky and get on with it, or I'll report your insolent conduct to the duty centurion!' Servilus took the tray grudgingly. He had no counter argument for the rebuke, plus the last thing he desired was to be reported to Iber, as only the gods knew what punishment the infernal sadist might devise.

With a final backward glance at the trotting beast, he left the kitchen wondering that if by chance, he were to take a single sip from one of the tray's half-dozen beakers before reaching the praetorium, would anyone notice?

FIFTEEN

THE ONE PIECE of weaponry the Roman army lacked; their opponent held in abundance. The chariot.

On the battlefield, pitted against both infantry and cavalry, the legions excelled on many occasions. But the vehicles used by the Britons proved harder to contain. Light in weight and built for speed, gathered in large numbers, they could be terrifying, their movements being entirely unpredictable. All this made them irresistible to an eager-to-learn character such as Gort.

At the age of fifteen he became smitten. Five years before, during one of the many festivals which enabled people of other neighbouring nations to compete in a variety of athletic and bardic competitions, was when fate beckoned. All nations involved had the opportunity to play host. On this occasion it fell to the Coritani to preside over the arrival of the god Imbolg and with it, the renewal of a bountiful spring. A time of hope and aspiration, and a waning one for Cailleah, an evil Hag who brought down the chill of winter upon mere humans by selfishly hording in the months of Summer all the available firewood throughout the land, ensuring she'd never go cold while others would, or so went the legend................

The name of the champion charioteer that day was Vixt. He lived in the land of the Parisi, way off to the north, long ruled by king Mogonus, sometimes called 'the Sly,' sworn enemy of its more powerful neighbour, Cartimandua. The Parisi had long association with this unique vehicle over which they'd acquired complete mastery. Watching how Vixt made a show of his skills in the traditional mock-skirmishes, put on for the enjoyment of the crowd, left Gort in awe and, such was his unbridled zeal, the charioteer took the Coritanian on board.

The moment he first held the reins, feeling the tremendous power of the brace of ponies pulling the wicker chariot, their energy entered him, and he knew that this was something he'd been preparing for all his young life. Vixt too, was impressed by the boy's avid interest and potential, so much so that after much discussion and bargaining, it was arranged that Gort be guest of his instructor for the whole of the following summer at his home in Petrava.

Mogonus, in return for such generous hospitality, accepted Volisios' gift of a bride, the maiden offspring of a deceased friend, designated to be the Parisi king's second wife. Sadly, she would later fall victim to a fever, though not before presenting the aging Mogonus with the gift of a son. The elated king named the child Mal, to whom he would become much devoted.

Looking back, Gort swore that in the first few days under Vixt tuition, he and fate would become irrevocably sealed. From then on, the champion charioteer would unveil to him every trick, every tactic and every move while learning just what a war-chariot, unarguably the fastest thing on two wheels in the hands of an expert, could achieve. It was, to an impressionable youth like Gort, a wonderful revelation!

Vixt set forth the basic principles, the first being to unnerve the enemy. A few charging vehicles might well cause consternation amongst an army facing them, even amount to a jaw-dropping moment. A hundred chariots arriving on the field of battle would be worrying but, raise that number to a thousand and the mood felt by an opponent could border on abject terror.

Secondly, these light-weight machines were also extremely manoeuvrable, carrying two men working as a team, here the driver of the vehicle would urge his nimble ponies at full speed up and down the front ranks of infantry while his passenger would hurl spears and other missiles into the packed ranks of infantry. Wheeling about they'd then charge again into what they were certain would be a confused mass. This allowed the second warrior to leap into the confusion of hand-to-hand combat. Later withdrawing, the chariots would then swing back, driving once more into the heart of the struggle to reinforce their compatriots on the ground.

On the face of it such tactics may appear over simplified, yet they'd the power to strike panic among those on the receiving end. Much to his delight, Gort was often privileged to ride with Vixt and a large contingent of Parisi charioteers who, with queen Cartimandua in mind, regularly practiced their warlike skills.

On his return to Rina, Armet admitted he'd been carried away by Gort's insatiable enthusiasm when describing the mastery of what this form war machine could offer and, had it not been for Volisios' refusal, he'd have set about building a few of the vehicles himself. As it turned out, with a strong friendship having developed with Vixt, Volisios and Armet were to see much less of the impulsive Gort.

With talk of rising tension in the south, the territories of the Trinovante and Iceni said to be on the verge of revolt, rumour persisted. It appeared each day brought more restrictions and the doubling of Roman patrols, while men found freedom of movement slowly tightening. With Paulinus' legions preparing to leave Lindum, all unnecessary comings and goings might prove foolhardy, if not perilous.

The coming march against Mona and its priesthood, a revered and ancient calling to whom many were drawn, dismayed many in the diverse nations of the Britons, especially those who saw it as openly hostile to the fundamental core of long-held beliefs, a less than subtle ruse dressed to hide Rome's real intention, a need to control a region rich in precious ores to be found on the isle of Anglesey.

Paulinus was, by his very nature and calling, totally insensitive to all such rumblings. he had but one aim, the draining of the coffers of a supine province of which, under Nero, he now fully controlled. For the itinerant peoples it would be a time when loyalty would be stretched to breaking point in a vicious struggle for the very soul of the land.

Meanwhile, regardless of growing resentment, Rome decided to add ever more laws and restrictions to those already in place. As for prince Armet, he could only hope that Gort would be lying low, wherever he might be, but knowing his brother as he did, such a wish was unlikely to be granted.

SIXTEEN

THE SMALL CLUSTER of round houses burned ferociously in the failing light. A group of legionaries, fifty veterans from the town cohort, the ones who had fired the huts, had nearly finished their work. The eyes and throats of some, those that had ventured too close to the flames, smarted sorely as they moved among the burning dwelling, looking for any remaining sign of life from those who'd vainly attempted resistance. Apart from a small group of bedraggled captives, there were none. The stench of charred bodies dominated as with a groan, the last wattle and daub hut collapsed, final proof that the arsonists had carried out their task with the usual efficiency.

The bearded centurion overseeing the operation, gladius unsheathed and blooded, his face flushed with rivulets of sweat from his exertions, prowled the perimeter. Kneeling to clean the short sword in water from the shallow stream nearby, he noticed the ring. Retrieving it, he saw depicted the figure of a long-haired woman riding what looked like a rearing horse. He sought to recall where he'd seen the emblem before, then as quickly remembered. One of those heathen bitches the barbarians called Epona, goddess of horses. The name gave him the shivers. No matter, the ring was silvered and likely worth a few sesterces. He rose, glanced about to make certain his good fortune hadn't been witnessed, but nobody appeared to notice. A few of the detail who'd suffered minor injury in the fight were being hastily dealt with by the single obligatory medic as others made ready for the march home. The centurion looked up at a darkening sky. It was growing late, and this was no sort of place to linger.

He eyed the surroundings with his dread emotions supressed. In over twenty-five years of service, he'd been involved in many such skirmishes. Yet this one was different and sat uneasily on the mind. The orders had been explicit and had to be acknowledged, especially when it came from the procurator himself who, next to Paulinus, was arguably the most influential power in the province.

Women and children, two score or more survivors, huddled in a circle before the ruins that had been their homes. Roped together they stared at the wanton destruction of their small settlement with vacant eyes, still not entirely comprehending. The assembled prisoners neither cried nor raged at the loss of their menfolk. Instead, the captives displayed unnerving stoicism, a trait greatly familiar to the centurion. He'd never admit it, but such acceptance of violence from these people seemed uncanny. He stared at their near nakedness in the gloom, saw their bodies streaked with blood and soil, eyed their garments, torn from rough handling. The women's hair, unkempt and matted, hung in lifeless strands. They appeared to him more like wild beasts than humans, perhaps the reason for his unease.

You're getting to damn soft, he told himself, turning away, not wanting to see the coldness in their regard of him. Most of the younger women would be raped before being sold into slavery, as was the usual custom in such actions. When they arrived back at the colonia, he'd make sure he had first pick of them before a more senior bastard got his leg over. Already he picked out several younger females worth a fuck. Later he'd make sure to select the best of them for himself, using privilege of rank and all that. And he now had something to celebrate, being a recent recipient of a well-earned plot of land.

That's what it's all about, isn't it, these bastard clearances, he told himself?

The operation was carried out in record time, reducing the Trinovante village to a funeral pyre. Twenty-five years of subjugating what he termed lesser beings had inured these men to suffering and what little opposition encountered was overcome with brutal efficiency. Even so, it was nothing to boast about, the centurion reckoned, though some loud-mouthed prick no doubt would. A few elderly beings, plus several dozen women and children. The centurion sniffed in satisfaction, cuffing his nose on a sleeve. Only several of the stronger males had managed to fight their way out, and he chose not to worry about them over much. Here, in this 'little Rome' chances of freedom were limited and eventually they'd be hunted down.

Hours later the spasmodic spit and crackle of burnt wood were the only sounds to break the silence over the scene of death. Tongues of fire still moved like writhing snakes about a litter of primitive weapons, corpses, contorted shapes of blacked limbs and the twisted attitudes of the fallen. For a while, would go the legend, no bird dared sing in such a place of slaughter.

A water rat, large and obese, later waddled up from the stream, sniffing its way cautiously through the wreckage. It moved only a few yards before its ears caught more movement in the undergrowth behind. A final snort from a damp snout sufficed before turning tail, and he left whatever unknown business he'd been intent on, unfulfilled.

Later still, out of the cover of trees, the small figure of a child appeared. She violently retched up a stream of vomit. Raising her head, she viewed the destruction of all she'd called home, sobbing convulsively. There was an agonising pain within her that she was incapable of understanding. In this wilderness she called the name of a mother who failed to hear. Bewildered, she finally sank into the agony of despair, lost to all feeling.

The wolf left the shelter of the thicket, sniffing the air suspiciously. Primal instinct told her that something out of order had occurred in her domain. A steady breeze blew dancing ripples in the puddles formed by the continual overnight drizzle. There were no sounds as the huntress gingerly advanced, picking her way through the wreckage of charred wood and scattered corpses that lay around. She approached the supine figure of the girl, sniffing, prodding with a paw. No movement. She eyed the form with suspicion, half expecting a retaliation. None came, and satisfied the beast closed in. Sharp fangs took a grip of a leg, at which, the child suddenly roused, uttered a cry of pain and turned vainly on her attacker. Startled by the unexpected sound and movement, the animal momentarily released its grip. Then with an angry snarl, it advanced again, certain now of the helplessness of her prey. Suddenly the huntress froze, senses sharpened. At once instinct told her she was in peril, and she began to retrace her steps back toward the cover of the trees. The spear thudded deep into her back, severing sinew and muscle, shattering bone as it embedded itself. It was now the turn of the she-wolf to feel pain. Rearing on hind legs, the beast uttered a howl of anguish before falling heavily, her spine shattered.

Rough hands lifted the girl, who being too terrified to speak, was only vaguely aware of the tall and shadowy figure looming over her. Strong arms held her close. 'No place for any of us to linger, child,' the man's voice spoke softly as they moved away from the desolate scene.

SEVENTEEN

UPON HIS RETURN to the colonia, Armet carried the report that Cerialis secretly suspected, yet never desired to confirm.

'Venutius! That bloody name again!' Cerialis looked enquiringly at the prince. 'Is the man dangerous?'

'He could be,' Armet answered, guardedly.

'Dangerous enough to give us trouble?'

The prince gave a shrug. 'I met him once. Sharp as a gladius point and intelligent. An equal match for Cartimandua, but you'd probably know that.'

If Cerialis identified with this casual remark, he failed to register it. 'He will have met up with Brennus at Dorona,' he carried on, choosing to avoid the half-forbidden subject of the Brigante queen.

'Looks that way, Quintus,' Armet replied. 'If he's sitting on Dorona, somebody will have to drag him off. My guess, he intends to stop your Paulinus right there.' He paused, looking up enquiringly at the legate. 'Something else?'

Cerialis rubbed a hand over his chin. 'No, not really, it's just that Paulinus' secretary, young Agricola, has arrived at Lindum in your absence.'

Armet shrugged. 'So?'

'He and I never got on in Rome, you know, even though we only met occasionally. He's a damn prig of a fellow, that's my opinion,' complained Cerialis, 'More than that, I've to be nice to him, the pretentious little bugger. It's all too bloody much.'

'I'll try not to like him then, for your sake.'

'Believe me, prince, you won't have to try.'

After a moment of silence, both men managed to grin at the absurdity.

The day before, king Tadoc had welcomed Armet and his men warmly, while his only son, Fomah, the prince's onetime friend, looked on with a sullenness bordering on the insolent. After ale and food was introduced around the group, the business of two legions moving through Tadoc's land was, to Armet's relief, agreed with surprising ease. The supply of certain items necessary for the coming campaign were assured, in return for Tadoc's being considered for status of client king. That settled, a more pressing problem began to be seriously discussed. Later, with the rest of the Coritani scouts retired to the comfort of a proper bed, the prince remained seated around the fire stones with his uncle, face to face with Tadoc and his, up to now, silent observer.

The subject of Brennus was quick to arise. It was taken with great seriousness, the recent invasion of Tadoc's land, and the ambush of Petra's Horse. The sheer daringness of the episode rankled. Rome was a disagreeable reality to be sure, but the Abrentii were the older foe, and both nations, Coritani and Cornovii, had good reason for dealing with them, once and for all.

'Brennus' days are numbered,' asserted Armet, decisively. 'The Abrentii live conveniently along Paulinus' line of march. I and the scouts will ride with them as far as Dorona to see the old man lose his head.'

'There is much to be avenged for all the harm done, I fear,' Tadoc said, gravely, 'a reckoning for both our tribes.' The old man tapped his swollen leg in frustration. 'Would that I might be going with you.' After a thoughtful pause, he added. 'I'm cheered that you're not going with the legions to Mona and our brothers there, at least. Feelings could run high in such circumstances. There are enough people of our own, as you well know, who'd oppose any move at all, against the sacred groves.

Armet nodded. 'You refer to the Batavi, I suspect?'

Since the reign of Augustus more than half a century before, the Batavians were seen as Rome's most steadfast supporters. Trusted with the emperor's life they'd shared this honour equally with his elite praetorian guard. Taken for granted, few men studied their history, including Quintus Cerialis who, for all his Rhine service, might have given more heed, if he'd found the time. There he'd have gleaned that this ancient Germanic tribe dwelling on the Rhine delta, were close descendants of the fearsome Chatti who, ironically, formed part of an alliance led by Arminius that brought about the demise of Varus' three legions, a disaster from which Rome was still recovering.

Tadoc sighed, shaking his grey head. 'Those perhaps, and others likewise strong in our faith. I myself, have a few misgivings about supporting Paulinus, and many of my people barely hide their unease over my decision. Whatever, things won't be for the good, and I fear mightily for the future.

Armet demurred with equal gravity, a little unsettled by Tadoc's sage grasp of reality. He, unlike Cerialis, had long know about this victory over Varus, wondering if such a leader as Arminius dwelt somewhere among the Britons. A major rallying figure, perhaps. Was the king of the Cornovii being prophetic in his random observations? Did he have access to the inner sanctum of prophesy?

Another question posed itself. Why hadn't Armet informed Tadoc that his presence in Paulinus' coming campaign had *yet* to be decided? Did his personal wish for retribution against Brennus take pride of place at the central core of his desires? There were some who'd think it so, including the calculating Cerialis. Others close to the prince knew his mind when it came to Brennus, yet

Tadoc appeared to have momentarily forgotten the need of the Coritani for closure of this continuing vendetta.

Was he going through a period of wishful thinking when it came to his own disquiet? He seemed to be walking a tightrope with no sense of balance, showing all the signs of a wavering mind. This king was not the fighting Tadoc the prince knew of old, neither too was Volisios. Naturally the thought of *any* of them aiding the destruction of Druidism, that ancient body of truth that had long sustained them, both spiritually and morally, made for caution. Yet Tadoc's reaction was strange. To Armet it was of little matter in the scheme of things how things fell out, just so long as he came out on top. With his mind made up, neither Tadoc nor Cerialis would lure him from *that* aim.

Later, when Tadoc retired to slumber, Fomah remarked sarcastically, after draining a third cup of wine. 'Why return to your Roman masters so quickly? Gela will be mightily sad, should you leave her without word?'

'My place is Lindum,' Armet patiently explained. 'It is Volisios' wish that I stay close. Gela will understand. Instructions to deal............'

'Instructions! From your keeper, Cerialis, I suppose. Tell me, why do you put Volisios' wishes above what, I'm certain, are your own inclinations? Is it honestly for the cause of Rome that you return?' snorted Fomah in disgust. 'If I didn't know you better, I'd think you rather enjoyed kissing Rome's dirty backside.'

Armet met the implied insult with a steady dark-eyed gaze, aware of Culchul's tightening grip on his arm. 'What I do is for the good of Tadoc, as well as that of my father.'

'That's not the feeling I'm getting, sitting here,' Fomah returned, tracing with a hand the faded battle scar still prominent on his forehead. 'I get the notion that you do it for yourself, degrading the Coritani with all this damn arse licking.' Fomah's eyes softened briefly. 'I respected you, once,' he muttered, his voice slurring. You're going against The Bear, I've no question with. The gods know our people, like your own, suffered much from him and his brood over the years. Nothing would give me greater pleasure right now, than to go on the war-trail with you. What I do question, is the way you're going about it, using the legions to do our dirty work!'

'You're making a grave error, if you think that, Fomah,' Armet retorted, his voice rising. 'I prefer to see things the other way round.'

'Seems to me, you want to see what you wish to see,' argued Fomah, with a sneer. 'Unlike your brother..................'

'Gort, like yourself, fails to see the reality facing us,' Armet responded, shaking off Culchul's restraining hand. 'Whether you like it or not, Rome at present has the edge...................'

'Yes, it does,' said Fomah, 'because of men like you, prince. But that edge is dangerous when put to the test. How short a time have the Romans been here? Enough to bring about your choice of clothing, the war-gear you've adopted, your shorn hair, all in all, you almost smell like one of their perfumed bloody tarts! Your brother, who loved you as deeply as I once did, must be mightily displeased. If truth be known, your stance is likely why he finally left Volisios and Rina behind, because he could suffer your actions no longer!'

Armet leapt to his feet, his eyes suddenly ablaze. Culchul Hud glared at Fomah while continuing to restrain his angry nephew. 'Enough,' cautioned the prince, 'enough! Gort would never betray me.'

'Forgive me, Armet.' Fomah stood unsteadily, and challenged Armet, eye to eye. 'I doubt you know anything of his thoughts, when it comes down to it!'

'I know all I need to know about the problems we'll *all* face, at some stage, if that's what you mean. You'd better mind what you say, as you're very close to forcing me into something one of us might later regret,' the prince spoke coldly.

'It's you that walks the tightrope,' Tadoc's son snapped. 'Let slip to Rome anything of what you know of Gort's whereabouts, and I'll come after you myself!' he spat. 'There are two reasons why I don't choose to do so right now! One, because my sister appears to favour you, only the gods know why, and second, your father has been my father's loyal supporter for many a year, and I'll not dent that fellowship.'

'You're over bold, Fomah, if you think that,' said Armet, relenting. 'You know little about my regard for my brother. I also value yourself more than you might think. How you regard me is less important than giving our peoples a fighting chance, should things change.'

'You've had a strange way of showing your values!' Fomah muttered, turning away, his face grim as he staggered from the room, aided by the arrival of one of Tadoc's household.

'Fomah should be punished for his insolence,' Culchul muttered, fingering the engraved torc about his neck. 'I'm sore tempted to squeeze his nuts.'

Armet shook his head. 'Beneath all the swagger he's a man of courage who has proved himself in battle on more than one occasion, both against Brennus and other such scum. Who can tell?' Armet then asked thoughtfully. 'I may need men like Fomah someday. Best leave him be, he's drunk too much is all, and in no fit state to understand.'

'He's not the only one. I don't think I understand, myself,' spoke his uncle, genuinely mystified. 'You mentioned king Obrig with old Tadoc earlier. What of him?'

The prince would not burden Culchul with all that he'd heard. This was neither the time nor the place to mention stories of the many souls, killed and enslaved in the tribal land of king Obrig's Trinovante, nor of the oppression that had lately overtaken many other unfortunates.

'Don't bother to ask,' Armet said, calmly, playing down his own fears. 'Some foolishness of Gort's, that's all. He always had these crazy fantasies at times. You know what he's like.'

'Don't I just,' muttered Culchul Hud, not unkindly, adding for certain measure a silent curse as the pair quitted the remnants of the fire.

After dawn Armet said his farewells to Tadoc and made ready to depart. Outside, in the light of a mist filled morn the small band of Coritani, after a welcome breakfast of hot fish soup and bread, were already saddling up.

'Shame on you, prince, for daring to leave without word?' Gela came running into his arms.

'I looked for you and you weren't there,' Armet admonished lightly.

Gela's face held a mock-serious look. 'I was visiting an aging aunt a few miles across the river. Anyway, I rode armed, like a warrior, with a most trustworthy escort.

'Your old crow, Ulvina, I suspect. Seriously, it's dangerous to be abroad while the Abrentii are reported to be about.' He bent his head to kiss her lightly on the cheek. 'I'll soon be back,' he promised. 'I suppose that mischief-maker of a brother is behind this. He probably sent you away, knowing I was leaving. I very much regret I'm so out of favour with him.'

The young girl nodded. 'Don't judge Fomah too harshly,' she said, taking his hand. 'I have spoken with him and already I believe he regrets what he said last night. You must go easy with him, perhaps later he will understand. I remember, there was once a time when you two were closer. It hurts to see the change in you both.'

'We were carefree youths then, Gela. Today's affairs have made us grow more distant. I can only trust a day will arrive when all may right itself.' Then, sweeping Gela up in his arms, he spun the lightness of her in a giddy circle. 'If it be not so, you may have my offending body chopped up in a hundred pieces for punishment.'

'What good would you be to me, piecemeal?' I need you whole,' Gela laughed.

Bending low he stayed her with a second kiss. The soft touch of her lips felt cool against his, before the pair finally broke away. 'Tadoc has promised to bring you to Rina when things calm down. I'll not disappoint.'

'Will there be such a time, I wonder?'

Armet noticed a tear in her eye. 'I'll try mightily to make sure there is,' he said, hoisting himself into the saddle. 'Unless you change your mind,' he grinned as he rode away.

EIGHTEEN

THE WELL-SPRING OF AMBITION rarely touched Volisios. Keeping his people fed, clothed and, as much as possible, out of harm's way, had largely been the summit of his desires. Through all the years of his kingship he had laboured for the advancement of the Coritani nation. As the she-wolf guards her lair, as the rich man covets gold, so Volisios zealously watched over his flock. For just such a reason he'd early on agreed to send his eldest son to Rome where he would be introduced to the uneasy privilege of belonging to an empire, a Janus-like gift but an honour sometimes granted to a future king, like himself. An undisguised bribe maybe, yet Volisios, to spare his people from any possible unpleasantness arising from a refusal, sought instead an arguable compromise. In light of recent events, he now questioned such a decision.

Uncertainty nagged at him constantly. When he himself was dead, what sort of ruler would his heir turn out to be? Doubtless Armet would be treading a fine line, serving Rome on the one hand while at the same time honouring an obligation to his people on the other.

The old king, weighed down with problems, juggled with the future even though he'd always had little option. Rome had cast a dark shadow over the proud Coritani, almost by stealth. Suddenly he'd found himself confronted with the choice of two uneven roads. Security for his threatened people by means of cooperation with the conqueror, with or without a treaty, or a protracted relationship with all its pitfalls. An eventual granting of a client kingship seemed preferable and, being a realist, he made the fatal decision. An uneasy peace, rather than a harsh subjection amounting to nothing less than abject slavery, was the answer. As a client king there should at least be mutual safeguards attached.

Yet, if what he'd recently heard was correct, that was no longer true, for Prasutagus had once accepted what had since been offered to Volisios. After the Iceni king's demise, it would seem Rome's attitude had fast taken things to another level, with rumour of harsh retaliation brought against his royal wife over unpaid debts and tribute. For Volisios another serious question now presented itself. What if something were to happen to the Coritani, if a like situation arose?

As if that weren't enough, there remained the ever-present unpredictability of the king's northern neighbour, the Brigante, a larger part of which favoured the anti-Roman, Venutius rather than his ex-wife, Cartimandua. She, being less popular with her subjects, sought instead to seek Rome's favour and protection.

There had been many days of heated argument from all quarters about the situations to be faced, with Gort proving the most belligerent voice.

Rising to his feet he'd banged the table angrily with his fist when Volisios had made his final pronouncement. 'Since when have we had to hide behind Rome?' He looked about him at those present, eyes glaring. 'This agreement with them will be shameful and do us small honour, making the Coritani nation little more than a bunch of beggars in their eyes and, by Astarte, they'd be right!'

'Things are different today, brother,' Armet interceded, calmly. 'In case you haven't noticed, we have a Roman army assembling not that far away, be wary of it.'

'And you seem only too willing to aid them, it seems, even though you're aware of their intent upon the sacred soil of Mona. Get too close, Armet, and they'll eat you alive!' With a last withering glare at the assembly, Gort stormed out. A little before sunset that evening, nursing a heavy heart, he and a large group of armed men rode away from the capital, their destination unknown.

As for Volisios, ever the hopeful man, still reckoned that given a few more years suitable answers might be to hand to quell all previous disagreement. But he knew he was close to death and didn't have the gift of time. Well aware of it, he lately imposed upon himself a nightly vigil where, beneath the light from several oil lamps in the small family shrine, he'd prostrate himself before the statuette set above the altar. The figure, oak-carved, carrying helmet, distaff and wreath, wore the trappings of Macha – healer and goddess of war.

She whom Volisios hoped would aid the Coritani in their hour of need was to the now-absent Gort, a matter of scorn. For him there was only one protector of the Coritani, and that was himself! Knowing his son as he did, Volisios feared that any good he'd accomplished over the years might one day fall into ruin because of the wayward impetuousness of his second son.

As it was, Gort had indeed disappeared, perhaps for the last time. The harsh words, bitter and fraught, were over, leaving an impossible situation unreconciled. Wherever Gort happened to be, one thing was certain, he'd not be alone. Dasal Hud had chosen to accompany him, for some hidden reason known only to himself. The priest now had a new title, calling himself 'Dasal the Wise.' he whom the child Gort once stupidly sought to challenge in the Druidical sacred circle.

Another matter. Reports of Brennus' destruction of Petra's Horse had been quick to circulate, and feelings of grief and anger stirred again in Volisios over lost family members at the hands of his perpetual enemy. Wife and daughter; their violated bodies, defiled and bloodied, had been found on the banks of the tiny river Soar, victims of Brennus' sons, Taghe and Varan. Volisios had since prayed daily for vengeance against his tormentors. Sadly, retribution had still to be achieved. Now the elusive Bear had taken on a greater foe, an act that would end, the king prayed, in final judgement.

Added to all this was Paulinus' soon to be mounted campaign against the Druse, the only real opposition to challenge the might of the legions. Volisios could only trust that no Coritani would be called upon to aid in the destruction of the ancient and sacred beliefs in the old gods! Armet, he was certain, would never be a part of it.

The pale moon – a grey orb, shone coldly down on Rina. Within the high hall a further council of elders was called to confront the king and again voice its complaints. It hardly mattered that this was the time of Condatis and the celebration of life, marked by the hammering of a new gold coin from the royal mint in Volisios' honour, so much had the situation deteriorated. Clearly, the king considered the matter of Brennus would have its place.

'King and lord', the assembly complained. 'You rule over a land of the humbled. Armet follows the eagle in Rome's service, minion in all but name, while our hereditary foes mock us, counting the once feared Coritani as willing slaves to be scorned. We are surely deserving better than that! It is small wonder that Gort has at last deserted you!'

Where was the Volisios of old, others questioned? What had happened to pride and dignity? It seemed to the grey beards assembled that the people had already bent the knee to Rome far too long.

Once where the ancient kings sat, there had been much that men praised. But those days had gone, to be replaced by a heavy mixture of open resignation, frustration and anger, which some of the younger fighting men remaining, found difficult to come to terms with. True to man's nature, some had ignored the unsteady balance of the scales, while others had sought to defy it. Openly, it was mooted that the king of the Coritani, who should have been the wolf's head, had become its tail instead. Talk of rebellion was growing fast, not only with Volisios' people, but also with neighbouring nations. The treatment dealt out by the imperial occupiers drifted somewhere between indifferent to severe, and feelings ran high due to the very real threat of the possible destruction of the oak-worshippers, mainstay of the Celtic Britons' religion.

If these concerns affected prince Armet, he did not show it and when he and his riders had visited Rina the previous week, reception was muted. His mind was on matters closer to home. He would soon have a new title, one which could hardly delight men such as Gort. Rome's governor, on the recommendation of legate Cerialis, was about to make it official. First commander of the first Britannic Horse!

'A man has many ways to get another to do his bidding,' Gort bitterly remarked, with a wry smile toward his boyhood friend and acolyte, Tove, on hearing the news.

As for Armet, Gort was almost a stranger, only partly understood yet loved. A man who'd chosen to cross a widening gulf. There were past occasions it was remembered, when Gort had harboured the hope there might be a chance for reconciliation, but after the many arguments and recriminations, there was little to be done. Perhaps Volisios was right when he prayed to Macha. Maybe their only salvation really did lie with the gods!

NINETEEN

S ET ON A GENTLE SLOPE beside the river, surrounded by a thriving commercial centre, stood Camulodunum, once the Trinovante capital, now the Roman centre of command for Britannia. More than a decade under her influence the settlement had the customary compliment of forum, basilica, shops, baths and a host of other municipal buildings, some inevitably still in process of completion. Dominating it all stood the great white temple dedicated to the late emperor Claudius, centre of hatred to the oppressed people of a once proud nation.

Stark reality had soon gripped king Obrig of the Trinovante. Brutally subjected to the fragile reality of client kingship, over a single act of protest he now sat ignominiously in chains in the dank cellar of that same Claudian temple. Another victim of Rome, the system that enslaved him had followed the usual pattern, a promise of financial and civic protection under the imperial hand. Further down the line it had failed to do either, leaving Obrig to languish indefinitely, while his only son Adomarus remained a hunted fugitive.

Many who refused to cooperate with the authorities were either outlawed or, like the king, enslaved on the smallest of pretexts, though a fewer number chose rather, to throw in their lot with the invader. Informers and traitors, they prospered under Rome's protection and became despised even more than their conquerors. Such divisions fed the growing atmosphere of resentment that spread throughout a land ruled by a power basking in its own self-regard that looked upon Obrig and his kind as a lesser breed.

Unlike his predecessor, Veranius, supreme governor Gaius Suetonius Paulinus didn't suffer fools gladly, and Catus Decianus, imperial agent and collector of tribute for the province, he'd long thought an idiot! This had been the main reason for delaying joining with main army at Lindum, making this unwanted detour in order to severely reprimand the procurator over the delicate matter of a recent clearance.

People like Decianus disgusted him. A fat, overblown autocrat, with an over predilection for a procession of young boys, so unlike Paulinus who basking in piety, would stay loyal to the fair Auspex, his boy lover. He missed the lad almost as much as he missed the set of dumbbells which some idiot slave had carelessly forgotten to pack. A health fanatic, Paulinus practiced with these implements, on a daily basis, appearing to thrive on the exercise, as there wasn't an ounce of surplus flesh on his body. Yet the absence of the bells was but one annoyance. Another was a hardly bearable discomfort greatly hampered by the necessity of this unwanted detour.

The procurator's ignorance of both young Auspex and the mislaid exercise implements, was only partly offended when his half-hearted offer of domestic hospitality to Paulinus was bluntly refused, the rough army tent he always slept in, when on the march, being preferable by far to the overweight tax collector's scented pillows. Now he sat tired and ill-tempered, forcing himself to listen to a grovelling litany of lame excuses.

What had occurred lately had nothing to do with him, the obese procurator protested. The senior centurion who'd committed the offence had done so with a few of his fellow comrades after too much wine. Ever ready to shift blame onto others, he pretended ignorance when he heard of such insubordination taking place under his nose, in violation of Paulinus' earlier written order a week before.

Quietly, on the spot, Decianus was read the riot act. He was then ordered to severely punish the leading culprit and all those involved in the clearance. With the coming assault against the Druse, Paulinus wouldn't countenance further disobedience in his absence.

The Iceni? A nagging reality!

King Prasutagus had been dead for some months. To gain the security of a client ruler, and to protect his land and people, a will had been lodged in which half of Iceni wealth after death would be claimed by Rome, along with repayment of all monies advanced by the empire as tribute for protection immediately upon the king's' demise. This included an eye-watering loan from the orator Lucius Seneca of forty million sesterces, which Rome now briskly demanded. Despite several threatening reminders, the agreement had not yet been properly adhered to and the Iceni widow, Boudiga, stoically confronted all those who thought it their right to invade her territory, the main warning being directed at the greater threat, Rome's troublesome legionary veterans. For the emperor Nero however, as far as he was concerned it was pay-back time.

'Make no move against the Iceni until I've settled with the heathens on Mona. I need *time!*' Paulinus stressed, 'dare to thwart me and I'll have you gutted like a hare, understand?' The procurator had a distinct feeling that the supreme legate wasn't joking.

Catus blusteringly protested. 'What of Nero's order regarding the threat here?' he countered nervously. 'The madman will..............'

'What that fool demands means bugger all to me!' Paulinus interrupted, his voice failing to hide his rising frustration. 'As far as we're concerned you never received such an order, at least not yet.' The legate poked a sharp finger in Decianus' chest. I'm the emperor's representative in all matters here, and don't you damn well forget it! More importantly, I'm here, whereas Nero, my dear procurator, is not.'

With that the governor, after a quick change of horses, gathered together his mounted equites, leaving behind a bewildered and extremely nervous procurator in his wake.

It wasn't long after Paulinus departure that the body of a centurion was found in a narrow side alley behind the Claudian temple. He'd been stabbed repeatedly, his throat slit from ear to ear. On closer inspection it was seen that the middle finger of his right hand had been neatly severed.

TWENTY

A SUMMER STORM burst over Camulodunum. To a background of persistent thunder, forked lightning carved jagged streaks across the sky, revealing for a split second the stone-built elegance that befitted the capital of the province. It was no idle boast that men named it, 'Little Rome'.

Cobbled streets, level and paved, ran between a growing number of comfortable villas along with public baths and other municipal buildings. Her forum and basilica rivalled any outside of Rome, sending a very visible message to the local inhabitants that Rome was there to stay. Commerce reigned as did the treasure house of this newly acquired province. Adding salt to the

Trinovante nation's wounded pride, a temple dedicated to emperor Claudius had become the latest symbol of alien rule.

The site had once belonged to king Obrig. Now its population only existed to serve new masters. Opulence, mixed with a strong dose of arrogance featured large in Rome's method of control, thus all buildings dedicated to the war god, Camulos, were torn down as they'd been at other sacred sites. In their place new edifices arose to serve other deities, shrines dedicated to Mars, Mithras, Diana, Venus and many others.

Camulodunum had grown rapidly in the decade and now boasted a population approaching fifty thousand inhabitants. Many legionary veterans, their twenty-five years of service completed, were settled on land filched by coercion or force from their rightful owners, while plots cleared of all woodland now boasted a host of dwellings, much of the changes taking place due to the brutal policies devised by the new procurator.

There was no denying the confidence and power. Yet unfortunately, amid all this prosperity, nobody had thought to build a defensive wall, such was the indifference to any threat from without, for who was there to oppose them?

In his riverside villa Catus Decianus, administrator and tax gatherer, lamps burned late into the night. Shadows flickered over the decorated walls of the small office room where he did much of his work. His bulky figure amply filled the chair in which he sat. At hand lay two dispatches, one opened, one sealed and waiting for the courier. The first, short and to the point, from governor Paulinus at Lindum, contained fresh orders concerning the pacification of certain areas of unrest in several client kingdoms. Catus had read the words with growing annoyance. 'Damn cheek! he muttered almost to himself.' I'm not a bloody soldier, I'm a sodding civil servant. Why couldn't that sly bastard do his own dirty work instead of landing it on me?'

He paused over the governor's words again. Maybe he'd misunderstood. Paulinus seemed to be asking the impossible! Didn't he realise the situation at all? The procurator could only count on a small garrison, perhaps a thousand men at the most to control a large chunk of valuable territory. Half of those enlisted were useless, being rookies recruited from the ranks of an untried, untrained militia of collaborating itinerates. Then there was the subject of the amount of tribute demanded from the Iceni. This business with the she-bitch Boudiga had gone on longer than planned, bringing little success so far. It was nigh on one year since the death of her husband and legal arrangements regarding a settlement of repayment had still to be complied with.

The reality was, for all the pomp and her supposed wealth, Rome was at this point in her history, financially on the skids, Nero's many public extravagances to satisfy the Roman mob, doing little to help where the price of organising more and more public games was enormous. Add to this the millions of subjects in this overstretched empire already wincingly over-taxed. Heavy investment in the new province had promised much, but early tales of untold riches had been greatly exaggerated, and the riches that Britannia had tantalisingly promised, had so far failed to materialise. The eye-watering cost of tying down four Roman legions when measured against any gain so far yielded, prompted the senate to consider the unthinkable, an abandonment of the fledgling territory altogether!

This then was the procurator's brief. To bring about completely the submission of the Iceni while at the same time enlarging the imperial coffers. Overseeing the success of this exercise would be an achievement and aroused his sense of importance. That sour-faced bugger, Paulinus, wouldn't dare to admonish him for disobeying an order to remain inactive until the supreme governor had dealt with the threat of the Druse. The second document on his desk to be addressed was the responsibility of the waiting courier. Brief and to the point, it contained the order to call up a cohort of semi-retired legionaries, reliable men whom he'd send into the Iceni capital.

Unknowingly, Catus Decianus, the provincial procurator, was about to set off a chain of events that would later prove unstoppable.

TWENTY-ONE

S OME MEN ARE GRANTED the gift of patience in a time of crisis. It must be said that G. Suetonus Paulinus, governor of a troublesome and unstable province, wasn't one of them. Drumming his fingers on the stained board of the table at the busy way station, a day's ride south of Lindum, he listened to the latest report, his mind already in a dark place.

What he'd heard was hard to believe, yet the casualty figures spoke for themselves. The loss of Petra's Horse followed by the failed attempt on Calinae had been serious enough, but for them to be pursued by a third such occurrence in the space of a week could barely be tolerated.

The slaughter of the small contingent at the unnamed outpost was indeed difficult to fully accept. Conversant as the supreme legate was with the tactics of guerrilla warfare, he was conscious enough to realise his predicament. Such outbursts, if they continued, might badly affect morale among the rank and file of the army, especially as the event had been carried out under the supposedly watchful eye of Lindum. Eager to be off and away, Paulinus immediately dispatched a galloper to the colonia, containing a hastily written order for legate Cerialis to immediately send a contingent to the luckless fort and glean any information he thought may throw a little light on the incident.

The morning proved warm but overcast as Cerialis' secondus rode into the ruins of the half-built fort. Accompanying him rode several alae of Thracians together with prince Armet and a score of Exploratores. Sitting his horse, surrounded by the stockade's charred and battered defences, Aquilla cast narrowed eyes over the scene, taking in the scattered shapes that had once been living men, the usual mutilated bodies, hacked limbs of the headless, all now a familiar scene to the watching prince.

'Killing is one thing,' Otalus, decurion of the Thracians present, spoke bitterly, 'but why dare to carry out such carnage so brazenly, under our noses?' He shot a suspicious glance in Armet's direction.

Aquilla nodded in agreement. Dismounting, he stepped over mutilated corpses, the contorted remains of an unlikely mix of infantry from Armenia together with a half-dozen Syrian archers. The total death count numbered more than thirty, 'These people must really hate us,' he said, turning to Armet, who'd chosen to sit Flavia's back without comment.

'Some of the attackers belonged to the Ordovici,' observed Otalus.

'Then they've come a good distance,' Armet said.

Systematically, using the fallen timbers of the breached stockade, a funeral pyre was hastily set up and the decapitated and limbless corpses, without ceremony, were consigned to the flames. No sacred words were said over the fallen during this mass cremation, as those present were uncertain as to which deity the dead had once worshiped, if any. Instead, the intruders trawled the ruined fort for any clues that might be found, any information that could be salvaged from the wreckage.

It was during this time that Armet's sharp eye noticed the bronzed object, half-covered by churned-over earth. Dismounting, he scooped it to him. He lacked time to examine it completely, yet it was no great matter. He'd seen it a hundred times before, encircling Dasal Hud's neck, a distinctive disc, worn by him alone, bearing two shapes of forked lightning, each fashioned in gold, converging one upon the other.

There had to be a reason for everything, however unlikely. Either Dasal had been robbed of the object by one of the fort's attackers or, even more mysteriously, he'd been present during the assault himself, a bold decision, even for a warrior Hud. After a final glance about him he pocketed the find. For the first time since obeying his father's wishes, reluctantly bowing to Roman authority, he felt a terrible unease. Supposing some hand other than his had retrieved the disc, a hand belonging to one who might be aware of the outlawed Hud's continuing support for Gort in his anti-Roman stance, and sadly there were some, Armet would then have been forced to fear the worst, not only for himself, but for Volisios, Gort, and the whole Coritani nation. Even so, the discovery was enough to starkly remind Armet of the danger he and his people faced, in these precarious days. He felt once more the cold of the tell-tale object against his bare palm as, leading Flavia by the reins, he re-joined Aquilla and the contingent.

Returning to Lindum the secondus accepted a welcoming cup of wine in the legate's office while making his report. Cerialis listened patiently.

'Well, this will stir the pot for old Paulinus,' the legate sniffed in disdain. 'What's the situation?'

'Prince Armet thinks it the work of Venutius and his damn Carveti!' Aquilla replied decisively, 'I see no reason to disagree.'

Cerialis pondered. 'Odd bed fellows, wouldn't you say secondus, a grizzly bear and one of our queen's jealous cast-offs?'

'Odd, maybe,' Aquilla intervened. 'But the cause is just the same, they wish to drive us back to Gaul.' He turned a nervous eye in Armet's direction as if for conformation, a move which didn't go unnoticed by the legate.

'If you want my opinion,' Hispanic's bearded fourth in command, Rufus Lippa intervened, scratching his stubbled chin thoughtfully. 'I suspect Cartimandua is his target, at least for the present. What better way to get at her and us Quintus, than by creating some diversion, away from Mona?'

'Too late for that, Rufus,' said Cerialis, firmly 'On that subject, the die is truly cast.'

Barely listening now, Armet stood quietly by, his mind still confused over the startling discovery of the disc and its meaning, wondering as to how Dasal's amulet came to be lying in the mud and litter of the remains of a gutted fort, many miles north of where it should be.

'There's always talk of it, though,' Aquilla continued. 'Every year we're threatened with the same rumours, the same blasted fears. There exists a whole plethora of worrying omens, prophecies and the like. Right, Armet?'

'Perhaps, by voicing these things, you help them grow more likely in the telling,' the prince answered, putting aside for a moment his bewilderment over events. 'Exaggeration can be the worst of enemies.'

Cerialis bit his lip. 'Well, we'll see about that, by the gods! Maybe the answer lies at Dorona.'

TWENTY-TWO

LATER, LEGATE AND PRINCE stood vigil at the high point of the parapet. 'Things always appear better from up here, when one's alone,' Cerialis said, staring down at the many fires peppering the landscape beyond the wall.

'That's a curious observation, coming from a man who thrives on the company of others,' said Armet.

The Hill provides us with a helpful view of things, Armet,' continued the legate, seriously, 'I fail to understand why the Coritani never made better use of it.'

Armet, barely visible in the gloom of a fast-falling night, drew his cloak tight around him. 'I recall, when as a child, Volisios would tell me many stories of a time long ago when my ancient ancestors, the Corieltavi, indeed built a settlement here. As of now, we are horse people, and it would appear strange for us now.' he said reflectively, a touch of melancholy in his voice. 'The plains are our fortress; open spaces our refuge.'

'Unlike Romans, eh? So uncertain of ourselves that we hide behind these damn defences,' Cerialis joked. 'Yet we can move, when necessary,' he retaliated lightly, unfazed by the barb. 'Paulinus arrives shortly, then you will see how fast we jump into action.'

'If you're referring to the power of Rome, I've experienced it at close quarters, remember?' Armet said. 'As for this hatred of our priests, what exactly is Rome's *real* purpose? Politics, religion, or is it something less obvious?' The existence of vast copper deposits on Mona's western hills, for example, an obvious prize waiting to be grabbed by Rome's insatiable lust, crossed Armet's mind.

'Religions, we usually tolerate,' continued the legate seriously, 'even if they include the barbaric practice of human sacrifice and wholesale slaughter used by the Druse. Yet when it comes to open rebellion.......'

'Such tales you frown upon are exaggerated, Quintus. You condemn the priestly right to punish murderers, rapists, criminals and the like,' Armet retaliated. 'Caesar spread those lurid stories that you seem so willing to believe; stories which greatly suited his purpose while fighting Vercingetorix,' he concluded.

'You deny them, these sacrifices?' Cerialis challenged.

'You justify the Roman way of taking lives by the thousand in the arena, feeding the twisted hunger of the mob, yet you speak of wholesale slaughter carried out by our people, based entirely on rumour. Such talk comes from an imperial lie based on separate incidents; completely demeaning beliefs Rome fails to understand. Even were the odd ritual occasionally to occur, it could never equal what I witnessed during my time in Rome.'

Cerialis stood silent beneath the failing light. 'Well, best let that argument lie,' he remarked finally. The words were said lightly and Armet accepted them, as he accepted many things about the legate, yet he wasn't entirely certain whether the man tested his loyalty this night, or no. The prince of the Coritani briefly thought of Dasal and his uncle, Culchul, aware that the act of harbouring known Hud's could carry a death sentence if exposed, even for a prince. Thus, both he and Gort were equally at risk. He made a mental note to be less outspoken on certain hot subjects, especially when trapped within the confines of a Roman fortress.

'You've come a long way since those days in Rome, Quintus, commander of a legion and all,' he broached diplomatically changing the subject.

Cerialis nodded as he stared at the twinkling fires below. 'It hasn't been so bad a journey for you either prince. Citizen of

Rome, holding equestrian rank, bestowed personally by Nero, himself............'

'I was a callow specimen prior to that.'

'Yes,' Cerialis said reflectively, 'we've both been cursed, with much to be learned.'

Two responsible individuals, both distant in background and habits, shared an unlikely alliance just as intently as they shared the catwalk at Lindum. With night falling rapidly it was difficult, from this high a level, to see the bend of the river and the pontoon bridges where Petra's severed heads were discovered. 'Did you really mean it when you boasted that a day may dawn when you might well be emperor?' Armet asked.

Cerialis smile broadened. 'It was a foolish thing to say.'

'I don't agree,' the prince of the Coritani stated. 'You have command of six thousand soldiers. Rome itself has been taken by a lesser number.'

'Like all the legions here, it is closer to five,' Cerialis complained, tapping his fingers on the tip of the timber palisade. 'Any replacements are slow in arriving, that's if they damn well arrive at all.' Here he deliberately failed to remind the prince of the reality. The Coritani, if called upon, might more than double that number in the field. A bitter truth, hard for the legate to swallow, and a good enough reason not to push the testy subject of the 'Hud's right now. He took one final glance at the river edge before darkness hid the tents of a host of itinerate traders and legionaries fully crowding the area between river and hill. 'That is partly my reason,' he added finally, 'for the formation of the Exploratores. Such an act might hopefully lead to a tighter working relationship between us. Your horsemen would go a long way to ferment it.'

They entered the warmer space of the praetorium where the legate called for wine. Armet was blunt. 'Has Paulinus yet granted my request, Quintus?'

'To ride with the advance-force? He'll come round to it, he's a practical man.'

'I trust you're correct, legate. I've a mother and sister to avenge, and I tell you now, with or without his agreement, I'll be there.'

CHAPTER TWENTY-TWO

You're dangerously stubborn, Armet.'

'As are you, legate.'

'Paulinus makes conditions.'

'Of course, he does,' Armet smiled. 'Like you, he's a Roman.'

Cerialis chuckled, then sipped wine before tossing Armet the small scroll.

'You really are a keeper of secrets,' said the prince, breaking the seal. Glancing at the governor's approval, he said accusingly. 'You must have known, all along.'

'He could hardly refuse, could he? Especially when I managed to convince him that the Exploratores were partly *his* idea.' Cerialis , once again, recalled a brief part of the conversation.

'What is so special about this heathen prince, Quintus,' Paulinus enquired during an earlier visit to the colonia, 'that you take such pains to recruit him?'

'Treat him well, and it will pay dividends for all,' the legate urged. 'I know the fellow's metal.'

Cerialis, because of a more than urgent desire to achieve personal ambition had continued, warming to his task. *Prince of a mighty nation, swearing allegiance to Rome, better to have such a man on our side than not. Rome would need to call upon men such as he, if it desired to prosper and spread the Pax, etc, etc, etc.* The verbal assault was relentless.

Paulinus reconsidered. 'If, as you say, he's such a remarkable catch, he might well be of use,' he said at last, 'especially when we begin to move the frontier north.'

So that was it! A valid point. Matters between the Coritani and Brigante being at best, grudging, the formation of an itinerate body of horse supporting an advance into Cartimandua's realm would certainly appeal to Paulinus' nature. Of course, something more than word of honour would be required from both parties, though what form this might take had yet to be mooted.

Armet accepted wine in silence, for a moment dwelling on what Rome saw as a prestigious honour and how Cerialis had persuaded general Paulinus to grant it, then he remembered Gort's dread words of caution. *"The legate, like Rome, is buying us! Buying you...............................!"*

'It must have been difficult for Volisios to adopt new ways.' Cerialis' voice brought him back to reality.

The Coritanian shrugged. 'It is what my father wishes. It's his fate and mine to watch over our people.

'But there are the discontented. Your brother for instance? I hear he is abroad.' Armet, ever alert, had long been aware that Cerialis regularly received communication from an unknown collaborator as to Gort's movements. This pointed to someone in his brother's service being a traitor. Whoever this person happened to be was exceedingly clever in hiding his identity.

'Gort is Gort,' Armet replied, adopting a forced easiness. 'He was ever wild in his actions. Possessed of a reckless nature he surely is, but he'd never overstep the mark,' he concluded, thinking it unwise to comment further.

'Find better methods to control him,' advised Cerialis with directness, 'for *his* sake, and for others, such watchfulness would be wise! The rash are ever a problem for someone though, are they not?' he mused, 'and they must be dealt with, eventually. A man can be foolish.' he added, somewhat reflectively. 'Especially when underestimating the enemy. Remember your first time at the arena and that business with Bacilon..........?

TWENTY-THREE

DURING THE FIRST DAYS SPENT in the capital of the known world, Armet had been introduced to many customs in that crowded city, a host of things that he'd never imagined but would soon realise it was no pleasure trip. Almost every day was spent in meeting with others like himself, all speaking a foreign tongue, all hailing from another part of the expanding empire. A rudimentary mastery of Latin was not an option, being regarded as essential. This included writing and reading, which he found frustratingly difficult. Strangely, his personal appearance was of great importance to the slaves who served him, hand and foot, but he was also well-aware that they were also his warders. His plaited shoulder-length hair he grudgingly allowed to be shortened to the fashion then in mode, in this place of constant change. The plaid breeches, linen tunic and fur boots were soon replaced by more suitable wear to fit the warmer climate, while the cramped and modest quarters overlooking the Tiber were adequate. Thankfully there was freedom to use the small public gardens below.

Another part of Armet's indoctrination, necessitated, under the supervision of his Roman guides, several visits to the games and the racing of chariots. The former he mostly shunned while the latter he found to be both informative and more exciting than he'd expected. The skills of the charioteers combined with the stamina of the horse-teams made him think of Gort's zeal for this war machine, which the Britons had much adapted to suit their needs, making for a lighter, more flexible weapon of mobility that proved most effective when pitched against a slower-moving enemy. Due to the expert instruction from the Parisi champion, Vixt, Armet reckoned young Gort the equal of any of the competitors he'd so far seen in Rome.

Perhaps the most renowned charioteer at the time was Xenaius, reported to be the victor of over eight hundred races, according to his Roman companion Fuscus Vecco, a senior officer in Nero's elite praetorian guard who doubled-up as the Coritani's guide and minder. Rising from abject poverty, according to Vecco, in less than ten years, Xenaius had accumulated so much wealth that it was said he rivalled some of the richest figures in the capital. Part of this claim to fame was the pair of horses which he personally owned and trained, each animal having won over one hundred races, each gaining the honorific title of 'centenarius.' Between the three of them, they'd made millions. Yet, opting to lead a very private life, Xenaius later married a woman without rank, siring several children and living in a modest villa on the outskirts of Rome alongside the Via Flaminia. Armet was only one of the many who appraised the charioteer, an extraordinary character to whom the prince would have liked to make himself known. Brother Gort, Armet thought again, would have loved him.

At his introduction to the Games, a large amphitheatre still undergoing an expensive renovation, was beginning to fill seats, but there would be many spare places that day, there being no large celebratory festival to commemorate, explained Vecco, apologetically, after purchasing the necessary ivory tags of admission to the better seats. Just a few second-rate contests were all that the embarrassed praetorian could promise. Armet, unsure as to what to think, was already feeling decidedly restless in this unfamiliar, and to him, unsettling environment.

Under an awning that protected them from the heat of the spring afternoon, they took their seats. The prince surveyed the scene. Slaves were raking the sand in preparation for the show and several men armed with hook-tipped staves patrolled the arena. 'Those are the fellows whose job it is to drag away the dead,' said Vecco, explaining the obvious. Minutes later the slaves departed as the wooden doors to one of the two entrances opened and the first pair appeared into the sunlight.

Both gladiators, Armet was quick to notice, were at odds. The first fighter, Vecco informed him, was known as a secutor. Armed with a curved short sword, he bore a round buckler on his bare left arm for extra protection. On his helm was engraved the sign of a fish, the recognised emblem of his gladiatorial class, men often referred to as 'chasers' or 'pursuers' by the mob. His muscled right arm and left leg offered bodily defence while a breastplate, decorated with the graven head of the god, Mars, protected his chest. This type of fighter was relatively new to the arena, only arriving on the scene some ten years before.

'The fish emblem,' queried Armet, indicating, 'is he one of those Christians men talk about?'

Vecco looked at the prince in surprise. 'You're well informed. What do you know of them?'

'Only what I heard,' Armet replied. 'They say they worship a single god.'

'Vecco laughed, as if he'd heard a joke. 'First class troublemakers prince, no more than that, but as far as Bacilon is concerned, nobody has ever yet accused *him* of turning the other cheek.'

Opposing Bacilon, a dark- skinned man armed with a large net in one hand and a wicked looking bullwhip in the other, the retiarius, stared nervously upward at the people in the stands. He wore the minimum of clothing, a loin cloth held by a broad leather belt, being his only garb, in contrast to the heavier protection given the secutor. This type of fighter marked him out as hailing from Syria from where the deadly skill first originated.

'The door of life,' the owner of the voice explained as he elbowed his way between Armet and Vecco, sitting without apology between them. The Coritanian, turning his head, quickly took stock of the newcomer. Clearly here was a man of some importance, for despite Vecco's high rank, the usually zealous Neroite made no protest. 'You must be the Keltoi, Nero's guest, the barbarian we've all heard so much about. Tell me, is it true that you once killed a wolf with your bare hands?'

Quintus Cerialis, dark haired, smooth faced, seemed gifted with charm and good looks. Of little more than average height he nevertheless, by his commanding manner, seemed taller. All Rome feted this man who'd made a name for himself as the victor over the Cherusci in Germania a few years back. Armet remembered now. He'd heard the stories. A feared tribe, part of a confederation lead by their champion Arminius, that once helped to destroy three imperial Roman legions, and of Cerialis, the impetuous diplomat whose skills were brought to bear during a threatening situation somewhere in the land of the hostile Traveri, along with other tales..................................

Cerialis' voice quickly jerked Armet out of his reverie 'You've not answered me, prince - about the beast........................?'

'You've been told a lie. I'm no wolf slayer.' Already, the son of Volisios had decided he didn't much care for this flamboyant Roman.

Cerialis gave a friendly grin, raising his beringed hands in a mock apology 'Pity, that. Anyway, you must accept an invitation to dine with me during your stay.'

Armet didn't reply, his eyes focussing on the scene below where the gladiator armed with the bullwhip advanced, making a purposeful move on the now crouching secutor.

'Inform him Fuscus, I represent Rome's future. Is it not so?'

'The secutor must win this contest,' Vecco muttered, hardly listening.

'Did you wager?'

'Too many sesterces,' the praetorian said glumly, looking on as the pair of gladiators circled each other. 'It appears I've already wasted my money.'

'Why so?'

'The dark skinned one, he carries a whip, not the customary trident.'

Cerialis made a face. 'Does that trouble you?'

Vecco shrugged. 'I don't happen to like innovation.'

'What is your opinion, prince?' asked Cerialis.

'These wretches, by Taranis, what is their crime?' demanded Armet, answering one question with another.

'Slaves, prisoners, prince. The one with the bullwhip ravished his master's wife. The other one is.........?' Cerialis snapped the fingers of one hand, momentarily frustrated.

'Bacilon,' said Vecco, finishing the sentence. 'I've already informed my friend here. 'An old graduate from the Dacian school.'

'Thought the bugger had chucked it in, long since,' Cerialis remarked casually, his eyes turning on the drama in the arena.

'Too many creditors on his back,' Vecco grimaced. 'He used to be one of the best, now look at him!' The Neroite spread out his arms as Bacilon narrowly ducked his head to avoid the switching snake-like flick of the trailing net's metal spikes. A matter of seconds was sufficient to prove that Vecco had maybe backed a winner, as the unfortunate slave and rapist, eager to go in for the kill, was moving within too close a range of Bacilon's sword.

'Well, this is going to be short,' Cerialis remarked with an audible sigh. 'What say you, prince?'

'We don't kill others for entertainment, Roman,' Armet retorted curtly as he carefully watched the circling pair. 'Anyway, the Syrian will win. Watch, I reckon the secutor's already dead.'

The secutor, thinking he had the measure of his adversary by avoiding the arc of the net, was carefully seeking the moment to strike, as the Syrian appeared to be taking too many risks, ducking and weaving in and out under Bacilon's guard while closely avoiding the point of the wavering sword. Eventually he saw his chance and with a vicious sweep of his bucklered arm he knocked the Syrian, spread eagled, to the ground. Roars of approval greeted the secutor's skill and shouts of 'Bacilon, mince the bastard, cut him up, the bloody swine's yours!' rent the air as he moved confidently in to finish the contest, Vecco's cries quickly joining in with the rest of the crowd.

Then it happened! Triumphantly Bacilon stood over the stricken slave while the crowd yelled for blood, urging the ex-champion to finish the job. In that split second the slave's bullwhip suddenly wrapped itself around Bacilon's neck like an angry serpent while at the same moment, his booted foot delivered a heavy blow to the secretor's unprotected crutch. It was a desperate move made on the spur of the moment, but it was enough to disable Bacilon who, clutching wildly at the strangulating whip, fell to his knees. The slave, now confidently taking his time about it, took hold of the secutor's sword and slowly guided the curved blade across the helpless gladiator's exposed throat.

The bulk of the mob were fair that day, with the majority voting to spare the victor, even if he were a slave. The wretch had, against the odds, unexpectedly bested a once famous performer. It wasn't always so; many a winner, for whatever reason, could be subject to the whim of the mob. As for Armet, not waiting to see more, followed by his constant shadow, Vecco, left the half-filled amphitheatre, purposely leaving the scene without one solitary word of farewell to Quintus Petellius Cerialis.

TWENTY-FOUR

S OME THREE MONTHS before Armet was due to embark from the port of Ostia and face an unenviable journey by sea, the invitation to dine at the house of no less than the lady, Domina Julia Felix, arrived at his comfortable abode. The prince's first reaction was to ignore the request until, advised by his ever-present minder, the senior praetorian officer, Fuscus Vecco, he reluctantly agreed to accept. Nobody turned down Julia Felix without valid excuse, Vecco encouraged. Armet himself, could think of several, but Vecco's continual shake of the head to any such thing dashed all hope of evasion. Not for the first time he had the uncomfortable feeling that he was about to be paraded once again, like some performing seal.

He voiced his apprehension to Vecco. 'Just what is her intention, apart from having a chance to examine the merchandise, up close. Noble savage, bit of rough, all that garbage...........................?'

'I really don't understand you, prince!' Vecco responded with a sigh. 'Anyone would jump at the chance of such a great honour. Recognition from her means you've really arrived. Just don't get any idea's, that's all.'

'You think I might?' Armet smiled sardonically.

'Don't let your guard down man, not for a minute. I've seen several visitors such as yourself come an almighty cropper. You're an exception, of course. That day at the Maximus.......................

The Circus Maximus lay in a valley between the Palatine - Aventine hills. The race that afternoon featured six competing charioteers over a traditional distance of seven gruelling laps. One of these contestants was none other than Quintus Cerialis, who, with his many connections and not being short of a sesterce or two, charmed the devious games factions for a place in the final race of the day. All this was going completely against the rules. What had the idiot done to get thus far, thought, Armet, and how many other idiots backed him? One thing he was learning about Cerialis was his total disregard for the norm, plus a continual desire to show off, a trait that Armet disdained and admired in equal measure.

When informed of this act of folly, he sought to dissuade. 'Have you raced before?' he challenged.

Cerialis shrugged. 'Enough to beat any in that feeble line-up. The team I'm driving belongs to Domitia Felix, horses bred and trained by the greatest trainer of them all, I can't go wrong.'

'You'll be flattened.'

'Thank you for your support, prince, but I can handle it. We are the blue team. You'd better damn well root for us, Armet!'

'A bloody amateur!' remarked Fuscus, dryly. Out of possible embarrassment, Armet chose *not* to admit that he knew little about it.

All seats at the Circus were taken that evening. It was the final race of the day. Cerialis, naturally thinking himself the centre of attention, imagined they'd turned out for him, but that was not the case, since the present champion Darius was also in the race. Armet suppressed a chuckle.

'Even a barbarian like me has heard of *this* Persian.'

Cerialis frowned, as if he hadn't considered this opponent before. 'Yes, I'd better steer clear of him then, hadn't I?'

The Domitia's 'triga' – the term for a team of three horses-- was indeed magnificent and rare. Usually, two or four animals were the norm in any race. But the occasion showed what a strong influence Julia commanded when she could persuade the masters of the games to bow to her whim. If it were she who'd purchased these animals, independently as was reputed, then she was a better judge of horseflesh than Armet gave her credit for. The team backing Cerialis were seeing to the final checks before the race. Armet was not at all surprised when he later bore witness to Cerialis' triumph, beating his rival, Darius the Persian by a quarter length, confounding the critics who'd broadcast that the challenger would likely get caught up in a shipwreck, in other words a pile-up. Yet it was at that very moment when things went awry. A wheel suddenly detached itself from the bouncing carriage, sending Cerialis sprawling onto the track, in front of the two remaining teams in the race. In the split seconds available to Armet, he leaped from his front-row seat, and recklessly running across the open space, dragged a half conscious Cerialis out of the path of the speeding cars, to the accompaniment of a frenzied roaring from the crowd.

With an arm dripping blood, seemingly oblivious to his condition, Cerialis leaned his back against the wall, with no thanks offered for the possible saving of his life. 'Alexander of Macedon did it Armet! Now, so have I!' he shouted in triumph.

If Armet's own name had been unknown before the brave act performed in front of a baying mob at the Circus, it soon became common coin among the plebs. Yet to the prince it seemed no great cause for celebration, as the approaching teams had been nowhere close when he'd helped a jubilant Cerialis limp clear from the shipwreck on the track. All was optical. Nevertheless....................................

'They are saying she is Cerialis' latest conquest, is that so?' The prince referred again to Julia Felix, still embarrassed for not knowing who Alexander and Darius really were. So much for this so-called imperial education which it seemed, had yet to fully come into play.

Fuscus shrugged, tight-lipped. 'Other way round, I'd say,' he muttered.

The prince and his minder were that evening, ceremoniously ushered into the triclinium of a handsome villa on the Caelian hill, not far from the via Flaminia, the very thoroughfare where the famed charioteer, Xenaius, had retired to. Had Armet been given a choice he would rather have been *his* guest, entertained by tales from an illustrious character, a man who'd fought for his place in the pantheon of his choice. Instead, from the moment he entered the atrium with its gaudily painted walls, Armet, not for the first time in Rome, immediately felt out of place and slightly uncomfortable, surrounded by what he thought was pointless opulence.

It was true what was said of the lady Julia, however, and Armet, certainly no expert in these matters, had enough of an eye to recognise why she carried the title of the uncrowned empress of the capital. Ignorant of her age, he would take her to be over thirty, but perhaps it was the sparkle in her dark eyes which made her appear younger. He would have to admit to himself later, that there was a desire to know her further, but it would be Cerialis who was soon to suppress that idea. 'She likes women,' he confided flatly, as if to rule Armet out. With obvious chagrin in his tone, he followed up with, 'Believe me Keltoi, I've tried.'

Armet sat uneasily on the couch beside her with the ever present praetorian Fuscus Vecco at his elbow. The low table before them groaned under the weight of food on display. Wild boar, venison, beef, fish were instantly familiar while quail, dormice and snails were not. There was much else in abundance, varieties of fruit, nuts, grapes but also other delicacies strange to the prince's pallet. Surely all this ostentation was not just for him.

He knew now that he should have thought more carefully as to his attire. Woefully tactless, he'd chose tartan breeches, boots and tunic instead of the more formal Roman fashion of loose-fitting toga.

Across from him a further half-dozen couches were occupied. He recognised some. Seneca the poet, Gaius Petronius the writer. Others he didn't know, yet all stared at him from time to time. He wasn't surprised, his presence was bound to raise eyebrows, especially after the incident at the games.

'Where is Cerialis? he asked after the usual acts of politeness.

'Quintus is always talking about you,' Julia ventured, avoiding the question.

'I'm surprised such a busy personage as himself can find the time.'

'I'm surprised that you're surprised. Can you not see how much he regards you, especially after what you did.'

'I suspect it was he who arranged for me to be here, lady, isn't it so?' he asked, steering her away from even more discomfort.

'Quintus may pull many strings, but I alone chose my guests. Do not begrudge us an opportunity to see you face to face, prince.'

Just then providence, in the name of Fuscus, interjected. 'Armet is set to return to his people in a short time. It would have been churlish of us not to have accepted your kind invitation.'

'You are fortunate, prince, to be in such good hands as Vecca's,' Domina Julia said warmly, yet annoyed with Fuscus for his interruption. She then, while placing an elegant hand on Armet's knee, offered wine with the other.

TWENTY-FIVE

A RMET WAS SELDOM at ease in Rome. At the time he was still grieving from the death of his wife, Tae, which happened too soon after the taking of the nuptial vows. Apart from the politics involved and the willingness of Volisios to comply with Rome's wishes involving the Coritani nation's future client kingship, his father thought this new world of Rome would keep his eldest son occupied long enough to return him to something like his former self. On Armet's part, he agreed reluctantly to comply with an aging Volisios out of profound love and respect, but above all it was ingrained duty that led him.

The size of the empire's capital was the first hurdle to overcome in the six months allotted him. Always he'd thought that nothing came larger than his birthplace of Rina, a town he was now made aware could be fitted into Rome's space a score of times. Language came second, finding the strange tongue near impossible to master after the crude camp-latin enforced in his conquered homeland. The third challenge however, far outweighed all else, coming in the shape of Quintus Cerialis.

After that first cold encounter at the arena, their paths, to the great annoyance of his constant guide, Fuscus Vecca, were to cross more times than might have been expected. Despite Armet's suspicions, Cerialis' interest might best be described as a little too overzealous in his desire to garner detail concerning the history and customs of Armet's people in Britannia. Only his easy-going character, mixed with a genuine enthusiasm to learn the slightest nugget pertaining to the Coritani, helped soften the prince's caution. Much later a more pertinent reason for all this inquisitive probing would come to light and a very different picture would emerge.

During this time of indoctrination Armet took a mistress, causing another vexation for Vecca. 'You have chosen badly,' he remarked disapprovingly. 'The woman is a public ball breaker.'

'A rich one too, I hear,' added Armet.

'If it was a bed mate you needed, I could have got you a girl more suited and less dangerous than Domita Julia.'

'A matter of opinion,' Armet retorted. 'Choosing a woman for comfort is one of the few things I can do without having to ask your damn permission, Fuscus. As I recall, it was you that dragged me along to meet the lady in the first place.'

'Was that really Vecca's opinion?' a naked Julia Felix asked, sitting upright on the bed, while Armet, from the balcony of her hilltop villa on the Caelian, stared out over the shadowed streets below. He vaguely heard her voice, but it was always the same after. He would take her delectable body with a desire he'd rarely felt with a woman. Even the love of his life, Tae, could never have given him such exquisite pleasure as this one. After, he would count himself a fool because of his need for a woman whose conquests among Rome's elite were legendary. In short, he'd been lured, tamed and beggared, at least on the outside.

His concerns were needless, for any man in the city would have been thought the lesser had they not performed sex to satisfy Julia Felix' openly voracious appetite. Seneca the poet, Polonius the arbiter, almost certainly Nero, were numbered amongst the lady's many other notable lovers, including, so it was rumoured, the emperor's insatiable wife, Octavia.

TWENTY-SIX

S UPREME LEGATE, PAULINUS, though it might appear different, wasn't a man to let grass grown beneath his feet. Having left Decianus presiding over a shape-shifting dilemma, he made it a point to keep in constant touch with developments, dispatching fast riding couriers to Cerialis at regular intervals along the way. The fact that the commander of the Hispanics was the recipient of the governor's messages only served to add to Balbilus' barely concealed dislike over what he saw as undisguised favouritism. Unfortunately for Cerialis, it was also another example of the legate of the Valerians mounting jealousy.

Straba the Greek, instinctively aware of the situation, climbed The Hill as quick as his thin legs could carry him. He was late for the briefing, having been absorbed in conversation with his new friend Demcal, an auxiliary serving in the ranks of the 'Golden Bow', the nickname given to the Cretan archers serving with 14th legion. He'd stayed too long, and his intuition told him something other than tardiness had taken over. The legate had generously given him time away to visit his friend, but only for a certain space. Now he was overdue, and the daily briefing must be well underway. His only wish was that Cerialis would be far too busy to notice his absence after receiving the latest news about Calinae and the second unnamed objective south of Segelocum. A forlorn hope, so it was with some trepidation that he sought to keep a low profile in the overcrowded room. He burrowed quietly into a place at the bench, hiding behind the broad back of the captain of Batavians, Nardon, while receiving hostile glances from two senior centurions on either side of him as he dug furtively inside the leather pouch for his tools, including waxen tablets and stylii.

After the recent disaster with Petra, last night's assault on the half-erected waystation came as another unwelcome bit of news. Both outposts lay on the edge of Brigante territory, Cartimandua's land, that regular hotbed of trouble for Cerialis. Thankfully casualties upon the first occasion were light and the attackers were quickly repulsed, whereas the dead discovered at the second fort were a different matter. Having only just been informed of the assault against the latter, the Hispanic's commander, cursing the absence of his scribe, sitting as yet undiscovered among the throng, angrily penned the message himself. A fresh galloper was summoned and despatched at speed to the governor. There was little more Cerialis could do to keep Paulinus up to date.

Aubanus, Hispania's senior centurion, a man as gruff as his rank demanded, having made a thorough report to the assembly sat down, relieved to let Cerialis continue with the daily briefing, his first subject being incongruously, hygiene. This usually drew disrespectful laughter and crude attempts at lavatorial jokes from some of those present when the subject was mentioned. But now the mood was more sombre, for disease was fast becoming a serious problem, almost on a par with all the unpleasantness over Petra and what followed, a fact that led to further unwanted sickness and death among the ranks. Progress had already been made to correct the situation, but overcrowding remained a problem, and the files of unwanted patients outside the medical tents saw no visible sign of it diminishing. The many itinerates mingling around the base of The Hill and beyond only highlighted the necessity to increase the number of suitable toilets for everyone, while the threat of disease drove the legates of Valeria and Gemina to again voice their complaints, a process they were attempting to heatedly thrash out when Straba made his entrance.

On the premiss that wars have been started for less, an unwritten instruction was quickly renewed. An extra force of pioneers from the auxilia would from now on, and in relays throughout the night, be employed exclusively on the construction of a further number of ablutions to be erected, wherever convenient, at suitable spots along the river. A few camp comedians would perhaps think there was a new joke to be had somewhere, had they time for humour. But the recent series of attacks on their comrades concentrated the mind on an equally serious subject. Hopefully a fresh effort would go partway to solving both these problems.

The men of the restricted Hispania, if hearing what their betters had discussed, might well have remarked with some acidity that the best way to remedy all the related issues would be, to quote optio Priscus, the happy sight of Paulinus and his sodding task force marching off to Dorona.

After several more domestic issues, Cerialis placed a light hand on the shoulder of the person at his side and cleared his throat dramatically. 'Moving on, I'll use this moment to introduce a young man who has lately arrived from 2nd Augusta at Glevum. Some of you know him, or of him. Son of the late senator, Lucius Julius Graecinus and Julia Procilla, recently raised to the rank of military tribune at the age of twenty-one, he's now serving as personal secretary to the supreme legate.'

Agricola, looking even younger than his age stood up, bowed abruptly and self-consciously, when dutifully acknowledging a mixed response of approval. 'Well, he puts our Quintus in the shade,' somebody quietly whispered in the audience, obviously referring to the tribune's lack of years.

When the assembly finally quietened Balbilus, unsurprisingly, rose to speak, aiming his question at Cerialis in person. 'Has anyone here pinpointed exactly where our esteemed governor might be, legate?'

Every man of equal rank usually addressed the commander of the Hispanics with the familiar 'Quintus'. Yet for reasons best known to himself, Balbilus continued to employ the title of 'legate'. Polite enough, yet when the older man spoke, the address came heavy laden with a large dose of open sarcasm.

'Paulinus is little more than a day's march away, Cerialis affirmed. 'Isn't that so, Gnaeus?'

Agricola remained slightly embarrassed as he nodded confirmation. 'I understand the governor should be with us tomorrow.'

'I'll say one thing about our governor, he certainly keeps the scribes busy,' remarked Tullius Roscius of legion Gemina. 'Never have I seen the like.' Roscius, a man soon to turn forty, poured water from a jug and parked his rear-end on the table's edge. Of the three commanders he was perhaps the most distinguished legate present, having conducted several successful military forays, not only in Mauretania, but several other equally difficult campaigns, Egypt and Palestine most notably, where his courage earned him high praise. Taking command of legion Gemina, less than six months ago, he was still adjusting himself to the vagaries of cooler climes, yet he'd quickly gained respect among the men for his fairness when dealing with those under his command.

'When he's not buggering his teenage paramour, the fair-haired boy, Auspex. That is the prick's name, is it not?' Balbilus chuckled as Agricola resumed his chair.

'This heathen prince, Quintus, is it right to trust him?' asked a grey-haired evocati, a re-enlisted centurion of the Valerians.

'With my life, centurion,' Cerialis replied so promptly than the older man sought not to press him further.

'It's not your life which is at stake though, is it?' Balbilus said, sarcastically. 'These supplies from the Cornovii, for instance. Can the bloody heathens deliver?'

'Get off his back, Julius!' Cerialis said, a little exasperated. 'We need people like Armet if we are to prosper. The prince knows Tadoc well, his father was a close friend, I believe.'

'Was?' questioned Balbilus, suspiciously.

'Volisios is ailing, perhaps dying,' Cerialis replied. 'Tadoc too. If that were to happen, *his* son Fomah will inherit. That individual has little regard for Rome and might well become a problem.'

'We have a remedy for bastards like that,' Balbilus spat, and all those other head-taking swine we choose to employ. 'If I had my way, I'd stick him high on a cross, together with all his heathen brood.'

'It is rumoured that Volisios can no longer sit a horse,' remarked Aquilla, absently.

'Then let the old bastard's arse suffer from a pox!' Balbilus blustered. 'I don't feel too good about all this damn fraternising. As for prince Armet, I don't trust him, and I trust his cocky younger brother even less. I saw him a year back at a review. An arrogant little sod, if ever there was one.'

'Gort, I consider no great threat,' spoke Cerialis. 'The prince and he are not close. In fact, he and Volisios have I believe, disowned the troublemaker. The fellow is merely a ranting boaster and can be easily handled. One day we'll catch him out. He'll make a mistake, they always do.'

'A heathen received by Rome with honours, doesn't make Armet a Roman in my eyes,' Balbilus swore an oath. 'Remember Arminius? If it were up to me, I'd have both their throats cut, and be done with it! Who knows, they may be planning some treachery, even as we speak.'

A silent Nardon of the auxiliary Batavi, who hailed from the Germanic Rhine Delta, glanced with cold eyes at Balbilus with such deep intensity over his casual remark, it didn't need words to express contempt at what he saw as an insult to his men. Self-consciously, the legate of Valeria for once, lowered his gaze and Straba the scribe, taking a mental note of this momentary interlude, confessed himself puzzled. Nardon, as far as rank went, even though he commanded two-thousand troops, couldn't hold a candle to the legate of a powerful legion, so why did Balbilus appear to back down?'

'I must back your judgement, Quintus, when it comes to prince Armet,' Tullius Roscius intervened in the exchange, after glaring with supressed anger at his subordinate sitting on the far side of the room, an unspoken reprimand aimed at the dark-haired Batavian for such insolence against a fellow legate. 'His conduct is a credit to the crucial business of absorbing barbarian people into the empire,' Tullius continued. 'He has one important virtue in that his people love him. Rome needs fellows like him, if we are to have any possible future here. As I see it, the founding of these Exploratores is a small, yet important step in the right direction. Make these Coritani feel a part of Rome instead of its enemy!'

'Bravo, Tullius,' chuckled Balbilus, sarcastically, back on form. 'Spoken like a true patriot. Yet I disagree. This bunch of swine are pure keltoi, in every sense, and they leave a nasty feeling in the gut. Wake up and take my advice, watch yourself, or your liable to find a knife sticking in your back.'

'I think the prince has other things on his mind,' mentioned the austere figure of primus pilus Aubanus, seriously.

'The witch, Gela!' Balbilus mused, a note of envy in his tone. 'I saw her once, on the arm of her heathen husband to be,' he smirked. 'Now there's a juicy prize worthy of the sport.'

'Then you must needs seek for your sport elsewhere,' Cerialis responded, sternly. 'Armet is an ally, and the girl, Gela, is Tadoc's daughter. Any thoughts you carry in that direction would be better worked off by renting a whore from the traders below, or it really will mean your waking up one morning minus your head.'

Another voice spoke up. 'Legate Balbilus is right though, when it comes to trust,' cautioned Arius Longa, senior centurion of Valeria. These untamed barbarians continue to test our patience with their treachery, and who's to know how many of them may be in league with the Coritani, or Tadoc's brood, come to that.' What so far is being done about it all?'

'Precious little, on the face of it,' Balbilus grumbled.

'We are all being put to the test, that's for sure, with these cursed affairs coming to plague us,' Roscius confirmed.

'Testing is too polite a word in my fucking book, my dear Tullius,' muttered Balbilus. 'I lost a squadron of fine cavalry with Petra, due to those pox-ridden scum. Now Calinae and this other damn place,' he swore aloud. 'Your chaps this time, Tullius, were they not? Thirty or more of them. Go on like this, and we'll have no damned army left. I already lack one of my damn cohorts!'

Balbilus referred to 6th cohort, still pinned down in Venovia by a band of local hostiles after several days of siege.

Roscius made a face and spread his hands.

'The situation at Venovia is bad, but by no means, critical,' answered Cerialis. 'When Paulinus gets here I shall send out Rufus or Gaius, with a relief force to see them off.'

'Why can't Paulinus do something?' interjected Roscius helpfully. 'He has to take the road bypassing the fort, not so?'

'A few mounted equites against an unknown force of bloody heathens,' Balbilus grumbled. 'No chance! Of course, if it were up to me, were I given the authority, I'd hit the bastards hard,' he continued bluntly. 'A couple of cohorts from my Valerians would do it, no problem! Anyway, question is, where is he? All this damn idleness will squeeze the seeds out of us if somebody doesn't shift his bloody arse.'

'I'm asking the same question,' Interrupted the balding Rufus Lippa, fourth in command of Hispania, speaking for the first time. 'Where is our illusive governor, Quintus?' he asked, scratching his stubbled chin.

'As far as I know, he's been delayed on imperial business with the procurator. Agricola answered Rufus Lippa's questioning a little too defensively, he thought.

At this Balbilus laughed, derisively. 'Fat Catus? Why don't we get him off his flabby backside and send him and his veterans to relieve Venovia instead, eh? And is that what they call buggery these days, 'imperial business?' What by Jupiter, were they doing, swapping cock suckers?' He stifled the mockery, rose to his feet. 'Why were we not informed earlier of the business with the overweight pillock?'

'It wasn't thought relevant, not with your understandable preoccupation with Petra.' Cerialis replied testily, becoming suddenly aware of the tardy presence of Straba who, head lowered, continued to make a clumsy show of being semi-visible when supposedly taking notes.

'I realise how frustrating the waiting has become,' confessed Cerialis turning away to move to the open window. 'Not counting my Hispanics, there are others down there,' he indicated, turning his profile to the assembly. 'Eighteen thousand men or more, ready to take Rome toward a victory over the Druse. It's been a long wait, but soon it will be over. Until then we must continue to sit on our backsides.'

'And shit on the riverbank,' Balbilus smiled coldly, referring to the previous argument concerning the lack of latrines.

Tullius Roscius intervened on another level. 'I'm afraid I don't like our situation as it stands. Moving the bulk of the legions from the south to the frontier vexes me. It leaves isolated sectors in many areas seriously undermanned.'

'Should there be trouble there are enough troops in our garrisons to deal with any further outbreak,' ventured Aubanus, confidently.

'Then your intelligence is better than mine,' smiled Roscius. 'I was thinking of the Iceni. There is rumour that its queen is once again causing concern. What's your opinion, Julius?'

Balbilus sat down heavily without replying, his mind being too busy on the extended list of complaints against Cerialis that he would slap on Paulinus' desk when given the opportunity. This upstart, for all his hands-on experiences with Rhine Army and Germania, must be brought down a peg or two and he, Balbilus, would delight in being the catalyst. All he craved for was a situation wherein this may be brought about. In answer to Roscius' question, he merely shook his head and uttered a bitter laugh. 'Like the Brig' queen, Carti' what's her name, just another heathen bitch!'

Late in the evening the fur-cloaked figure of Cerilalis stood again on the catwalk, his favourite spot now. Stretching away into the twilight the usual host of newly kindled fires flickered like so many stars. The scene dropped away from his vantage point on The Hill and yet, despite its familiarity, this example of the potent power of Rome, never failed to inspire.

Superbly equipped and organised, led by the most ruthless and efficient of the empire's generals, a contemporary of such brilliant leaders as Corbulo, Geta and Vespasian, this flexing of muscle, Cerialis thought, must deter even the bravest of Rome's foes. Yet that night, confident as he was, he failed to overcome the mounting sense of unease which at present hung over Lindum.

As for Straba's earlier absence at the briefing, it had not gone unnoticed, and the expected punishment had still to be given. Though it appeared that the legate, his mind engaged upon more immediate concerns, had so far turned a blind eye to the slave's conduct, the scribe's imagination could feel the sting of an inevitable lashing to come, being sensible enough to know that such a careless lack of timing would ultimately have its price.

TWENTY-SEVEN

GNAEUS JULIUS AGRICOLA, son of the late senator, Graecinus, worked far into the night. Not until the trumpet sounded the conclusion of the second watch, did he finally sign away the last document and dismiss the weary scribe. Alone, the tribune drank a welcome cup of wine and relaxed his body against the cushioned spine of the chair. Tiredness strained every muscle. Aware of the silence he rubbed sore eyes, blinked at the flicker of the table-lamp, stared at familiar things – stools, desks, a military stand that supported field armour.

Approaching his twenty-first birthday he'd recently been appointed to this new post, private secretary to Paulinus, whom he'd most likely be accompanying to the west in a matter of days. From his previous position with 2nd Augusta, he'd been ordered north a little time ahead of the governor who, because of the latter's detour to Camulodunum, was scheduled to be arriving in Lindum within the next twenty-four hours. At least, that's what he hoped.

On the desk a pile of paperwork, piled-up already, much of it to do with the business of building progress in the colonia, where things appeared to be as good as could be expected for a growing frontier settlement. At first Agricola had been pleased enough with the honour granted him at such an early age. Unfortunately, such enthusiasm was soon dashed. He didn't exactly resent being dumped in a dull and miserable northern outpost on the fringes of civilisation, he'd only himself to blame for that, having sought constantly for change. But he'd not expected to become a glorified secretary to a man who thought he could treat a person of his breeding like some lowly minion.

He bit his lip at the thought while running the palm of a hand over the wooden arm of the chair, caressing the polished surface as tenderly as he might caress the inner thighs of the slave-girl he'd only a few hours before purchased from a hard-bargaining, but reliable itinerate trader who did most of his business in and around the colonia. His sexual inclinations were normal for a young man, and he hadn't had a woman since leaving Glevum ten days ago. There had to be some sort of consolation for being assigned to this miserable place, he told himself. Taking his mind off the girl, he poured himself more wine, his thoughts now moving on to how Paulinus would react to the unwelcome news regarding Calinae and the destruction of this second fort; both incidents following hard on the earlier tragedy of Petra's Horse.

Legate Quintus Cerialis appeared to accept these setbacks without too much concern, although Agricola was not at all sure exactly what the fellow thought, beneath that devil may care attitude he seemed to adopt in public. Agricola had met Cerialis briefly a year or so ago at the banquet in Rome, given by his mother to celebrate her son's coming promotion. Their paths crossed only briefly, but there was no mutual bonding, a case perhaps of the privileged aristocrat verses a man whose background was, to put it politely, obscure. Only hours before, Cerialis had appeared just as friendly and annoyingly affable as he remembered him. A character Agricola found difficult to gauge, and he wondered if it were possible to look up to a man like Hispania's legate, a person he himself would never wish to emulate, having chosen his own way to attain power. Yet he hid his ambition, never wanting to pose a threat. His youthful face, smooth-chinned, with an engaging mop of light-coloured hair above dark blue eyes, could be a great aid in cloaking his true self.

As for his take on Cerialis, he must be cautious. He might well be depicted as a single-minded go-getter and a godly gift to women, but Agricola didn't buy into that. A man who'd climbed to a position of commanding, arguably the finest legion in the army at such a young age, had to be possessed of other merits. There were rumours. Had he really bedded queen Cartimandua? Just one of many salacious stories abroad.

On another level there was the business of Rome's relationship with the local Coritani people that interested the tribune, above all was that of their leader, prince Armet, and the familiarity he had with Cerialis, especially over a unit of tribal locals recently formed, the Exploratores. Something altogether new, and a matter for investigation if ever there was one, a subject that might well be pursued by the newly appointed secretary at some later time. Although hesitant in judgement, the newly arrived aristocrat was soon to share his envy along with that of 'man from the ranks', legate, Julius Balbilus.

None of this was any business of Agricola. If he'd learned little else during his twenty-one years of life, he'd taken on board one fundamental lesson. How to keep one's nose out of any trouble which could affect him personally, at least until, like a boxer, he'd found his feet. With the keenness of youth on his side, combined with a dogged sense to achieve, these were assets he might well call upon, to gain personal advantage.

He laid aside the several pieces of correspondence awaiting Paulinus' counter signature, those he had so recently dictated. The letters contained more than the usual messages. The receiving of necessary supplies from king Tadoc's Cornovii on route, apparently arranged by prince Armet, orders to the fleet assembling at Portus Adurni, to be on standby, ready for the 'big push', plus information about the exact number of flat-bottomed boats needed for the treacherous crossing of the Menai Straits, the stretch of water guarding the last stronghold of what Rome called, 'the Druse'.

Then perhaps the most important letter of all. Instructions to his recent mentor, the camp prefect of 2nd Augusta, Poenius Postumus, with whom he had earlier served in another capacity. Should it be necessary, in the absence of its legate, Postumus would have to provide extra military support, if needed. Agricola was already well-aware that this last decree carried with it a major problem posed mainly by the warlike Silures, dedicated followers of the betrayed Caractacus, who still posed a very real threat to the remote Roman fortress lying beside the Sabrina, a continuing menace to Glevum's security.

Ever since he'd disembarked onto the shore of Britannia, the same question that Cerialis and others had long asked, would come up again and again in the head of Agricola. Why, by the gods was it taking four legions to hold such a small province, when the troublesome populations of much larger lands needed only two? He reached for the roll containing the legionary musters within the conquered territories, giving particular attention to 9th Hispanics. What he learned as he studied the figures, worried him. From the first day he sensed things were not up to scratch in the province, all four legions being way below strength. This information of the true number came as a shock and didn't make for good reading. Nearer five and a half thousand held in each combat unit rather than the official six. A discrepancy that the zealous tribune would soon attempt to rectify.

It was the weakness of Hispania that brought it home. To go by the figures, this unit was a fighting force in name only. Overall control seemed precarious and too thinly spread to be effective in an emergency. Agricola became even more disturbed as he studied the muster rolls. Garrison duty alone was disconcerting. Stretching from the northern border, isolated units of Hispanics, together with their auxiliaries, occupied the five major holding stations along the Great Way, also known as the via Claudius, as far as Londinium to the south, the largest of these being Verulamium. When constant patrolling of the land between Lindum and Cartimandua's frontier region were tallied, Agricola reckoned that after the imminent departure of legions Gemina and Valeria for the coming assault against the enemy, Cerialis' command would have to be extra-vigilant in its handling of any likely trouble spot.

Six months earlier Agricola had been assisted to gain his position on Paulinus' staff by those men who still had the ear of Nero, one of the more notable being no less than the prefect of the elite praetorian guard, Onius Tigellinus. The report placed before Paulinus concerning the young man's ability and noble birth was enough for him to be given the position he now held, secretary to the most powerful man in Britannia, an envious post for anyone seeking advancement. Now sitting isolated in an uncomfortable administration building, he had a momentary thought that his presence here amounted to a ghastly mistake. Better it would have been perhaps, to have remained in the familiar comfort of his comfortable villa in Gaul.

If he'd but known it, destiny and the province he viewed so disdainfully, were to become inevitably interwoven and, like a struggling man caught in the flood, he would need all his cunning to stay above water.

It was to say the least, a little ironic how fortune cast the dabs for, as night followed day, Agricola suddenly felt a tweak of home sickness. On the desktop, shining up at him sat a small amulet of fine gold. Crafted upon its surface was a familiar theme, a young man in the process of slaying a bull. The Mithraic emblem, a present he had lately received from his beloved mother, Julia Procilla, *'a lady of singular virtue,'* as one famous poet described her, in celebration of his birth. Beside it lay the letter he'd personally written in reply, the one item of correspondence that didn't need the approval of the governor.

He re-read the words scratched into the wax tablet. In no way exceptional, they probably matched many such notes written by any member of the garrison camped beside the Witham. *The latter days of spring promised much, deceiving us by its mildness. Now I fear it sends us rain by the bucketload so that I begin to think that our army might very soon drown under the flood, I along with it. No matter. I thank you for the kind and thoughtful gift. In return I send a small token to you, my first from this strange place............*

The brooch was brightly enamelled and depicted a leaping horse. On its back rode a warrior armed with shield and spear, around his neck a gold torc. *This I bought from a native trader, one of the many taking up residence at Lindum,* Agricola wrote. *These barbarians seem to have an unholy love of horses, which they prize above all else. Not without reason are they known as Epona's children. She is thought to be a popular goddess locally.* He did not write, sparing his mother's sensitivity, of the ritualistic decapitation of their enemies.

For a moment he thought once more of his father, the noble Graecinus, a man he never knew, murdered by the deranged emperor, Caligula, over some obscure legal tussle less than a month after Agricola was born. It had been a loving marriage, marred by tragedy. To date, as far as the young man was aware, his reclusive mother had never seriously considered any future partnership.

He stuffed the tablet and brooch into his deerskin satchel. He hadn't pursued the matter of censorship in great depth. Although staff officers mail was supposed not to be tampered with, there was no absolute certainty that his wouldn't, at some time, be under scrutiny.

Suddenly a sound low and far off entered the open window of the small room assigned to him, startling him from his reverie. Thunder growled in the distance. Agricola strode to the open window. To the east he saw flashes of jagged light. Carried on the rising wind, drops of rain splashed his tunic. Two men of Cerialis' Hispanics on duty outside the praetorium, grounded javelin butts and came to attention. The young tribune casually returning the salute, stared south along the river-route toward Crococalana, only a few miles away, where the holding camp of Armet's Coritani, the four hundred Exploratores lay, his mind deep again in thought as to where the heathen, prince Armet figured in this, it being an uncommon practice to allow auxiliary captains such close intimacy with those of higher rank. The prince was said to have been sent to Rome, where he was taught Latin and later, gained Roman citizenship. Even so.........................

While warm rain wet his face, aware of the watching presence of the guards he started off, draping a cloak over him, the satchel over his shoulder, making his way through the narrow streets of the darkening colonia. Eventually he would find his billet and the inviting arms of the young girl he'd so recently acquired.

The date of Agricola's introduction to Lindum came two months after the eight hundred and fourteenth anniversary of the founding of Rome. He recalled the noise of celebration heard throughout Glevum that evening as revellers from 2nd Augusta paid dutiful respect to twins, Romulus and Remus.

Another cause for carousal appeared to be taking place tonight, only yards from his room. For one hesitant moment the Agricola felt tempted to join them, but he was weary and there was much work still to do, his destiny being to accompany Paulinus' army on its long-planned march on Dorona. But for now, the girl was waiting...

TWENTY-EIGHT

AT A COMFORTABLE distance from the restless frontier, Catus Decianus decided to enjoy his usual afternoon at the baths and have his few remaining strands of hair trimmed during the process. The departure of Paulinus had left him in an extremely confused state of mind, and the recent murder of the town's useful centurion didn't help. There was one good thing about it though. The supreme governor hadn't been around to hear of it, being on his way to that stinking disgrace to Rome which discerning men called fortress Lindum.

'What by all the gods are you trying to do, Tarma?' Catus winced, testily 'My head isn't made of marble!'

'Forgive me, your excellence,' The tonsor remarked. 'The gel is not as flexible as it used to be. We're awaiting a fresh delivery.'

Decianus grunted, shifted his bulk with irritation upon the cushioned stool and kicked out at Tarma's nubile young attendant who'd begun to anoint his fleshy legs with an oil that smelt to him a little like rancid pork fat. 'No, this is not good enough!' The procurator protested. 'Just how long must one wait for the mere basics of simple pleasures?'

'Relax, eminence!' Tarma answered, patiently, coating his hands in a suspiciously thick, dark ointment from the bowl. 'When we've finished with you even your own mother won't recognise you.'

Catus Decianus slumped even deeper into the cushions, longing for the torture to be over. 'If such a miracle could be, brave Tarma, I would gladly salute you and your lowly profession, after I've had you flogged that is.' He flicked a drop of moisture from a plump knee, his action almost dainty. 'Thank the gods, you never knew my mother. She thought me ugly, damn her spleen.'

'With all due respect, she could not have meant such an insult, dominus,' Tarma said smoothly, his hands raised in mock horror. 'Let me dare to be honest. Is it not a common fault for some mothers to fail to see their son's potential?'

'It is true,' Decianus acknowledged, thinking wistfully of how much faster he might have advanced without the constant criticism from the she-wolf who'd given him life. May the gods give her pox! 'Go easy on the flattery, slave,' he admonished. I don't need to remind you, you're a long way from manumission.'

Unseen, at the procurators back, Tarma dug his fingers into the thinning scalp of the procurator with extra pressure, his lips displaying an expression that would frighten a gorgon. Later the tonsor would receive the obligatory ten lashes for some other minor domestic mishap. What would take place was a harmless ritual planned to humiliate, the thongs of the whip being strips of velveteen and the punishment administered by a ten-year old boy whom Decianus had found orphaned in the town and was buggered regularly in pursuit of his appetites.

Such then was the way of things...

Later that evening, after he'd Indulged himself with his new-found plaything the procurator or 'old moneybags' as the townspeople termed him, surveyed from his window the dark weave of the river and the fading land beyond. By his side stood a small dish of grapes. At times of nervousness, he indulged in them continuously, as if he were being paid by promotors to do so. But these came from his own vineyard, established some time ago when he'd obtained his important position. Worryingly, tonight he felt a cold touch of uneasiness, having never before felt in any way unsafe in his exalted status. Why should he feel out of sorts when guarded by two-hundred veterans?

Several weeks earlier, there'd been rioting within the precincts of the Claudian temple! In the ensuing brawl several Britons in the procurator's pay, suffered severe injuries, one of them dying from his wounds. Those of the opposing faction, well-known causers of disturbances in the area, when apprehended, suffered death by crucifixion. Since then, an angry mood had prevailed in the form of a dangerous mob now calling openly for the procurator's blood. Catus had a good idea as to who was causing this sacrilege, and the name of Adomarus son of Obrig, a rebellious king who languished in a cell of that same temple, stood out. Such a flagrant flouting of Roman law could well make a man of Decianus' sensitive nature, extremely nervous, even though the cause of his troubles had long fled with a price on his head.

He stood convinced that something beyond his control was abroad. Just exactly what this something might be could not be explained, and he wasn't at all sure with all the rumours going about what he ought to do to curtail these recent seeds of unrest. The soldiers allocated to keep order were barely enough to contain anything but minor disturbances, let alone a substantial area of the province. He could kick himself for not having tackled the undernourished looking snob of a governor about his grievances when he had the bloody chance. Would it really have been too much? Half a cohort, perhaps an extra one hundred, two hundred, perhaps one damn half of one damn cohort, whereas Paulinus commanded two whole bloody legions and the gods knew how many damned auxiliaries, just to hold down a few heathen lawbreakers. Adopting an air of sageness that he hardly possessed, he again contemplated the present situation.

Mona! That was its name. A hotbed of sedition wherein resident priests spawned from the mouth of Orcus practiced the foul rites of human sacrifice! Like most Romans, Decianus had heard second hand of many bloodcurdling stories concerning the foul creatures who worshiped alien gods, and Decianus believed them all. Such heresy fully deserved to be put down with all the severity Rome could muster, following the example employed by Julius Caesar against the Gaulish Druse and their leader

Vercingetorix in the age of the republic. Yet was this barbarity really the prime reason for Paulinus' overriding obsession? The need for precious metals was paramount if the province were to be properly controlled. By all accounts it had failed to yield sufficient returns on its investment, and feelings were running hot enough for some to talk of abandoning the islands for good.

Decianus, though regarding the country as the most miserable place in the world, while at the same time seeing the profit to be made, was not in agreement with this opinion. Rome, having already sunk a fortune into the province, desperately needed a mountain of vital resources to keep a wayward Britannia financed, and the procurator was shrewd enough to realise that this could not be obtained by putting down a few wild-haired Druse. As for tales of human sacrifice, were these accounts enough to unleash two crack Roman legions into what could be an extended war? More likely the limitless gold and copper deposits known to exist in the west and elsewhere, was the predominant reason for the long-planned assault. Besides, on a personal level, Catus wanted his share.

Was it fate that only hours after the departure of the governor, a second sealed letter from the emperor arrived on Catus' desk, following hard on the first? The procurator scanned its contents for a third time with growing approbation. The commands completely countered Paulinus' own, and this time a second signatory, that of Nero's advisor, Seneca, philosopher and statesman, had been added to the scrawling hand of the emperor. The collection of the promised tribute, including that eye-watering loan owed by the Iceni under its obligatory agreement with the dead king, must with all speed be settled as soon as possible, without undue delay. The procurator's pudgy hand shook with nervous trepidation as he again reread the letter. Caught between the machinations of three powerful men, what in the name of Jupiter must he do?

TWENTY-NINE

D ASAL THE DRUID, he who had been so boldly challenged by Gort all those years before, had more than one notch to his stave, as those rash enough to make the mistake of underestimating him would find to their cost. From humble beginnings within the priesthood, only son of a slave, he rose to become one of the most powerful spiritual leaders in his class. Fed by an increasing ambition, within a decade he'd extended his influence well beyond the misty shores of Roman controlled Britannia, including Gaul and Ireland. But it was to Anglesey that Dasal Hud had brought his organisational skills to bear. Aware that time was moving events at an unnatural speed, he was perhaps the first of his brother Druids to recognise a greater need for defence regarding the sacred sites of Mona.

The latest report received told of a fleet of twelve Roman triremes quietly approaching the western side of the island's Hibernian shore. This, together with earlier information regarding the construction of several score of specially adapted boats with narrow draught, meant for one purpose only, to enforce a successful crossing by assault troops over the narrow waters that divided Mona from the eastern mainland. To wipe out the cursed Druse, a threat to the empire for over a century, a pincer movement difficult to avoid, was put together. Cunningly devised by Paulinus himself to eliminate this dangerous cult once and for all, it had all the hallmarks of tactics used successfully in Gaul. It was expected they'd work just as well in the supreme governor's favour.

Several valid-sounding reasons would be given for the needed wholesale liquidation of the cult, but the more important one would not be admitted. A prize was to be had in Mona's mineral bearing western hills, large deposits of precious copper being top of the list!

There were three levels of Druse throughout Britain when governor Paulinus faced the risky task of subduing Druidism.

CHAPTER TWENTY-NINE

First came Arch-Druids, mostly men, occasionally women. These were the more influential and respected of the faith, those who'd served a long apprenticeship immersing themselves in the many mystical complications of sacred lore. Caesar was said to believe that the Druidical world was one of ridged discipline, describing their priests as, among other gifts, teachers of wisdom. This didn't stop him from vanquishing its members in Gaul however, along with their defiant protector, Vercingetorix.

Second to the above were healers and physicians, famed for their care of the sick, men and women who would rather prevent ailments at source if possible. Ironically, a few males were chosen for harsher duties, the execution of serious wrong-doers, rapists, murderers and thieves, a ritual which Roman propaganda was quick to pick up on, hypocritically labelling such acts as bloody pagan sacrifices, a legacy that ensured their lurid place in history. Like those on the higher level, they were teachers of wisdom who believed implicitly in the existence of the immortal soul and the power of the cosmos. Others in their following were bards, preachers and healers, founts of learning for all seekers after truth.

The third kind of mystic was of a quite different hue. Men like Culchul and Dasal, bearing the distinctively dangerous title of 'Hud,' were of warrior class, trained since an early age to learn the necessary art of combat. The latter, despite their calling, were permitted by the Arch Druids, the oak knowers, to use their skills whenever alerted.

Rome was the major enemy, a very real threat to existence itself. This led in effect to many renegade priests and priestesses dwelling in the pacified lands to defy Roman injustice wherever possible. They were by any description, the other side of the coin. The designated term 'Hud' also meant defender and, aided by tribal leaders to maintain their real status they instinctively hid their true calling from the alien power and its traitorous collaborators. These warrior priests were thus hardened individuals, ready to sacrifice all for the cult's survival should necessity demand it.

Almost two decades before, when Roman troops arrived for a third time on the island, many tribal groups in the south chose to resist stubbornly, only to be trampled underfoot by a ruthless conqueror who, like all conquerors, was only interested in gain. But as Caesar predicted, complete peace could never take place while Druidism remained, thus was their power scattered to the four winds, their shrines and temples, overturned. Gradually, as a matter of policy, Rome began a disciplined persecution with their usual indifference to personal suffering. Over the years, those Huds that chose to remain among the vanquished, risked losing both freedom and life. Some travelled north to take shelter with those who'd not yet been completely subjected to Roman rule, finding safety with tribes like Volisios' Coritani. Dasal, now the rebel Gort's advisor and mentor, was one of these mysterious members.

Many watchful people of the midland nations became aware early on of the unfolding situation regarding Paulinus's planned assault. The treatment recently dealt out to Adomarus, son of Obrig and prince of the Trinovante, together with rumours of Rome's attitude to Boudiga's Iceni, didn't go unnoticed, being a cold wake-up call, if ever one were needed, to previous similar events throughout the Roman empire.

For more than a year, Dasal with a few followers, visited all four corners of the province and beyond, closely avoiding Roman patrols in order to recruit to their cause all who nurtured a common hatred. Gort had, to the chagrin of father and brother, proved an eager convert to Dasal's influence. But as far as he saw it, this was a chance to break away once and for all from the bonds with which Volisios had, by agreement with the conqueror, entrapped him and others when taking the giant step toward the ambiguous status of client kingship. Many more would follow and, when Gort finally departed from Rina, a frustrated and disillusioned number of fighting men chose to accompany the youth.

If Dasal Hud was their spiritual leader, Gort in a very short time became the unchallenged warlord and many, stung into action by the sharp words of seasoned agitators such as the Hud, meant he'd little trouble in gaining more supporters. As weeks passed, a formidable war-band, with Gort at their head and Dasal Hud, roamed the land unopposed, continuing all the while to enrol others to their strength.

It was during this time that Gort chose to revisit an old acquaintance in the shape of king Mogonus, king of the Parisi, the man who'd been instrumental in giving the Coritanian a chance to enhance, with the aid of his champion driver Vixt, his skill with the chariot. Riding with him were a small group of warriors, including Dasal Hud and Gort's long-time companion, Tove.

THIRTY

PAULINUS ENTERED LINDUM with a turma of trusted equites, arriving by night under a forest of hand-held brands. The column, personally met by Cerialis, together with a strong escort of legionaries, intercepted the group several miles south of the colonia.

Accompanying Hispanic's commander, the newly designated young aide-de-camp to the governor, tribune Agricola, rode out to meet him. No trumpet announced the supreme legate's arrival, no drum or fanfare. Once arrived in the praetorium he summoned all senior commanders. Sixty-one years old, every inch a campaigner, both as soldier and administrator, a hard man, he exuded fear and respect in equal measure to friend and foe alike.

A long list of past victories left him well equipped to deal with any trouble from those facing him in the land of the Druse, and his presence alerted fighting men to the realisation that there'd soon be action. At this late hour, cloak and gear splattered from head to toe after the long ride north, he scanned with a soldier's eye a rough-drawn map.

The report concerning the massacre of a tiny group of defenders south of the military base at Segelocum, did little to cheer the black-dog condition that had pursued him north. This latest disappointment only added to the irritation.

A typical answer to military setbacks was to catch the enemy on the run. After the expected arguments, opinions and disagreements, a strategy finally lay on the table. Legate Julius Balbilus would take three cohorts – one from each legion involved, Valeria, Gemina and Hispania. These, accompanied by a like number of auxiliaries, made up of infantry, Tungrians, Macedonian archers and Balearic slingers, plus one-thousand cavalry, would be the cutting edge of the 'big push.' Their objective lay some seventy miles west of the Trisantona, making the march from the river roughly a three-day journey, half of it through forest, the legionaries curse!

'Up to you, Julius. I'll back your judgement. If you decide the place can be reduced with just one assault, then do it. If it fails, dig-in and wait.'

'I'm already there, eminence,' Balbilus said, drawing himself to attention.

'I mean it, Julius,' Paulinus cautioned with heavy emphasis on his words 'On *no* account attempt a second attack without back-up. Should you encounter a problem you can't contain, fall back on Deva, we'll meet you there.'

Balbilus hid his thoughts on that suggestion. Deva! A muddled, half-built excuse for civilisation, a nowhere on the lip of nowhere, manned by half a century of undisciplined criminals, serving part of their stretch there rather than choosing to rot in captivity at Lindum. Besides, the dump possessed no bathhouse, or so he'd heard, and no whores either. No, you can stuff your Deva, eminence!

'We shan't fail, sire,' Balbilus emphasised.

Secretly the legate only half listened. The chance of action was pure gold to the old campaigner. He was to be given free rein. As to the odds to be faced, he knew he'd overcome them. There would be no need to wait for Paulinus and a second chance. Best of it all, he thought with relish, he'd have complete authority over a cohort of Cerialis' Hispanics, presenting him with the means to settle a long-awaited score.

The problem of Venutius, now the premier focus of attention, was a matter of growing concern, and for good reason. The Brigante king was a figure far bigger to tackle than Brennus, mainly because the real power he wielded remained a mystery, with his ability as a leader, untried. As for the strength he commanded, men spoke of a thousand or perhaps, ten-times that number. Paulinus had ever remained undaunted by rumour. In his experience there was no way undisciplined fighters could raise such a large army, and he remained confident that his seasoned legionaries in the field, were more than capable of dealing with anything that lay in store.

'Dorona,' Paulinus sniffed with satisfaction. 'If Venutius hinders our way we will have to remove him, quickly. Not so?' He paused, glancing meaningfully at the small assembly. 'Now, gentlemen, regarding the little matter of the boats.'

The assembling of the necessary means to obtain a foothold on Mona had proved particularly frustrating. The marines working all out to provide the flat-bottomed craft were plagued by the constant menace of sabotage. As soon as any of the craft were readied, despite their being put under guard, adherents of the Druse found an ingenious variety of means to wreck them, many sacrificing themselves in the process. The growing number of hastily erected crosses facing the Straits were grim witness to their efforts. Built for the purpose of an eventual bridging of the watery barrier separating the Roman army from the island, these boats were to play a vital part. Without them the Druidical groves and sacred sanctuaries would be that much harder to breach.

It had been an idea agreed months before, this sea-born crossing of these unpredictable waters. Paulinus took an especial interest in the scheme as his nephew, Aulus Glaborus, was in total charge of the tricky logistics involved. At least there were better tidings received from elsewhere to balance Paulinus' temper. Twelve triremes, dropping anchor in Hibernian waters facing the western shore of the island, had neatly completed the pincer movement, drawn up by him some months before.

Further orders were to follow that night. With defiance coming from certain peoples, the Iceni becoming especially uncooperative, Paulinus instructed Cerialis to reinforce the five major forts between the colonia and Portus Londinium, doubling the strength of the Hispanic's garrisons, if required as an extra precaution against any trouble. But there was no doubt about it, the problem with Decianus had managed to unsettle the general. He didn't trust the procurator in the business regarding the clearances. Increasing fortress garrisons might appear an unnecessary knee-jerk response by some, but if the worst were to happen, and there were other potential hot spots, a stronger presence might well act as a deterrent, one that 'fat Catus' must be forced to take note of, reminding him perhaps that the all-seeing eye of Paulinus watched from a far lesser distance than that of the emperor.

Cerialis wasn't overly pleased about these instructions. The Hispanics were already stretched to the limit. Only a few miles north of Lindum, two cohorts reinforced control of the unmarked frontier with queen Cartimandua's, Brigantia, by far the most powerful and ambiguous nation that Rome had yet engaged with. Other imperial troops, auxiliaries, stationed at further strategic points, amounted to another thousand troops or more being scattered, leaving the legate with a much-depleted force with which to defend his base at Lindum. To lose yet another five-hundred good legionaries to Paulinus' old campaigning friend, Balbilus, however temporarily, was yet another setback he could have done without.

The supreme legate leaned over the map and drew Cerialis close. 'In confidence, Quintus,' he whispered, 'get your scribe to draft the orders.' The legate was sore tempted to say, I would, if I could find the bugger. Where was the little Greek, anyway? Cerialis cursed inwardly.

'I want a brace of our fastest gallopers to ride to Glevum at dawn with instructions for legate Galtiore,' Paulinus continued. 'If he's ill, get him to instruct prefect Postumus to rendezvous with me there,' he indicated a spot on the chart with a bony finger, 'at a place they call Cymbroda, or is it, Four Ways? Tell whichever of the two that can walk to get off their sodding backsides, ready to march north to meet with as many men of Augusta as can be spared.' Paulinus' hand gripped Cerialis' arm tightly. 'Yes, I'm aware of the trouble with the Silures,' he argued, as if knowing what Cerialis was going to say. 'This is of the uttermost importance, you understand, he *must* come. Much depends on it. Tell him I trust to meet him there in thirty days. Underscore that! Thirty days!'

They would long be remembered, these instructions sent to Glevum at a pregnant hour. Men would ask later if Paulinus possessed the gift of foresight, prior to the battles at Dorona and Mona, to be so accurate in his forecast or was he given some prior knowledge as to what was to come? A warning from a traitorous informant, or from others closer to home, those who followed the eagles and were well in favour with the governor? These were of course, questions that would never provide answers.

The legate of Hispanics understood that, however many of 2nd Augusta might leave their base and proceed north to join up with main army, they'd leave Glevum greatly exposed, with all the possible risks involved. The legion's legate, whatever decision he made, would find himself on the horns of a dilemma. But little had been heard from him recently, it being reported that he remained confined to his bed with an unknown sickness. Knowing Gaius Galtiore's liking for hogging the limelight, Quintus Cerialis, taking into consideration the man's egocentricity, had to conclude that the vain fellow must be very ill indeed.

Many days later, after Paulinus' departure in the wake of the advance guard, a galloper would arrive at The Hill delivering a weighty leather pouch into the hands of Cerialis who unceremoniously up-ended its contents onto the desk, his lips parting in a grin while staring at the sight of a pristine set of dumb-bells.

THIRTY-ONE

MOGONUS SAID WITHOUT MIRTH, 'Old Volisios must have lost his wits to have sent you here, cub.'

'Volisios' life nears its end,' spoke Gort bluntly. 'My father now rules in name only. Armet's the one who holds the real power.'

The round house of the Parisi was large and, despite a roaring blaze, Gort felt chilled while praying to his god that the cursed fever, which continued to plague him, would not recur at this critical moment. Mogonus thoughtfully picked a morsel of pork from between broken teeth while staring hard at Gort, who sat on the far side of the fire. The wily chieftain, king of the chariot folk, a defiant opposer of the neighbouring Brigante and a constant thorn in their queen's side, grinned wickedly. He sat resting his hunched frame against the high-backed chair. While the travellers were given welcome food and ale the king spoke again. Now his voice took a lower note, sounding harsher than before, like to a raven's croak. 'It is said you've raised many fighting men, yet you come here without the support of prince Armet. To me that seems strange.'

Gort shook his head. 'Don't underestimate my brother, king. I had thought that he and Volisios might see things differently. Yet for the sake of the king, he has persuaded himself to believe that cooperation with Rome will keep us all safe.' Gort smiled at the thought. 'I think I am stronger than my brother now and, though I love him dearly, I believe he's wrong in continuing blindly to follow the dictates of Rome.'

'And what of Volisios? Where is his mind on all this? '

'Because he grows old and afraid, he feels his people will be better served if he cooperates with Rome.'

'And when your old king has gone, do you intend to take his place?'

Gort was hesitant. 'Given the right circumstances, yes, I might take his place.'

Mogonus wiped a greasy hand along his thigh and, belching noisily, reached for the almost empty jug of ale. Gort sensed that he was playing for time, as if he were waiting for the younger man to set his own trap, to become ensnared in his own words. Despite his irritation at being taken for a fool, Gort felt calm inside, glad at least that the ever-suspicious ruler of one of the smallest yet fiercest fighters in the north was painfully predictable, at least so he thought. 'You must hate prince Armet very much,' Mogonus muttered.

'I love my brother more than life itself,' Gort said, stretching his hands toward the fire's warmth.

'Then why...................?'

'We cannot be reconciled. Since our last meeting the void has become too wide,' Gort concluded, a hint of melancholy in his voice.

'These warriors you lead, what exactly do they want?'

'What most of us desire, king; to defeat the Roman and send him back across the narrow sea with his breeches down.'

'Is that all?' Mogonus chuckled. 'I'll say one thing, cub, you certainly don't lack ambition. By Tiranis, you might even have won me over a few years ago.' The king leaned forward toward the fire, warming his hands and rubbing them vigorously together. 'And how, if it ever takes place, will your brother react to this rebellion?'

'Armet as always, will continue to follow my father's wishes.'

'Which are?'

'I've already explained. To protect Volisios and my people, he'll continue to bend the knee,' Gort muttered, the bitterness in his tone apparent when he spoke, adding softly, 'but that will change. That's why I'm here.'

The risks were formidable. Gort, were he taken, would suffer the same fate as the Huds, Culchul and Dasal, meaning certain torture and death on the cross. Yet this concerned him less than the thought of what pain might also come to those he loved, were things to change. As an act of goodness, not hatred, he'd deliberately distanced himself from his kin. Armet may still be held above suspicion by Rome, no matter what happened to himself. After the last violent argument, he'd no choice but to quit Rina, for the final time. Though there was much regret in his heart over deserting both brother and father, there was for him the greater challenge, to defeat Rome, then hunt down the murderers of his mother and sister, Alorad, a task he would swear the gods had chosen for him.

Mogonus spoke bluntly. 'The Romans are marching west, they've already left Lindum for the sacred groves, so I'm informed.'

Gort, brought back from his contemplation, nodded. Signs of rebellion were fermenting, he knew. What had snared the once independent Trinovante was but a foretaste of things to come. Adomarus, son of Obrig, leading a war-pack of several thousand men, similar in number to Gort's followers, had set up a refuge not too distant from the land of the Iceni some weeks before, not long after Rome had paid their bloodiest visit yet, to the queen. Half the Iceni dwellings still smouldered when he and Adomarus had appeared that day. Many of its citizens had been slain, its men butchered, the women raped or enslaved. Even Boudiga herself was subjected to the humiliation of being forced to watch the violation of her daughters before the greatest insult, her own scourging.

Using old roads, Gort and his childhood friend, Tove, accompanied by his advisor, Dasal Hud and a score of followers, carefully avoiding legionary patrols and ubiquitous check points, had ridden north to reach the lands of the Parisi, choosing for safety, to travel by night. Traversing the forest known as 'Angst,' the place of great oaks, they had finally arrived, unheralded, in king Mogonus' territory, a place which the Romans would later call Petravia. Leaving their small group of riders camped a few miles from the Parisi capital, the trio were soon challenged by heavily armed warriors, carrying lighted brands and riding a dozen war chariots.

Some would say that it was a bold move on Gort's part towards a people who had never been friendly to outsiders, especially their closest of neighbours the Brigante. But Gort was no stranger to the Parisi, and he knew Mogonus well. In less fraught times the king had taught him the art of charioteering under the practiced eye of their tribal champion, Vixt.

From him Gort had long ago learned about the fighting qualities of the Parisi. Also, he had come to know the character of their leader, a man who against all odds had led his people through ten years of hostility with the common enemy Cartimandua who, despite vigorous opposition, continued on a regular basis to raid the Parisi borderland.

'Well, cub,' Mogonus' stare hardened. 'This time I hazard you've not returned to us for more chariot lessons, and that it's you who could now teach, seeing as, since we last met, you've made a bit of a name for yourself.'

'I'm glad to use any event, as an excuse to see my old friend, Mogonus.' Gort spoke slowly, still not having completely mastered the near unfathomable dialect of the Parisi.

Mogonus grinned. ''We have closely followed your progress among the tribes, and you speak openly of your intentions. I respect your honesty especially as you've no doubt considered that I could hold you and your followers at my will. I reckon Rome would pay a great deal in ransom money for your safe return.'

'Do that and you'll earn the enmity of those whose ambition it is to throw off the weight of slavery, 'Gort replied easily, sipping ale. 'But that won't happen, will it? You're not Cartimandua, any more than I'm Caractacus.'

Mogonus chuckled while his bloodshot eyes jigged like devils. 'You're a good talker, I'll give you that. Yet you speak of slavery, forgetting we Parisi are a free people.'

'How long will you be able to say those words?' Gort countered, leaning forward again toward the warmth of the fire. 'While we drink your ale, a large Roman army sits a few miles from this land, watching you carefully, as does the she-wolf who befriends their power at Lindum.'

'We are well supplied with information about Rome's cock sucker. Tell me something I don't know, such as, what is it you want from me?'

'We wish one thing only,' Gort leaned back. 'We want you to listen.'

'And just who are *'we'?'* Mogonus countered. 'Dasal, I know.' He looked at Tove, coldly. 'This cub I don't.'

'Tove is my secondus, my right-hand man.'

'Your secondus!' Mogonus laughed, stifled a cough before slapping a thigh. 'A strange word. Just like your brother, it would appear the Romans have got inside you at last!' He stared hard at Tove. 'Do you love your master?'

Tove, after a fleeting glance toward Gort, spoke only one word.

'It is good to love your leader,' Mogonus agreed, wiping his bearded chin.

'Rome hasn't got me at all,' Gort then said, hiding his annoyance well, saying, 'If such were the case, I'd not be here at all.'

'Well, cub, what exactly *are* you here for?'

'We're in need of your chariots,' replied Gort, flatly.

Mogonus sat in silence, as though stunned. Then, in sarcasm he said, 'is that all then, my chariots?' He paused before continuing. 'We are not as completely adrift from human affairs as you seem to think. I'm aware of the troubles with the Iceni and Obrig's people, as I am in all else around.'

'Then you have heard about what took place with Boudiga. Doesn't that make you a little fearful?'

The king nodded. 'A bad business to be sure, to flog a queen, and a terrible lesson learned about the danger of cosying up to Rome.'

'What happened to her will come to you eventually. Your present freedom cannot be taken for granted,' Gort urged. 'I have seen, first-hand, what Rome can do. Also, you must also be aware, if the priests go down, you'll be next!'

'Gort is right!' Dasal Hud spoke in support for the first time. 'All must prepare for war and drive the invader back to Gaul.'

Mogonus closely studied the warrior-priest, his eyes moving to the sword at his belt, then to the hand-axe suspended by a leather strap from the Hud's broad shoulder. For the first time the Parisi king looked uncomfortable. 'I respect your words, holy priest.

But I must be plain, like you I have a duty toward my subjects. What you are about is a fine thing, but you must agree that you could fail.'

'We'll not do that,' spoke Dasal with confidence. 'With two legions tied up against our brethren in the west we may never have better chance of success. As Gort says, we are already many in number.'

Gort nodded approvingly. 'From Camulodunum and Icenorum to your border', he agreed, 'the Catavellaunians alone have pledged many warriors. I'd like to see Rome get the better of *them*!' Gort paused. 'We all know what Paulinus has in mind. Mona's sanctity lies in the balance. My brother and four hundred Coritani riders, Exploratores they call themselves, are set to join the advance force, ahead of the main body. Dorona alone, bars the way west. After them follows the main army, two legions moving against the holy Drus-Wyd!'

Mogonus scratched his chin, thoughtfully. 'Who will be in charge of the Dorona mission, Rome or Armet?'

Gort, choosing to ignore the sarcasm, answered. 'Under the eye of Cerialis, he professes to aid them, yet I believe my brother's main quarry is the same as would be mine. Brennus and the Abrentii, no less.' Gort leaned back, recalling the dark day he lost Alorad. 'There are old scores to settle,' he muttered. 'I would be with them, even aiding Rome, had not my cause taken me to other places.'

'And after Brennus?'

'I'm no seer. I don't predict,' Said Gort finally, signalling to his companions to leave.

'I must confer with my advisors,' Mogonus answered, slowly clambering to his feet, his bloodshot eyes level with the young Coritanian. Taking Gort by the arm he took him out of earshot of the others, whispering confidentially in a low voice. 'Take care, choose your friends wisely, for I sense there are those amongst your following who mean you great harm, so best be watchful.' Mogonus steered him back to the fire, continuing to address him affably. 'I'll say again, we too are more aware of the situation than you appear to think and, as true followers of the old beliefs, what you say can't be ignored.' The elderly king slowly resumed his seat. 'I'll tell Vixt of your arrival. He'll be happy to see an old pupil after all this time.' Mogonus paused in thought. 'Meantime you must know, it's a hard thing that you ask. Any decision cannot be mine alone.'

'Mogonus is a wily old fox,' whispered Tove later from the opposite bed. 'And all your nonsense about these Catavellauni, where does that come from?'

Gort tapped his forehead. 'Mogonus is Mogonus,' he answered under the dim flicker of an oil-lamp.

'You don't think you've won him over?'

'You do not win over a man like Mogonus,' Gort mused. 'You bargain with him. We wish something from him, he will in return want something from us. Yet I know him well enough to throw the dice that he's hiding something. He just doesn't trust us enough to tell all, yet.'

'It's a risky business,' Tove agreed.

'No Tove, It's diplomacy.'

If Gort pondered only a little while over Mogonus' strange warning, it was the hovering presence of his life-time curse that vexed him more, like the fear that visited him earlier that evening. He never knew when or where he might be caught out during these bouts of helplessness, and he prayed that no one would be with him should it chose to strike. If he had enemies, as the king appeared to believe, then so be it, no surprise. One didn't walk on hens' eggs without cracking shells. Nevertheless, he would pocket the king's advice and be doubly vigilant in future.

Morgonus himself would admit he was no diplomat, but he was good at masking his true feelings when it came to it. Gort in his turn was clever, yet he failed to get inside the old man's head. Already the king had half made up his mind. In the space between receiving news on Dorona and the hour when Gort took his leave the following morning, Morgonus was sending gallopers out to mobilise his considerable force of charioteers. Here, given the opportunity, was a perfect time for him to settle old scores with Cartimandua, her supporters having seriously been reduced in number by the forcefulness of Venutius' argument concerning his own right to rule the Brigante. With her Roman supporters, Cerialis and the Hispanics otherwise preoccupied, the embattled queen had conveniently become a tempting target to put out of action. With this in mind, the Parisi leader began moving his fleet of war-cars in the direction of her borders and the nearby imperial colonia of Lindum.

THIRTY-TWO

'I KNEW IT, I bloody well knew it!' exclaimed Philo, one of five others who shared a tent with the recruit, Servilus. 'I'll wager that pigswill, Iber, put the legate up to this, and that's why we've been lumbered.'

'What the hell's your gripe?' Verra answered with sarcasm. 'I thought you were the one who was all for action, you're always wishing for it enough.'

'I doubt Iber had much say in this,' observed Priscus reflectively, drawing on a boot. 'This order comes from higher up.'

Philo laced the lorica segmentata across his chest, short temperedly muttering an oath. This flexible gear had recently been distributed to only some of the front-line units so far, the 9th Hispania being one of the chosen. Lighter, more unrestricting than the rigid breastplate, designed to allow for greater mobility in battle, it was to many a great improvement. Inevitably the other ranks quickly gave this new defence the nickname of 'crab armour.' But old grunts like Philo had several less polite names for the experimental design, most of which would never be found in any military manual, and a few long-time servers would continue to curse the change.

The recruit Servilus struggled nervously with the straps that held the sheathed dagger and its companion the gladius, a wicked edged short sword made for stabbing, a weapon that helped carve an empire. Ornio smiled, taking hold of the belt to disentangle the cords. 'I've even heard rumour that our revered commander was overruled by a second legate,' said Priscus, making last minute adjustments to his new gear.

'Yes, agreed,' said Glabas the joker, grinning. 'I reckon we *all* know his bloody name, don't we?'

'That dick head Balbilus always had it in for us,' Verra said with conviction.'

'He's definitely got it in for legate Quintus, that's for sure,' shrugged Priscus.

'Same thing,' agreed Glabas.

'But why hit on us?' Philo grumbled. 'We're always bloody well under strength.'

'So is the whole bleeding army,' Ornio muttered, 'or haven't you noticed?'

'I wouldn't let Iber hear you, soldier,' Priscus warned. 'He'll stick you on fatigues for a month, that's if he doesn't cut your bollocks off first.'

The complaint about the failure to bring the legion's numbers up to strength was a fair one. On paper the soldiers of 8th Cohort, 9th legion, were a fair example, once mustering six hundred and twenty rather than, as they now stood, five hundred and thirty-seven. Discrepancies were not uncommon within the ranks, reasons of conflict and sickness being a constant 'up front' issue.

Paulinus' decision to hand the command of the advance guard over to Julius Balbilus was just what Quintus Cerialis had secretly been waiting for ever since the governor's arrival. The casual information passed on to Servilus while delivering the wine had eventually proved correct. It appeared that a sudden change of mind on Paulinus' part was most likely brought on by recent events when a near successful attack on the way station of Calenae, an assault only averted by the quick reaction of its small group of defenders, may have hastened such a decision, that and the latest one, closer to home. Although Cerialis felt a twinge of envy at this news, he had to admit that this was the only sensible course. As legate of the Hispanics, his first responsibility lay in the defence of Lindum, not heading an advance unit against distant Mona. Keeping watch on the frontier would now be paramount in the extreme, what with preparation for the final push against Ynys Mon and the tiresome Druse, being all but finalised.

Add to this package of uncertainty, the she-wolf, Cartimandua, whose marriage, having ended in bitter acrimony, took out her spleen on Venutius' family, imprisoning them and taking her armourer Vellocatus to her bed for good measure. Now she looked to Rome once again for protection from a vengeful ex. As for him, a formidable successor to Caractacus, he was already proving a thorn in Rome's underbelly as commander of a large war-host. Now he seemed to be joining hands with the queen's troublesome half-brother, the reckless Bear of the Abrentii.

Only the gods knew what mayhem might erupt because of these fast-moving events. Cartimandua, for all her promises to Cerialis about seeking a further treaty with Rome, might yet take advantage of the splitting of the imperial legions to do some underhand work of her own, and was not to be completely trusted. Meanwhile the combined number of the rebels, Abrentii and renegade Brigante alike, were at this stage impossible to assess. Paulinus with his customary arrogance, brushed aside any rumours going the rounds concerning such matters and legate Balbilus, only too ready to agree with anything Paulinus said, meant governor and legate shared the same opinion as to the fighting ability of the heathen barbarian. One thousand or ten thousand, the number of the pitiful rabble would make little difference when coming up against a trained and well-disciplined army in the field.

Balbilus having been given the job of organising the order of march, quickly made the selection, two of the cohorts being instantly named. As for the third, Cerialis' own, this required a bit more thought. What would most annoy the young legate of Hispanics, Julius calculated over a cup of wine? His idea was a good one and he congratulated himself on the choice. It would be the cohort Cerialis prized above all, his precious 2nd, most of which was comprised of legionaries who'd once served under his command with Rhine army.

Servilus was unsure as to how he felt when the order came down the line about his cohort's inclusion in the march against the Abrentii. Despite the warning from the decurion, he felt a little guilty that he hadn't informed his comrades with the news. As it happened, it didn't matter. Apart from Philo, the others made no secret of their chance to finally have a crack at the enemy, indeed, *any* enemy. Action, that was the point. Optio Priscius kept repeating the words like a mantra as he finally dressed and grabbed the rest of his gear. 'Yes, but why us?' Servius wondered. 'Why us?'

'Because we're here, lad, because we're bloody well here,' Priscius grinned as he hefted his shield, 'and we just love the bleedin' legion like our mothers, don't we?'

The three cohorts leading the task force parading on the busy Martial Field, eyed the first of the cavalry units crossing the pontoons at the point where the heads were discovered. Was it such a short time ago? Centurion Tullio Iber, strutting round like a peacock, prodded viciously with his vine staff at any target unlucky enough to cross his path, and took great satisfaction from it. After months of waiting, just like proper legionaries, they were finally leaving the confines of Lindum and moving out against whatever fate awaited them. As far as disciplinary enforcer Iber was concerned, this would be a wonderful opportunity to further his chance of promotion.

THIRTY-THREE

A N ARMOURED MACHINE cut a narrow swathe like the grim reaper through low-lying mist that hid the scrub land west of Lindum, a shadowed column of cold bronze and iron, bearing a relentless path toward Dorona. The marching men, each one a vital part of the machine, glad to be liberated from the tedium of the camp with its constant monotony of the drill field and boring fatigues, set a good pace.

A mile or two out of the confines of the colonia they skirted the sprawling settlement of Noventum, which the natives thereabout called 'Nardus'. It was there beside the low-built mud and wattle round huts of this unimpressive village that the newly surfaced road terminated. Although the site marked the edge of Roman engineering, the ancient trackway continued, following a path well-trodden long before the arrival of the invaders.

The Keltoi knew it as the Ancient Way – the path of the gods, the road where Lugos, lord of fury, with his helper the raven, hunted souls and where goddess Epona sought for boar on the back of her favourite stallion, Orm, possessed of golden tail and mane. Straight and purposeful ran the path, thrusting like a sharp-edged sword through forest and moorland where soon it would vanish into the wilds of Brigantia, leaving the continuing construction of the legion's engineers, far behind.

None of these things meant a flea's arse to stocky legate Balbilus. As far as he was concerned, where the cobbles ended, so did security. Any observations that he may have paid regard to, were dirty piss holes like Noventum, marking the northern border of Rome's empire. Here the still to be completed outpost of Segelocum, ten milestones north, cast an all-seeing eye over queen Cartimandua's realm, a place unfamiliar and unpredictable.

The solid ranks of cohorts passed rapidly through the village and its smells. Nailed boots kicked at yelping dogs as unremittingly as they would have treated their owners, if they found themselves in the way, but it's Coritani incumbents merely stood alone, or in scattered groups, eyeing in silence the moving column, their faces entirely devoid of emotion.

Some way further on, the well-worn path dipped gently toward the unwelcome forest where trees, close and forbidding, parted for nothing but the narrow way through. Four hours out of Lindum, Balbilus ordered a halt while awaiting prince Armet's scouts and the squadron of Thracian's to return from up ahead, standard procedure now for legionaries, having learned lessons the hard way, taught by the Germanic Arminius with his massacre of Varus' three legions, half a century before. Now, whenever legionaries negotiated such terrain, where woodland featured, this tragic event would be uppermost in their minds.

With the cavalry returned, having met with no resistance, Balbilus pushed the column forward. The legate already knew from earlier reports that the woodland ahead, although dense, was of no great size, being only a few miles deep, and he calculated he'd have his troops through in quick time. Yet it was in such places that uneasiness took hold.

To heavily armoured men the encroaching presence of a forest was indeed hostile. All their training, all that drill, everything they'd learnt about battle order, didn't apply here. The average legionary favoured more open terrain where he could fight shoulder to shoulder with his comrades, see their strength, be conscious of the power that came from near proximity to those trained and trusted. Densely wooded places offered no such assurance. Instead, they were dread regions that only served to feed their fear, and the men on the march would have to undergo this ordeal of shadows more than once.

The cohorts from Gemina, Valeria and Hispania – carried the well-tried weapons of the legion. On their shoulder, the pilum, a seven-foot length of wood and iron, a javelin, sharp-tipped and deadly with a killing range of twenty metres. Some soldier carried two of the latter. Its shaft was slim, designed to buckle on impact, making it almost impossible to be thrown back in the heat of battle. When used singly it was an ugly tool, employed en masse, it became the ultimate destroyer.

To compliment the pilum, strapped by leather thongs to the arm, was the shield. Tall, half cylindrical, fashioned from plywood, bound in tough bull-hide, the edges reinforced with bronze and its centre covered by a metal plate, decorated with the legionary numerals, they offered protection from knee to chin. This item, though ponderous, was reassuring, as were the leather baldrics that hung at the chest, holding short sword and dagger. In addition to these destructive weapons, they carried an entrenching shovel, a pair of palisade stakes, two mess-tins, plus enough rations for several days in the field.

The auxiliary support cavalry divided their strength between selected gaps made by the marching legionaries, as well as squadrons to front and rear. These were lightly armed, being protected in sharp contrast to the crab-armour, with flexible leather tunics pitted with iron studs. Their spears were shorter than their sister, the pilum. Yet, with their broad, leaf-shaped, blades, they could be just as terrible when it came to killing. On each man's back was strapped an oval shield, in the centre of which a metal boss was nailed – a weapon in itself.

There was little else that was different in the rest of the armoury of these proponents save for the Pannonians, men recruited from the regions of Lower Hungary who, disdaining the usual sword, carried instead a pair of long-bladed daggers in their belts, weapons in the use of which they excelled. As for the Vascones, who brought up the rear of Balbilus' infantry, enough was already known of their courage in adversity. Tough little Basques, from southern Gaul, experts in mountain warfare had, whilst based at the fortress of Glevum with 2nd Augusta, gained much praise through their persistence against the native Silures. Overall, a messy campaign. Six weeks later, because of a favourable report sent to Paulinus – himself an expert in mountain warfare - from camp prefect of Augusta, they found themselves pursuing another enemy of Rome, the Druid!

Armies have a way of doing inexplicable things.

At the tail end of the column, slow-walking their mounts, along with the Vascones, came the rear-guard, the remains of luckless Petra's Horse accompanied by an ala of Asturians who, with their gaily tasselled saddle cloths, link-mailed tunics covered by azure-blue cloaks, provided a welcome flash of colour in sharp contrast to their surroundings.

Two hours after the departure of Balbilus' three cohorts, Straba the Greek, together with a heavily tattooed Pannonian dispatch rider returning to Segelocum, rode casually across the pontoons, leaving Lindum in their wake. Following in the direction of the column, sitting a shaggy pony beside his reticent companion, a cloak wrapped close around his thin frame, the ever-present stylus and boards of wax in his travelling satchel.

They'd gone only a short distance when the Pannonian reined in, casually dismounting to adjust a loose saddle-girth.

The Greek halted a little ahead of his companion, swinging the pony round, staring thoughtfully back along the way toward the safety of Lindum. The comforting, almost homely sight of the palisaded wall on The Hill, might have made him turn back, there and then, thereby dismissing his foolish mission and the accompanying risk. Yet he couldn't turn back now. Stubborn pride wouldn't allow it, imagining the ridicule such a change of plan would bring. He'd become an even bigger joke and the butt of any jibe. This would prove especially true when it came to the Hispanics whose legate, and the nameless whore lying with him, he'd almost dragged out of bed to make his latest plea, receiving an eyeful of fist for his untimely arrival. No, he thought to himself, better the unknown than that. Cerialis already harboured the belief that his scribe was more than a little mad, and this venture would undoubtedly confirm it.

What would be the leg-pulling and jibes to come were he to creep back to The Hill, before he'd even begun his search? That he was indulging a whim, a dream? Straba spoke silently to the air. Surely, it had to be a little more than mere folly, for what he was about to do must be necessary if he were to write the truth. He had to know the reasons why men fight, why they were prepared to die in this blighted spot where even the clouds frowned hate. For certain he'd never find the answer within Lindum's protection.

As for the inevitable punishment, he dared not dwell on it. Straba, like any man, had no wish to die. Yet what kind of person would he be if he shunned his one big ambition? Yes, underling he was and most likely, if he were to survive Dorona and Cerialis' retribution, he'd continue to be one, living under the insufferable yoke of slavery. The reality was clear, people like himself, if lucky, only got one real opportunity. This one was his!

CHAPTER THIRTY-FOUR

By that reckoning, he had little choice.........................

His thoughts had wandered, and it was only now that he became aware of the Pannonian staring directly at him. The Greek would swear that the man was smirking with his eyes, making him wonder if the stranger could see the shaky trepidation present in his own.

Pushing an oatmeal wedge of bread into his mouth. the horseman re-mounted, offering Straba a grudging portion. In silence the Greek, turning his pony's head, politely declined, striking out on a trail to whatever fate decreed.

THIRTY-FOUR

T HEY ENTERED THE LAND of Cartimandua unannounced, like ripples on a calm sea, bringing a touch of colour to the empty borderlands of Brigantia. Free for a time from the restrictive woods, the advance cavalry happily found open ground. The four hundred Coritani, Armet's light riders, the Exploratores, cantered along the ancient way, piercing the air with their wolf-headed lance-shafts, to follow the scouts' lead rider. Patux the signifer carried on this occasion an imitation of the Roman vexillum, a square cloth banner mounted on a tall shaft of stout wood. Topping the shaft, a carven figure of Epona, goddess of horses gazed down, a second proud insignia belonging to the prince. Darting from under the hooves of proud horses, dun dappled hares sprang from the cover of tall-growing grasses. Luckily for them, those who rode by were bent on much larger game.

Only when they reached the twisting snake of water did they slacken their pace, fording the river. Slow running and shallow, its bed alive with reed- mace, it presented no obstacle. The giant stag slaking its thirst, startled by the horsemen, swerved away. One of the young warriors fitting arrow to his bow took aim, only to be stayed by a firm hand, before his missile could be launched. The rider muttered an oath, yet obeyed the stern and disapproving eye of Culchul Hud, recalling the order that hunting on this march was forbidden, no delay, being the command of the day.

At this point the horsemen came to a halt. The prince sat the mare, Flavia, in silence, his body bent low as he leaned from the saddle above the crouching figure of his uncle. In the sudden hush, broken only by an impatient rattle of harness, Armet waited patiently while Culchul sought for any tell-tale sign the churned-up soil might give. After a final satisfied examination, the Hud resumed his seat in the saddle. 'What do you see?' Armet asked.

Culchul scratched his grey beard thoughtfully. 'Riders, a great number.'

'How many is great?'

Culchul shrugged broad shoulders under his mantle and wiped a grubby palm over plaid breeches. 'Hard to tell, three, maybe four hundred. There are wheel marks too.'

'Chariots, or carts?' The voice of legate Cerialis' secundus, Aquilla, asked. The serious mannered Roman, ordered by Suetonius Paulinus to ride with Armet's scouts for the duration, sat his horse beside the prince, the promised 'observer', in person, the supreme legate's price for his giving a favourable nod to Cerialis' request for the Exploratore's inclusion in the vanguard. Or, as Culchul dryly remarked, well out of Aquilla's hearing, *'the watchdog'*.

The Hud now snorted disdainfully and looked up at Armet with finality, 'By Alator, these marks can only mean one thing. It's the wolf queen's cast-off. It will be Venutius.'

'It's true then?' Aquilla, muttered haltingly 'He *really* has escaped from the wolf's lair!' The secundus spoke haltingly, in the unfamiliar Coritani tongue, a strange language which, valiantly, he was attempting to master, having given up in disgust all attempts to digest the confusing camp Latin used by both itinerants and Roman's alike.

'For a second time, the poor, hen-pecked bastard!' Culchul chuckled. 'These marks were made recently. It seems they're moving west. The Carvetii leader is without doubt, making his way to Dorona.'

'So,' Aquilla remarked, 'not a hunting party then?'

Sub-chief Culche, suspected by some, but never confronted with being a shadowy agent of a mistrusted and subversive priesthood, laughed darkly, a harsh sound likened to gravel crunched beneath one's boot. 'That depends on what the swine are hunting. Perhaps someone like *yourself,* I shouldn't wonder, secundus.'

While Aquilla pondered on Culchul's well directed sarcasm, Armet twisted in the saddle and called a name. A youthful warrior trotted his pony forward. 'Ride to the column, Ulvas, give old legate Balbilus the news that Venutius is, by now, nearing Dorona. He'll inform you as to what's to be done.'

'This should quicken the imperial pace a little,' remarked Culchul, a wicked smile flickering under red-rimmed eyes as he watched Ulvas' rapid departure. 'Nothing like a dose of fear to make a Roman walk a little bit faster, isn't that so, secundus?'

At this Aquilla threw a look at the grinning Coritanian, trying to do a translation of what seemed to him to be another half-hidden jibe. Meanwhile the prince fixed his gaze ahead, eying the serpent twist of track that wended across the undulating downland, his eyes searching for scattered shapes that he thought to see in the distance, shapes that should have told him of the disposition of Bowen and the forward scouts. Yet there was nothing, save for a few stunted trees on the near horizon. The prince summoned another waiting rider. 'Find Bowen, tell him to halt at his present position, and to stay there!'

As the horseman became a phantom form in a descending mist, Armet turned his head as a hard knee touched his. Culchul, sidling up beside the prince, still grinning through stained teeth, observed. 'Bowen behaves like our Gort. The more he's taught, the less notice he takes.'

Armet glanced down at the fingers holding the reins. To his astonishment his hands shook just for a second, and jerking the bridle of his mount, he made Flavia toss her maned head in protest. He soothed the sensitive animal with a word. Should he be anxious over the wildness of some of those he'd chosen to form his group of scouts, or overlook it?

Some had more than proved themselves, like Patux for instance, a cousin he'd rescued from a torched hut during a series of forays on Coritani holdings and now his signifer, lightning raids made by thieves seeking stray livestock, or anything else that could be filched. It pained the prince to know he received more regard and respect from young Patux, than he ever got from his brother. Gort preferred now to go his own way, explaining clearly that he wanted no part in the business of his father's pathetic efforts to secure Rome's pleasure. Volisios, for his part, while loving his sons in equal measure, remained deeply sad, seeing the rift growing, ever wider, between them.

Without doubt Gort harboured a wild streak, yet one day, he might understand just what he and Volisios were attempting. He'd but to mention just one instance of what men could suffer if they dared to challenge the empire. The Trinovante in the south, like the Coritani, were once proud people with a good man, king Obrig, to lead them. Now they were little more than slaves, because they once defied the mightier power. And signs of recent trouble brewing in the land of the Iceni after Prasutagus' death, could bring to the table a whole new set of challenges.

A sudden breeze stirred Armet's short hair. He wore no helmet to compliment his Roman armour, silver cuirass, scaled and flexible, hiding a leather tunic, greaves, scarlet cloak, the baldric of linked metal discs that supported the long sword of a cavalry commander.

'They will learn,' he at last muttered, to Culchul.

His uncle made a face. 'Given that we all live that long.'

The prince reproved the Hud with a slightly disapproving glance, then indicated the way ahead. 'Pray to the gods we do.'

'I reckon Bowen is a little over eager, Armet, maybe he forgot to halt at the big river, as you ordered,' said Culchul, pursing his lips.

Armet tugged at his bridle. 'That we will shortly know.' Turning in the saddle he stared to where the dark smudge of the forest met the skyline, his eyes narrowing as russet shapes moved into his view. The first units of Balbilus' column, a glimpse of armour caught by a setting sun. The prince's eyes moved upward. Darkness would soon be upon them.

'You appear worried, cub.' Culchul observed as they rode on.

'It's Gort, damn it!' he forced a smile. 'I can't forever be his keeper, let him be.' he countered, as he felt Gort's recovered disc from the unnamed fort still burning away in his pouch.

Culchul, knowing his nephew well enough to sense a lie, said nothing.

'Tell me uncle, how's your sense of smell?'

'I smell the dampness of nature, nothing more.'

'The Bear is closer though, I feel it,' remarked Aquilla, finding the words.

Culchul raised an enquiring brow and spat contemptuously onto the earth. 'The reek of Brennus and his kin never leaves my nostrils, Roman. I've scented the bugger everywhere. Here, there's nothing.'

'Maybe the scent of Venutius will be even more overpowering,' said Aquilla.

'I wager some of these tracks don't tell the whole story,' muttered Culchul, ignoring the words of the secundus. 'Well, what of it? No need to worry about that,' he shot a look at Aquilla, 'especially when we have the power of Rome at our back.'

'I'm not thinking of ourselves.' Armet reined in.' Culchul, you were present when we had the captive questioned.' He was referring to a seriously wounded man found along the line of march. Boasting the familiar bear tattoo on his arm, he was instantly identified, but just how he happened to be lying. unattended and alone along their path, was a mystery. A useless and messy attempt to extract even one iota of information was doomed, the prisoner being already three parts dead at the time.

'Your inquisitor left little more than crow meat,' Culchul muttered, disappointedly. 'We couldn't dare apply our *own* persuasion, for fear he'd give in on us, the bastard was that far gone.' Culchul smirked at Aquilla who tried hard to comprehend.

'He must have said something, Keltoi,' prompted the secundus, hesitatingly.

Culchul flicked a contemptuous hand. 'Wild talk from a wretch already on his way to an unwelcome embrace from the Morrigan. His senseless blabbering came from the pain of wounds and would have been of little worth.' He pulled a face. 'Anyhow,' he added, 'it's done.'

The forlorn blast from a Roman horn came on the warm evening air. Pressing heels gently into Flavia's belly, Armet rode off at a canter toward the sound. Aquilla, Culchul Hud and the others fell in behind. In the mind of the prince were thoughts not now relevant. Yet he knew it took a multiplicity of events to fill a tale, and this story had yet to be acted out.

THIRTY-FIVE

A SMALL KNOT OF RIDERS gathered on the sun dappled hill crest to gaze down on the moving legionaries of Julius Balbilus' column, resembling slow moving dots from this distance. Cartinmandua, resting her manicured hands on the warm mane of her horse, stared avidly, her dark eyes narrowed with ever-deepening contemplation. Silently she sat, her slim body hidden beneath a richly embroidered mantle. From this vantage point, no pace-drum could be heard, instead, only the deep throated groan of a lone horn carried on the chill breeze, denoting the progress of the cohorts.

'The vain fool!' the queen muttered, quietening her restless mount. A shape moved from out of the group and drew in beside her. A hardened hand touched her knee. 'I doubt you'll ever know a bigger idiot then Brennus, my Vellocatus?'

The tall figure of her armour bearer, now her lover, smiled below a broken nose, legacy from earlier days as the nation's champion pugilist, as he shifted in the saddle. 'Only your husband that was, perhaps.'

'If the Romans don't succeed, I'll seek for the heads of both those sorry fools, myself,' the queen replied with venom. 'Brennus and my dear fool, Venutius,' she managed a scornful laugh. 'They might have been made for each other.'

'What if the Roman's lose the fight?'

The Brigante queen, ruler over the largest territory in Britannia, rounded on her companion, eying Vellocatus as if he'd completely lost his mind. 'Lose? Rome *rarely* loses, does it? Why do you think I struggle hard to stay on friendly terms with that vain dolt in Lindum? It's the power he wields on my border, that's why. I intend to make use of that power, to great advantage, when I have need.'

'Cerialis?' joked Vellocatus. 'It seems I have a rival.'

The queen sighed quietly. Vellocatus, though a champion in bed, was to Cartimandua, in all other respects, no deep thinker.

'We both have mutual interests, that's true,' the queen coldly replied. 'The legate has done us favours more than once regarding threats from my darling husband. As for what your dirty mind is thinking, yes, it is true. I may, or may not, have favoured the commander of Hispanics with my attentions. Either way, that's no reason to grovel before him, like a beggar. Co-operation with Lindum allows more time to consolidate our position.'

'Which is?'

'At the moment, to play the lamb, then,' Cartimandua swung her horse about, 'only the gods can tell.'

Vellocatus hesitated, indicating the disappearing column of men. 'Are we not sending a galloper to warn the rebels?' he questioned. 'Good or bad, Brennus is still our kin.'

'Half-brother,' the queen corrected, scornfully, 'and a lousy one at that, with all the damned trouble he's causes me. Besides, brave Vellocatus, I'd hazard a guess that he already knows.'

With that, Cartimandua, putting elegant heels to her horse, cantered away, her agile mind already planning her next move in the hazardous game for power.

THIRTY-SIX

A S EVENING DREW IN, the advance force halted at a predesignated point, the crumbling ruins of a half-built waystation, proving that Rome had at least advanced thus far before thinking better of it, leaving instead a weed choked wreck. After calling in most of the forward scouts, fatigue units erected a defensive stockade, while the army cooked a late meal and prepared to settle for the night. Sometime, toward the last hour of the third watch, Balbilus was tentatively shaken awake by a reluctant decurion, the legate being a heavy sleeper. Blinking his eyes against the flickering rushlight he raised his head from the hard leather saddle serving as a pillow and sat upright on the edge of the makeshift bunk. 'Well, what is it?' he demanded with open irritation.

The decurion stepping back, pushed a dishevelled figure into the circle of light. 'Your pardon sir, but a sentry just found this wretch crawling along the outer ditch. He's lucky to be alive, one of my boy's took him for one of the Brig's, and may have stuck the stupid bastard, had I not intervened. As it was, the guard accidently tapped the intruder's leg rather roughly with a spear-butt, hence the limp. Centurion Rufio said you might wish to interrogate the renegade personally.'

Balbilus grunted, stretched himself then peered closely at the prisoner. 'You appear to have caused my men a lot of trouble.' Balbilus scrutinised the visitor closely in the light of a pair of flickering oil lamps. 'I feel I ought to know you.'

'He confirmed he's the scribe to legate Cerialis,' the decurion interrupted, still staring at the slave with suspicion. 'But he don't look like no scribbler to me, more likely some silly bugger on the run, I'd say.'

The legate stood and poured wine into a cup on the makeshift table, held up by three legs and an improvised javelin shaft. After swallowing its contents, he stared blankly. 'Well, this fellow thinks you're an escaped slave. Are you?'

'Not exactly, legate,' Straba muttered, wishing he could sit for a moment and rest his bruised limb.

Balbilus sighed. 'As it happens, I already know who you are, but I'd rather you told me, yourself.'

The begrimed secretary wiped mud from his cheek. 'It is as your man says. I'm Straba.'

Balbilus peered closer. 'Of course, I've seen you skiving about headquarters many a bloody time, may the gods give you pox.' He indicated for the hovering decurion to leave and, after giving Straba a final look of deep distrust, he made his exit. 'You look different to the last time we met, Greek.' Said the legate. 'As I saw it then, you were trying to dodge your master.'

Straba winced, rubbing his sore leg. 'The matter of the latrines, yes.' He paused. 'I could do with a bath, since we've mentioned it,' he added.

'You cheeky fucker!' Balbilus, now fully awake, exploded. 'Just what in the name of sodding Jupiter, are you doing here?' he questioned, ignoring the slave's impossible request, while pouring more wine.

'I came merely to observe.'

Balbilus uttered a stifled laugh. 'Did you now? Observe what, pray?' he drained the cup. 'Didn't you find enough discomfort in Lindum, without looking for more elsewhere, and now you add insolence to your crime. Tell me, who was the bold creature that ordered you to spy on me?'

'I'm not a spy,' said the Greek. 'Something else led me.'

'Exactly!' Balbilus chuckled. 'Your master being the 'something,' right?'

'Legate Cerialis knew naught of my leaving,' replied Straba, defensively.

Balbilus stared in astonishment. 'Well, I reckon he knows now.' The legate stretched himself. 'You *do* know the penalty for absconders?'

Straba felt a weakening of the knees and wondered how long his legs would continue to support him. 'Something unpleasant, I expect.'

'It's death on the cross, damn you! Isn't that unpleasant enough? If I possessed any sense, I'd order one to be set up, here and now, miserable tosser that you are! Yet crucifixion is a bad thing to manage before a battle, stuff like that can upset those who might, themselves, be dead meat by the end of the day.' The legate chuckled. 'I begin to think you're either very brave or extremely dumb,' he remarked with a snort of contempt. 'Looking at you now, I'm drawn toward the latter choice.'

'At this minute, me too,' Straba agreed, a weak smile crossing his face.

'How did you arrive here. Not on foot, I fancy?'

'Rode, or at least I began to. If it weren't for my pony going lame, I may have got here earlier.' The scribe's tone sounded almost apologetic, so much so that Balbilus *really* did begin to think that he had a madman on his hands.

'A pony! A thief as well as a runaway, eh?' the legate of Valeria scratched his chin. Don't tell me you made it on your own?'

'I had an escort to start with, a Pannonian dispatcher on his way to Glevum,' the scribe explained.

Balbilus looked at the Greek in puzzlement, his thoughts of a sudden switching to Gaius Galtiore's 2nd legion.

'Where is he now, this phantom rider?' Balbilus probed suspiciously.

Straba shrugged helplessly. 'On his way south, I guess, he seemed prepared for a long journey.'

'Had the fellow a name?'

'I never asked.'

The legate decided to let the matter stand. After all, gallopers came and went constantly, especially with an army on the march. 'I repeat, you're a damn fool, the whole country is crawling with Brig head-hunters who'd love a prize dumb- head like yours nailed over the door of one of those flea-ridden huts of theirs.' He rubbed his bearded chin. 'Point remains, what do I do with you?'

'My companion,' said Straba, ignoring the question, 'did talk of king Venutius.'

'Go on.'

156

'He talked of Brigantian support for Brennus, the one you seek, the Abrentii leader who intends baring your way to Mona. He says Venutius was coming to Dorona with a large host of fighting men.'

'Bah!' Julius Balbilus chuckled contemptuously. 'I've heard all the lies, before. Brennus and his stinking heathens won't get in the way for long, I'll see to that. As for their number, exaggerated stories often circulate among those, feeble-minded enough to believe them.' The legate eyed a shivering Straba and shook his head. 'Is that all you've got to tell me, slave?'

Straba looked a mite puzzled. 'I thought you'd might investigate further. I thought you had the right to know, seeing as you command the column. The Pannonian spoke of ten thousand.'

'Damn nonsense! No heathen in the province could muster such a strength. A couple of thousand, perhaps, no more.'

'This man seemed very sure of what he said.'

'And why would he share this knowledge with such a creature as yourself?'

Straba shrugged.

'Are you armed?'

'I observe Scapula's law. You know I'm not allowed to bear weapons of any kind,' the Greek said wearily, tapping at his crumpled satchel containing several rolls of papyrus, together with a set of stylii and waxen tablets. 'I carry out my duties with these.'

'Of course, I've heard, avoiding proper tasks ordered by your master while, at the same time, scribblin' away at your damn histories.'

'No sir, if you'll forgive the correction, I'm *also* scribbling yours.'

Balbilus stared at the bedraggled figure who seemed impervious as to his possible fate, and shaking his head disbelievingly, he summoned back the decurion. 'It appears you are prepared to die, slave.'

Straba shook his tousled head. 'No man is prepared to die, legate,' he winced as the pressure on his leg kicked home. 'Have I leave to go, sir?'

'Go where? The legate spat, ill temperedly.

Straba straitened up. 'I wish to speak with prince Armet. I believe he is somewhere here.'

'That Coritani heathen! By Mars, you really are bereft of all sense!' Balbilus fell to pacing the derelict room for several minutes before making his decision. 'I'm as big a fool as you are, for doing this,' he muttered. 'Get my man to take you to the cavalry lines and out of my sight. You may find the Keltoi bastard there. But take care he doesn't slit your throat and eat you for supper.' smirked the legate, waving a hand in dismissal. As Straba limped slowly away, Balbilus caught the decurion by the arm and spoke quietly. 'Get this knob-head out of my sight, before I do him an injury. Keep him close mind, we don't want commander Cerialis' personal slave to get hurt, do we?' he added with amused sarcasm. 'Before you do that, tell Gallinus to take him to a quiet place and administer ten measured lashes, for his lying soul. Tell the fellow to go easy mind, so as not to break flesh. I'll think about what to do with him later.'

Left alone, Balbilus poured yet more wine, his mind now fully awake. Why would a common galloper wish to share any knowledge with a dolt like Straba? Ten thousand warriors! An exaggeration, surely. The slave was indeed raving mad. Just what was the purpose of the mysterious Pannonian in filling Straba's head with impossible rubbish? Also, what business did a Greek have with the prince of the Coritani, unless.........?

Balbilus didn't normally find difficulty in sleeping, even if that sleep be interrupted, yet his jumbled suspicions would keep him from any further slumber for what remained of the night.

THIRTY-SEVEN

IT SEEMED AS IF THE BOY had been driven to the world's edge.

The man and the youth, the one-eyed, single-handed, Orsobis the Druid, together with his pupil, Halgar, after being set ashore, sought shelter of the first welcoming dune. Even to this young boy's vivid imagination such behaviour seemed to be bordering on madness. It appeared to young Halgar that they were miles from anywhere, that the pair had been off-loaded in the wrong place. Orsobis nevertheless appeared unfazed. Squatting on his haunches, he unlaced the strings of the pack to bring forth food. There was bread, not yet stale but getting there, plus several wedges of goat cheese, two slithers of pork and a few left-over beans. Halgar fell upon his share avidly as he'd scarcely taken anything edible since dawn the previous day.

Second level Druid, Orsobis was both a healer and dealer of justice. With zealous consistency he supplicated himself before his war god Taranis with the fervent promise to make sacrifice, no matter how futile, for just one more sun-kissed and pleasant day. While he prayed, he recalled with uncustomary nostalgia a time when the terraced vines of Gaul, which he'd occasionally visited, groaned under the weight of succulent grapes – every bunch a many-breasted woman to be tasted and – oh so greatly – to be enjoyed.

The breeze blew diverse patterns in the tuft grass above the pebbled beach as indifferent sea birds strutted imperiously at low tide. Where would he find anything to cheer him in such a place as this? At the shores edge the tiny boat, its unfurled sail catching the wind, was whisked away rapidly by its two- man crew like a low flying gull. In this lonely spot there were no witnesses, man and youth being cast alone into an unfamiliar place. This presented a keen edge of realisation to their purpose, like a knife blade's caress over taut skin.

Asked Halgar, between each grateful bite. 'How far must we go?'

The one-eyed Orsobis picked at the bread as if it were a banquet, selectively, with no outward show of urgency. 'We'll rest up for now.' He probed with his fingers amid the sliced onion lying in his lap with studied care. 'Perhaps one day's march will take us to where we ought to be.'

At first, Halgar didn't appear overly upset by this, being long used to his master's vagueness, though there was a growing sense of unease taking place within him. Even so he did pose a further question, striking while the iron was at white heat, as the saying went, for he sensed Orsobis was in a listening frame of mind. 'Why then,' he ventured, 'did the boat drop us here, and not farther south?'

Orsobis wiped his one remaining hand on his sleeve, brushing crumbs from his lap in a dainty manner. All that was lacking, thought Halgar, was a clean cloth and a water bowl, luxuries that the youth hoped might be available for them at their destination. Then the priest, in a deep voice such as water makes in a flooded cave, said, instructively, 'Halgar, it would be good for your education to learn that for a man who boasts of being of the Carvetii people, as am I, this place can be akin to hell. To be honest, I don't usually feel at ease this far south. They reckon the gods of the Romans will swallow them and send their bare bones to their emperor Nero in beribboned bundles.' Orsobis grinned. 'Luckily, I'm the exception.'

'Then such men are barbarians and cowards,' Halgar spoke with emotion. He glanced back over his shoulder at a cold and alien sea. 'We must still be a long distance from where you wish to be. So far, you have not told me what we're here for.'

'True,' Orsobis agreed, with a mirthless grin, giving Halgar a knowing wink with his solitary grey eye. 'Yet where we are sitting is still to the south of them. This is the territory of the Ordovici, lad, here Ogma rules. This is the place where I believe Roman ships have brought men of the legions to our land. It is our task to find out what's in store.'

'Spies?!' muttered Halgar, incredulously.'

Orsobis' eye was penetrating. 'If you like.'

Halgar's look generated bewilderment then, dropping the remainder of the frugal meal onto the ground, he stared unblinkingly at his smiling mentor. 'So, you've brought us in this forsaken place for what?' He rose to his feet, pulling the tartan shawl about his thin frame. 'To search for a few Romans?' He returned Orsobis stare with his own. 'I may be silly, master, but I believed you've tortured yourself many a day over the details of our mission. Yet you tell me little of it.'

Orsobis of the Willows smiled. 'Many tribal elders and other haters of Rome have put their trust in what we may discover,' the elder man said, standing. 'Whatever knowledge we gain of the invaders plans will be of tremendous help when the hour comes.' He hefted the sack over his thin shoulders. 'Word has it their ships will have landed at Mona for a reason,' he said finally. 'It's up to us to find, then report, yet I'll tell you this much. The Romans are setting themselves to building special boats to cross the narrow waters that separate us. For that, young Halgar, speed is required. Eochu puts his trust in our efforts, let us not disappoint him, and lastly,' Orsobis said testily, 'I haven't abandoned us. I know *exactly* where I am.'

Orsobis strode away swiftly, and Halgar was obliged to fall in beside him. 'So, this is the reason, the boats?'

Orsobis glanced up at Halgar with an unblinking eye. 'How old are you?'

'Master, you know my age.'

'Maybe one day when I'm feeling generous, I may pass to you the wisdom that most grown men do not possess, perhaps never will possess. '

'I know it, master,' Halgar said, partly humbled and only a little satisfied.

Orsobis, reaching out, brought down his stave on Halgar's head with a none to light blow as they walked. The strength of it brought tears to the boy's eyes. 'Why do you think I've given my life to the pursuit of imparting knowledge to dolts like you? Think you it was some personal ambition that I let you inherit the light and power of the oracle?' he breathed. 'A large Roman army is about to descend on our sacred groves of oak,' he continued. 'Our job is to find out how they propose to do it. To cross the water, one must build boats with shallow draught. I suspect they are doing this not far from here. We must find out exactly where, what size and how many. The task will be difficult, maybe dangerous, and time is short. That is why we are here.' Orsobis, setting aside the stave, reached into the sack and withdrew a bundle, drawing forth two sheathed short swords, one of which the youth, after an initial hesitation, nervously accepted.

'You should have told me that I may have to kill, master,' Halgar muttered, thrusting the weapon into his belt. 'I have never killed a man, for any reason. Unlike you!'

It was the wrong thing to say, and Halgar was already regretting it.

'You dare censor me?!' Orsobis, executioner of criminals, growled menacingly, his single hand taking a tighter grip on his stave. 'What I do sometimes has to be done. There is much evil out there, sick souls who commit terrible acts, who, by law must forfeit their lives, that's how it is. As for yourself, I offer prayers to both Tiranis and Cernunnos that you may never have to use that blade. Now boy, enough is enough! As of this moment, you are way out of my favour. Speak another word and I'll flog your hide to the bone. Maybe, a few hours silence will allow me to assemble my plans into some semblance of order. After that, I shall spare you, my attention.'

THIRTY-EIGHT

T HE HOLLOW NOTE of a horn announced the third watch of a shortening night, a signal sound within lesser sounds, when Straba's escort finally located prince Armet in the horse lines of the Exploratores. Wincing with pain at every movement from a sore leg, coupled with the burning sensation spreading across his back from the flogging given him by an over-zealous Gallinus, he was left to fend for himself.

Armet, with a shadowy group standing with him around the glowing embers of a fire, looked up curiously as a stumbling Straba approached. This early in the morning the air carried with it a faint smell of scented wood smoke. Cerialis' runaway slave trembled from an overwhelming bout of apprehension as, once again, he questioned why he was putting himself into another unknown situation.

Several men accompanying the prince looked the beaten figure up and down, silently. 'Ah, our fugitive,' Armet's voice spoke. 'I'll tell you something, Greek, when I was informed of your presence here, in the lines, I could hardly believe my ears. Nor I suspect will Cerialis, when he gets to hear of it.' Armet regarded the redundant scribe so menacingly that he wanted to crawl into a hole. 'You really are bloody mad, you know? I ask myself why old Balbilus didn't nail you to one of his wooden babies, rather than giving you a mere scourging.'

'What the legate said, about my being mad, is possibly true, but I'll not count myself a fugitive,' Straba answered defensively, his lean body shivering under the inadequate cover of a torn cloak, lent to him reluctantly by a member of Balbilus' staff to hide the evident welts received from the late flogging. 'It's all part of a plan,' he added.

Someone in the small gathering stifled a laugh. 'Gods, the slave has a plan!' It was Armet's cousin Patux, half-hidden in the gloom. 'We can't wait to hear more, scribe.'

'We'll take the wretch to my tent,' Armet instructed.

The contents of the prince's space were even sparser than that of legate Balbilus. A straw pallet and a makeshift bench covered with a soiled blanket was the sum-total of the furnishings. The prince wiped his brow with a cloth, then tossed it unceremoniously to Straba. 'You've been beaten! I see blood on your neck. Clean yourself up a little,' he indicated, adding, 'Are you hurting?'

Straba stood immobile on unwilling legs. 'I've been whipped before.'

'No doubt with good reason, but that's not what I asked.' Armet sat looking the dishevelled slave up and down. 'You look even more pathetic now than when we last met,' he commented, easing himself from his leather cuirass. 'I hope you think your gross insubordination worth it. You surely realise the danger you're in? A slave leaving his master without the master's consent is never a good move to make. In short, you haven't got a leg to stand on.

A bad joke, Straba thought.

'Perhaps, as an obviously educated man, you rate yourself higher than the rest of us, even so, I'd still risk a few Coritani coins to discover the *real* reason for you so carelessly valuing your life.'

Straba, surprised that their mint was allowed under Rome's overseers, to continue to forge its own currency, covered his lack of knowledge with a painful shrug. 'Prince, I wouldn't want you to waste your money,' he replied. 'My reasons are simple.'

'How simple?' Armet asked, feigning patience.

'May I sit?' On a nod the scribe gingerly squatted, cross-legged. 'I want to understand why free peoples choose to serve others, the way your people serve,' he began. 'The only way I think I might fathom this would be to record, in writing, a history for those generations yet to come. Think of your time in Rome, for instance, prince. You might well have seen things in the city that you found disagreeable. The legate told me, you once met with the tyrant Nero, on a day of chosen gladiatorial bouts especially arranged in your honour. That must have been a moment of which I would learn more.'

'A snort from a restless horse within the nearby lines seemed to echo Armet's half-laugh of amusement. 'For an absent slave, you're dangerously impudent. The games you speak of, wildly miss the mark. The honour was for the bard, Seneca, whose presence I was regrettably obliged to share that day. As a reporter of fact, you really must try to be more accurate in what you record.'

Straba stood in the half-light of dawn, admonished and now, hopelessly tired.

Armet looked askance at Culchul Hud. 'Well, what should I do?' 'The idiot it appears, wishes to immortalise us, maybe turn us into gods with the written word of Rome!'

Culchul eyed Straba up and down again with open disapproval. 'If you're stupid enough to keep him, you've got two choices only. Either we slit his slave's throat now or, somehow, we try to make use of the idiot.' The Hud paused. 'How will you square it with the legate, though? He's his slave, not yours.'

Armet shrugged, 'I'm here. Quintus Cerialis isn't.' Straba looked as if he were about to faint, not certain as to whether the jibe about throat slitting was just that. A jibe!

Said Armet, 'Are you prepared to ride with us, scribe?'

'I'm not much of a horseman,' the cleric stammered, nervously, leaning on one elbow, trying not to be sick.

'That's easily remedied,' Culchul growled, 'even if I have to nail your skinny arse to the saddle myself.' He shot a grin at Armet, as if sharing a private joke.

'The slave can ride well enough, Culchul, or he'd not be here,' observed Patux.

'Remember this, I'm only going to say it, once.' Armet cautioned. 'Until I return to the colonia, your life is entirely forfeit to me. I alone, will decide your fate. Cross me, and you're a dead man, understand? You might play your games with the legate, but such tactics won't amuse me.'

A weary Straba could only give a tired shrug.

'Get the slave a horse, suitable clothing and something to eat,' Armet ordered. Then he stared down at the Greek. 'Remember, none of us will cry over your dying, scribe. That is the lot of a slave. Yet I'll let nobody say Armet refused to test a man's metal, not even yours. I'll give you a chance to redeem yourself. You'll ride beside me! I've decided!' Armet threw a glance at Culchul who, still not really comprehending, secretly wondered who the *real* madman was.

As it fell out, the dumbstruck slave was, without ceremony, enrolled into the service of prince Armet's scouts, at least for as long as he lived. A Damocles' sword hung over Straba's aching head. The risky throw of the bones he accepted with resignation, when soberly contemplating the dark alternative awaiting him at Lindum.

THIRTY-NINE

THE NEWLY DUG TURF-DITCH, bristling with sharpened wooden stakes was clear for anyone to see, even at this distance. Along the man-built ridge protecting the settlement, armed figures stood ready for battle. Yet the besiegers greatest worry were the numbers of rebel spearmen on both flanks of the deep ditch and steep bank of Dorona's outer defences. An accurate calculation was impossible, but the Brigante-Abrentii alliance looked disconcertingly formidable. It was glaringly obvious that Brennus, with added support from Venutius' reinforcements, had used the time given to repair and reinforce the settlement's massive stockade. A brief survey was enough to confirm Julius Balbilus' worst fears. Unless a quick end was made possible, a lengthy and costly siege beckoned. That must not be allowed to happen, but the legate was already overtaken by the growing feeling that he and Paulinus could have been wrong in their final estimation of enemy strength.

Calculated to further irritate, a follow-up on the slave soon reached the legate of Valeria's ear. Straba, that miserable object, was now enrolled in Armet's scouts, serving as a field runner – message carrier – whatever, under the close protection of the prince. Soon this crafty Greek would have much to answer for, as too would Cerialis' favourite heathen, Armet, swore Balbilus.

The legate of the advance party arriving at Dorona, had to come to grips with yet another reality. If a two-day old report was a guide, Venutius had evidently thrown in his lot with Brennus almost as soon as the three chosen cohorts had left Lindum. A sudden decision or a reckless one? Either way, the last communication from Paulinus was unmistakably clear.

Trample every inch of Dorona! Destroy all living things within the settlement. Be thorough, ruthless, grant no mercy, unless it is to interrogate. Let these scum be in no doubt as to our intent. Every defender, man, woman or child, must be slaughtered, even the livestock. All trace of the stronghold must be levelled,

*expunged. I repeat my earlier order. Should your first attack fail,
forget the heroics and wait for myself with the main force.*

All well and good in theory, Balbilus mused. This was his
old comrade at his most pompous. Caution, always bloody
caution, typical of the man he'd served under all those years back
in Mauritania, a service from which he'd received, in his own
estimation, the smallest of all nuggets by way of recognition.

Forever plagued by the losses his command incurred during
one of the countless sieges undertaken against some resistant city
in that god forsaken country, had led to the governor's hesitant
nature. To the restless Balbilus, these instructions infuriated. Does
the man *really* think I'm that incapable? The legate made up his
mind. Given his chance, he was going to flatten Dorona, his way.
After many frustrating months of idleness, here was a chance to
show these fools why he was legate of 20TH Valeria, the finest
legion in the armies of Rome. As for patience, he'd had a gut-full
of that. Look where patience got you. Had he been in control, he'd
have destroyed this poxy cult of Druidism much earlier.

But Balbilus was also a military realist. Soon it became evident
to him that the rumour spread at large within the army ranks was
regretfully true. An easy victory was not assured. He guessed at
numbers once again. There were other fighting men bolstering up
the rebel strength, if the tattoo marks found on the dead proved
accurate. Worryingly, a few of the corpses were identified as king
Tadoc's men, Cornovii, the very people who had, only days before,
promised to provide the march with needed supplies.

Tadoc was being set-up for client kingship, that was certain.
Yet he was also a friend to his future son-in-law, prince Armet of
the Coritani, another nation so prescribed. Coritani or Cornovii,
Balbilus trusted neither. This was all exceedingly troubling,
prompting ambiguous danger signals. Further bodies, he recalled,
found slain on the march, bore a variety of different insignia
carved into retrieved gold, silver, bronze, and ivory torcs. The
owners of these were at most, dissident bands, carrying a personal
grudge, aimed at their reluctant leaders.

There was more. Evidence had it that members of the usually passive Deceangli, over whose land the cohorts now marched, were joined with others from further afield, including dark-haired Silurians from west of the Sabrena, a long way from Dorona, all of which smacked of a worrying international alliance.

As the sun rose on a hazy morning, the legate ordered up his archers, dark-faced warriors from Syria, expert users of the composite bow, their numbers reinforced by slingers from the Balearic Islands. The Syrians were instructed to aim their arrows high so that the missiles would clear the walls and find their victims beyond. At the rear of the Roman legionaries, four mobile catapults and ballistae, powerful spring-guns, operated by tension ropes and laboriously dragged from Lindum, had been deployed. Quickly it became clear that their deadly missiles would fall well short of their target by many yards.

Along the length of the Roman front, centurions took up their places. Cavalry alae sat their saddles watching as the stocky frame of Balbilus, gladius drawn, rode to the head of the lines of waiting legionaries. The assembling ranks, like the legate, waited in near silence as Balbilus' cherished babies, the mobile scorpions, took up positions either side of the serried lines of men. Nervous and touchy as an open wound, all wished to untie the hard knot that gripped their bellies, wanting to relieve the tautness in their bowels by making some other poor devils suffer.

Sharp words of command to prepare javelins came along the lines, while groans of frustration could be heard as the men of the artillery adjusted then re-adjusted their sights. 'Bloody idiots!' optio Priscus swore, throwing a look of disgust to the recruit Servilus. The recruit returned Priscus' remark with a nervous imitation of a smile. This would be his first real taste of battle, and he wasn't exactly sure whether he felt up for it. Unlike the older companions of the contubernium, now beginning to show signs of impatience at this drawn-out prelude to death, Servilus could only wish for a swift victory over those that manned the daunting rampart of Dorona.

FORTY

'**I** FUCKIN' WELL KNEW IT!' grumbled Philo, as the ballistae bolts and fire arrows finally began to find their mark. 'Never rely on the poxy engineers!'

'It's being so wonderfully cheerful that keeps him going,' said an anonymous voice from behind.

'Next swine who speaks will get my staff across his dirty mouth!' Iber barked. 'Do you bloody hear me?'

'Up yours!' came a mingled chorus of unidentified voices.

The mobile artillery, having moved forward under a shower of arrows, now battered at the earth walls with greater accuracy, and black smoke from a dozen burning huts rose quickly, under fire from the bombardment of four giant catapults. But the effect hoped for was short lived, as the cumbersome machines looked to be soon overrun by a mix of enemy cavalry and foot who stormed towards the waiting cohorts with unbridled fury, heading directly for the wall of shields.

This wasn't supposed to happen!

A second horn blast echoed in the ears of farmer's son, Servilus. Gripping the javelin with a sweaty hand, hugging the comfort of the shield across his chest, he longed for something not quite understood, while his eyes focussed upon the rampart ahead, teeming now with a host of warriors, who appeared recklessly unafraid of the missiles raining down on them. To the recruit, at this distance the enemy moved like insects swarming about a giant anthill. Ordered to advance, shield locked to shield in the first line of the machine, he asked himself what had brought him here to die in a harsh land.

Blurred shapes rode at speed across Servilus' front, confusing him. They made a brave showing, with their silver trappings and the cross barred wolf-tail staves of the standard bearers. These were some of the men he'd seen last evening. Prince Armet's scouts, the Exploratores! Long hair plaited or hung loose; they shunned helmets. The bared arms of many of the riders displayed intricate tattoos. Servilus also noted the gold and silver torcs, arm-rings worn with a flamboyance almost unknown amongst the largely subdued tribes of the conquered southern nations.

There was a great skill in the handling of the mounts of the Exploratores, Servilus noticed in the dawn light. Watching them, the horse-loving recruit briefly put aside his fear and could only admire, for it was plain that they had little to learn in the way of horsemanship.

A shouted command brought him back to grim reality. A repeated order to advance came down the line and the ranks of all three cohorts moved ahead. As they set off, he would swear that he'd spotted Straba the cleric, riding at the prince's side.

'This is it!' Priscus muttered above the rising clamour voiced by several thousand throats, bringing the recruit rudely down to earth. 'Mithras and Mars protect us!' he yelled, encouragingly.'

There came a sudden surge of activity to the right of the Roman line. Racing ahead were six maniples of Vascones, some seven hundred men. Balbilus was creating a diversion, a ruse to tempt even more of the enemy from the protection of the rampart. In one solid wedge, their centurions leading, they closed the distance at a trot, spears piercing the warmth of the early morning air. Turmae, groups of mounted Asturians, rapidly crossed the front spears of the Vascones and the mass of advancing men. Armet's scouts followed the Asturians and were soon swallowed up in the throng. Servilus, searching again for Straba amid the swaying wolf-tailed banners, was soon unpleasantly diverted as massed ranks of Abrentii Brigante threatened to completely engulf the disciplined cohorts awaiting the order to 'Loose!' Almost immediately one and a half thousand deadly missiles began to fall every few seconds into the charging groups of oncoming flesh and bone.

It happened suddenly, the whole episode taking but a few moments. The Vascones, a little ahead of the legionaries, met the furious onslaught with sword and spear. Hopelessly outnumbered they were about to be hurled headlong into the shields of the oncoming cohorts, who were forced to a halt. The command

'Shields!' rang out. The fleeing Vascones, their eyes fear-crazed, came pitching into them. 'Let the bastards through!' yelled the centurions. 'Let them go!' Making gaps in their ranks the legionaries obliged as the panicking troops charged on, one almost bowling Servilus over in a frantic eagerness to escape. Another came close enough for Servilus to hear the man's harsh breathing, see the slashed face of him, feel the fear, see the gushing blood.

Again! 'Front rank, javelins!'

Servilus hefted his second shaft. He sensed rather than saw outlying alae, fast- moving horsemen on his right. Arrows began whipping overhead and about him as he moved. Men staggered and fell. He knew one of them was optio, Priscus, a feathered shaft now lodged in his throat. Oblivious to the shield wall the renegades kept coming in droves. Behind them a threatening sound came from the many voices of those still atop the rampart. The ex-farmer from Tarraco, felled to his knees by a body-blow from something unseen and losing consciousness failed to hear the high pitch sound from the enemy throats. Having seen a heartening sign of the outnumbered Roman force failing to fight their way into Dorona, the enemy set to chanting the victory paean of Andraste, goddess of war and death. To many of the seasoned troops within the Roman ranks, it was a sound remembered only too well from their campaigning in Gaul, and they dreaded the words conveyed. The triumphant baying matched the din of battle. In the ancient tongue of the Keltoi it translated into 'No Quarter!'

Legate Balbilus, crouching in the saddle, pulled tight on the reins, shouting orders for horns to sound recall while cursing, with an angry oath, his failure to achieve what he arrogantly considered to be a simple, mopping-up operation. Perhaps he should have heeded the heathen prince after all, sensing the odds were no longer weighing in his favour. Ignoring all advice, an unpleasant fact had to be faced. The storming of Dorona wasn't at all going to plan.

Yet he consoled himself that all was not yet lost. The task force had suffered an unfortunate setback, nothing more. But he'd likely sacrificed, in the past few hours, half a thousand men and gained nothing, while the enemy well outnumbered his strength by at least three to one. Worst of all, this would have to be explained in detail to Paulinus on his arrival with the main army, only a day's march away.

Even before he'd reached the relative safety of the base camp, the frustrated legate's mind was made up. He'd make his second attempt to take the initiative the following day at dawn. A twenty-year veteran with the legions and a future governorship of the province in the offering, fate must not be allowed to turn against him in a casting of the dabs and the prize of glory. He was, after all, commander of a Roman legion, five thousand crack soldiers, seeing himself as the second figure in the province and perhaps its future leader.

By this coda, Dorona *had* to be taken!

FORTY-ONE

FIVE NAIL BITING HOURS had been all it took for Julius Balbilus to realise that both he and Paulinus, despite words of caution, would be guilty of a major error of judgement when it came to judging the strength of the opposition. Had it not been for some quick-witted initiative shown by Armet's scouts, joined by Thracian and Tungrian squadrons, the struggle for a foothold on the muddy slope below the rampart and its stockade might have ended with an even greater loss of men. As it happened, the violent impact of the counterattack on the Brigante centre cleared a wide path, allowing the Roman foot to adopt a semi-disciplined retreat from what could have been a bad situation.

Retiring at a respectful distance, Balbilus troops now regrouped to lick their wounds, leaving the worried legate to reassess this unforeseen set-back. The precious artillery, cumbersome ballistae, were overrun and sabotaged by the enemy at the very start of the battle, only a minimum number of missiles being launched until put out of action by wave after wave of determined infantry. Only 'Balbilus' babies', the scorpions and their crews, managed to extricate themselves from the tide then threatening to overwhelm them.

Here was an enigma for the legate. How was it possible that a mob of heathen savages could possess such co-ordination and discipline under fire? Someone in command of the rebels had obviously closely studied the Roman art of war. This was no disorganised rabble. Better armed and disciplined than was usually the case, they almost proved the legionaries equal upon occasion. A sobering realisation that the enemy's extended front proved imminently capable of outflanking the Roman formations and rolling-up their centre, also came as a shock, a severe oversight, hardly given credence within the safety of Lindum's distant praetorium. It was lucky for them that Venutius hadn't used the obvious advantage of pursuit, instead preferring to regroup and await a second Roman assault.

There was later, more unpalatable news. Due to the fierce fighting at the rampart, a rough count told of sixty legionaries, and twice that number of auxiliaries, either slain or missing. Add the seriously wounded to the mix and a hasty estimate showed a further several hundred members of the legate's task force being classified as useless non-combatants, a disproportionate showing belonging to those of Cerialis' Hispanics. With that in mind, Cerialis' secondus, seriously concerned over the losses, those of 9th Legion in particular, without Balbilus' consent, sent a fast galloper to Paulinus and the main army enroute, carrying the unsavoury news. Balbilus, though senior in rank to Aquilla and a loyal friend to the governor, could hardly make objection. Not only would it look bad had he prevented Aquilla's sensible action, his already bruised credibility, would surely be called into question.

That was his position after the disastrous first assault. Paulinus would have to know the result sometime. Better honest and upfront, rather than hesitant. The legate of Valeria's problem was, how to come up with something at least half credible in order to redress the balance and save face. Feeling victory almost within his grasp, with the enemy badly weakened by the ferocity of the day's attack, Balbilus, without conferring or accepting advice, made his fateful decision. He had possibly twenty-four hours to recoup, he reminded himself, long enough to snatch the initiative and escape possible humiliation. With the arrival of the main army so near, it was an approach which did not go down well with the level-headed Aquilla and most of the advance force's senior commanders, when belatedly informed.

Armet's reaction at Balbilus' failure to take the settlement was certainly in agreement with the majority. Yet his personal aims had to take first place. The legate's second stab at Dorona would bring with it a renewal of hope for the Coritani prince, knowing he might never get another chance to bring down the old enemy while using the aid of Rome, and he intended to make the most of the opportunity.

Away from the divisions soon to divide the pensive atmosphere already present within the Roman camp that night, soldiers nervously patrolled the perimeter of the temporary stockade, alert for any possibility of a counter- attack taking place under cover of darkness.

FORTY-TWO

WHATEVER THEIR DIFFERENCES, prince Armet and Cerialis' secondus, Aquilla shared one great fear, failure had no place in their philosophy. Within an hour of Balbilus' decision both men, together with the several commanders of all cavalry units, assembled in Aquilla's tent. There, a bold addition to Balbilus' head-on assault, from which none could persuade him to forego, was reluctantly agreed.

'The legate won't like being overruled,' said Clomos, general of Tungrian Horse, stating the obvious.

'He won't have to know, until it's over,' Aquilla responded.

CHAPTER FORTY-TWO

'What if we don't succeed?' muttered Otalus, lately a decurion and now, after the sudden demise of his commander on the scarp, in charge of the Thracian contingent. 'What you propose is not good, we could all be accused of mutiny.'

'Then we'll have to answer to Paulinus as to our reasons,' answered Armet.

'It's insubordination,' said another.

'It's necessary,' replied Aquilla. 'You saw what happened today. Balbilus, if he's allowed to carry out a repeat of his tactics, will recklessly sacrifice many more of us, all for his own glory. As for our mounted arm, they were uselessly employed, supporting the infantry when most should have been elsewhere. Only prince Armet's decision to intervene allowed the infantry to make a successful withdrawal.'

'A mass cavalry attack from the rear was advised by Aquilla, but Balbilus chose not to respond,' Armet said in support. 'The legate wanted praise to go to the cohorts, especially the Valerians. It was his decision that added much to today's failure. It mustn't happen again. Give the cavalry a chance and show the bastards how it's done and take Dorona.'

'It's still insubordinate,' said the earlier voice.

After much argument, sworn to secrecy, although a vote was duly taken, there was still reluctance as to the validity of deceit. Only Aquilla's promise to assume full responsibility for their decision finally swayed the assembly to his side, leaving Balbilus in total ignorance of this covert strategy.

All in all, a remarkable thing had come to pass. The auxiliary cavalry arm, in one action, eclipsing though only temporarily, the invincibility of the legions. All concerned would carry one vital thought in their minds during the next few hours. What they were undertaking incurred a great risk. If they failed, their lives were on the line, knowing what view a staunch supporter of discipline such as Paulinus might make of it. Balbilus, the 'go get 'em' soldier of the victorious Mauritanian campaign, versus an untried heathen and a middle-rank officer, serving under a fellow legate he all but despised.

FORTY-THREE

'I THINK YOU SHOULD see this, legate!'
The morning came as a blessing for the unsuspecting Balbilus, having slept fitfully through what remained of the night, and he was relieved to be roused. Outside the tent, dawn approached under a cloak of mist. Following the anxious centurion, the legate found himself standing on the hastily constructed wall of overturned carts and felled trees where the camp's defences faced toward a still shrouded Dorona. Having slept uncomfortably in their armour, men were quick to assemble, taking up their posts behind the wall, while a lone horn sounded a belated alert. Archers snatched up their bows and gathering ranks of infantry hefted javelins in preparation for an imminent attack. Surprised to see so many other figures standing at the same spot, Balbilus instantly recognised Sextatus the evocati, recently promoted to the rank of his primus pilus, for the duration of hostilities.

Also present, he noticed suspiciously, standing close together, were secondus Aquilla and Armet, 'the heathen Brit'. He cast a sly glance at the two opposites, wondering what, by all the gods, each had in common. At the prince's elbow, supporting himself unsteadily with the aid of a makeshift crutch, stood Straba the slave, the fellow he'd so recently instructed Gallinus to administer a flogging. On second thoughts he convinced himself he'd been far too lenient with this impossible idiot. A fugitive slave mingling with his betters, like a freedman! Snorting disapproval, his gaze wandered over the silent and empty plain to probe the mist, to see a vague shape slowly emerging.

A single wicker chariot, carrying two figures, emerged at a rhythmic pace from the swirl, swerving several times while travelling back and forth directly across the Roman front, the vehicle's driver expertly avoiding the still uncollected corpses from the previous day's slaughter. As the growing number of mystified spectators formed an audience, the chariot swung alarmingly in their direction, then slowed to a walk as it approached. On command, archers raised their weapons, focussing on the oncoming target, waiting for the word 'Loose'! The passenger standing beside the driver could be clearly seen, and the order was immediately given by Aquilla, to lower bows.

'Exhibitionist!' observer Glabas to Servilus. 'She's got a bloody nerve.'

'Cartimandua!' Aquilla spoke softly, almost in awe, after exchanging a perplexed look with prince Armet. 'How in all..........?'

'What, by the gods, is that damn bitch doing here?' Balbilus muttered, cutting in angrily, his frustration showing. 'She's dishonouring the battlefield, damn her to buggery!'

All watched as the chariot came to a halt, as close to the front rank of soldiers as space would allow. The queen of the Brigante, dressed head to toe in a tartan check of blue, red and yellow, held in her right hand a long-shafted spear. At her waist a cavalry sword, the regulatory spatha, swung from a finely wrought and bejewelled belt at her slim waist. Her hair, dark, braided and meticulously set, hung half-way down her back. Her beauty, especially in this dire spot, was undeniable. When at last she spoke, she employed a passable command of Latin.

'Where is Julius Balbilus?'

The legate jumped down from the wall with surprising agility for his age, elbowing men aside amid a barrage of excited voices, forcing them to create a corridor. Aquilla, Armet, the advance force's primus pilus, Sextatus, and the limping scribe, followed behind. Cartimandua meanwhile, made no move to step down from the chariot.

'You have no business here, unless you have news that might be useful to us,' Balbilus said loudly.

'I have more business here than yourself, Roman. Must I remined you that this is my land. Venutius and my brother happen to be *my* problem, not yours.'

'As for this being *your* land, I don't believe it's present ruler would agree with you,' Armet interjected, drawing himself up, his eyes momentarily challenging those of the queen's charioteer, Vellocatus, who acknowledged the Coritani prince with a smile of contempt. 'This land belongs to king Setane and the Deceangli nation.'

'Setane?!' the queen laughed harshly. 'An underling and a flabby idiot who no longer knows his elbow from his dirty backside!' She appraised the Coritanian. 'You are, Armet?'

'That is my name.'

'Have we met before?' She pointed with her spear.

'Once, a year back.'

'With legate Cerialis?'

Armet nodded, guardedly.

'I thought so. One of Volisios' two cubs, but not the rebellious one?' Armet ignored the jibe. 'And how is little Gela now, your betrothed?'

'She is well, queen,' answered the prince, startled for a moment by her unsettling knowledge of his affairs.

'I hear she communes with dark spirits. Best beware, prince, one day she may use those spells taught her by the hag, Ulvina, and turn you into some foul creature, if you should displease her!' The queen turned her attention to Balbilus again, who'd watched this brief interchange with barely suppressed ire. 'Old governor Paulinus is wrong, you know,' Cartimandua continued. 'His might should be concentrated to the south, rather than on foes dwelling in sacred Mona. My sister-queen, Boudiga, is mightily angry. She, unlike me, is not of a forgiving nature and could well spell trouble for you.'

'Not half as much trouble as I could bring down on you, you damn she-witch! I've a good mind to have you whipped out of here!' shouted Julius Balbilus, his temper rising. 'I repeat, you have no business here, unless you wish to take part in the mopping-up operation, when we've done our work. I hear you Brig's are excellent scavengers!'

It was not the right thing to say. 'Behind that hill over there,' she indicated a large mound a mile away, 'I've positioned several thousand of my best fighting men, men like Vellocatus, here,' she put a hand on her paramour's bare shoulder, squeezing the flesh, intimately.

'The slut has even got the gall to bring her latest bit of rough along,' observed one of Balbilus' optios to a companion, giving an accompanying smirk in Vellocatus' direction.

When you engage with my brother today, we'll be watching,' the queen's voice intoned in the ensuing silence. 'If by some chance you fail yet again in the assault, I shall as you say, do the mopping-up.' As if on cue, Vellocatus tugged at the reins attached to the brace of horses and the chariot reversed. 'You people should make a point of feeding your slaves, legate Balbilus. Straba there looks as though he's in need of a good meal. He'll need all his strength when legate Quintus finally catches up with him.'

'Damn her!' cursed Balbilus as the chariot sharply turned and sped away. 'The sorceress must have ears in every damn cohort in the blasted army. How could she know all that stuff? What means had the witch employed to learn of his decision to attack Venutius again, when he hadn't yet passed down the order to his troops? Undoubtedly, some evil business was at work! 'I should have clapped the bitch in irons while I had the chance,' he finally muttered angrily.

'Had you done that, legate, you'd have had several thousand *more* hostiles to deal with this day,' said Armet, just as perplexed.

'She could be calling our bluff,' Aquilla remarked, gravely.

'You heard the queen. Would *you* take that chance?' Armet posed. 'She and her Brigante are by far the stronger power in these parts. Most importantly, her followers worship her.'

'A goddess, then?' Aquilla asked.

'If she be so, then she's a treacherous one. I've heard stories you wouldn't believe,' Armet replied, seriously. 'It's common coin, there's more to her than outward show.'

For once Balbilus, before moving out of earshot, was totally in agreement.

Behind them, Straba, leaning heavily on his crutch, made a mental note of these exchanges but sensibly remained silent.

FORTY-FOUR

AFTER THE DEPARTURE of Cartimandua, an odd silence descended over the encampment. Stranger still, was the fact that the enemy, though still possessed of superior numbers, had made no effort to launch a counterattack during the night, as Balbilus and others half expected. Whatever the reason, the advance force lost hours of precious sleep, being ordered to remain on standby as the legate prepared to announce his decision to renew the attack on the settlement.

'You want to know what our trouble is?' Legionary Verra asked at random in the early light, over a bowl of barley soup.

'Not really,' said Ornio, I've had enough trouble already, seeing that witch- queen of the Brigs, up close.' He lifted his eyes heavenward in mock supplication. 'But I suppose you're fuckin' well going to tell me, anyway.'

Verra ignored the interruption and scanned his half-empty mess can, declaring, statesmanlike. 'We've been trained to think we're invincible.'

Ornio, now quickly promoted overnight, to replace the unfortunate, Priscus, grinned. 'Varus and the twenty-thousand buggers who copped it in Germania, might well have taken issue with that stupid observation, soldier.'

'That was then,' boasted Verra, 'this is now.'

'We can't afford another set-back,' Lentilus said, soaking up his share of soup with stale bread.

Philo looked up enquiringly. 'What do you mean, another set-back?'

'There are rumours going about, I should have told you,' Ornio replied. 'Myself, I think it might be official. But we'll know soon enough, anyway, damn it!'

'Well, bugger his bollocks!' Verra swore in astonishment. 'Someone should give the mad bastard a very nasty disease.

'Disease or not,' said Ornio, 'it's typical of him, isn't it? To save his dirty arse we're about to become his sacrificial lambs. If you ask me, yesterday's business was only a skirmish. Today may be different.'

'So, he's going to make another attempt?' moaned Philo. 'I knew it, I bloody well knew it!'

Verra's look of astonishment remained. 'With Paulinus and the main force only a spit away, it's bloody insane!'

'I reckon that's what brought queen, whatever her name is, to Dorona,' spoke up Glabas. 'I overheard Iber saying she knew everything about our movements, before even Balbilus decided.'

Verra chortled.' I bet she don't' know about Iber's.'

'Or Lindum's dire lack of shit holes,' Lentilus added, cocking a leg, dog-like.

'Can Balbilus *really* do that, make us try again?' Servilus asked, nursing his head as he stood upright. He'd been lucky during the previous day's debacle, only his helmet saving him from what could have been a death dealing blow aimed at the back of the neck. Thus, he reckoned himself doubly fortunate to still be with his comrades that morning, a survivor from the first blooding.

'Balbilus is still legate in command, sod our luck. He can, and likely will,' grumbled Ornio. 'Yesterday was bad. If the news is true about a second assault.........'

'He's a bloody dickhead,' spat Verra. 'He's not even *our* legate. Cerialis will have something to say about it?'

'Our wonder boy isn't here though, is he?' said Glabas. 'What happened to Varus and his legions could bloody well happen to us, and we'd all be massacred, end up in the wolf's belly.'

'Let's hope you're mistaken,' said Verra, standing, 'I don't want another bastard day like yesterday.'

'There's something I can't work out,' said Servilus, silently contemplating the rising wood-smoke.

'Is there anything you could ever work out, bird brain,' Philo mocked.

'Why is it whenever we win, it's a victory, yet when the heathens beat *us*, it's a massacre?'

Ornio threw the last twig of wood on the dying fire. 'How long have you been with the Hispanics, lad?'

'Over a year.'

'Then you've still time to learn, should you live,' said the optio, rubbing his hand along a cramped thigh.

'Which won't be long, I fear,' Philo said seriously. 'It's in the air. I sense it.'

'One of your silent farts, is it?' grinned Ornio.'

Mist continued to cloak the camp as men hastily rearmed, echoing Philo's unease. 'Armet rode out of here, a little after daybreak,' someone said suspiciously.

'One fucking barbarian looking out for another, if you ask me,' Philo grunted.

'That's a real shame you pessimistic sod,' chimed in Verra, mockingly. 'I hear the bastard speaks very well of you.'

'He may clothe himself with Roman arms and gear, cut his bloody hair, Roman fashion,' muttered Philo, ignoring Verra's bad attempt at humour. 'But that don't make him a Roman.'

'Well, at least he's been to Rome,' stated Verra, 'which is more than any one of us has.'

Ornio's remarks regarding sacrificial lambs was about to be put to the test. Balbilus stood poised to make the biggest open decision of his illustrious military career. The shame of Paulinus and the main force arriving with the business of taking Dorona still unresolved, was more disturbing for the legate than ever. The problem had to be sealed by day's end, if not, his future and with it his reputation, would take an undignified tumble into obscurity. But confident that he could pull it off, and going recklessly against character, he was throwing all he possessed into the arena. Should he lose, he'd have to explain himself. That morning he prayed fervently for the gods to give him a chance to conclude the whole bloody business.

There was one other matter just as important. Cerialis' Eighth cohort! Of course, putting them in the most vulnerable position in the assault, the more perilous centre, a position where men were most likely to suffer the brunt of fierce in-fighting, was a small satisfaction!

Aquilla's frustration at the legate's earlier indecision had showed in his face, his character finding it hard to hide his disgust at Balbilus' narrowness of thought, unbefitting of an experienced legionary commander. One fact alone gave the secondus cause for cheer, his association with the prince. In the last few days, the secondus had formed a growing respect for the Coritani leader. In the coming confrontation they were to fight side by side, and he saw much merit in it. Aquilla, a cavalry man through and through, had decided to join Armet, taking his place within the four hundred, which he regarded a privilege. Armet's uncle would scratch his head once again, perplexedly. 'First Armet takes on a useless idiot as a cavalryman, now he joins with an equally useless Roman aristocrat, their ever-present 'observer'! What, by Epona, would come next?'

With their cover fast dispersing, with the grassy sward heavy with dew, the cohorts, again in three solid wedges, fifteen hundred legionaries and an equal number of auxiliaries, advanced once more in near silence toward the unseen rampart, scene of their bloody encounter the previous day. The sharpened staves, bristling along the face of the scarp, were the first things that came into view. In contrast to the pattern used the day before, few horsemen were seen guarding the cohort's flanks. To seasoned foot sloggers, this was immediately worrying, as should enemy cavalry decide to launch a lightning strike, exposed and open to attack as they were, they risked being cut to pieces even before getting anywhere close to the defenders.

Servilus, now positioned in the second rank of Hispanics, felt sweat on the palm of his hand as he gripped the javelin. Perhaps Ornio was right, he thought, when he said that what happened yesterday was only a skirmish, that today would be the *real* test of their courage. Certainly, the air was fully charged with an unsettling menace. No battle-horn split the air, nor beat of a drum. Only the tread made by booted feet and the rhythmic sound of metal scraping metal, announced their movement.

Like Priscus previously, the recruit prayed to Mithras that whatever happened in the minutes ahead would see him favoured by this bull-slaying god, so that the end might be swift. It hadn't helped optio Priscus though, he mused, all the praying. He momentarily realised that he'd *really* miss that man's comradeship. Drawing the shield resignedly across his chest, he looked to his front, imagining far-away visions of his native Tarraco, to help allay the fear.

FORTY-FIVE

ALONG THE LENGTH of the Roman front, centurions and other senior ranks fell into their allotted places while others picked up the pace. Horsemen of the remaining cavalry units, those not part of Aquilla and Armet's pending attack on Dorona's unprotected rear, made a colourful show riding the flanks of advancing foot-soldiers for the benefit of an unsuspecting Balbilus who, sword unsheathed, rode up and down between the armoured ranks of men. The triple strength of the legionary cohorts halted momentarily in the centre of the host, protected there by several alae of Asturian Royals together with one of the two survivors of Petra's Horse; men with a vengeful axe to grind in memory of Lucidius Salva and their fallen comrades. These last riders made a telling display as to what to expect from the enemy, having been the first to be introduced to something never imagined.

The deep note of a battle horn close to his right startled Servilus. Striding forward again, wedged between the pessimist Philo and the joker, Glabas, he again strove to suppress his fears.

His eyes focussed nervously as they looked toward the distant enemy, awaiting the inevitable, realising there was no way out until the end, whatever that end may be. He wondered how a man like Verra, a veteran of half a score of such encounters, could blindly accept the fact that this could be the day he took a one-way trip to Pluto's realm.

A sharp order to prepare javelins, jerked Servilus into action as it rapidly came down the line. At that moment another group of wild looking riders trotted past the cohorts in the opposite direction, away from the coming fight!

'What is the legate's bloody scribbler doing among the damn Brits'?' Philo observed, raising his voice and pointing with his javelin, attempting to be heard over the rising tread of advancing soldiery.

'Just how would we know it, idiot?' returned Glabas with an oath, 'why don't you ask the bugger before he falls off the bloody horse?'

Servilus, barely hearing, instead was filled with one great desire. If only he were the Greek and not as he really was, just another type of slave. With no time to speculate on this question, he shot a final glance at the horsemen as they gradually faded to the rear. A familiar order to prepare to launch their weapons came from the guttural voice of Iber, followed quickly by other shouted commands as the machine neared a waiting scarp suddenly bristling with spears. A screen of Thracian riders, wearing plumed helms that wouldn't have disgraced Thermopylae, crossed in front of them to quickly disappear. Staring above the rim of the shield, the boy from Tarraco saw the ditch with its protection of sharpened wooden stakes. A thunderous growl, coming from many throats, became the grim accompaniment to the rhythmic clash of weapons as the columns of legionaries, closely following their screen of auxiliaries, drew closer. Soon, enemy missiles came raining down and Servilus swore that every single one of the barbs was heading personally in his direction.

As the arrows flew, the men of Hispanics raised shields over their heads, forming a tortoise like canopy, the tight-knit testudo. To Servilus' front, the bodies then began to fall, earliest victims of the bloody assault. For a second time that day the recruit uttered a quick prayer to Mithras, deity of soldiers and light. What was about to come, he would have to meet, yet it did no harm to have at least one watchful friend on his side.

FORTY-SIX

YESTERDAY WAS YESTERDAY thought Julius Balbilus, legate of the Valerians. Today will be different!

Shield to shield, a moving wall, rank on rank of lighter armed Vascones and Tungrians, continued to devour the distance with speed, knowing time was of the essence. Following close behind, striding with measured tread came Balbilus, having now dispensed with his horse to personally lead the cohort on foot. Valerians on the right, Gemina to the left and lastly, Cerialis' Hispanic's who, grudgingly following Balbilus' explicit instructions, were conspicuously positioned in the dangerous centre. The legate had considered other ploys, such as keeping his own Valeria in close reserve, in order he'd say, to plug up any gaps, were it not that such a ruse would have been blatantly obvious to all.

Reinforcing the cohorts was a large contingent of Black-Sea Dacians, responding to a familiar cry of 'Javelins!' rippling through their ranks. Simultaneously the first barrage of Balbilus' babies opened-up, this time with deadly accuracy over the heads of the first wave of attackers racing toward the heavily defended ditch at the foot of the rising climb to the rampart. Nimbly avoiding hundreds of sharp-pointed stakes that porcupined the ditch and scarp, they engaged with the defenders, both sides colliding ferociously in a desperate struggle for possession of the rampart. With the last of the concealing mist almost gone the cohorts viewed a seething mass of men locked in close combat. On either flank of the cohorts, more auxiliary infantry ran ahead as a continuous cloud of missiles rained over the heads of the second wave, fast closing the gap between themselves and the wrestling mass of combatants.

A murderous hail of projectiles gained momentum as spears, arrows and deadly slingshot, flesh gouging and bone shattering, fell continually without distinction on friend and foe alike. Seeing the rapid success of Balbilus' infantry advancing beneath this ceaseless barrage, many of the defenders quickly overwhelmed the leading auxiliaries full on and, with a mighty clash of arms, fell upon Balbilus' oncoming cohorts.

Events then passed at increasing speed; all previous plans forgotten. Alerted by a signal from a deep-throated battle horn, what the attackers perceived as Venutius' horsemen, choosing to seize the moment, appeared from hidden positions, left and right of the mound. This unwelcome force, wildly slamming into the thinning ranks of the unfortunate Vascones, drove them back to be spitted by their own momentum onto a myriad of sword points of the oncoming ranks of support. Servilus' group, as yet unscathed, hunkered down where they were, behind a solid wall of shields.

Adhering closely to a strategy hastily prepared, Armet's four hundred, together with as many auxiliary turmae as could be spared, sat their horses in concealment at enough distance from Dorona's rear as to be unseen, awaiting their signal to move. The position they occupied thus went unchallenged, and no activity was seen except for a small band of horsemen who veered away to disappear into the cover of encroaching woodland. The group were too far distant for recognition. Only their trappings and the prominent stave carried aloft by their signifer raised Armet's suspicions that it might have been somebody of rank. Immediately he sent off Machai with a small number of Exploratores in rapid pursuit.

The prince was unsettled by what he'd seen. Was this his enemy, Brennus, fleeing the fight? If not, who else? Secretly he hoped it might instead be Venutius, the man cheated from a throne by a faithless wife. But what little Armet knew of the Brigante leader told him that such a brave fighter would never leave the field of conflict, not while there was the slimmest chance of victory.

Venutius' name was already legendary. Having taken up the war against Rome waged by his predecessor, Caractacus, he challenged his enemy at every opportunity, appearing and vanishing at will. Armet had no quarrel with such a man, even though he supported the Abrentii. Rather, he admired him, both for his reputation and dogged persistence, two things to which the prince could never aspire, owing to his father's continued loyalty to Rome.

A third possibility then entered his head, those horsemen he distantly saw before the charge could well have been there on the orders of none other than Cartimandua! Yet that was surely impossible, not even the she-wolf would take such a risk. Then again, if the prize were worth it.............. Armet recalled her brazen presence at the base camp before the renewal of fighting, a further question unanswered.

What if an attempt had been made to ensnare Brennus? Armet tried to dismiss such a thought. It could not succeed, not with The Bear surrounded by so many dedicated followers, could it?

Yet Dorona beckoned him now, and he put speculation behind him. In the distance, under a billowing spiral of black smoke, the settlement burned. Sitting silent in the saddle, after an hour of hard riding, a mass of assorted cavalry had circumnavigated their target by a wide margin, in order to reach this spot.

Machai returned with unhelpful news. Riding as fast as their skills could take them, the Exploratores had little chance of intercepting their quarry, whoever they might have been, and not wanting to miss the action, they'd raced back at speed.

Resting uncomfortably between Culchul Hud and the prince, Aquilla, looking a little anxious at the disturbance, removed his helm, mopping his forehead with the end of the coloured cloth tied about his neck. Behind them, astride a recalcitrant animal, its reins now tied loosely to Gralos' mount, Straba the cleric, armed with sword and round shield, inwardly feared a loosening of the bowels, for the sound of conflict wasn't so distant that it failed to reach his ear.

What was obvious to Armet was that if Balbilus' forces were attempting to take the scarp a second time, they were taking a long time about it. Straba, glancing sideways, delivered a nervous grin toward a slightly amused Patux, sitting close which prompted the wayward scribe to think the Coritani signifer had scant hope for his survival.

'You wanted your damn war, Greek,' growled Culchul, turning his head. 'Now you'll have it. Won't be pretty, perhaps, but stick with us, maybe you'll live to boast that you once rode with prince Armet and the four hundred.'

The scribe fought back a reply that he didn't mind riding with them, it was *dying* with them that was the problem.

'Don't fret, Roman,' spoke Armet to Aquilla with a light-heartedness he didn't feel, as he patted Flavia's neck soothingly, noticing the man's stare. 'Whatever happens, we have the advantage of surprise.'

'That's not it,' muttered the secondus. 'What awaits us if our plan fails? Then we'll be in the same damn situation as Balbilus,' he replied as his horse began pawing impatiently at the turf.

'We'll soon find out,' Armet said encouragingly, looking to his front and taking a tighter grip of Flavia's reins as he heeded her eagerness for the chase. Right now, he badly wished for Gort. What, if after all the years of waiting, both could have shared in the satisfaction of this moment, and what would his brother have made of it?

An agreed signal, the deep throated call of several warhorns, brought a return to reality, the sound that the three cohorts had finally breached the rampart wall. With a wave of an arm the son of Volisios led a thousand riders toward the spiralling cloud of smoke curling black above the embattled fortress men called Dorona.

FORTY-SEVEN

UNDER A THIRD FIERCE BARRAGE from fire arrows, fast penetrating dry thatch, several score of round houses quickly exploded, covering much of the plateau with roaring flame and smoke. The farmer's son from Tarraco, shoulder to shoulder with Philo and Verra in the second line of the armoured wedge, his eyes stinging from running sweat while seeking to focus to the front, fought his way up the steep slope, slowly pushing back the retreating defenders, while many forsook the crowded rampart, staggering under a heavy and murderous fire as they sought to escape from the continuous volleys of javelin, barb and shot falling among them.

Still a few frantic metres from the rampart's lip. Servilus and his team trampled over a human carpet of the fallen. Verra was the first comrade to fall, his helmet lost in the melee, he received a lead shot in the head and was clearly dead, before his body hit the soil. Unconscious of the sudden loss, the recruit continued to stumble, stabbing forward blindly with the gladius, ducking, weaving his body behind the shield.

Sure-footed Vascones and Balearic slingers, their stones deadly accurate at a hundred yards, continued to advance to left and right, delivering a merciless bombardment from hand-held catapults. For those already trapped between the mound and the nests of dwellings, including many women and children caught up in the horror on the bloody lip of the rampart, it was just another mode of death suffered amid the ongoing mayhem.

Struggling clear, their feet finally on level ground, Servilus and the men of Hispania, were suddenly confronted by a further group of wildly leaping figures, a blurred vision of tattooed arms and braided hair which continued to come at them, manically. Lentilus was the next member of the contuburnium to fall, calling out in agony for the mother he never knew as he collapsed at the recruit's side, stricken from two random arrows piercing neck and shoulder. Servilus stumbled ahead to collide with another fierce shape launching itself on the point of his gladius. It happened so fast that seconds passed before the realisation of impact. Breathing deeply, he viciously beat down his screaming attacker with his dented shield while everywhere the air around him exploded like shattered glass. A round shield smashed into him with such brutal force it almost drove him to his knees. Servilus then took the full force of the short axe wielded by his ferocious opponent, the man's eyes glinting wickedly in anticipation as he moved in close for an easy kill.

Discipline drummed into him by sadistic officers like Iber kicked in, the recruit automatically dodging aside as the falling axe glanced off his helm. Quickly he plunged beneath the Brigante's guard, blindly thrusting with his sword-arm. A brutal collision of blade on flesh and bone jarred his wrist, sending a sharp pain up to his elbow, a momentary spasm that made him cry out, a sound going unheard amidst a thousand, equally frightening sounds. In blind retaliation he stabbed again and again. This time the sword found yielding softness and he felt a sucking impact as the blade found the man's unguarded belly. Then the youth heard a terrible noise, a drawn-out squeal, more animal than human. Later he would recall with disgust, that the frightening utterance had come, not from his opponent, but from himself.

Horns tore the air above the tumult, the order to disengage and reform. Many of the near-beaten enemy fell back to create a large defensive circle in the centre of the settlement, an area littered with many scores of dead from both sides, sprawled amid burning buildings and other detritus. Servilus was startled to see more women, even children, joining the defenders, many of them carrying any weapon that could be salvaged in order to share a determined last stand alongside their men.

'Ornio yelled above the din, breathing heavily, a blood lust possessing him while his own trickled down his cheek, 'Bitches and whores!' he yelled wildly. 'Let's sort the buggers out!'

The fighting groups continued vainly to resist, small knots of defiance now, fair game for cavalry. Behind separate pockets of shields, those on the edge of the scarp yelled encouragement to others struggling alone, only to be run-down by encircling horsemen.

Barely heard above the noise of war-horns, Armet's horsemen suddenly appeared like a flow of molten lava, thundering around the chaos of death that was the killing ground. This could no longer be termed a battle, more resembling mass slaughter where the discerning killer could choose his own victim. Amid the confusion the prince and his uncle sought out their *real* reason for their being there. Brennus!

'He's here, he must be,' Culchul Hud later said hopefully, when the killing slowed. He turned over a blooded body with a sharp pointed stave.

'One of them is found, Armet,' Drada, a recent recruit to the Exploratores, yelled gleefully, reining in, a severed head hanging from his saddle. 'By his garb and the trappings of the horse, I think it may be either Taghe or Varan, but not knowing what they look like.....................'

'Let me see it,' Culchul interrupted, relieving Drada of the blooded object roughly by the hair. The Hud then contemptuously threw the gruesome find at Armet's feet. 'It's been a long time. I can't be sure.'

Culchul may not have been certain, yet Armet was. With the chaos still surging about him the prince of the Coritani stared down, mesmerised by the sight of the scarcely recognisable face, for men killed in battle didn't always resemble how they looked in life, not of Varan, but of his brother, Taghe, scourge, rapist and enemy. Volisios would be greatly cheered by this devoutly wished for event, the head of one of the murdering scum responsible for the brutal death of wife and daughter.

'It's Taghe,' Armet said, tight lipped.

'No sign of the other one,' Culchul spat. And how can Brennus not be here, damn him?'

'Find a sack, Drada!' Culchul ordered, remounting. 'We can at least take this fine trophy back to Rina!'

'Is that necessary, prince?' came Aquilla's voice at Armet's back, disturbed by the barbarity.

'You should be pleased, secondus, Armet answered. It isn't only me that's partly avenged. This man was also responsible for ambushing Petra's Horse!'

Aquilla, sitting his horse in silence, nodded. 'At least Paulinus will be happy at that.' Around them as the secondus spoke, the last of the defenders of Dorona, fought and died. Whatever the Coritani thought about their hereditary foe, they would never later deny that the alliance of those in defence of Dorona, lacked courage.

Gradually the remaining Brigante were worn down and, in less than an hour the process of mopping up began. Women and children, all who remained alive, were forcibly herded and gathered in one large and terrified group. Prowling about the burning ruins of Brennus' settlement men began the bloody business of slitting the throats of those of the enemy whose injuries prevented them from having any chance of escape. At the same time, they stripped both living and dead of any valuable torcs, trinkets, rings, or any such tokens they might possess. Amid cries for mercy and lamentations coming from the circles of women and children came another sound, a noted keening from the victors, a triumphant offering released from many a thousand throats in gratitude to the gods for survival.

Against this background, Armet's riders searched vainly about the huts of a Dorona in flames, frantically scouring between the burning ruins, searching vainly for any sign of Brennus.

Culchul shook his head in frustration as he reined in beside the prince. 'Armet, I fear he fled with Venutius. Perhaps he sensed defeat, and decided to quit the battle early on, to cut his losses, cunning fox that he is. Even if he hadn't, it would be a hard task to find them amid this mess,' he indicated the mayhem surrounding them. 'I'll tell you of another rogue we can't find, it's you're damned Greek!'

It was the wrong time to disillusion his uncle about Brennus, Armet decided. If Brennus was anywhere, it certainly wasn't with Venutius.

'We got separated,' shouted Gralos in explanation to his friend, Culchul, barely hearing the words above the clamour.

In the confusion Armet had completely forgotten the Greek scribe, but his concern was short-lived. After hunting the area, Gralos and Patux came upon him keening in his native tongue, a muffled dirge over the body of a slain Brigante. 'It was self-defence,' spluttered the scribe,' throwing aside the blood smeared weapon held in his grip as they dragged him to his feet, his thin frame heaving uncontrollably. 'He fell on his own weapon,' he kept muttering repeatedly. 'I didn't' ....'

'I reckon we'll make something of you yet,' said Culchul, grinning from ear to ear while clapping a heavy arm around Straba's shoulders.

'That old bugger Balbilus should be well pleased with today's work,' observed Patux, nodding as his hand shook the wolf head stave. 'He's even managed to get the slave to fight for us.'

'The legate might indeed be pleased, even if Straba isn't,' Armet nodded.

'Too bad, we missed Venutius,' ventured Aquilla. 'His body is not among the slain, at least, not so far.'

'Nor will it be, secondus. 'I fear he's long gone,' the Coritani shrugged, recalling the sighting of a small group of riders fleeing the scene of conflict prior to Armet's advance.

'You don't appear very upset about it,' remarked Aquilla, dryly.

'I've no quarrel with the Brigante king. He's Rome's enemy, not mine. 'Its Brennus and his crew that I hunted.'

'Well,' sniffed Aquilla, a mite put out, 'it looks like we've snared neither one of them.'

Several thoughts now occupied Armet's mind. Unlike Cartimandua, Venutius had been seen, albeit at a distance and not by Armet, fighting at several threatened areas atop the scarp and later, amid the burning settlement itself. Had the queen observed from a safe distance, as she implied, or was the she-wolf bluffing? The answer lay in the presence of Vellocatus, a relief for Balbilus perhaps, but a puzzle for the prince, and he asked himself, just what game pieces was the queen holding in her manicured fingers?

Did she have only a passing interest in a Roman victory, or did her presence herald something a little more disturbing? Over Venutius a state of confusion later existed, some sceptically hinting that Venutius had never been at Dorona in the first place, deserting the field at the first sign of battle, a scenario dismissed immediately by Armet. Whatever the answer, he was certain Rome hadn't seen the last of either Venutius or his one-time wife.

Amid the carnage of the day, Balbilus showed much pleasure by putting to death several hundred prisoners, men and women, some of them being handed to his Scythian archers for target practice. A scattering of the younger women and children were, countermanding Paulinus' extermination order, rounded up and shackled. It would be for some of them, an introduction to an unpredictable life of dishonourable servitude. Regarding the dead on both sides, they were finally united in a half-score of pyramidic funeral pyres, leaving the ashes to be cast to the four winds. Soon it was put about that the bodies piled high on the burning platforms were so great in number that the all-consuming fires continued to be stoked for several days. Thus ended the fighting at Dorona. As for Cartimandua, it would soon be proven that her presence in the area hadn't been solely out of curiosity, as prince Armet had so rightly thought.

The bloody business of Dorona, finally achieved, the road lay open for Paulinus' army to move on west. Yet, Venutius of the Carvetii, for it could only have been he, had delayed Rome's legions by three vital days, giving Mona extra time to organise its defences. The cost of the operation would never be fully calculated, but in terms of lives lost, the numbers were staggering. Of the three cohorts employed, together with its support auxiliaries, those of the slain well-surpassed four figures.

One week later, Cartimandua's half-brother, Brennus the Bear, weighed down by chains, as Caractacacus had once been, found himself unceremoniously handed over to a very puzzled Cerialis, before the gates of Lindum.

FORTY-EIGHT

DORONA HAD FALLEN, but the price paid would not please Paulinus. Balbilus, even with its successful conclusion, had gone way beyond his brief in blatantly disobeying orders, doing what he was precisely told *not* to do with his second attempt to overcome the defiant settlement.

It must be said that the legate of Valeria expected some sort of dressing down, followed by an obvious caution from his old friend and veteran, Suetonius, but if he thought that would be all, he seriously miscalculated his position.

The stocky commander guarded by a pair of his trusted centurions, faced his first unpleasant surprise. No quiet summons, no shared jug of wine and customary sweetmeats within the governor's private space. Instead, publicly on view to all, after being confined to quarters, he stood stiffly at attention before Paulinus under the wind-blown canvas of the governor's filled pavilion. The group present included Aquilla, the Coritani prince Armet, together with several of Balbilus' staff officers, who stood noticeably apart.

Three serious questions had been levied against the legate regarding his conduct. One, why a flagrant disregard for orders, two, why did he decide to place legate Cerialis' Hispanics in the vulnerable centre, where combat would doubtless be at its fiercest, rather than employ his own Valerians, as was normally expected? Lastly, and perhaps most damning of all, why had he chosen to ignore all reliable evidence regarding Venutius' power?

Paulinus, an ill-tempered man at best, as Decianus, procurator, had earlier discovered to his chagrin when reading the casualty list for a second time, while watching as the commander drummed bony fingers on the table with ill-disguised frustration.

The large pavilion had been hastily set up, draped in various hangings and military paraphernalia, and furniture and tables accommodated the many maps and open scrolls. Heavy stands of bronze supported military vexilla, a splendid display of standards showing an equally impressive number of battle honours and plaques. Sacred icons and vestments, religiously displayed, they hung proudly. When finally completed the whole tent presented an oasis of ordered disorder, imperial style, counteracting the noisy confusion without, as endless groups forming the task force continued to arrive, at what was until then, Balbilus camp.

'I commend your success, Julius,' the supreme governor glanced yet again at the hastily written list he'd been handed, 'I really do, but I'm puzzled as to how you can lose so many of our soldiers to an untrained, undisciplined mob?' He placed the written evidence aside while resuming his gaze on Balbilus. 'Perhaps you can enlighten me with an explanation as to your thoughts yesterday, given that you so readily ignored my order to await my arrival before mounting a second attack?'

'With the greatest respect, eminence,'.................. the legate replied with supressed anger, 'I carried out your instructions to the best of my ability, and I really must..'

'My agents say otherwise, legate,' Paulinus interrupted with barely concealed frustration. 'You make your protest, vigorously. Yet I placed three veteran cohorts, plus two and a half thousand auxiliaries and more than fifteen hundred horsemen, under your command. Over five thousand men! Why was it so important to countermand my order, when you failed the first time? Is your connection with the gods superior to mine?'

'Balbilus paled, yet he stood automatically at attention as he defended himself. 'In war there are sometimes sacrifices.........'

'Sacrifices?' Paulinus slumped back in the chair, shaking his head vigorously. 'These losses are appalling!' He snatched up the crumpled list before tossing it aside. 'Valerian cohort, 106, Gemina, 133, Hispania, 190. Do you wish me to remind you, yet again?'

After that there was little appropriate defence that could be mounted, but Balbilus, being the man he was, certainly tried. 'We could hardly reason out their strength until we neared the settlement. Even then.......' he protested.

'Not so Julius, it won't do,' Paulinus interrupted, tut-tutting while shaking his head. 'Secondus Aquilla informs me that you were well acquainted with this knowledge but chose deliberately to ignore it. You even went so far as to dismiss further reliable information from my Exploratores, out of hand. Above all, legate, you saw fit to disobey *me!*'

Balbilus shifted uncomfortably under the governor's icy stare, presenting a brave front, while at odds with himself. He took the few seconds available to cast an angry glance in the direction of Armet and Aquilla, both standing at a distance to one side, being fully convinced they'd played a large part in his betrayal. 'They were merely a heathen rabble, weren't they, eminence?' he continued, an instinctive hold on survival kicking-in while defending his corner. 'In war there will always be the unexpected......' he added.

If it were a remark to push Balbilus' point home, it didn't go down very well. 'Our losses were damned inexcusable, almost one whole cohort in number!' Paulinus voice grew harsher as he retrieved the crumpled document. 'You forget who you are talking to, I know only too well about war.' Paulinus shook his grey head. 'No, Julius, you're the one at fault, small blame to others. You should have waited. As it is, too many of my soldiers died in a personal folly of your own making!'

'Isn't the noble governor forgetting that I *actually did* capture Dorona.'

'Just you alone, legate?' Paulinus answered sarcastically. 'I hear tell that secondus Aquilla, here, together with Armet's forward scouts, plus a large section of the cavalry, also led the enemy a pretty dance.'

Balbilus flinched, then for a second time he threw a hostile glance at a silent and uncomfortable looking Aquilla. 'The cavalry did their duty, I don't deny, but it was my cohorts on the scarp that gained the final victory.'

'A little more than that, the cavalry broke Dorona's back, just as you should have done on day one.' The governor sat back. 'I have one final question to ask, Julius, and it's a pertinent one. Why was Hispania made to hold the centre of the advance rather than, as is customary in such circumstances, men of the commanding legate?'

'I thought Hispania the suitable unit, being the one legion issued with the new-fangled crab-armour, which I'm told offers better protection,' said Balbilus, unapologetically.

Paulinus again shook his head. 'Armour that until yesterday was untried, Julius. *Untried!*'

The publicly disgraced legate was an unforgiving man, who bore a grudge to excess. Sensing conspiracy, he was already plotting vengeance. Somebody had organised this humiliation and he would have their bollocks on a spit, just as soon as more evidence was disclosed. As it was, Paulinus deliberately relieved him of his command with instructions that the matter be examined in more detail, meaning it wouldn't take place this side of ongoing hostilities. This made his part in the coming assault against the Druse altogether unlikely. His mind in turmoil, he swore retribution upon lesser mortals, men like Cerialis' lapdog, Aquilla, and prince Armet, wolf hunter and upstart heathen of the Exploratores, a man first in line for special treatment when the right time came.

He'd faced setbacks before, fought his way out of them, and would do so again. As it was, one thing only occupied his deliberations. Two men in particular had made the legate their mortal enemy by not acquainting him with their cobbled-together strategy at Dorona.

Armet, together with the secondus, had secretly determined that the mistakes suffered on the first day at Dorona would not be repeated. Secretly and together, they'd formed a different plan, and their scheme, luckily, had paid off. A small unit of horse, flanking the advance of the leading infantry in the assault, acting as decoys, mostly for show, gave the impression of greater numbers involved, making themselves as conspicuous as possible by riding back and forth along the flanks of the advance. Meanwhile, Armet, Aquilla, with the greater number of cavalry, under cover of a helpful dawn mist, departed silently from the horse-lines, the hooves of the beasts, muffled with sackcloth. Silently they led them on foot, departing in small groups as they made for the prearranged point, all done with a maximum of secrecy. So maximum, thought Balbilus, deep in his fury, that they never bothered to inform their commander!

Relieved of his position, on the return to the colonia, under escort from men of the Hispanics and Armet's Exploratores, was but one more humiliation to be endured. But for Julius Balbilus, patience was the key, a time to set a trap, invent a ruse. Pacing back and forth in his temporary quarters below The Hill, rebuffed, cast aside, consuming more wine than he should, the stood-down legate began work on his modus operandi.

FORTY-NINE

AFTER DEPARTING main army, a return to Lindum occurred without event, except that legate Cerialis saw fit to draw up a detail guard of honour for all the one hundred and ninety Hispanics who'd died taking the settlement.

Over the stinging embarrassment of legate Balbilus, Cerialis shed no tears for a man who'd deliberately ill-used his men when choosing the battle order, rather than his Valerians who, to their credit, quickly expressed their shame for not holding a time-honoured position. As things turned out Armet and Aquilla were personally chosen by Paulinus for special commendation, which only served to enrage Balbilus the more.

'A word of advice, Armet,' Aquilla warned in parting. 'Add caution to your habits. Julius will be after your hide likely enough, given the chance. He may even invent a trumped-up charge with which to snare you, vindictive old bastard that he is.'

'The man is under constant guard, and can do no harm,' Armet spoke.

'That's when he might be at his most dangerous,' replied a concerned Aquilla, 'The old bugger has been openly shamed. We have deliberately gone against him, dented his pride. He won't forget it.' The secondus paused. 'Your being close to Quintus can hardly help.'

'In that case you'd better watch out for yourself, secondus.' Armet advised. 'You know,' he reflected, the one sure thing that Rome taught me was not to be *over* generous when it comes to matters of trust. It was a gladiator in the arena who showed me just how one must at times, play dirty.'

Aquilla's answer was a shake of the head as he led 2nd cohort away. He knew of the first meeting of his legate with Armet, and the story of Bacilon was often recalled over cups of wine.

Nevertheless, Armet would indeed be cautious. Although both men shared the blame, if blame it were, Balbilus' ire was more likely to turn on him, he a Keltoi prince rather than an aristocratic Roman secondus, like Aquilla. The fact that Armet was now a citizen of Rome would cut little ice with a man like the commander of the Valerians. The prince's fingers felt for Gort's discarded gift from Volisios in his pouch, for reassurance, suddenly feeling a dread of some future thing without name or form.

Such was the way of things, on that day.

Before his departure from the holding point of Crococalana to revisit king Tadoc, a last chance to see Gela before their betrothal two-weeks hence, the prince performed another task. He found Straba doing time for his gross disobedience in a narrow cell lit only by a small single window. Generously, Cerialis hadn't taken the lash to him upon this occasion, but a two-week diet on stale bread and water would, the legate hoped, sober the scribe sufficiently enough to curb his wanderlust. A small price to pay, the scribe considered, for gross insubordination. After that, it remained uncertain as to whether more punishment awaited him further down the line.

'I have a question before you leave, prince,' said Straba, sitting up slowly, his back still sore from his previous beating from Gallinus. 'Why did the legate not have me flogged this time? What stayed him?'

Armet grinned. 'Two reasons. For all your strange ways, and I find it difficult to say this, I have an interest in you, and I told the legate so. Let's face it, you showed more courage at Dorona than I ever gave you credit for. I thought it merited a small reward, rather than another beating.'

'I was damn useless, both of us know it, prince. Yet I doubt such praise or reward would be enough. I've seen our legate when he's upset..........'

'I mentioned two reasons Greek, which I thought it fair to mention. I suggested that you're being continually beaten on the slightest whim wouldn't look so good if you decided to incorporate the legate into your precious histories. Yet I'll gift you with some advice. If you value life, don't go wandering again. There's a limit to Cerialis' patience and to my support of you. I doubt if you'll be so lucky again.'

Later, leaving Straba both relieved and bemused, Armet and an escort of scouts journeyed to Tadoc's settlement. News there proved to be both good and bad in equal measure. Meeting with Gela, he listened to her preparations for the betrothal and about her attempts to persuade Fomah to be present at the festivities. 'He's not as sour as he pretends,' she laughed, and all was soon arranged for the ritual handfasting. Tidings of Gort's whereabouts however, were mixed, all reports conflicting, as well as puzzling, with a great deal of rumour in circulation as to whether he too, would attend the joining.

Continually, he had been reported here, there, and almost everywhere, even as far as Gaul. Various other destinations did get a mention, Parisi, Mogonus, Iceni and its queen Boadiga, plus a few others less familiar to the prince. It was quite an impressive list, but one piece of information appeared most credible. Gort had been seen in the south. According to his informer, he'd travelled in illustrious company, that of king Obrig's son, Adomarus of the Trinovante. It appeared that together, he and Gort were fast inducting fresh fighting men in support of Boudiga's cause, people greatly aroused by the Iceni's brutal treatment administered by the procurator's veterans.

'Give it up, Armet,' Culchul advised later. 'We have about as much chance of locating Gort now as it would be to find a pin in a rockpool.'

'I sense danger! My brother's cutting the meat too thinly,' Armet implored. 'For that he might bleed, with me not there to bind his wound.'

Culchul smiled. 'You worry unduly, cub. 'One day he'll turn up again, you'll see. He won't be too pleased about our failure to get Brennus, though.'

'The bastard will be found, one day,' Armet replied, a prophesy speedily confirmed by The Bear's arrival several days later at the colonia, when he was handed over to become Cerialis' unexpected prisoner.

There was other news. A late despatch from Paulinus, forwarded on by Cerialis was not what the legate of Hispanics or Armet had expected to read. The name that stood out from the report was Batavi, and they would prove to be the root of all troubles for king Volisios.

It was information of the direst sort. It appeared that a large section of Batavians had deserted Paulinus less than two day's march from Mona, one report telling of defection on a grand scale. Rome had not expected it, likewise Paulinus. But worse was to come. Within hours the deserters returned to fall upon the column with unexpected ferocity, killing many and making off with those luckless enough to be captured. Unbelievable stories of torture and mutilation were rife. When prince Armet learned of these things, one name immediately sprang to mind, that of the Batavi leader, Nardon, a man he'd encountered only briefly within the confines of Lindum.

On reflection, these acts of disloyalty weren't surprising, considering the delicate situation of religion. Ties that bind can bring about the most unusual happenings, and the relationship between Batavi and Druid covered a long period of history. It would have been wiser for Rome to pay attention to these salient facts. Ironically, she also recruited Batavi mercenaries from the European southern lowlands, connecting the relationship between them and the Druids over the years. A meeting point for dialogue, rather than the sword. All in all, perhaps their most fundamental reason, for a change of mind.

FIFTY

S TRABA HAD NO IDEA how long he'd been sleeping under the soiled blanket some considerate soul had thrown over him while he lay on the hard floor. There were no shutters at the tiny window, yet he failed to register what time of day it was. What did it matter? The scribe had the feeling that legate Cerialis hadn't done with him yet, despite the prince's interceding, only half believing he would not again be punished. Better to think nothing of what discomfort might lie ahead. To the scribe, for some reason, it no longer mattered. What he'd bravely set out to do was more than achieved. Nobody could take that away. His histories would now have substance, if he lived. The visceral terror experienced at Dorona, would mark the beginning of his work. Were he capable of smiling, he would have, but with a mouth that tasted of dry leaves and his desire for water so far going unheeded, the smile wouldn't come. Was this then to be his punishment, starvation?

Water did later arrive. The legionary lifted his frail body upright, pressing the crude chalice to Straba's parched lips. The slave whimpered at the sharp stab of pain caused by his sudden movement, a constant reminder of the supposedly lenient beating given by gladiator, Gallinus. Was it really just two weeks ago? He gratefully swallowed several gulps. 'You really are what they say you are!' said the soldier, drawing bread from his pouch.

'Mad?' the scribe choked. 'Yes, I know all about it.'

'Too bloody mad for your own good, if you ask me,' said Servilus, not unkindly. 'Look at you. existing on stale bread and slops. 'I'll say this, scribbler, for a non-combatant, you can certainly take your punishment.'

'No choice of mine,' Straba gasped, catching with his tongue, the last drops of water.

'Hey, not too much! You'll kill yourself!' Servilus warned, cuffing the frail Greek gently. 'I've been assigned as your keeper. Servilus, 2nd cohort, Hispanics, and I'd be happier if you didn't run away again, not on my watch, or I'll be severely shafted. Not that you're in any state to crawl, never mind, walk.

'You were there, in the centre?' Straba grimaced.

'Got it in one, scribbler, the bastard Brigs'. The last charge of prince Armet's heathens really saved our skins though. You were part of it, they tell me. Makes me wonder why you're still stuck in this filthy dump.'

Straba shifted his frame delicately. 'Long story, Servilus,' he replied. 'But what more of my friend?'

'My friend?' Servilus echoed. 'You ain't' got no friend, scribbler.'

'Armet, the heathen, as you put it,' The Greek stuttered.

Servilus stared down at Straba in astonishment. 'Just what is it with you? How's it done?'

Straba gave a puzzled look. 'I swear by the gods, yours and mine, I know not what you mean,' he coughed.

Servilus straightened, his brow furrowing. 'These tricks, how do you get the great and the good to your bedside? First the Coritani prince, then our legate. Both of 'em paid a visit last night, as if you were the bloody Brig' queen, and you fit as a dead 'un.'

'I've not been too well,' Straba stared up, shaken momentarily out of his semi-stupor. 'Did they really do as you say, visit?'

Servilus shook his head. 'If it were up to me, I'd be thanking the gods that one of them didn't hang me up on the cross, or maybe make me a good target for the archery butts, or worse. I'll tell you something though, scribbler, I'd throw the dice in your favour any time. I could do with your sort of luck, no bitching'

Receiving no coherent response, the lad from Tarraco withdrew. The Greek had fallen once more into unconsciousness, 'dropping off like a baby' as the recruit described later to the remaining members of the contraburnium, not surprising, considering Straba's situation. Unfortunately, the slave's slumbers were to prove even more fretful than his waking hours.

There came in his delirium a hazy dream of his parents who lived in one of the Greek inhabited townships bordering the Adriatic, part of the early poverty into which he'd been born. Later, things grew better, when a generous merchant- client enabled his father to apply his skills as a rope maker to best advantage, moving into the large southern port of Brundisium, where he was to enjoy a reasonable income for his all-too-short life. His amiable wife meantime made, then bargained, her cheap trinkets on festival days in the city's agora. They were never rich, but both businesses combined gave them enough coin to support a small family and in time, along came a daughter and then a son who they named, Straba.

It seemed he was destined for a safe, if repetitive life.

Disaster however struck eleven years later, when a vicious outbreak of plague descended on the thriving town and other coastal settlements bordering the Adriatic. With fearsome speed it carried off a substantial proportion of inhabitants, including all three members of his family, leaving him alone. With no trade or likely means of employment, his late father's rented property was seized by unscrupulous landlords, and the boy quickly fell prey to exploiters who chose to sell him into slavery.

From there, destiny saw him taken by merchant ship, along with a dozen boys of roughly the same age, to an unknown destination where a specialised market for this type of merchandise was appreciated. The ship carrying him dropped anchor at the coastal town of Catania, lying at the foot of Mount Etna. Founded a thousand years ago by Chalcidian Greeks, it would later turn out to be his saviour.

His new master, Tsabo by name, also a Greek, purchased him for an undeclared sum, probably a knee-jerk reaction of solidarity for a fellow countryman, rather than the glaringly obvious reason for such a transaction. Probably, as Straba later found out, Tsabo's cruel emasculation while a child, had much to do with it, there being rising demand for castrato singers, a fact of life encouraged early in the empire by emperor Tiberius and now much used by his fellow countrymen. This forever labelled Tsabo a 'spadone' or 'half-man,' a fate that had happily bypassed the thankful Straba. Yet his new-found mentor, obviously possessed of a character that made the best of a limiting situation allowed him over time, to acquire moderate wealth, not uncommon for certain talented castrati. No millionaire, he'd at least had the sense at the height of his musical career to buy his freedom, enabling him to indulge his commanding passion as a devoted seeker after knowledge.

Yet there remained one mysterious question for Straba. Why would a retired spadone, by dint of his profession and sexual limitations, show the least bit of interest in such an unlikely purchase as himself? Later, when the answer finally arrived, it was explained by its simpleness. Tsabo had seen in Straba a gift not often noticed by others like himself, said gift being that of a fellow spirit.

Under his guidance, Straba slowly became what Tsabo hoped he'd be, a willing pupil sharing with his protector a growing interest in the study of the stars and other mysteries, later to include a study of volcanoes and other natural sciences.

For seven years Straba was to devour many more wonders from his middle-aged mentor. How to scratch words and discover what their shapes meant, how to calculate and predict the actions of the heavens, much like that greatest of astronomers, Hipparchus, whose teachings he was destined to follow, assiduously. Yet it was the volcano that was to dominate Straba's attention while living under the shadow of Etna. Magma, gases and hot ash became no secret in his study of the mountain. For this he had to thank the dramatist, Aeschylus, of whom he became greatly enamoured. His words described the volcano's interior as the workshop of Hephaestus, and the restlessness that at times made the earth tremble was due to the angry movements of the giant Typhon, imprisoned by the great god Zeus.

Impressive stories made legend.

Yet all these things shattered, when Rome intervened!

An uprising in the town had brought its soldiers to Catania and the outcome proved exceedingly brutal. Amid the confusion, his mentor, like a thousand other inhabitants, died among the ruins of the city and Straba found himself, yet again, in chains. But something else happened that day which would leave an indelible mark. Before he was overwhelmed, desperate to defend himself, he'd picked hold of an old knife of Tsabo's, one used for the gutting of fish. Thus armed, he hopelessly prepared to take on the raiders.

His feeble effort lasted only minutes. Being overpowered, he lost consciousness from a well-aimed blow to the head. It was only much later, many miles at sea, that he learnt of his innocent mistake. The boy's name he never discovered, but he'd often seen him about the town, a cheery youngster no more than nine or ten years of age, ready to give a friendly nod in passing. His captors later found the incident amusing, as to how the Greek, lunging out at the first confused shape to enter the room, turned out to be the terrified lad who being snatched up bodily by one of his captors, cowardly used him as a shield. Straba's blade, instead of connecting with his opponent, found the heart of the boy instead. For this terrible error he was to be constantly reminded by his callous gaolers at every available opportunity.

It was from that day that he swore to the gods that he'd never allow himself to use weapons again. A noble if forlorn gesture, as it later turned out.

How he landed up in the northern wilds of Britannia, so distant from the island of Sicily, he owed to the incomprehensible logic of military statistics. Shipped to Rome, expecting to be singled out for sale in yet another marketplace, some chinless wonder of a cleric, in search of promotion, discovered that the lowly scribe could write, as well as tally and form numbers, virtues greatly appreciated by any army paymaster. Finally, he found himself transported to the alien world that was frontier Britain, controlled by Quintus Cerialis' and his Hispanic legion.

Straba awoke from his reveries in daylight. An early morning sun breasted the high sill of his cell window. A cup of wine, fresh bread and an apple lay on a platter beside him. He stared at this feast in astonishment.

'Servilus?' he muttered, but the recruit had disappeared.

Gingerly he turned, though not too much, his sore back still niggling like a thousand wasps in a nest. He was gratified for the thought, though. Real food and even wine! If they were taking the trouble to feed him, they wouldn't be about to kill him, would they?

No matter. To this Greek slave the risen sun, at that moment, rarely looked so wonderful.

FIFTY-ONE

GAIUS SUETONIUS PAULINUS, supreme governor of Britannia, stood up to his bony knees in cold water beside the inhospitable shoreline of the Menai Straits. Gazing ahead into the mist he saw little to fire the spirit. Overtaken by a dark mood regarding the near shambles at Dorona and the disobedience of his trusted friend, Balbilus, another problem niggled.

The Batavians! Or at least, enough of the bastards to cause great mayhem!

It was the last thing expected. Yet it happened, causing death and disruption, delaying the campaign, much to Paulinus' growing frustration, by several weeks. The number of deserters at first count, proved to be overstated by half. For this he made sacrifice to the gods, a precaution which gave the governor a fresh feeling of confidence, as the auguries promised total victory in the coming assault. Yet nothing could gloss-over the seriousness of the previous day's event. This wasn't merely a betrayal; it was open hatred. How else might a civilised man describe it? What vexed him more was the reality that the rebels were mostly men from the precious cavalry, tried and trusted. In his book, and he stood with Cerialis on this point, cavalry was another word for speed, and without speed an army was like a vehicle without wheels. Apart from that, the business with the Batavi was already breeding doubt throughout the various units of the task force as to its solidarity. Moral was high on the agenda, meaning that the task force must be ordered into action as soon as possible.

Every man would be needed, especially now after the desertion of the rebel Batavians. Although Paulinus possessed a credible breakdown of the opposing strength, such knowledge remained superficial. After Dorona, he was taking no chances. Then there was the ongoing problem of the boats. Upon his arrival at the crossing point, he discovered that less than half of the flat-bottomed vessels were in a state of preparedness, many others having apparently been sabotaged by Druse supporters, some of which were taken captive.

One such, naked and shivering, bleeding profusely from the lash, sagged between two troopers waiting at the governor's elbow. The name that the inquisitors forced out from him was, Halgar. Earlier, he'd deliriously mentioned a single name before losing consciousness. Orsobis! Was it this wretch and others like him who, literally, had zealously punched a hole in Paulinus' plans, boldly scuppering a sizeable number of landing craft. When put to the questioning, the boy at first feigned ignorance. Regarding the heathen as a complete lunatic, he ordered Halgar to be hamstrung, leaving him to crawl from the waterside, a meal for carrion.

Over on the far side of the Straits, hidden by grey sea-mist, sat the object of much meticulous planning, Mona. Shortly, Corbulo's successor would lead his soldiers to cut down the sacred groves of oak, fiercely cherished by the Druse. The eyes of Rome would surely be watching the event and luckily, despite earlier disappointment, Britannia's governor was set on the task ahead, furthering his reputation with an already impressive list of past victories.

He also drew heart from the timely news that his twelve triremes, with a full muster of marines, now lay anchored on the shore in Hibernian waters, off the western coast of Anglesey. Encirclement was complete! He wanted no escapees to worm their way out. On the morrow or soon after, the cult known as Druidism would be destroyed once and for all, a dangerous menace to Rome, wiped out of existence.

Optimism if well placed is a fine thing, but if over confidence emerges, the price can prove difficult indeed. His Batavians had already cost him dear, both in valuable time and expense, and for a man who was unarguably, the most powerful Roman in Britannia, doubts would be cast, and events occur in a way that even the proud victor of Mauretania, for all his vaunted fame, could possibly have forecast.

FIFTY-TWO

JUST WEEKS BEFORE the assault on Mona, two armed men rode deep into the midland forest, avoiding enemy patrols, distancing themselves from the busy military road that stretched north. The path they chose was ancient, so old that nobody alive could tell who'd built it. The Old Boar track, men called it, although a travelling Adomarus failed to see any such creature within the surrounding woodland. The pair gave their mounts free rein, avoiding easier paths, leaving them to pick their way gingerly through dense undergrowth. When the red light of dawn showed itself, they knew they must be nearing the border with the Iceni, and the wind that had blown all night, suddenly slackened.

They paid little attention to the elements, their journey consisting of a series of setbacks brought about by differing opinions and argument as to their whereabouts. 'You were right, Adomarus,' owned his young companion, Viga. 'We really had no choice but to come the longer way.'

211

'It's not so difficult when one knows the route,' answered the prince, confidently, pulling the cowl of his cloak tighter about him to help shield the burden beneath, reluctant to admit that at times he wasn't sure himself of the direction taken. 'It's what happens when we arrive, that's what vexes.'

'The babe, she does not stir?' Viga asked.'

'She sleeps.'

Finding a sheltered spot near the base of a gentle hill, they dismounted. Viga unhooked the leather pouch hanging from the saddle, drawing forth pork and bread, the last of their meagre supply. They ate in near silence, broken only by the rustle of trees.

'Are you going to wake her?'

'She needs rest. The people of the Iceni will tend her,' Adomarus said hopefully, looking askance at his companion with a hint of a smile. 'She will one day thank you though, for your aim that night, Viga. Without your intervention, that old wolf would surely have enjoyed a good supper.'

Viga managed a nervous chuckled. 'It runs in my kin,' he boasted. 'We were ever masters with the spear. Anyway, the animal was old and an easy target.' He looked down at the child again. 'She doesn't stir. Are you sure she lives?'

'She sleeps well,' said Adomarus again.' I can feel her breathing.'

'Good,' answered Viga, with a satisfied nod.

Remounting, they finally left the cover of the forest as Adomarus, only son of the imprisoned king Obrig, carefully eyed the beginnings of the track with caution. The storm arrived suddenly when the first crack of thunder rolled overhead. His horse alarmed, whirled in a circle, panic stricken, flaying at the air with its forelegs, snorting in fear. A second clap followed, causing the beast to tug frantically on the reins. Hard leather straps cut into Adomarus' palms, drawing blood. He reeled in the saddle, holding tightly to the child at his chest. Viga, coming abreast, caught with his free hand the bridle of the frightened beast. Luckily the outbursts overhead passed as quickly as they arrived and Adomarus calmed her with a light caress of a hand, whispering soothingly until she finally ceased her trembling.

When night again drew in, the pair took their rest in a glade, concealed by a grove of birch trees and Adomarus woke to the welcome sight of the rising sun. Also, the vague outline of the man blocking it. Quickly roused, cursing his lack of caution, he reached for the sword lying at his side. The stranger beat him to it, grasping the spatha by the hilt, pushing the Trinovanti none too gently away with the toe of his leather boot.

'This is no place for slumber, prince Adomarus,' the stranger warned, examining the finely wrought cavalry weapon with approval. 'A Roman patrol lies up ahead, just waiting for fools like you,' he smiled, handing back the weapon.

'How do you know my name?' Adomarus asked, relieved, though a little anxious, as he got to his feet.

'We overheard your companion mention it yesterday. You know, for a son of a brave old warrior, you appear to be a little careless.'

'Overheard?'

'On your way to the Iceni queen?' The stranger did not wait for a reply. 'Well, I too, as it happens.' Come, ride with us, you will be all the safer for it.'

Straddling horses at the bottom of the grassy slope, half-hidden by the cover of the birch, a numerous group of armed men waited in silence. Adomarus couldn't tell how many, although each seemed well provided for. Obviously, a war band. He delivered a gentle kick to Viga's ribs to awaken him, only to rouse the child also. Immediately she began to whimper while Viga, scrambling to his feet, grabbed the girl and cradled her protectively.

'Let's get moving!' the stranger said, mounting, not questioning the child's presence. 'Enough time has already been wasted.' Here he paused. 'I gather you *are* still going our way, prince?'

Adomarus replied with a slight decline of his head, a little disgruntled at being caught so lacking in vigilance.

'Safer,' the stranger said flatly. 'This way, you'll be safer. Anyhow, there's only one direction for renegades like us, right?'

Adomarus paused, 'At least, give me a name.'

The stranger smiled. 'A name? Is it that important to you?'

'Names can tell much and by your speech, I believe you've travelled south.'

'Indirectly. I'm Gort of the Coritani nation, son of king Volisios...............' For some seconds the Coritanian lowered his tousled forehead against the horse's withers, gripping the edge of the saddle, silently cursing the inconvenient return of his old malady, as he groped like a blind man until his loss of vision departed as quickly as it came.

You might have added, *also brother to prince Armet,* Adomarus inwardly mused, silently ending Gort's sentence for him, being entirely ignorant as he was, to the youth's curse. Then, no more being said, the group turned east in the direction of the Iceni capital.

FIFTY-THREE

WITNESSES WOULD LATER SWEAR that there was barely sufficient wood on the island to supply the number of crosses needed to crucify all those taken captive after several days of savage conflict.

As in Gaul, so it was now. In a short space of time the island had been reduced to the sorry status of a primitive wasteland. Ancient sites, sacred altars, together with other revered sites of worship, were systematically obliterated in a blind fury, never before experienced on such a scale. Many of the dead, their mutilated remains left to nature and the elements, would never be counted. Every human being, man, woman, child, including the new-born, lacking means to flee, had been routinely put to the sword. At many places heaps of corpses stood proof to those making a final stand against the killing machine, leaving the earth littered with scores of those who'd made the final desperate stand.

CHAPTER FIFTY-THREE

Especial treatment had been directed toward women, who not only suffered the ignominy of rape, but agonising death on the stone altars, a mockery to cement the falsified claim of human sacrifice. It would also be claimed that, not since the time of Cassivelaunus had there been such unimaginable slaughter as that carried out on Mona.

With the evening darkening, under the lurid light of blazing brands, blood flowed freely into the once unsullied streams and rivers of Anglesey as the task force began, day and night, going about the grim business of total slaughter.

Being the most powerful man in Britannia, it was expected that Paulinus would order his pavilion to be raised at some distance from the bloody carnage he'd personally created. But that would have been truly out of character. Tasking himself to see that his orders were carried out to the last letter, he commanded his tent be set up within the largest oaken circle on the island, each giant tree deputising for lack of crosses. Nailed hand and foot, the leading Druid leaders, unlucky enough not to be killed in the main battle, died lingeringly, one by one. It was here, against this background of hell-on-earth, that the governor read and re-read the news. Hands trembling with rage, ears seemingly oblivious to the agonising screams penetrating the open tarp, Paulinus silently called down the wrath of all gods on procurator, Catus Decianus, who, in his gross stupidity, had provided the governor with a situation more fraught than that of the Druse. The little Paulinus knew of Boudiga and her previous non-cooperation with Rome, after her husband's death, was enough now to force him to act with speed, leaving little further time for celebrating the victory just gained.

Salivating over what might be a suitable punishment for the traitorous wretch of a procurator, moved him considerably more than the destruction of a dirty bunch of heathen scum ever could. The crime of disobedience must be doubly repaid, he fumed. The tidings he held in his unsteady hand said all. Instructions as to the temporary halt to clearances within Trinovante lands, had obviously been ignored, an imbecilic folly that would guarantee the one thing that Paulinus had striven to avoid, a war on two fronts!

To a large extent the pincer movement used in the past fortnight, Paulinus' personal strategy had proceeded as expected. The triremes, carrying their full quota of marines, prowled back and forth on the western edge of Hibernian waters, ready to intercept any wretches who attempted to flee over the narrow stretch of sea to Ireland. Others chose to take the slim chance of escaping north into Brigante territory, a decision carrying the added risk of having to avoid watchful Roman patrols fast blocking any ways of escape.

Suetonius fully enjoyed a moment of satisfaction before its being spoiled by news of the clearances. Earlier he'd visited the circle of tall oaks where three-score ancient trees had been set aside for the most prominent of the heathens. Many bodies hanging there were already dead. Yet a few remained in the last agonising stages of life, including the one-eyed Orsobis, tutor to Halgar, who, with a last reserve of strength, launched a volley of untranslatable invective against his persecutor. On a nod from the duty centurion a legionary using the shaft of a pilum, broke the Druid's legs. His body, weakened by hours of hunger and torture, sagged instantly as he breathed his last.

Britannia's governor issued fresh orders to pursue the remaining rebels without pause. Being of a conceited disposition, a man who preferred to do things his way, he rarely delegated, yet he'd decided that Agricola take up the reins in his place and tie up the loose ends concerning the business of Mona. The tribune, surprised, accepted, although not quite certain in his mind as to how he should go about it, preferring, perhaps, to be running things from behind a desk rather than a saddle. In the long run, looking on the bright side, the experience could lead to a future promotion for the ambitious Roman.

Throwing untried men in at the deep end to see how they'd perform might not have been Paulinus' normal style, but at this moment he reckoned the young man up to the task of doing a job that any fool of a decurion could do. But there was a greater reason, a more pertinent decision for his conduct.

That evening against the continual backdrop of debauched savagery he dispatched messages to Cerialis. Being that bit closer to the centre of Iceni rebelliousness by more than a hundred miles he decided that the Hispanics were the only force strong enough to deal with the troublesome queen until he intervened. At dawn on the following day Paulinus, after a curt farewell to Agricola, left behind him several squadrons of cavalry, one legionary cohort, plus a like number of auxiliaries to make a fully functioning garrison to control the territory.

That done he turned 20th Valeria and 14th Gemina away from a vanquished isle to face the journey of two hundred and fifty miles, normally a twelve-day task for legions. Paulinus, hedging his bets, despatched word to Augusta's commander at Glevum to meet him at the half-way point of High Cross. Characteristically optimistic, he then determined to do the whole distance in ten.

FIFTY-FOUR

IN RETROSPECT, THE DRUIDS fought a surprisingly stubborn resistance against a greater, more ruthless opponent. Yet it soon became obvious that Paulinus had greatly underestimated the odds, and it was a fearsome sight that first greeted the unwanted legions, prior to fording the narrow stretch of water.

The coastline at this narrow point in The Straits facing the Romans was crowded with a vast number of defenders, many of them women, their aspect of the latter terrifying to behold, men later vouched. Those in the first assault wave confessed to feeling an unfamiliar doubt in their own ability to overcome the odds, such was their sense of shared fear. Gaining the far side, scrambling ashore, they were immediately assailed by deadly showers of missiles of all kinds, enough to force them into the shallows had not a support wave speedily hit the beach.

Those boats not disabled by Orsobis of the one-eye and his gang of helpers, were furiously pushed ahead by the oars of their crews, all the time at the mercy of a constant hail of missiles, Challenging the narrow waters, the small craft floundered precariously, rocked by the cavalry swimming amongst them. These expert riders, especially trained for crossing rivers, adopted tactics involving both horse and man, working as one. With riders swimming alongside their mounts, gripping tightly with both hands either the tail or mane, such a manoeuvre allowed for a swift negotiation of a watery barrier. But by their efforts, the churning waters toppled several craft, drowning many of their occupants.

A vicious no-quarters hand -to-hand struggle then ensued as more and more soldiers of Valeria and Gemina, aided by their back-up of auxiliaries, fell upon the defiant population of Mona. From then on it was only a matter of time before resistance crumbled under the onslaught of hard-headed professionals who'd been well taught the bloody game of war, and how to play it. Scattered groups of the enemy, dispersed and driven over the island were, in the following weeks, either put to the sword or made captive.

The brutal defeat of the Druid was the cause that severely weakened Rome's hopes of assimilation with the people of Britannia, as news of Paulinus' savage assault spread steadily to all the oppressed regions of the island.

Volisios, fearing for the safety of his people, suppressing hope while conquering infirmity, reluctantly turned to a different plan, his mind haunted by something that had not yet come about. Thus, on an impulse, setting his face south, using a recently completed part of the Via Claudius for speed without even informing Armet, he proceeded to Rina taking as many armed men with him as could be gathered, where immediately he set to work strengthening his capital's long-neglected defences. So, the man who'd for so long sought peace for his people, now turned his thoughts to war.

FIFTY-FIVE

JULIUS BALBILUS, legate in absentia, was on a mission that day. With a few bribes directed in the right quarter allowing him to make his escape, things went without a hitch. Satisfied that his name still went for something, he set his sights south with gladiator Gallinus and several long-serving followers at his command. Though he was working on a basic strategy, he'd be relying a lot on chance and flexibility when considering the overall plan.

As far as it went it depended a lot on timing. Kept sketchily aware of Paulinus' daily location after leaving Anglesey, receiving reports even while confined, enough information placed the supreme legate with some certainty at a place roughly middle distant between Mona and his supposed destination, the strongly garrisoned town and settlement of Verulamium in the territory of the Catuvellauni. With his humiliation still rampant, Balbilus fled Lindum with a positive urge to reconcile himself in Paulinus' favour while seeking to regain his hard-earned place as commander of Valeria along with his dignity.

If it were merely seen as a race, Balbilus saw no contest. The governor, together with two hard-pressed legions, encumbered as they would be by baggage laden vehicles and possible prisoners, given the distance involved, would never arrive at the destination, prior to himself. His mind racing as fast as he rode, supplied with constant relays of fresh mounts from still functioning waystations, he considered an even bolder concept.

Venovia, home to 6th cohort, Valeria, distance from Lindum, one hundred and thirty miles away, was the key.

Because of that outbreak of unrest among the local incumbents, Balbilus recalled that it had been impossible for the cohort to leave their base at the time of Paulinus' march, Venovia still enduring a daily siege, a predicament barring the cohort's physical presence from the rest of Valeria at Lindum. Five hundred legionaries! Balbilus almost salivated. There was a further attachment to be added, taking the form of a wing of auxiliary horse, and Tungrians, at that! Another four hundred. He drew strength from this, these last mentioned were no traitors like the Batavi, who'd violently turned against Paulinus' army. Rather they were a unit above suspicion, seeing as he'd seen to their training personally. Their Roman senior centurion, Titus Lucanis, was another who'd served under him in the old days of campaigning in Mauritainia. Whether he or the garrison had knowledge of the legate's present humiliating situation, he was totally ignorant, but he was nonetheless certain of Lucanis' loyalty.

Passing Ratae, which the Coritani called, Rina, he quickly gave Volisios' recently reinforced defences the once-over, feeling reassured over what he saw as the old king's hasty attempt to protect his capital in case of emergency. The process of rebuilding several gaps in the outer wall didn't go unnoticed under Balbilus' trained eye. As he saw it, the whole place was begging to be attacked. As to how many men of fighting age he may have to face, that was a guessing game. Who knew, perhaps he'd have the luck to capture prince Armet, himself, a sweet revenge. He would be the first victim. Whatever, it didn't matter, 6th cohort would, under his orders, do what was necessary, and Balbilus wouldn't disappoint. Out of this, just one hitch. For all his plotting, he hadn't been able to get close enough to slit the throat of Cerialis' scribe, also imprisoned in the colonia, the sniffling slave they called, Straba.

Had he been aware, events in the province were gaining ground swifter than any team of horses in a chariot race, more than anybody could ever have predicted. Even as Balbilus approached Venovia, seeds scattered long since were about to rise, children of the dark-cloaked grim reaper, the mythical Casi summoning an unseen force poised to end the tyranny of the alien occupier squatting in their sacred domain.

As far as Suetonius Paulinus was concerned, doggedly racing ahead almost before the blood of a thousand Druse had dried on his sword, this amounted to unfinished business with procurator Decianus over a nit-picking argument about a few pox ridden Trinovante. A far greater problem was about to upset Balbilus' plan. Paulinus, on being handed a hot report on the march, swiftly redirected his thoughts. His army now had a different objective which superseded the first, namely the bustling settlement and port of Londinium.

FIFTY-SIX

GUILTY OF A SUBLIME CASE of bad timing, Catus the procurator, greatly fearing the wrath of Nero, defiantly disobeyed Paulinus' instructions regarding the clearances, releasing his rapacious legionary veterans upon the ancient tribal capital of the Iceni, the day after Nardon's discontented Batavi turned against Paulinus' task force in the west. Picking a time when the bulk of Boudiga's fighting men were absent from the tribal capital, therefore unable to stave off further encroachment from a second force of intruders, there was little left in the way of effective resistance to Decianus' latest harassment.

Most of the defenceless Iceni unluckily in the capital that day consisted of women, children and the elderly. Many were killed, the women raped or taken away in chains to be auctioned. What men were discovered, were put to the sword. Queen Boudiga herself, after suffering the humiliation of a flogging, was forced to witness the brutal violation of her two teenage daughters.

With flames licking at the straw roof of the hall – a Roman style building standing largely untouched beside it, the procurator's men went about the serious business of looting. Hours later, with the ancient seat of Iceni power in ruins and open to the sky, Gort and his followers arrived.

During the past few months, accompanied by Tove and Dasal Hud, he'd taken many risks, riding back and forth over much of the midland sway, drawing men from scattered settlements, north and south, to the cause, rumour having become common coin over Paulinus' threat to the ancient priesthood dwelling on Anglesey.

Within a surprisingly short period, a force combining a dozen nations began converging in places where even Rome's eagles had yet to venture. A diversity of tongues voicing the desire for change, and with it, the lifting of the Roman yoke. Gort, a man driven by unquenchable will, spoke words men had long waited to hear. He held no illusions, being brother to Armet gave him a greater credence than he might otherwise have possessed, and the controversy surrounding Armet over his apparent willingness to concern himself too keenly with the oppressor went counterweight to a respect for the prince's honesty. Gort reminded himself of one basic fact, the Coritani, the proudest of the proud, children of Epona, would cleave to him, no matter what befell.

With this thought uppermost in his head, a second visit to Icenorum would be hopefully, more successful than his first. Then he'd promptly been dismissed by Boudiga, as a shallow, bootless youth, a loner without authority, blighted by bitter argument and disloyalty to father and brother, being told to go home by the haughty queen herself.

Gort's successful fortunes had changed all that. Now, in the short space of three months that ended in this shame of Icenorum, support from other nations would be welcome. In effect Decianus' veterans had unwittingly done him a favour. Until then, Boudiga's land had been a fearsome guardian of its territory, a dangerous place for Gort and other outsiders. Now, with a mix of a thousand Coritani, Cornovii and Trinovante at his back, the younger son of Volisios was confident of a better reception from the haughty, red-haired widow queen, having learned something of prudence during a busy three months. Discretely, he left the bulk of his war-band encamped a safe distance from the capital, seeing no point in provoking any knee-jerk reaction from an extremely nervous people.

Gort, together with Tove and prince Adomarus of the Trinovante, entered the crowded hall. Standing in what remained of the queen's palace, impatiently awaiting her appearance, he kept reminding himself of the many occasions when he'd tried so ardently to convince Armet to be more heedful of Rome and its power.

Do not trust Rome, lest she devour you, went the mantra.

Such was the belief. Inhuman treatment meted out to Boudiga more than backed such distrust. Thoughts of the Coritani and his father at Rina, a place not that distant from Cerialis' controlling Hispanics, continued to cross and recross Gort's mind, especially after receiving dark news from one close to Armet, that spoke of Volisios' fast-failing health. This prompted him to send a messenger to Rina in the hope of arranging a meeting with Armet at a time and place of the prince's choosing. Although to date he'd heard nothing, surely now was the time to sink personal differences.

Rough treatment experienced by the Iceni would become bleakly familiar. Offer a tribal leader a massive loan, in the case of the Iceni amounting to forty million sesterces, then owe it to such a personality as statesman, poet, and Nero's chief fixer, Lucius Seneca. Such a demand would carry with it an equally massive repayment of interest, well-knowing the sum would be nigh impossible to raise in the time usually granted.

In the Iceni's case, a carefully crafted will stating that, in order to ensure the nation's independence, Prasutagus would be advised to make over, upon his death, half of his considerable assets to Rome's reigning emperor. Unluckily for his widow, procurator Decianus was the authorised collector.

Lured by a mixture of greed and a chance for advancement, the procurator finally decided to ignore the intention of the will, fiddling the figures while pocketing a generous sum for his future needs.

What followed was inevitable, even though Rome obviously didn't see it that way. Boudiga's several rebuffs of Nero's agents gave him what he sought, an excuse to send in his land-stealing legionary veterans, mob-handed into Iceni territory. They carried through their task with a complete lack of tact, arresting members of the nobility who'd opted instead, to reject Rome's unjust decree. An immediate confiscation of property by any means, followed. Robbing the royal treasury of every available copper the procurator, for good measure, stepped-up the practice of the 'clearances,' a move extending authority into further holdings that legally, lay well beyond his personal jurisdiction.

The ultimate humiliation followed. Only later was it reported that those involved in rapine and murder were the same individuals seen running amok within the land of the Trinovante.

Adomarus' frame of mind was perhaps more deep-rooted than Gort's. As the exiled prince of his nation, he was less than surprised by the harsh treatment endured by his neighbours, knowing full well what it meant to be trapped under the iron claw of the eagle. In the space of a decade the Trinovante had gradually been subjected to similar treatment. Ongoing clearances, killings and rapine, driving into slavery those that sought to resist, bred nothing but hatred. Nobody was immune, Adomarus' family had to face ignominy and insult, notably king Obrig, betrayed and imprisoned at the request of a growing number of the worst kind of Briton in the shape of pro-Roman collaborators.

Obrig, like Prasutagus, had been one of those afforded the status of client king, even though the Iceni were an autonomous state, a fact ignored completely by both rulers who would then be forced to pay a hefty price for the folly of misjudgement. Obrig was abducted under cover of night a month before, and Adomarus hadn't seen or heard from him since. With the king's household confiscated, his would-be jailors sought to apprehend the outlawed prince, along with his close friend, Viga.

'The child was lucky and thrives with a new mother,' spoke Adomarus, his attention captured by the brace of collared hunting mastiffs seated either side of the throne on the raised dais awaiting

Boudiga. 'Viga and I were fortunate too,' he referred to the incident with the wolf.

'I'm happy that she thrives,' Gort muttered. 'Pray to the gods that things work for all of us,' he responded, fingering the cold comfort of the iron hilt of his sword as he glanced up at the heavens, now visible through a roofless hall.

With gratification he recognised familiar faces in the throng, Prototonis of the Dobunni, grey haired and bearded, standing in silent dignity, alone. Present also were others scarcely known to Gort, chieftains of the Atribates, a people absorbed by Rome at the beginning of the oppression, but who now had second thoughts as to their future. Yet perhaps the most outstanding figure yet to arrive was the famed Granacos, nephew of the already legendary Caractacus of the Catuvellauni, still waring with Rome's 2nd Augusta at Glevum.

And there was one other prominent absentee. Mogonus of the Parisi, ruler of the chariot folk, an annoying thorn who'd been piercing the flesh of Cartimandua for years, was not to be seen. Gort could only hazard a wild guess as to which way the wily old bastard was leaning.

The Coritanian eyed everything with renewed hope, convinced that many other warriors were now prepared to face the might of the overbearing enemy that was Rome. In Boudiga's hall that day, standing shoulder to shoulder in this place with such determined men, he no longer had cause to feel alone.

FIFTY-SEVEN

A SOLITARY HORSEMAN paused at the gate as the decurion stepped forward, tired eyes shaded from a ruddy glow of incandescent brands.

'I've come to interrogate the prisoner, Brennus.'

'The one to be crucified, prince?' The decurion held out a hand. 'You have a pass?'

Armet, dressed formally in his uniform of a senior equestrian, produced the written order, a small favour forged by Straba two days before.

'The legate, is he alright about this?'

'He should be, he signed it,' lied Armet.

The decurion paused, inspecting the prince under the light. A moment of closer scrutiny and recognition seemed in order. 'There are certain conditions.'

'Of course,' Armet replied, abruptly.

'We'll look after your weapons. One of my men will escort you in. We don't risk anything with those heathen scum, especially this bastard. I've come across a few murderous Brigs' in my time, but this one................'

'Gives you trouble, does he?'

'Nothing that a taste of my whip won't manage.'

Due to the gear the prince wore, along with a decent grasp of Latin, the guard commander was a little over condescending, perhaps aware of Armet's familiarity with his legate. Armet opened his cloak. 'I'm unarmed.'

The man chuckled. 'You're a brave un', and no mistake. You don't know the Brig very well, obviously. Given a half chance, he'd tear your throat out with his fingernails. That's why you're getting an escort.'

The news that he'd been thwarted in his search for Brennus hit Armet like a thunderbolt. Cartimandua had been way ahead of him. Now he knew why the queen had paid Balbilus' advance guard a royal visit the morning of the second assault. The irony of all this was the fact, later discovered by an equally furious Aquilla, that the leader of the Abrentii had been snaffled speedily away by Vellocatus and a band of the queen's loyal followers at the height of the battle, which meant her plan had been concocted just prior to her unexpected appearance.

Armet, having been cunningly cheated of his quarry, felt bitter shame and disappointment and couldn't be pacified. 'That damn she-bitch got the better of all of us,' Culchul swore. 'Nobody caught on to her little game. I'm just as much to blame, perhaps even more so.'

Despite this setback, Armet had to raise a cup to her calculated temerity. On tackling Cerialis on the subject he'd come up against a stone wall. For some reason any dealings with Cartimandua often brought out the legate's testy side, and he privately forbad Armet not to go within a hundred yards of Lindum's, still half-built prison. Hence Straba's false pass.

Inside the dimly lit cell block he heard the outer door close, waiting while one of the jailers produced the appropriate key. Not for the first time he asked himself why he was here, in this dank and hopeless place. What was the purpose and what would be gained, unless it were some conscious inner salving.

'You've already crossed Cerialis on this matter, cub. Whatever he plans, he has his reasons,' spoke Culchul Hud, catching a firm grip of Flavia's bridle. 'What craziness makes you think you can get away with it? What words of any sort can pass between you and that Abrentii swine that can serve any purpose? The bastard hates us as much as we hate him. The bear and the wolf, that's what it amounts to. It was always so.'

'You fret too much,' Armet said, pulling the bridle forcefully away from his uncle's hand.

'You're beginning to sound too much like young Gort,' Culchul admonished. 'Do you really think the Romans won't get wind of this? Are you a lunatic?' he continued in frustration. 'What did you learn in Rome that lifts you so high in her affairs?' The anger in the older man's voice was subdued, to be replaced by a pang of bitterness. 'You return to us, you wear the gear and mouth their damn tongue, thinking you possess the answer to all our ills. I tell you, in the eyes of a man like Cerialis, we are merely servants to be used, where and when he chooses.'

'Easy for you to talk, uncle,' muttered Armet, a mite unkindly. 'Like Gort, you don't have to lead.'

Culchul grimaced. 'Of course, you are right, cub, I don't. Instead, I'm left with a heedless Coritani prince to make useless council with.'

Admitted to the cramped room, lit now by a single oil-lamp, he regretted his churlishness with Culchul, a man who'd almost taken the place of his brother, the fast-ailing king.

Before him a vague shape sat, arms upraised where iron rings held both wrists in chains. The legionary kicked the figure roughly with a studded boot. The form stirred and shifted, leaning his back against the wall. Eyes stared out to pierce the pale luminosity like two angry darts. Armet, removing his helm so that the prisoner could see his face, bent forward. 'The heathen's all yours, sir, best to watch him, though', said the jailor, adding, 'We'll both be outside, should he need a slap.'

In silence the prince of the Coritani stared down at the almost unrecognisable figure of a man who'd been his nation's enemy for twenty years or more, a man he'd never actually met face to face, till then. Armet felt blood rush to his cheeks while his heartbeat increased. He tried stilling all emotion, yet his hand trembled.

Brennus was known by many names. Sometimes called Artgenos, the red haired one, he also answered to 'The Bear', Ring-Giver and scion of the Abrentii Brigante, half-brother to queen Cartmandua. When Brennus spoke, the hollowness of it took Armet by surprise, sounding a little strange to his ear, not being familiar with the harsh northern dialect.

'The gods told me that the day could arrive when I'd meet with the Roman lacky, prince Armet, first cub of that doddering old fool, Volisios,' Brennus said, his voice gathering strength. 'I chose not to believe them, then. I see now, I was wrong.' Brennus swallowed, licked a dry lower lip. 'Last time I saw you, you were lying on your belly, grovelling in shit. Had I known what I do now, that you would give yourself over to Rome, I would have killed you, there and then.'

The prince continued to stare, vainly attempting to fathom what lay hidden behind the heavily lined face of this man, bruised and scarred as he was. This renegade was the creature he'd sought for so long, the mother and sister killer, yet it hardly seemed worth it all now, not for this.

'For someone soon to die, you seem very calm,' he found himself saying at last.

'You think I fear death, Coritan?'

'No, I don't think that.'

'Perhaps you've come to gloat, like my damn sister?'

'I never gloat over fallen enemies.'

'What *does* bring you here, then?'

'Perhaps the gods have sent me, out of curiosity.'

Brennus squinted, blinked, shook his red head vigorously. 'Tell me, whose gods are these, Rome's or mine, Mars or Andraste?'

'The gods are the gods,' Armet answered, icily.

'I see they taught you well in Rome, for that is what I thought you'd say. Yet I ask again, why come?'

'You know about me, about Rome?' Armet asked.

Brennus managed to wipe his chin, despite the shackles. 'Who does not?'

Armet hesitated. 'I've hunted you and your murdering clan for many a year, and you've ever managed to slip from my grasp, even at Dorona, where I still held hope.'

'Brennus managed to make what sounded like a laugh. 'Many lesser men have sought me. Count yourself fortunate prince, that it's happened at last.'

'You slew my mother and sister after Taghe and Varan had violated them, and then you left my father, crippled,' said Armet, quietly.

'Your old Volisios' spawn, for sure, easily spotted, despite your gear,' Brennus grunted. 'Well, if you've come to kill me, do it. Rather it be you than those Roman pigs. If you can't, sod off and send your brother instead.'

Armet looked startled. 'Why him especially?

'Because he's like me in taking our fight to Rome,' Brennus croaked. 'You could do your nation a mighty favour by following him. Flog Roman arse, not kiss it!' The Abrentii leader made a sound that might have been a laugh.

'I do Volisios' will,' Armet returned, defensively.'

'Volisios is wrong!' Brennus replied, eyes blazing. 'Maybe I should have killed him too, when I had the chance!'

Heavy chains rattled in their iron grips as Brennus shifted, scorn glazing over his eyes. 'I've a good idea who sent you, and I understand that you must lap dog fashion, do Rome's dirty work, or find yourself beside me on a cross. It could happen, you know?' he added, with a wide smirk.

'Nobody sent me.'

'I'll tell you something for nothing, no bargaining,' Brennus whispered, confidingly, as if there were such a privilege, ignoring the jailor and gripping Armet by the sleeve. Up close, the smell of him invaded the nostrils. 'We all bear wounds inflicted by others, including us Brigante, ask my bitch of a sister, that efficient betrayer, Cartimandua. A week ago, I lost Taghe. Later that same day I learnt that Varan too, died from a fatal wound. That's how it is. Our fates were written long before my people and your nation began their feuding. We have been wrong in that, but things will change.'

'I know one thing that won't change, my disregard for you and your breed,' Armet spat, still attempting to tug his arm away. 'I only wish it was my sword that had sent them and you, to Arawn's realm.'

'I'll take hate rather than sympathy from a dog's body to Rome, any day,' muttered Brennus, finding new-found strength as he attempted to rise. 'Yet change is close. Ask one of the Barddas, if you can find any alive, after what happened on Mona. Soon you'll be forced to choose between head or heart. That, I and my friend, Venutius, can promise you!'

'How did your sister manage it?'

Brennus leaned back against the wall. 'When you're fighting up front, you don't expect a blow from those behind,' he spat. 'Vellocatus was quick, I'll say that. He and his minions carried me to the rear, as if to treat me for a non-existent wound. Instead, they had me trussed up like a chicken and, before I knew it....................'

230

CHAPTER FIFTY-EIGHT

'Difficult to believe.'

'You were not there,' grunted Brennus with undisguised satisfaction. But should there be an afterlife, I shall laugh about it for eternity, and how, for the rest of your existence, you'll curse yourself for being robbed of vengeance after all those years seeking it.'

'No more time, sir,' the legionary cautioned, entering the cell with his companion. 'I've already gone against orders, as it is. The optio in charge will have my nuts squeezed if you stay longer.'

Armet ignored the jailor. 'Crucifixion's no death for a warrior.'

At that, Brennus laughed harshly while the prince pulled away, wresting himself at last from the prisoner's grip. 'Neither is shame, Coritan.'

One of the legionary's, half drawing a knife from his belt, came forward and viciously kicked out at Brennus, knocking him heavily against the cell wall. Armet intervened, pulling the man away. 'You'd do better by giving the prisoner some food, rather than beating him,' he advised with a nod in the prisoner's direction.

The legionary grinned down at the condemned man and jangled his bunch of keys. 'Where's the bleedin' sense in that?' he grinned. 'The Brig will be food for crows this time tomorrow.'

'I hope it's quick,' was all Armet said in parting. A wry grimace was the only sign of acknowledgement from the prisoner as the closing of the cell door returned The Bear to stygian darkness.

FIFTY-EIGHT

THE MILES STRETCHED ahead for Paulinus. A challenging journey for cavalry, even more so for those on foot. It would prove to be a gruelling trek for the army. During the first few hours, hounded by hostile skirmishers riding sure footed ponies, Paulinus already began to question his rash decision.

Riding briskly ahead, already annoyingly behind schedule, the supreme legate at last reached the isolated fort of Cymbroda, or High Cross. To his disappointment he found the site completely abandoned, no sign of any support from legion Augusta, a dire situation begging for answers. The reason was soon forthcoming by messenger. Either legate Galtiore or prefect Postumus, whichever one of them being in charge, apparently ignoring Paulinus summons while juggling the odds against a constant threat from the Silures opted, in the interest of Glevum's security, to keep 2nd legion confined to Glevum. Paulinus now felt a burgeoning situation beginning to thrust its entire weight upon him, and not in his favour.

After weighing the miserable lack of choice available, he had no option but to press on with the cavalry, his need to link up with Cerialis' Hispanics at some convenient spot now gaining urgency with every passing hour. From the number of reports coming down the line, it seemed obvious that Paulinus was about to encounter a full- scale rebellion.

Trailing almost two day's march behind him, the infantry received orders to abandon the cumbersome wagons, a command that was thankfully obeyed, though not without complaint from some. A few oxen-drawn vehicles carried assorted religious items of gold, ivory and silver, collected from Mona, much of it looking to be sold in the marketplace. Several others, weighed down by weapons, horse trappings, oaken spear-shafts topped with burnished heads, torcs of silver and bronze, copper ornaments and trinkets, all robbed from the sacred shrines, would be saved for later evaluation. All other traffic would be discarded, including a sorry group of captives. There weren't many that had escaped the days of the killing frenzy, perhaps roughly a hundred in number, those who for various reasons, might have fetched a comfortable price. But because of an instinctive desire for haste, plus an awareness that every hour was vital, Paulinus viewed his prisoners as nothing more than unwanted burdens. After selecting a dozen of the more attractive specimens from both sexes, those remaining were immediately put to the sword.

Back with Paulinus, another galloper came at speed along the dusty track that eventually led to Glevum. The perspiring rider fetched-up before the governor and slid, tired and exhausted, from the saddle. He recognised the officer immediately. This man was no ordinary carrier, his name was Clodius Nerva, senior advisor on prefect Postumus' staff. His sudden appearance only heralded further trouble along the way, with the news worse than even Paulinus himself could have imagined, though it did give him a few answers by way of exchange.

In truth, 2nd Augusta *had* staged a mutiny, Clodius Nerva explained. Facing down their officers and refusing even to consider leaving the relative safety of the colonia, was an unforeseen move. This went partly to explain their non-appearance at Cymbroda. Relieved of his post, the camp prefect was being restrained. As for Augusta's legate, the indisposed Galtiore, nothing was known as to his actual condition. Paulinus could only promise a greatly vexed Clodius that, when the time came, responsible heads would certainly roll.

Not knowing how long it would be before reaching his personal take on civilization he drafted an order that all remaining edible food salvaged from the wagons was to be shared - a scorched-earth policy having been adopted by the rebels - which meant each man had now to carry extra weight along with his gear, plus an added instruction to eat sparingly.

Another setback plagued Paulinus, another score to settle, his being further angered by the actions of Catus Decianus, the procurator. Apparently, he now faced an insurrection led by king Obrig's son, Adomarus, at Camulodunum, most likely the result of the flagrant disregard for the governor's explicit orders regarding the clearances. Another order recklessly ignored and a further head to be added to a growing list. More worryingly, Adomarus hadn't sufficient power to make such a reckless challenge to Roman authority without support, and Paulinus didn't have to throw the net far to suspect her who gave it.

Heat continued to be an annoying constant, yet the driven army, greatly discomforted, trudged on. There was only one consolation, most of the annoying raids carried out by shadowing war bands had petered out. Over time it grew harder to measure which of three conditions were the worst, hot weather, the enemy or slow starvation? Inevitably, before long, sickness began to plague the straggling column, dysentery and sudden fever, spreading fast among all ranks. Things may have been easier had Paulinus possessed the usual medical detachments assigned to a legion in the field. For reasons disclosed only later, these proved to be woefully inadequate when tackling a rapidly changing situation.

Another three days saw the bulk of the army gradually eat up the distance. Paulinus, placed well up front, eager to reach the centre of action wherever it might be, led them on. That given morning, after he and the cavalry finally crossed the official frontier, the Roman Limes south of the Coritani capital of Rina, Paulinus allowed for one brief stop-over in order to make sense of the latest batch of reports concerning rebel progress. There he made a snap decision, one that would alter everything. Hastily scribbling further instructions to legate Cerialis as to his intentions and calling up a fresh horse, he hurried on his way.

His objective, a disconcerted Cerialis learned, would no longer be Verulamium, but the imperial port of Londinium.

FIFTY-NINE

B OUDIGA LEFT THE HALL to return later. She wasn't alone. Dressed in gaudy attire of a lightweight tartan cloak and breeches and accompanied by two large hunting dogs who squatted dutifully at her feet, either side of her chair, she silently surveyed the scene. Two pallid teenage girls, dwarfed by the decorated throne of oak on the raised dais, took their places to sit silently upon cushioned stools, heads lowered, braided hair reaching down to their waists. For one moment Gort could have sworn that one of them nervously caught his eye, only to realise later that it was a trick of light from the many blazing torches encircling him. 'Which one of you answers to the name of Gort of the Corieltavi?' Boudiga asked, searching the assembly with a roving stare.

Gort, hearing his name pass Boudiga's lips, exchanged a brief look of surprise with Dasal before pushing his way through the throng to reach the base of the dais. 'Corieltavi?' he questioned, 'that was indeed my people's ancient title, queen, long out of use by the time Rome came. Now we are known as Coritani.'

'Well, Gort of the Coritani, let's get up to date. Why is Armet, brother and prince, absent from this gathering?'

'He seeks Brennus, our detested enemy,' Gort answered, hoping he sounded confident.

'Yet I hear Brennus is Rome's enemy, too?'

Gort stood silent, he felt naked before the widow of king Prasutagus. How was he to answer that? He was uncomfortably aware of his sudden vulnerability before the watching host. Not for the first time, he inwardly cursed his older brother for landing him in a compromising situation, not of his making. Typically, whatever occurred, he was still treated like the infant of the family.

'Is it not correct, that prince Armet and Volisios still favour Rome?' the queen prompted.

'In what they've always seen as a vain hope to protect our people, then yes,' Gort retorted, damping his anger, 'as your husband at one time believed.' He was on edge and aware that his tongue shouldn't get the better of him. 'It's complicated,' he blustered at last, fronting up to a woman clearly more than a match for himself. *But don't goad me like an animal*, he thought, even as he replied. 'I've laboured hard for every man who follows me,' he uttered, his voice rapidly rising despite himself, causing Boudiga's two attending mastiffs to lift their heads, one of them growling menacingly, already half-way to its feet.

'That is so, I will vouch my life for it.' Adomarus of the Trinovante, who'd stood silent in the hall of the Iceni beside Gort all the while, now came boldly forward in support. 'For many months,' said Adomarus, 'my friend and Dasal Hud have been sounding out loyalty to our cause, travelling the byways of many nations, giving heart to all who wish to throw off the yoke that seeks to make minions of us all. Gort is thus a worthy man in my eyes, and above suspicion!'

'You are fortunate to have such a stout defender as Adomarus, for a friend,' Boudiga spoke, her voice rising until the clamour of many tongues fell away. Her voice softening, she gave a half-smile. 'I have ears too, as well as eyes, young Gort. I already know your worth, even if your brother does not.'

'The prince will as ever do whatever he thinks is right,' said Gort, defensively.

Boudiga nodded. 'You are all witness to the shame the proud Iceni have endured. You see for yourselves that the Romans are not only common robbers, but they also wish to enslave all in the process. We'll need men like Gort and Adomarus now the fire is kindled,' she raised her voice again so that all assembled might hear. 'Today we have news that the priests and the folk of Mona have fallen to the unnatural beast, Paulinus. I also have it on good authority that he's ordered that playboy and Cartimandua's latest plaything, Cerialis, to join forces with him. He means to put us down, thoroughly. Rome will be in some hurry, so the cavalry will leave Lindum first, if they haven't already. It will be you, friend Gort, who must delay them, any way you can, to give us precious time. Can you do it?'

Gort hesitated, then nodded.

'There are plenty of fighting men backing you, more than enough,' said Boudiga, a mite sarcastically, annoyingly addressing him like some adolescent, he thought. 'The Iceni are decisive people when roused and we are many. Just delay Cerialis yet be heedful. Sadly, some of our people nearer home, those that give Rome aid and comfort, will be watching.'

Later, when Gort sat alone, he pondered on the Queen's last remark, remembering a similar concern voiced by Mogonus while at Petrava. There were many traitorous Britons serving Rome in one capacity or another, and without up-to-date confirmation,

Armet might still one of them. If there were traitors in his war band, he would deal with them. The bigger question was, with legate Cerialis on his way, would Armet's command, many thousand strong, side with Cerialis or oppose him? Most of all, could this be the situation he'd secretly dreaded all along, ever since the brothers last bitter exchange in what seemed a lifetime ago? These were all questions to which Gort had no answer.

At least there was news of a better nature, recently received from his uncle. Brennus, scourge of Volisios, had finally been apprehended, though sadly not by the Coritani, and The Bear lay rotting in Roman Lindum rather than Volisios' Rina, a prisoner of Cerialis.

Not knowing quite why, Gort immediately dispatched a rider carrying a word-by- mouth reply to Culchul's tidings, together with a near-friendly message for his brother as to his intents, the latter of which he'd already began to regret.

In the early light of morning, over an untidy breakfast consisting of cold pork followed by a generous amount of ale, further plans were made at Icenorum as to how and when to unchain the British wolf waiting to devour Rome's eagle. By the light of dawn, more than fifty tribal chiefs and their followers had made the pledge. One such, the Dubonni leader, Prototonis, joined with Gort, bringing with him over one thousand men. All that was needed now, was a welcome sign from the gods.

This was the time when Gela's ever-present illusions shifted rapidly in the direction of reality. The phantom horsemen, so often filling her dreams, were wraiths no longer. Indeed, for it would be blindness not to notice the arrival of a constant procession of strangers who sat encamped outside her father's hall. The speakers for many peoples from other nations conferred with king Tadoc and her brother Fomah. Much of what she heard passed over her, but she could still use her eyes. Over the days many scores of fighting men, mounted and on foot, using hidden paths, had found their way to Rina. Once she thought she caught a glimpse of a slight figure she could have sworn was Gort. But the sighting was brief, and she couldn't be sure. But that is what the wayward

Gort had become to those who knew and loved him, an indistinct mirage to be imagined in many places across Britannia, whether being there or not.

The time for Gela passed snail like, for she was desperate for news. Where did her beloved Armet stand in all this? Was he really a traitor as some suspected? Why had he not yet come to her as he'd so faithfully promised? On impulse, with all these questions buzzing about in her head she saddled a horse and, under cover of a cloud covered night, left Tadoc's settlement accompanied by two trusted men in the king's service, and made her way in haste south toward the Coritani capital. At daybreak, when her absence was discovered, the king conferred hastily with Fomah. Clearly uneasy, no amount of comforting calmed his fears. His land had suddenly become part of something else, and he no longer felt he was in complete control, his position being governed by forces stronger than his. The news that his old friend, Volisios, had fallen into a serious sickness, didn't help. The times were changing, and he would be forced to change with them, for good or ill.

There were other concerns to be addressed. If and when trouble came, his people must be ready to meet it. Naturally Tadoc's greatest worry was a mere day's ride and three words away, *Cerialis' Hispania legion*! The king had learnt enough about the legate's of-the-cuff tactics from Armet, to make him ever more wary.

Cerialis was extremely impulsive and was indeed known for bucking the trend. At times it paid off, as it had done with Cartimandua, she who possessed like Janus, two opposing faces. It was rumoured that he'd bedded her. But salacious stories become the richer in the telling, while the legate, uncharacteristically, chose reticence. Three years before, her one-time husband, Venutius attempted to finally topple his wife from power. He may have succeeded, were it not for Cerialis' unexpected intervention. Going against an order of Didius Gallus, a previous governor, not to intervene, he instead responded by moving one third of his legion into Brigantia. There with reassurances to the queen he restored her to power, temporarily leaving his soldiers to guard her capital until sure that sufficient order was restored. As things stood, with Suetonius Paulinus busy in the west, the only realistic power within a large area of the province lay under the control of the legate of legion Hispania, a situation of which he was well aware.

The deployment of such a large army could not go unseen for long, meaning it would be a matter of hours before Rome's agents alerted Cerialis. Meanwhile Fomah organised contingency plans. All non-combatants, women, children and the frail were immediately evacuated into the depth of the forest that covered most of Cornovii land. War-bands would then be called in, ready to support the Coritani. Should all end in battle, the gods would decide whether or not Tadoc's people would survive.

Thoughts of Armet too, raised questions, while the absence of his daughter was a further vexation Tadoc could have done without. A mad minx indeed, so anxious to be with her prince that she chose to desert her father now, when the times were uncertain. She'd left him, riding with only her companion, Ulvina and two trusted warriors for protection, leaving the king burdened with worry.

Earlier Fomah, with a score of followers had ridden out to intercept Gela but, possessing little indication as to exactly which path she'd taken, he reluctantly felt obliged to give up. Muttering many a curse, he angrily swung his horse back along the fruitless trail he'd ridden only a few hours before. Now, he must help Tadoc. prepare for a probable war.

SIXTY

THE NEWS CERIALIS RECEIVED proved as bleak as it was unexpected. Details of the problem with the Batavi had trickled through like water from a leaking gourd, each hasty message appearing more confusing than any previously dispatched, hardly good tidings to slap on a legion's daily order board.

The action of a trusted auxiliary unit wasn't enough to alter the present situation, though it did signal that all bets regarding a status quo, were off! Later dispatches announcing the supreme legate's defeat of the Druse failed to lift his spirits, but news indicating growing unrest in the south, immediately put a different slant on things. The need for urgency was paramount, yet whatever Paulinus' situation, it would do little to change Cerialis' personal gripe, one that had plagued him throughout his entire tenure at Lindum, namely the numbers game. In the early hours of a dull morning, he ordered Hispanic's senior commanders to attend the noisy praetorium, where a heated exchange took place over the options available. It was there, historically, that queen Boudiga's name was first recorded in the busy toing and froing of dispatches.

Like ripples in a pool, the business of treachery was enough to send alarm bells ringing through every imperial post in the province, large or small. At Lindum the effect gave a particular cause for concern. If the garrisons within Cerialis' sphere of influence were alerted, it followed that others would too, and daily there were palpable signs of unrest getting ever closer to Lindum. At integral areas of the border, units facing the unpredictable Brigante were placed on high alert, a wise and precautionary measure.

Greater cause for worry was the recent incident at the cavalry holding point of Crococalana, much closer to home. There a sudden confrontation between men of Hispania and Armet's scouts erupted into a violent scuffle. After the Coritani departed, leaving one dead and several wounded legionaries behind them, Cerialis ordered their immediate arrest. The main culprit was named Machai, a long-time friend of the prince. The legate, still trusting to the benefit of the doubt, drew on the side of caution that Armet hadn't yet been informed of the incident, and a full explanation was still forthcoming. There was only one problem, Armet and the Exploratores seemed to have evaporated like corn-chaff on the wind.

Cerialis had Machai brought before him. The legate had only one question to put. In which direction had the prince gone? To this enquiry, on receiving no satisfactory answer, the prisoner was returned, this time in chains, to the dank cells below Lindum.

An added headache, internal this time, arose in the management of Julius Balbilus, a lesser event than that involving the Batavi, yet one that Cerialis could have done without. Ironically, against better judgement, he'd already planned to release the disgraced legate from close arrest, for with things as they were, there seemed little sense in guarding the prisoner forever, having no idea whether Paulinus would even plan a return to Lindum.

But as so happens in life, fate had taken a hand. Not waiting for any show of clemency from his jailor, Balbilus, somehow bribing the guard detail, under cover of night and accompanied by the gladiator, Gallinus, together with several loyal gallopers, had already shown Lindum a clean pair of heels. Part of his strategy was a bold one - take back 20th Valeria from his long-time deputy, Arius Longa, with or without Paulinus' say-so. A risky move, by any admission. Cerialis' response was to inwardly shrug shoulders while raining down curses on the departed veteran.

Regarding the future of slave, scribe and would-be historian, Straba, Cerialis decided that the insolent Greek's solitary confinement should continue for a while yet. Keeping him in his meagre cell, living on scraps and watered-down wine from the legionary cookhouse might, the legate hoped, go some way in curing him of his compulsive nature. By doing so Cerialis knew he was once again bucking the system. Under Roman law, he had every right to condemn his prisoner to crucifixion, a not unknown punishment for lesser crimes. The legate couldn't even explain such unusual conduct himself, only in so far that he perceived there was something more to his unfortunate scribe than he'd yet discovered. In not severely punishing Straba's odd conduct, the legate displayed what could only be described as an inexplicable fondness for his habitual defector, though he'd never admit it.

All those who'd plied their trade along the overcrowded riverbank were the first to sniff out changes in Lindum's fortunes. Two days before, acting on an uncanny scent for trouble, they performed a near-supernatural vanishing trick. In doing so, they did Cerialis a favour, allowing him to create a clear field of fire for the archers, which later turned out to be necessary. Thus, a large area of humanity, under the shadow of The Hill, a self-sufficient shanty town, crammed with garish multicoloured tents and ragged awnings had, in less than twenty-four hours, become open wasteland. A bustling area of activity, awash with a mixture of camp-followers, chancers and pimps, had fast disappeared, as if by magic. Little was left, apart from a pile of discarded detritus. But the crosses would remain to jog men's memory, half of them remaining still haunted by their lifeless corpses.

Written down, the changing situation indeed looked dire! Take away the few larger garrisons administered by the Hispanic legion along the via Claudius, plus an assortment of smaller forts consigned to vulnerable areas of doubtful loyalty, the colonia's remaining strength, including auxiliary units, amounted to less than six thousand men. Had the legate been possessed of more legionary muscle, he might have faced the present threat with greater confidence. The order to meet up with Paulinus near Verulamium, a hundred and thirty miles distant, with a part of the route reportedly occupied by rebels, was challenging. He hoped reinforcements from those several military stations along the way would assist him on the march. A somewhat dubious hope, as things stood.

Reluctantly these dangers, from that day, now included the usually obliging Coritani, on whose land, eleven years before, the seeds of Roman Lindum were first sown. Cerialis had from the start of his tenure, put a lot of trust in young prince Armet, a relationship based on fragile respect and necessary tolerance formed in a very different place, the word 'fragile' being uppermost. Now something very strange was entering the landscape. Just how strange, the over-stretched legate was about to discover.

SIXTY-ONE

S ERVILUS' CONTUBERNIUM had been especially selected to oversee the punishment of the Abrentii leader known as Brennus the Bear. All were aware that selecting the group of men for the messy task of crucifixion was centurion Iber's doing, another vindictive way of petty revenge for the humiliation brought upon him by the young recruit from Tarraco, who continued to spurn a stream of unwelcome advances. It went without saying that the decision hadn't made Servilus the most popular man in the cohort, crucifying someone not being one of the most sought-after duties of the day.

The few legionary witnesses about at this early hour were unimpressed by a not unfamiliar sight of an execution squad marching with the condemned to the point where the crosses waited, most of the early risers still possessing sore heads from the consumption of too much strong wine recently arrived from Portus Londinium. For some it had been a heavy night. Now they were paying for it.

'You should have let him get his bloody leg over,' was the major criticism the recruit had to endure from his companions as they dragged their stumbling burden to meet his fate. 'Had you not been so bloody high and mighty,' muttered Philo, accusingly.

'Make sure you take another cup of drink with the rest of us,' had been the advice of the cross-master in charge, 'you'll be glad of it when your man starts to blubber.' This officer wasn't familiar to the men of the contuburnium, but the importance of their prisoner merited the attentions of a specialist, much to Iber's regret. Although he'd gladly have accepted the post, he could at least gloat over Servilus' discomfort, even if only a muted sadism could be got. Best of all, he'd pulled a few strings to be there.

'Make it clean and make it quick!' advised the cross-master.

With the approach of day, they arrived at the row of vacant crosses. Five unusually, stood empty. The sixth lay on the ground, ready to receive the prisoner. Close to the river a stout timber whipping post awaited. To this a silent, some would later say, too silent, Brennus, was immediately manacled. Servilus had seen a few such punishment posts at various places on and around The Hill. Over time, all had been well used.

Iber, leering, came to stand over the recruit, a cold smile of triumph crossing his pitted face before being shoved aside by the cross-master. Servilus took a small box from the master's hands and set it down. The supervising decurion stooped and removed a trio of nails, placing them in a row upon the earth, each laid in unison with the final rhythmic falls of the lash.

Far out on the marsh came the doleful boom of a bittern as dawn invaded the slobland, while Servilus and the rest of the contubernium silently brought all known blights down on Iber's head, for they knew he'd come to witness their discomfort. The recruit searched his mind for a reason as to why he was there, but think as he may, he found none. He was there, and he'd been ordered there, that was the reality.

At his feet the Witham flowed, a silent witness. A gentle breeze cooled his brow as a small group of riders suddenly drew rein before him. Unsurprisingly, as the colonia's senior officer, legate Cerialis was among them. Oddly, Armet of the Coritani, mortal foe of the condemned, seemed to be missing from the small assembly, there to witness justice to be carried out in Rome's name.

Brennus, a pair of blooded breeches his only garb, dragged roughly by Hastas and the decurion to the post, was hastily shackled. Another opened a scroll containing the reason for the coming execution, an act which seemed hardly necessary, given the circumstances.

Nervously, Servilus stood awkwardly by, while his comrades laid the now naked Abrentii parallel with the wooden instrument of death. The bruised brow of the condemned furrowed as his lacerated back came into raw contact with the cross beam. Servilus looked away while, with Hastas, he blindly assisted the placing of the Briton's wrists against the wood. This man was, despite the flogging, strong enough yet to resist. Servilus felt sweat running into his eyes as they struggled. Words poured in a torrent from the rebel's swollen lips. The tongue he spoke sounded like a bad attempt at camp-latin, but Servilus couldn't be certain. Only one word sounded familiar to Servilus, that of, *Armet*.

Someone leaned forward, dealing a heavy blow to the Abrentii's face as Glabas the Joker grabbed the iron nails. 'Hold him!' ordered the sweating master. 'He'll start jumping like a jackass in a minute!'

The hammer fell as the first of the wrist spikes were driven through flesh and sinew. At that moment the captive uttered a scream, quickly followed by a hellish keening as the second nail was driven home. Vomiting what contents remaining in his gut, Brennus grunted, tossing his head from side to side, growing momentarily silent as he drifted in and out of consciousness.

'What in the name of the gods are you doing, soldier?' scolded the cross master, grabbing the hammer from Glabas with a frustrated curse. 'Give it here, damn you! Hold the bastard's legs, someone, or do you want to be here all bloody day?' The third and largest nail, driven through his ankles, finally secured his feet to the base of the cross.

Several of them lifted and set the base of the crucifix into the deep hole dug for it. For a moment the cross juddered, bringing a further cry of agony from the victim. A little later the twisted figure sagged. Somebody pierced the body with a sword. There was hardly any sign of movement. The man might have been drugged, as there was so little life still to be seen in him, a strange reaction in one so strong, thought the cross master. Tamping down any loose earth round about, their task completed, the contubernium turned away. Of Cerialis and the recently arrived horsemen there was no sign, making Servilus wonder why the buggers had bothered to show in the first place. Feeling unsteady, he stared down at hands covered in the blood and spew of the rebel, finding it extremely difficult not to throw up on the spot.

When Cartimandua later received news of her half-brother's end, she said prayers to Taranis and her favourite of favourites, Arianrhod, goddess of rebirth and fate, her own precious silver wheel. The *fate* was Brennus's while the *rebirth* was a life without a troublesome and embarrassing relative, once allied to the menacing presence of a strong Venutius who, in happier days, once shared the northern queen's bed and throne.

SIXTY-TWO

IT IS STRANGE how dangerous circumstances can at times work in one's favour. Against a background of fast-moving events, legate Balbilus had pushed aside all odds, to reap a personal whirlwind of unimaginable luck.

His arrival at the small wayside base of Venovia, on the via Claudius, was to present a chance to free himself from the indignity of Paulinus' response to the legate's open disobedience. Linked to a burning shame from the combined accusations of Cerialis, the lapdog secondus, Aquilla, and the devious Coritani prince, the injured Balbilus considered he'd been unjustly served.

Miraculously, due to some unexplained oversight when calling in Valeria's legionaries from their posts within the province, two imperial centuries of 7th cohort, three hundred men when the usual auxilia were added, had been inexplicitly missed from the final muster. At the time of decision, little protest was made, not even from Balbilus.

The situation was of the kind that fired the determination of a man like the legate. Stuck in the kind of limbo that was Venovia, although news of the taking of Dorona had filtered through, men remained conveniently ignorant that Balbilus no longer served as their official legate. Mentally rubbing hands to celebrate his possible good fortune, he laid his plans. With one extra throw of the dice, he might regain the dignity he believed was his due.

The day before, he and his small group bypassed the Coritani capital and hopefully on the morrow, he would return heavy handed, his confidence further boosted by the welcome addition of a detachment of Gallic horse who had, only three days earlier, been assigned to the fort. Their centurion was not unknown to Balbilus. His name was Titus Lucanis. It was from him that the legate learned the real reason for the unit's non-appearance at Lindum.

'We thought you'd heard, sir,' said Lucanis, surprised. 'It's all of two weeks now.' The story didn't take long in the telling, for the answer emerged with but one name.

Iceni!

Balbilus' original scheme about arriving at Verulamium ahead of Paulinus, still many miles away, would have to be put on hold. The idea of racing to reach the distant settlement wasn't so great a prize as prestige gained in putting down a rebellion. The fact that there'd been little sign of hostility around Rina wouldn't stay his hand. All the better for it. In his estimation, the Coritani were nothing short of black-hearted and treacherous head-hunters. Knowing Rina was weak in its defences, suggested he could reap enough damage on king Volisios' capital, sufficient to weaken any threat to Rome from that direction. He had to hurry. Knowledge that Armet's betrothed had arrived recently, only added fuel to Balbilus' fire. Blame would be laid at Cerialis' door, both he and his damn Hispanics. That would be the tale put about. In no time at all Balbilus knew the ruse would quickly reach the ear of prince Armet. A wild scheme, yet fate had been known to weave such a web.

Having kept busy the loyal gallopers travelling with him from Lindum, Paulinus' progress was being observed, albeit, from a distance. He calculated three days hence would put his army within reach of Durovigutum, some fifty miles north of its goal.

Balbilus fully intended to be there, but only after he'd dealt with Armet's heathen dung heap.

SIXTY-THREE

THEY HAD COME in the night without warning, carrying lighted brands and death-dealing weapons, the unexpectedness of the attack easily breaching Rina's part-repaired wall of timber. It was a classic lesson in the art of abduction. To disable the opposition, select the target of their assault, then strike before the enemy be roused from their sleep.

It was an act of pure revenge, and Julius Balbilus, for obvious reasons, because he couldn't vent spleen upon secondus Aquilla, found instead a way to get at prince Armet, thereby targeting one closely linked to the prince, in the shape of Tadoc's only daughter, Gela. To make certain that the centurion Lucanis didn't waver in his assignment, he'd attached gladiator Gallinus to the ranks of the raiders for reassurance.

Roused from her bed by the sudden clamour without, she snatched up a spear, the nearest weapon to hand, and met the threat, head on, proceeding to stand her ground in defence of the stricken figure of Volisios sprawled at her naked feet. The king was barely conscious having fought, sword in hand, in a brave attempt to protect his future daughter-in-law. Due to an old wound, coupled with his frailty, he was clearly incapable of defending even himself, and one sideways blow to the head from a shield edge was enough to render the old man incapacitated. Gela's long-time servant and companion, the healer and diviner, Ulvina, already lay dead across the open doorway, her throat cut from ear to ear. With her weapon wielded ferociously, while she stood her ground, it seemed a new Gela was born in those wild moments. No longer the dreamer, but a warrior. Had Fomah been witness to her courage, he'd have found it difficult to believe that his baby sister had such a determined fighting spirit.

Throwing burning torches onto the thatched roof of several round houses, shadowy figures from Venovia, delivering a parting shot, set ablaze other dwellings while stumbling away in haste, a rear-guard creating further confusion in their retreat. Faced with strengthening opposition from the appearance of armed Coritani warriors, the legionaries fell back from Rina in disorder. Last of the night raiders to leave, centurion Lucanis, tossing the ring onto the surface of the central shrine to the gods Teutates and Esus, fled from the lurid glow, swallowed up in the darkness from whence he'd emerged. The object bore the unmistakable mark of the Hispania on its crown, that of a prancing bull, misleading evidence as to who would be blamed for such a cowardly attack.

Earlier in the day, the scenario involving Machai, now having played itself out at 9th legion's holding centre at Crococalana, proved to be an event that would bring greater unease than the violent assault on Volisios' capital, as if that episode weren't cause enough. The incident, had it presented itself in a different place and time, might have been more delicately handled. Unfortunately, the incident morphed into a face-to-face brawl between members of the Exploratores and a group of Cerialis' personal equites.

The reason for the argument wasn't difficult to discover, recent news of Paulinus' subjection of the Druidical cult on Mona, filtering through to Lindum, being the cause. Weapons having been drawn, a serious incident ensued resulting with one eques dead and several others receiving a variety of wounds. After the melee five of Armet's men, the prince's friend, Machai among them, were promptly set upon and shackled together before being shown the inside of a cell on The Hill, there to await the judgement of a much-displeased, legate of Hispania.

SIXTY-FOUR

T HE DISTANCE FROM LINDUM to the heartlands of the Iceni by road roughly measured a hundred and twenty miles, five days march for a legionary. As for Armet, with his cavalry, it was accomplished in three, making a search for Gort no longer necessary. Yet his uncle, Culchul, urged caution over the timing of a reunion, never having any great desire to approach Boudiga's territory at any stage, fully believing the prince would be about as popular there as an outbreak of pestilence.

Boudiga couldn't be blamed for her dislike of the Hud. He'd committed himself, along with nephew and brother, to place himself under Rome's influence, against better judgement, which took courage. The fact that Prasutagus had been similarly guilty of much the same thing would be considered, when the time was right for argument, all nations having felt compromised by the oppressive weight of Rome heel on their necks, at some stage or other.

The drunken incident between members of Armet's Exploratores and Cerialis' Hispanics over governor Paulinus' handling of the Druid question made no small contribution to further dark clouds on the horizon. Suspicion, never far away, found a quicker pace. A multitude of rumours regarding Armet's position with Cerialis, including a possible attempt to apprehend the former, may well have prompted the prince and his Exploratores to distance themselves from the centre of trouble hovering around Crococalana.

A furious Armet's reaction to events was instantaneous. Alerting his father to events at the holding station, siting the arrest of Machai and the others, Armet then spoke of Cerialis' supposed treachery over the attack on Rina, giving Vosilios the cast-iron reassurance that Gela was now safe from harm. The prince then advised a very concerned Tadoc to be on his guard and prepare his settlement for possible assault, shoring up its defences without delay. Fomah, after making full apology for the unsuccessful attempt to apprehend Gela on her way to Rina, fell to assembling the greater part of his personal following, swearing he would from that day be Armet's man. The prince, when later riding away, recalled several previous fiery encounters with the Cornovian, and drew much comfort from such a pledge.

Torn between fears for her father and love for Armet, Gela's desire to fly to Rina and the comforting embrace of her betrothed, without ever being sure he'd be there, was an act of recklessness that might well have turned into something more, endangering everything she loved. She realised it now. It was never to be an easy option, yet, amid rising uncertainty, plus Ulvina's earlier prophesies of doom for Armet and his kin, still fresh in her ears, she wanted to be with him more now than at any time since the day of their first meeting.

In the fraught hours that followed, Armet sent a fast rider to Rina with a reassuring message. Yes, he would very shortly come to the capital. What he failed to inform her of, was the necessary foray back to Lindum. The province would become extra hazardous from this time on as Roman occupied Britannia, due to long neglect and arrogance, became gripped by rumour and counter rumour.

There were other contributors, a total disregard for the spiritual beliefs of the indigenous population, being paramount. If the imperial hierarchy had seriously set out to fulfil its role, it might have considered the history of ties that bound the island's nations to Druidism for over half a millennium. A growing realisation that Rome's intentions included the destruction of these ties, was more than partly responsible for a sudden about turn of the usually loyal Batavi, in a land Rome had so swiftly come to treat as its own.

Cerialis, with many of his Hispanics scattered in a variety of bases between Lindum to distant Londinium, being largely static, would be greatly restricted in the following passage of events. Other units now on the alert, such as the vital one at Segelocum, were already fostered out to several important frontier sites lying within Cerialis' jurisdiction.

Inside the praetorium, after a sleepless night studying the latest reports, he fell to carrying out Paulinus' orders, over the rendezvous. He did however give a little time to what was happening with Tadoc's Cornovii, a group which the legate never completely trusted. Promises which in hindsight, were never fulfilled. Informers consistently informed him of the recent movements of a faction led by king Tadoc's anti-Roman son,

Fomah, though little of event was yet cause for worry. Why then, his unease?

On a whim, he dispatched half a precious cohort, more than could be spared, to monitor the area for any sign of suspicious movement. At the same time, he sent a smaller force, led by a centurion, to the holding point of Crococalana, reinforcing the small and now very nervous security unit stationed there. From him he received more unwelcome news of Armet's defection, with sizable groups of Coritani and Cornovii moving south along the very route that Cerialis had no choice but to take.

Quickly despatching yet another galloper in the direction of Rina, hoping against hope that he was in time to alert the isolated garrison of Thracians monitoring king Volisios' capital, he ordered them to be ever vigilant until relieved, unaware that in retaliation to Balbilus' attack the night before, it was already too late.

Lastly, after a fervent prayer offered up to Mars, he began preparation to depart the confines of Lindum. From there he'd ride ahead with the cavalry to disperse and hunt-down those seeking to deny his vital link-up with Paulinus. As many men of legion Hispania that could be spared, would follow. Thus, in the legate's mind, a combined force of cavalry and infantry should be enough to slow the rebellion. He even hoped he'd apprehend Balbilus along the way. All well in theory, yet Cerialis was soon to find far bigger problems arriving on his watch than those of the disgraced legate of Valeria.

SIXTY-FIVE

EVERY TWENTY-FOUR HOURS the world turns full circle and humanity revolves with it. For most, the time signals little change in everyday living while for others, no two days are the same. So, it fell out for prince Armet after what had happened at Lindum's holding station.

CHAPTER SIXTY-FIVE

With a better atmosphere prevailing, things might have been handled differently, but the public stage men were about to enter was far from that. Britannia's governor had almost daily lent heavily on Cerialis, urging him on without delay. The legate felt Paulinus' impatience. With the growing unrest gaining ground in the south and the refusal of 2nd Augusta to reinforce Paulinus, the odds were being whittled down to chaff. Bluntly the current situation meant the legate of Hispanics was fast becoming the harassed governor's sole support against a very real threat. Later dispatches, each one more desperate than previous reports, continued to reach the walls of Lindum.

One of the five Coritani arrested by the legate's soldiers was Machai. Being a close childhood friend of the prince, this particularly unsettled him. At once, making use of terms agreed under the 'special alliance' to cover such misunderstandings, he demanded his immediate release. Cerialis, busy mustering the Hispania to fulfil Paulinus' demands, gave a just as immediate refusal.

Also, long-held suspicions of Armet's uncle now came to the fore, suspicions confirmed by a growing pile of evidence supplied by itinerate agents. It was as the legate had long thought. Culchul was finally unmasked as one of their cult's major conspirers holding the title of 'Hud,' a fact played down by his once trusted colleague, prince Armet.

As for the matter of Gort, undisguised hater of Rome and a renegade, other spies in the legate's employ had tracked him to a certain area of a recently dead king now ruled over by his rebellious widow. Cerialis, several times, had admonished Armet to bring his maverick brother to heel, requests which had fallen on deaf ears. Now proof of betrayal was dropping like over-ripe fruit from a tree into his lap and he began to feel he'd been duped, used by a man with two faces; someone honoured with the gift of Roman citizenship and other privileges he thought, with bitterness.

'Armet is bound to react over this,' Aquilla commented worriedly. 'Especially when he finds out you've already sent them to the archery butts.'

'Damn well hope he does,' Cerialis cursed. 'As for the prisoners, they were guilty of killing one of my legionaries, and a Roman at that! It's a fair punishment for murder, secondus. If I allow such crimes, others will naturally look upon us as weak and seek advantage.'

Aquilla listened but didn't respond, perhaps mulling over the consequences. For good or ill, the secondus' personal opinions in this case didn't side with those of his superior. This was Armet of the Coritani being condemned out of hand, an itinerate power to be respected, leader of the most well-regarded light cavalry in Britannia, possibly beyond. Had Cerialis forgotten these facts?

In the mind of Aquilla, with the risky situation as it was, a touch of leniency might have been used. As to what might happen now, amid the business of organising those sections of the army selected for the march, neither he nor the legate would have to consider the question for long.

SIXTY-SIX

'YOU LOOK WORRIED,' remarked Cerialis, irritably eying Aquilla's dishevelled state. 'What's wrong?'

'You're not going to like this, Quintus, not one bit.'

Crowding the Witham's far bank a large company of horsemen sat motionless. A few vaguely familiar faces told the legate a little of what he needed to know. The arrivals belonged to the Coritani, prince Armet's men. Included in this host he also recognised their leader, the tall, grey-headed figure of Armet's uncle, Culchul, the now confirmed, Hud. He and a companion urged their mounts from the group, coming to a halt a few feet from the water barrier, all that separated them from the dominating presence of the colonia.

The young rider, Patux, sitting his horse beside Culchul carried a decorated stave. Gracing its honed tip was mounted a human head. Cerialis watched from the saddle, his horse the twin to prince Armet's Flavia, as summoned legionaries, Servilus and his contubernium among them, doubled into line as five score Cretan archers rushed to man the timber walkway of the stockade. Aquilla trotted his horse almost to the water's edge and joined with the legate. Apart from the harsh rasp of weaponry and the snorting of nervous beasts, all became silent in an eyeballing face-off.

'Do you recognise this creature, legate,' Culchul shouted hoarsely, in halting Latin.'

'By the god of gods, its Gallinus!' Aquilla exclaimed. 'Balbilus' henchman!'

'Before my patience runs out!' Cerialis shouted in reply, 'and I arrest you or send you packing, tell me why you dare to challenge us in this warlike manner? I'd also like to know what you're doing with the head of Balbilus' gladiator, Culchul Hud?! And where is prince Armet, that he sends you to do his bidding?'

If the designation, 'Hud,' coming from the mouth of Cerialis, meant anything, it didn't register, not now, not after all that had happened. 'When I left, the prince had already ridden to the fort at Vonovia, where he believed the Hispanics had attempted to abduct his betrothed. The fort is now taken and the guilty one awaits death. The gladiator's head is prince Armet's gift, a reminder of what can happen to murderous scum, like your Julius Balbilus.'

'That is nonsense! None of the Hispanics have been anywhere near Vonovia. Also, he's not *my* bloody Balbilus!' Cerialis vehemently protested.

'We know the truth, yet there is another matter to resolve,' replied the Hud. 'You hold five of the Exploratores, prisoner. One of them goes by the name of Machai, the prince's man. He demands their release, unharmed!'

'Unfortunately,' Cerialis shouted, as sitting knee to knee beside him, Aquilla blanched, 'you're too late. But if you're interested, you'll find them awaiting you, further down river, cushions for archery!'

Culchul shook his greying head as a rider returning quickly from the known area of the butts, nodded to the Hud his confirmation. 'You've made a very grave error, legate,' he solemnly replied.

Cerialis was about to make a further retort, but even while Culchul was speaking, the first brands were lighted. Almost immediately flame licked at the edge of the pontoons and Aquilla, not waiting for a command from Cerialis, shouted the order. Within the space of the time taken to down a cup of wine, the fire had taken hold. Through the smoke the bruised and bloody head of Gallinus spun and bounced across the watery divide, to land with a dull thud at the forward hooves of Cerialis' pale and motionless horse.

What happened then would supply the Fates with a fresh set of dice, as showers of arrows flew from the barbican wall. One struck Culchul with full force, piercing the renegade priest's exposed neck in the narrow gap between armoured shoulder and helm. This was a strike that might have knocked a lesser man instantly to the earth. Instead, honed by instinct, he still attempted to draw sword as his final breath escaped him. The youth, Patux, who'd been protecting the Hud's flank, himself took a barb in his exposed back, the force of which pitched his body forward to slump over the neck of his horse.

Cerialis, attempting to calm his now restless mount, shot an angry glance in the direction from which the deadly missiles had suddenly been launched, without his having given the order to 'Loose!'. In that one short moment he accepted things were too late to be reversed, the die having irrevocably been cast.

Nobody had even suspected Armet's reaction to the arrests of his scouts would occur this rapidly. But with Culchul, assuming the position of emissary, suddenly appearing across the river opposite the stout gates of Lindum, a certain amount of confusion had then taken place. The biggest surprise was the size of the response, possibly five-hundred horsemen, fully armed and war-clad. So menacing was the possible threat of violence that Cerialis thought fit to meet it with an equal show of strength, ordering several ranks of infantry to deploy between the river and the colonia's hastily closed gates. The outcome, though messy, proved to be inconclusive, yet it nevertheless sent a chilling message. As for Culchul Hud, the wound received proving fatal, the Coritani prince, once a valuable ally, would be impossible to reconcile.

SIXTY-SEVEN

T O BEGIN WITH, Balbilus attack on Rina really hit home like a prize-fighter's blow to the solar plexus. The garbled account given by the eyewitness was so muddled that Aquilla, sitting the rider down, gave him a cup of wine and waited impatiently for the flood of words that eventually gushed forth. They hardly made for easy listening, each word spelling out a complete betrayal of one fellow legate by another. Undeniably, a deliberate flouting of military protocol had taken place. Attacking the Coritani seat of power without authority, then seeking to blame the incident on one not a party to it was a deliberate affront aimed at both Cerialis, and legion Hispania.

The legate, though beset by the main threat coming from the south while concentrating on the vital business in hand, ever the optimist, despatched gallopers to wherever Armet was reported to be, carrying with them an offering to thrash things out between the prince and himself, a cooling off period being the language he used.

'That damn prince of heathens,' commented Philo disparagingly, polishing his sword sheath. 'I knew it, I damn well knew it!'

'Looks like the legate picked a wrong un' there,' agreed Lentilus, lying back on his bunk.

'First Crococalana, now this,' Lentilus remarked, 'Who were the buggers this time? He was referring to an attack that had taken place beneath the timber walls of the colonia itself, the previous day.

'7th cohort, the unlucky 7th.'

'How many?'

'Several wounded, so I'm told,' Lentilus muttered. 'So much for Coritani cooperation.'

Philo laughed harshly. 'That bastard barbarian and Cerialis were never going to being bosom friends, a marriage of convenience was more the like. If I were legate, I'd crucify the whole bloody lot of the murdering bunch.'

'What would you know about marriage, dummy?' chuckled Glabus. 'A quick poke in a tart's bedroom is more your style, I reckon.'

'You'd be surprised,' muttered Philo.

'The poor sods of the 7th were ambushed, unprepared, just like at Crococalana.' Lentilus quietly complained. 'Not a fair fight, Armet's bullies had it coming. I just wonder who the bastards may be about to murder next?'

'What's fair with them heathen swine?' Philo spat. 'Next time it could be us, I shouldn't wonder.'

As it happened, they'd not have long to wait for the answer.

SIXTY-EIGHT

'WE SHOULD HAVE DISARMED Armet's uncle and kept him here until stubborn heads cooled,' Cerialis later bitterly reflected.

Aquilla pursed his lips in contemplation, then shook his head. 'Not a good idea, Quintus. Not a good idea. We've already insulted the prince, over much. Keeping his relative at Lindum against his will, wouldn't have bettered things.'

Cerialis thumped the table with a fist. 'Jumped-up heathen, dictating to me! Who does he think he is, harbouring a renegade Druse, right under my nose?'

'We all know who this 'jumped-up heathen' is,' Aquilla echoed with emphasis. 'A man who instantly thought *you* responsible for the attempted abduction of his betrothed. Also, should you need a reminder, he commands a formidable number of warriors who could have been helpful in the present situation.'

'You have a gift for stating the bloody obvious, secondus,' Cerialis retorted with vigour. 'The prince shouldn't have been so eager to blame me for the assault on Rina, should he, when he should have concluded, it was legate Balbilus? The old bugger must have lost his damned mind, and it seems he's not the only one!'

'The legate's pride has greatly suffered,' Aquilla answered. 'He lashed out, blaming Armet and myself for his disgrace in the eyes of his old comrade, Paulinus. We stole his glory and I fear he won't easily forget it.'

'A loosed barb!' Cerialis nodded. As for the prince, Aquilla, it seems you side with him despite his traitorous defection.'

'I fought alongside him at Dorona, remember?' There was a genuine seriousness in the voice of the secondus. 'His men think of him as a god. Being mere mortals, we ought at least to use the benefit of the doubt.'

'I can't trust the fellow, not after this damned affrontery, today,' Cerialis confided, slumping sulkily onto a chair. 'He should have trusted me, more.'

'Now you're sounding like old Balbilus,' the secondus chided, familiarly. 'There are others to beware of, other than prince Armet, some of our auxiliary units, for example.................'

The legate pursed his lips, the business of the treacherous Batavi being a warning sign. 'As far as that goes, we have to use the men Rome supplies us with, even if some be at odds with their loyalty.'

He sat and took the cup of wine the secondus offered, secretly aware that Aquilla, ever a sensible character, damn him, was right. Looking at the latest batch of orders lying on the desk, was a reminder that this was neither time nor place to seek further trouble. Arresting Armet's men so rashly had been a stupid mistake, while their hasty execution amounted to nothing less than a knee-jerk reaction to the false accusations made. Yet right or wrong, Roman law had been served, and seen to be served, plus the legate was administrator, as well as soldier. A line had to be drawn in this matter, and men would regard him as weak, had he acted otherwise.

In addition, the governor's orders were stark in their urgency. Boudiga's name was gaining prominence in almost every dispatch. Cerialis recognised rightly the failure of the victors of Mona to join up with legion Augusta, a major reason for the governor's fears. With his soldiers apparently tied down by rabid, war-seeking Silures, prefect Poenius and the 2nd were loath to leave Glevum further weakened by their absence. Obviously, Paulinus' call for reinforcements from that direction, however crucial, would have gone largely unheeded, meaning all reliance for back-up would fall upon Cerialis and his Hispanics. There being no other units that could be called upon. Cerialis knew it, and Paulinus took pains to make it abundantly clear.

The legate, holding the very latest report tightly in an unsteady hand, had long run out of curses. Didn't Paulinus realise he himself was in the same situation as Augusta's prefect? Yes, Poenius did have the damn Silures on his back. Tough! But he, Quintus Cerialis, had Cartimandua, plus her vengeful spouse, Venutius and the Brigante to vex him. not to mention the unpredictable Parisi king, Mogonus, all of them waiting to see which way the wind blew. Now he must regretfully add prince Armet to this growing list!

For a moment he had an uncomfortable vision of Venutius joining the Parisi leader's war-chariots and overrunning Lindum in his absence.

With the rendezvous point for the combined force yet unnamed, any further information from Paulinus would have to be intercepted on route. Cerialis was saddled with a grim challenge in the shape of a tricky military operation mounted without delay, a feat which the legate, under the circumstances was forced to admit, would need nothing short of a logistical miracle.

The thought that he really needed Armet and the Exploratores weighed heavily! And the ultimate question remained, what would the Coritani prince do by way of retaliation after Balbilus' crazy move against Gela, coupled with his own reckless decision to order the execution of five of his followers?

SIXTY-NINE

JULIUS BALBILUS sat silently brooding within the damaged fort of Venovia, a forlorn half-wrecked place he'd come to regard in the short time available, as his own. The remnant of the only loyal troops left to him were being gradually decimated by a series of attacks from a determined group of rebels, intent on the fort's destruction. Strategically it stood where two major highways converged, east and south, a day's hard ride to Verulamium for cavalry. If Paulinus meant to engage those at the heart of a growing unrest. Balbilus calculated that this was the route he'd likely take.

Almost unbelievably, such being his state of mind, the shamed legate impatiently awaited the return of Lucanis with the prisoner, Gela, fully expecting his order to have been successfully carried out to the letter, with little expectation of failure. When the centurion finally arrived, he brought with him a very different account as to what occurred at Ratae. Resistance had been fiercer than expected, and the cost in terms of his command had been high. Worst of all for Balbilus, his loyal servant, Gallinus had failed to return with those involved in the assault, another unexpected price to pay for such small returns. But at least a part of the plan had been achieved, if Lucanis was to be believed. The ring thrown beside the shrine to Tuetates and Esus should implicate Cerialis' Hispania in the violation that had taken place. Hopefully this would be sufficient to implicate his rival to such an extent, that any remaining tie with prince Armet would be seriously undermined.

A satisfaction, nevertheless. He anticipated his next move, the rightful reinstatement as legate of Valeria. To say he was taking a major gamble an already greatly damaged reputation, would be an understatement.

In the real world from which he was in danger of departing, one more error meant he'd be fried like meat on a griddle, having put great reliance on the flimsy possibility of his being right when all about him said otherwise. It may have been a bout of helpless madness that had taken hold, blurring the sense of reality, but he really believed that by seizing Armet's betrothed and harming the allegiance, he could claim a right to command his beloved legion once again and at the same time, achieve vengeance.

Balbilus had proved to be wide of the mark on *all* counts. First, Paulinus would take a different road other than the one the legate thought obvious, and the only Romans the dispossessed legate would be likely to meet would be Cerialis at the head of Lindum's hard-riding cavalry. Second, a furious prince of the Coritani, his mind set on murder, offered yet another dangerous obstacle to any future reconciliation with Paulinus. Thus, the hazardous picture was complete. Half-deranged, the legate's lack of reality in all matters was beginning to resemble a fallen leaf carried away on the breeze.

SEVENTY

WITHIN A DAY AND A HALF of events at Venovia and Culchul's sudden death, a very different Armet reined-in on the far bank of the river to face the fully alerted gates of Lindum, a smaller war-band than that of his late uncle accompanying him. The prince was a man not easily brought to anger. But the loss of Culchul, Machai and others of the Exploratores, men he'd held to be exceptional friends, demanded explanation, it being difficult to accept these unwarranted affronts coming from a man like Quintus Cerialis. Difficult or not, these insults took second place to Armet's rising fury, when he first received news of a failed attempt by the Hispanics to lay hands on Gela. He'd long known the impetuous character of this Roman, but he had never reckoned him to dare go this far. This oversight would make for even more anger within the prince, much of it launched against himself for past misjudgements.

Not since the loss of his young wife Tae, had Armet carried deep feelings of love for another woman, but Gela had turned him. At first, it had been difficult to gauge the depth of his desire, and only later did he find himself drawn to her, in a way not easy to define. She was nothing like Tae, yet he'd taken to Gela's innocence and gentleness in a world daily dominated by decision making and the continued business of necessary tasks when controlling a vibrant and independent nation like the Coritani. With Gela he found solace from the cares of his world, if only briefly.

Yet one important happening had now occurred, and that was the sudden heartening appearance along the way of Fomah, accompanied by several hundred Cornovii horsemen who, soon acquainted with what had threatened his sister at Rina, road hastily to meet with a furious Armet.

The fact that such a man as Cerialis should threaten the one person the prince cherished above all others, seemed oddly inexplicable, the legate being an honourable man, or so he'd been fool enough to believe. Now, feeling stung like the thrust from a pointed barb, he sought revenge for Gela and others he held close; a settlement to the whole sorry business must be made. The alternative was obvious. Should his demands be refused, he would, given the first opportunity, kill Cerialis.

With their differences in belief and culture, a feigned attempt at commonality between Rome and proudly independent people like the Coritani, would amount to a rough ride. Deep down a part of Armet had even shared Gort's disdain of a ruthless war machine that no longer felt it necessary to cover its true intent, preferring instead to unveil the realities of all the trappings of a superpower. Yet it had been his father's fervent desire.

Now, with his hands at last untied and strengthened by Volisios' overnight change of heart with Balbilus' attack on Rina, the die was cast on both sides.

From their position on the high palisade at Lindum, those Romans that had known him as a helpful negotiator could visibly see the prince's altered stance. Gone were the sartorial trappings of Rome, the engraved armour and matching helm. Instead Armet adopted the dress long worn by his followers, a many-coloured weave of tunic and breeches. Also, a wooden stave, much scorned by Paulinus, held aloft by Patux's replacement, Cartivel, boasting eight wolf-head tails nailed to the crossbar rather than the usual six, one Coritani tradition not recognised by Rome, the extra number of animal appendages being displayed only when a decision to wage a total war had been decided. Sitting Flavia in its shadow, Armet demanded reasons for the Rina assault and the brutal slaying of the five men unwisely put to death, throwing in the matter of the recent untimely slaying of his uncle, for good measure.

The reception the prince received at the colonia was as cold as that given earlier to the unfortunate Culchul. Cerialis, ignoring Armet's request for dialogue, blaming instead members of the Exploratores for causing the fatal brawl, was characteristically defiant. With this came a demand that Volisios, as king, in his own interest, should continue to honour the 'on the nod' agreement to obey Rome's requests when required, aiding the legate or his subordinates whenever, or wherever necessary. Cerialis added that a further threat of armed punishment clearly directed toward Volisios' capital at Ratae would be undertaken should his recent demands go unheeded. As for the incident with Gela, Cerialis went so far as to express his pleasure that she'd escaped unharmed while, also in the same breath, blaming Armet for the false allegation that he, rather than an obviously sick and deranged Julius Balbilus, was the *actual* culprit. Finally, he reminded Armet that he was still a citizen of Rome.

Armet's following reply was icily shorter, by a mile. Any past agreement between Rome was from this hour, dead in the water, all previous pacts being instantly revoked. Also, the prince no longer put his trust in Rome or its false promises, adding that as from this day, seeing scant honour to be gained in its possession, he instead preferred to remain a citizen of Rome no longer. Further, when the legate chose to march the legion south, he'd have to find a second route outside Coritani territory. He doubted also that Cerialis would receive any aid from other Keltoi nations. At his side, as if to add weight to the threat, Fomah now stood in full agreement, all past animosities openly set aside.

Later, in the confines of Cerialis' office, Aquilla sat biting his lip in frustration, fully aware there was no such thing as a *second* road. 'Armet came right to the point though, I'll give him that,' he muttered, pouring wine, offering a cup to a thoughtful Cerialis. 'Well,' he sipped, 'what now?'

The sitting legate of Hispanics drained his cup in a single gulp and immediately poured another. 'Ignore the threats,' he said with sudden determination. 'Orders are the same as those drawn-up yesterday. Half our strength remains here, with you in command. I'd like to take more men, but I can't afford to lose Lindum, on top of everything else, or Paulinus will have my bollocks boiled for breakfast.' Cerialis, uttering a bitter laugh, drained what remained of the wine with a flourish, and rose. 'I shall leave with the cavalry before nightfall, followed by the five chosen cohorts, the selection of which I will leave in your capable hands, Aquilla. Aubanus will be your secondus!'

'The senior centurion is capable enough to command here without any help from me,' argued Aquilla. 'Let him remain instead, while I ride with you.'

Cerialis shook his head. 'You're my eyes and ears, Aquilla. I trust nobody more than you. That's why I want you to defend Lindum.'

Aquilla paled, visibly disappointed. 'The odds are stacked heavily against you, Quintus.'

Cerialis donned a helm, shrugged as he reached over the stool for his sword belt. 'Paulinus want's me in the south, and in a few days, that's where I damn well intend to be.'

'And the prince?'

'What about him?

'Something tells me he means to delay you.'

'I *know* he does, and he won't be the only damn traitor, either. There'll be others, I'll wager.' He grimaced at the secondus. 'No matter, eh?' He drew the gladius from its decorated sheath, stared thoughtfully at the blade before thrusting it home again. 'That after all, is what we're paid for!'

As both men hurriedly left the coolness of the praetorium for what promised to be a warm summer evening, they briefly acknowledged the salute of the twin guards outside. Cerialis, turning his head, then made a surprising remark. 'Your first duty as commander of the garrison!'

'Yes, sir?' the secondus paused in mid-stride.

'Release our scribe!'

'Free Straba?' the secondus visibly showed surprise. 'By the gods, why?'

'Firstly, knowing the bugger as I do, he'll probably attempt to escape during my absence, anyway. Secondly, I can never make up my mind about the halfwit!'

Aquilla lips half-parted in a smile. 'Truly, the fellow's an enigma, I'll concede that.'

'See to it, secondus! When I'm gone, draw up the manumission.'

Aquilla paused, the lines in his worried brow deepening. His legate was about to face a daunting task, one that could upset the balance of power in an already volatile land, and his mind seemed focussed on one solitary slave. 'Are you *really* serious about this, Quintus?'

Cerialis, offering no reply, left the secondus shaking his head in puzzlement.

SEVENTY-ONE

IN A TROUBLED SLEEP Armet wrested with problems. His options were not easy to dwell upon and in the jumble of visions that flitted from scene to scene, he remained confused.

The prince was a child of four when the legions waded ashore a third time to colonise the island on a more permanent basis. Growing up, Armet grew used to their presence and the site of the colonia they called Lindum. He recalled several emissaries visiting his father's capital in the early days, bringing with them the promise of protection offered to his father in return for certain conditions. The latest negotiator had been legate Quintus Cerialis, a man whose association with Armet began in Rome under the giant awning circling the arena in which gladiator Bacilon met his unexpected end.

Volisios was slow in responding to advances at first, but the reality of changing times could not be ignored, despite his caution. Above all, having fought an almost constant war with the more belligerent of his neighbours, not least of them being Brennus, for much of his life, he desired peace and looked to Rome and the legions to supply it. Cerialis and the Hispanics had done so twice, for the vixen queen Cartimandua, now they might do it for him and deter any that might do his people harm.

The king's argument with his younger son, Gort, over his drift toward what the latter saw as something to be strongly resisted, had fractured relationships to breaking point between the two, while Armet reluctantly sided with Volisios. Yet Gort's reasoning proved popular with many. Why should the rightful ruler of a proud and powerful nation yield anything at all to a people who, like other tribes only a short time before, regarded Rome as no more than a lucrative trading block with whom they dealt peacefully for countless years, he argued? It was a premiss hard for some to refute.

Then a day arrived when Rome walked again in the land, a very different Rome, this time carrying weapons, not trinkets.

A time inevitably came when the imperial war machine, dealing harshly with any resistance, including several fierce confrontations with the Coritani, ventured further north, their legions ending up on the wild border of Volisios' neighbouring Brigante. Further south, to consolidate their power, Rome began to establish a second stronghold on the bank of the river they called Aqua Linite, fifty miles north of the Coritanian capital of Rina, which they quickly dubbed, 'Ratae'.

It was by no means an easy take-over. Resentment of the invader would be a constant threat to imperial exploitation in the region, the almost feverish need for precious metals, deposits of which its several consecutive governors swore the island would provide in abundance, being uppermost in their minds.

Four years before, when prince Armet was a youth, Rome came for him, shipping him off to the imperial capital for 'indoctrination', part of the deal negotiated with Volisios in return for certain safeguards, never fully accepted by the Coritani elders. Upon Armet's return the transformation was visible. His command of Latin being more than passable, and his hair, once grown well below the neck, now cut short in the manner of a fully-fledged Roman aristocrat.

Gort was appalled by the change in his brother. It didn't matter that Armet was duty-bound to obey his father. In his mind, a selling out of the people was what it was all about.

Looking back, Armet understood Gort's rage. All that had happened since, fully justified it. Volisios had clearly supplicated himself to save the Coritani from Roman encroachment on land that wasn't their own. Now a boil that had been festering for years was about to burst. Gela's planned abduction on the orders of Balbilus, the subsequent death of Culchul, the arrest and barbaric execution of his men at Crococalana, one following quickly upon another, hastening events.

The shockwave over the treachery of Nardon's Batavians hit Lindum like a thunderbolt, yet it hadn't in any way weakened Paulinus' resolve, the atrocities committed on Mona going only part-way to equal the bloody balance, as his soldier's mind viewed it. But what had been lost was the half-accepted value of trust and a fear that others would follow Nardon's deadly decision in the days to come.

A fresh wind gained strength outside, making the skin of Armet's tent flap noisily. From somewhere close, not being fully awake, he felt a spiritual presence of the goddess, Epona. Outside Flavia snorted as if to remind the prince that the figure was her goddess too. A fleeting image of his dead uncle flashed before him to join with that of the goddess, both sacred things now adrift in his thoughts.

A firm hand woke him, and with half open eyes he saw a familiar figure leaning over him. 'It's time,' said his youthful cousin, Cartivel, a relative chosen to replace Patux as signifer and carry the wolf-head standard of the Coritani.

Armet sat up and splashed his face with water from the bowl on the stool beside him. Cartivel, already fully armed and helmeted, carried at his belt the traditional spatha – a cavalry sword.

'Is all ready?' Armet asked.

'Everything goes well,' spoke Cartivel, 'especially now.'

'Why, especially, cousin?'

'Tidings of Gort, by messenger from the south. He says he's heard rumour that you've started to let your hair grow like a warrior. He'll meet with us soon, at a place of your choosing.'

'I thought he was lately with old Mogonus!'

The signifer shook his head and grinned wildly. 'Better than that, the scourge of the she-wolf has come over to us, the old bugger. With luck, promised chariots could soon be moving our way!' He paused. 'What now,' he asked, 'we must move fast if we're to join with Gort.'

'I could try to stop Cerialis leaving Lindum.................'

Cartivel stared in astonishment. 'Do that and you're a dead man, don't give the swine a chance to snare you or you'll find yourself looking at the world from the height of a cross.'

'You are right, better I settle accounts with the creature Balbilus first. As for our legate of Hispanics, we'll meet with him soon enough I fear.' Quickly arming himself he walked with his cousin to join with the waiting band of Exploratores. A satisfied smile momentarily brought a lightness to his face as he mounted Flavia, a natural expression such as young Cartivel had rarely seen, till now.

SEVENTY-TWO

'HERE'S YOUR PROMOTION, GAIUS,' Aquilla recalled Cerialis stating with cheerful confidence, fully armed and leading his white horse. I reckon there are enough heathen swine about who may have the idea to put Lindum under siege in my absence. Just make sure they don't succeed. Understood?'

The secondus leaned forward in the saddle, silent and downcast. You don't look very happy with your new job,' observed the legate earnestly.'

'I'm uneasy, that's true, Quintus. Nothing seems right.'

'I agree, but no cause to look so glum. Keep your wits about you and we'll both be laughing about all this buggery over a cup of wine a few days hence.'

The previous morning Servilus and the remaining members of the contubernium formed-up in line of march, one small unit of Cerialis' hastily assembled army, leaving Lindum one day earlier than the bulk of the cavalry. They took their place in rank as the column moved out, their flanks escorted by small contingents of Thracians, Asturians, mounted archers from the Danube and light squadrons of spearmen from Dalmatia. The recruit watched their easy progress with envy, imagining he were one of the riders, lucky bastards!

Later, leaving the familiarity of the colonia behind them, the cohorts fell in behind the eagle-topped vexilla, five under-strength units, two and a half thousand men at best, under the command of their newly appointed officer, Rufus Lippa. The pace set would yield them twenty-five miles a day or, as they were lightly armed, perhaps a little more when walking normally. Such was the speed proposed, yet it wouldn't take long before this calculation began to appear wildly optimistic.

From his vantage point atop The Hill, where he and Cerialis had often viewed the once bustling scene below, Aquilla eyed the marching column until the last cohort vanished in the distance. Almost too suddenly for the secondus, even before Cerialis' departure with the cavalry the coming morning, Lindum began to feel a decidedly strange and isolated place.

SEVENTY-THREE

THAT NIGHT UNDER THE GLARE of a myriad brands, men hastened with their tasks, the disturbing news still filtering through from Mona adding to their urgency. Tadoc's contribution of Cornovii, under Fomah's command, after shoring-up the badly neglected walls of their tribal seat against possible Roman attack, joined with Armet's Exploratores. The preparations seemed to give strength of heart to their endeavours as the final meeting between Armet and Tadoc took place. Soon after their conjoining an unexpected group of warriors rode into the capital of the Cornovii, seeking prince Armet. Emissaries from Venutius, no less, who told of a sizeable force of warriors massing in the west, standing ready to back the prince in the coming challenge.

This welcome promise of support nevertheless came as a surprise and was, on the face of it, approached with no small degree of caution. Just what were the Brigante king's intentions in making this peace offering, so soon after his retreat from Dorona and the surprise abandonment of Brennus? Was he diplomatically searching for a new set of allies in his ongoing altercations with Cartimandua, or did he genuinely want a share in any victory against Paulinus? Be that as it may, Armet's reply was necessarily ambiguous. He would not pretend the offer from Venutius, though generous, would in any way alter his intent, which he forcibly made plain, adding as a salve that the struggle which the Brigante had long endured in their opposition to Rome, was already legendary. Thus, if he wished to send a war band, they would be welcome, providing they served under prince Armet's leadership. Exactly how Venutius would react to this independent reply, remained to be seen.

Later, after all the talk and the making of decisions, Gela appeared in the half-light of torches, her slim figure dressed for war. A leather tunic, especially made to cover her frame, together with sword and dagger hanging from the bronze-linked belt at her waist, completed her attire. It was notable that since Balbilus' abduction attempt, she'd become a somewhat different Gela. Tougher, certainly more assured, aware of her own strength, so much as to make a difference, she held in her hand the same spear that she'd defended Volisios with during the Raid on Rina. 'When you make your plans, all of you, include me,' she stated coldly, her voice fully prepared to rebut any argument.

Armet turned abruptly from conferring with Fomah. 'That would be foolhardy,' he replied.

'Foolhardy or not, I'm here,' she persisted. 'Since Rome appears to think of me as they do their sluts, I see it as my fight too.'

'Where we're going, you cannot,' he countered. 'In the next few hours fatal decisions will have been fulfilled.'

'Armet is right,' said Fomah determinedly. 'You'll be safer out of it, sister. Rome will be busy elsewhere and won't have the manpower to spare to risk an attack on our home. Stay with father, he may well have need of you in the days to come.'

Gela gave a dismissive laugh. 'Father has many another to do his bidding.' She glanced about the scene. 'I see other women here, and I can't believe what I'm hearing.' Her eyes met those of the prince defiantly. 'Is it because I'm your betrothed, or the daughter of a king, that you choose to shoulder me aside? If these are your arguments, I won't recognise them,' she continued. 'Neither does it bother the Iceni queen, from what I hear.'.

'Boudiga is a leader mightily wronged. Only creatures less than animals could violate a queen. She *really* does have more to avenge than yourself,' Armet argued.

'Gela stood her ground. 'That is so, my treatment can never equal hers. But defending honour and losing a close friend in Ulvina, along with the saving of your father, must give me at least some small right in the making of decisions.'

'Yet Armet is right to be cautious, Gela,' the voice of Patux, wounded protector of Culchul warned as he was gingerly helped from the saddle. 'There's more news coming from Lindum and the eagle's poised to fly. Cerialis is marching south as expected, with at least half a legion!'

'Then we will see that he bites off more than he can chew,' said Fomah.

'We know he intends to aid Paulinus,' Armet said, 'and we must make certain he doesn't,' he added. 'We'll be leaned on,' he admitted, his mind for a moment on Gort, who he had yet to find. He turned to Fomah. 'You know what to do?'

Fomah rose to his feet, 'The Cornovii will be the first to attack. We'll slow him down, at least as far as Rina, from there the Coritani can take over.'

'Tell Tadoc to take all non-combatants to the western forest for a few days, Fomah, where they'll be safer,' Armet suggested.

'That won't be necessary,' Fomah replied, 'he already knows what to do, even though he'd rather fight along with the rest of us.'

'Tadoc will aid us better if he stays,' Armet countered. 'When do you suppose the Roman force will reach Rina, Patux?'

'That depends on your Cornovii,' Patux replied, acknowledging Fomah. 'The legate's force are a mix, cavalry, infantry and archers, auxiliaries for the most part. Those on foot, the cohorts, his crack troops, will follow later,' the former signifer calculated. 'They'll be our problem. From Rina, the distance to the joining point with Paulinus is nigh on eighty miles, three days in my reckoning for foot soldiers - perhaps a little over two day's hard ride for a horse.'

'Then we'll try to shorten their journey and meet the enemy halfway.'

Amid all this movement of people, Gela reappeared, leading a long-maned pony. Armet and Fomah exchanged glances. 'She's *your* sister,' said the prince, deflecting the issue.

'And *your* betrothed,' Fomah reminded, with a shrug.

Gela, staring into the dying light of the campfire, hid her smile while choosing to remain silent.

'Clearly, events have overtaken us,' Armet released a smiled, 'now we've acquired our own Boudiga?'

Every mile of the road south to Paulinus would be peppered from then on with a flexible army of men and women from various nations along the route, every yard being bloodily contested. For Cerialis every hour, like every mile, would be vital and the legate, only too soon, could find that a strategy hammered out within the relative safety of Lindum, to all sense and purpose, might well be made redundant after the very first hours of campaign.

SEVENTY-FOUR

IT TOOK A BRAVE MAN or a particular fool to slight prince Armet of the Coritani, the latter description turning out to be more the case for Julius Balbilus.

A possible taking of Venovia wasn't in the end, given to Armet. With things being as fluid as they were, another war-band had become the prince's erstwhile helper.

The smells enveloping the way station, blistering from the previous day's heat, would have upset the stomach of any man. As it was, Armet and the Exploratores received fair warning. A brief scan of death and destruction that had become Venovia, told of a depth of ferocity that even the warrior prince found difficult to take in. Those that had conducted the assault, spared none of Valeria's two hundred strong unit, their cavalry then being absent. Naked bodies lay everywhere, quite a few decapitated or mutilated in various ways. Somewhere within the midst of this carnage they found the remains of the once ambitious Julius Balbilus, veteran of the war in Mauretania, and one of the first Romans to cross the Atlas Mountains along with his old comrade, Suetonius Paulinus. If he'd wished for a soldier's death, he must have been greatly disappointed, for those who killed him cared little for his military fame, and there'd been no Gallinus to protect him in his last moments. Instead, what was left of him would serve as food for hovering scavengers attracted to an unexpected feast.

Disappointed at being cheated of his quarry, the man who'd overseen the cowardly attack on Rina, whose minions badly wounded Volisios and attempted the abduction of Gela, was now beyond all reach.

Armet sat Flavia amid the charred ruins, his mind on other matters. Culchul Hud had fought gamely for life, so the prince was told, but the wound he'd received at Lindum proved too much, even for his tenacious spirit. They'd laid him to rest with as much ceremony and respect as the hour would allow, yet Armet already felt the loss greatly, his uncle proving almost as much a father to him as Volisios, perhaps more so, for he'd often accompanied the prince in his dealings, cunningly evading any attempt by a suspicious Rome to snare him, thereby constantly risking his life in the prince's service.

Here was yet another slight that would have to be repaid. King Volisios, already ill, was prevented from taking part in the rites to his brother, stricken as he was by the wound taken defending Gela during Balbilus' assault.

Men said that Armet seemed almost beyond anger, yet there was little time to consider rage, given the daunting challenge facing him. This reality goaded the prince to leave the blighted Venovia, a place now manned only by the dead. News placed Cerialis closer than expected, for although Fomah's Cornovii had slowed his cavalry, he was too wily a character to be beaten by just one nation alone, however persistent.

Now it would be the turn of Armet to delay the legate, and promised support, including a large band of Silurian guerrilla fighters from the west, wanting a piece of the action, gave him heart. There was another thing that cheered. Fomah, son of Tadoc, now regrouping from the previous day's foray, would shortly be met with at a prearranged spot.

SEVENTY-FIVE

CERIALIS HAD DEPARTED LINDUM with mixed emotions. Although escaping a desk, glad to see action at last, he remained greatly disturbed over the business with Gela. Knowing that Balbilus and his minions must have been behind the abduction failed to ease his mind, and he could only wonder at the hatred of the one man who dared condone it. Worst of all prince Armet had presumably, like himself, been completely duped.

Never could the business with the Coritani leader have come at a worst time, yet Cerialis, for all his casual attitude, was a pragmatic man and could when challenged, rise to meet adversity. What happened now would put every ounce of leadership to the test, faced with the unpredictable. Not only had he the fate of his command to worry about, locking horns with a further threat in the shape of a hostile prince Armet hardly helped him in his dilemma.

The legate's cavalry strength was formidable, five turmae of equites plus assorted squadrons of Asturians, Tungrians, Thracians and others, numbering two thousand or more. But there were gaps. Several otherwise needed units were ordered to remain in the colonia to help bolster its defenses. Other mounted wings he hoped to pick up as he went along, making up the shortfall, but the latter were unreliable statistics.

Why had he suddenly decided to grant manumission to his scribe, Straba? To be honest, he found no answer to the question, sure that the curiously likable fellow hardly deserved it. Was it a prevailing thought that he himself might die in this coming struggle against what he already considered to be vastly superior odds, was that it? Or was it a report telling of a growing number of nations coming together to challenge the ongoing presence of Rome after almost two decades of occupation?

Then there was the prince, a man in whom he'd earlier put his trust. Surely it was instantly clear to the Briton that the legate of Hispanics had no hand in the abduction of Gela. He had sent messages of denial, both written and verbal, to Rina and beyond. So far, no response. He also knew of Armet's wayward brother, Gort, how he'd raised a formidable force to accompany queen Boadiga in the south. None of this was conducive to putting Cerialis in a comfortable frame of mind. In short, he had no answers. All he could do now was his duty, assuring the cavalry met with Paulinus.

A Roman cavalryman was expected to average forty miles a day, a three day's ride that covered the one hundred and thirty miles to Verulamium in normal times. But it soon became obvious that such accuracy would never apply during this time of uncertainty, making the designated hour of contact with the converging army of Paulinus vexingly uncertain.

Uncertain too, was secondus Aquilla's position. With more than half the Hispania marching south with Cerialis, he'd been left with barely two thousand troops to defend the walls of Lindum. He was worried too about the threats surrounding the colonia, not only from the Brigante but also unexpectedly now, from Armet's people. Then there were the Parisi and their old ruler Mogonus' who, watching carefully, must have viewed Cerialis' departure with some approval. What was to stop him now with his fleet of war vehicles from making the best of a welcome advantage so generously presented?

The evening was calm and the near silence surrounding Lindum seemed, after the recent departure of the colonia's traders, slightly unnerving. Occupying the spot where, before retiring, he'd so often shared a draught of wine with Cerialis, the secondus witnessed yet another night descending. The ritual displayed the self-satisfaction of a conqueror, sure in the knowledge that he could hold the furthest point of empire at arm's length until the confident order came to 'up tents' and move the border north, into Brigante territory.

That night though, things felt different. For the very first time since his appointment as secondus, Aquilla ordered the doubling of the guard at every look-out post around the colonia, while he himself decided he was in no mood to find sleep this night or any night until this looming fermentation of possible rebellion was stopped dead in its tracks.

SEVENTY-SIX

S TRABA IN HIS SHORT LIFE had mastered a host of skills, including how to deal with stubborn door locks. Never had there been a better occasion to use this acquired knowledge than now. After offering up a prayer in praise of Tsabo of Catania, the mentor who'd instructed the scribe in these especial tricks, he applied himself to the matter in hand.

Just how long he worked on the means that led to freedom he couldn't answer. No matter how diligent his attempts, the disappointing result was plain. He would remain entrapped! His new friend, the recruit, Servilus, might have aided in some way but he'd already departed Lindum according to his reticent replacement.

So, it came as a surprise to find himself standing before the absent legate's desk later that day, waiting puzzledly for secondus Aqulla to speak. 'Well scribe, what shall it be this time?' He paused to pour a cup of watered wine. 'If you're looking for a place in prince Armet's employment you're too late by a bloody mile.'

The Greek glanced full circle, staring about him at the walls of the familiar office as if it were new to him.

'Lost something?' Aquilla enquired lightly.

'I'm a little concerned, secondus, as to why I'm here?'

'By Jupiter, I bet you are. But given time, knowing you, you'd probably have found a way out without my say so.' Aquilla half-smiled at his own jest. 'By my reckoning you ought to be looking at a view of the river from the giddy height of a crucifix!'

'I agree, I've been more than stupid.'

Aquilla tapped his forehead with a finger, drawing a deep breath. 'You know, scribe, you keep coming back like a familiar tune. Only two realities have kept you away from death. First, for some unaccountable reason, the legate has a fondness for you. Secondly, you found enough courage to ride with me at Dorona! It takes a brave sort of fool to do that.'

Straba would have liked to reply that the choice wasn't exactly voluntary, more likely fear rather than bravery had found him riding with prince Armet's Exploratores, and he might have done so had the secondus not pushed a small scroll neatly bound with red ribbon, across the desk. 'I'm obeying Cerialis' instructions, you understand?' Straba paused, hesitantly. 'Don't look so dumb. It's your manumission, Greek. He wished it on you, before he left.'

The scribe untied the ribbon and slowly scanned the sheet of papyrus before returning it to Aquilla. 'That is most generous of the legate, but I think I must refuse.'

'Refuse?' The secondus echoed, surprised. 'You refuse your freedom?'

Straba spread his hands. 'Where would I go and what would I do with it?' Almost everything and everyone I know is here in Lindum.'

Aquilla's reaction was one of incredulity as he slumped back in his chair. 'It's true, isn't it? You're a bloody fool.'

'For a long time, my days have belonged to the legate and the legion,' Straba replied without hesitation. 'Therefore, I possess few friends and have no home to go to.'

Aquilla laughed without humour. 'You call us 'friends', we who've had the power of life or death over you, as well as you're being the butt of insults from those who can barely string a coherent sentence together.

The scribe nodded.

'And what about this damn history you profess to be engaged in?'

'I can write words anywhere, especially when history is happening around us as we speak,' said Straba, doing his best to explain the inexplicable. 'I wish to follow those I've come to know and join them on the march. Just to be there, you understand. I hear the cohorts have left the colonia or are preparing to do so. I have a dear friend, Demsal, an archer with Gemina, if he lives. All I ask.....'

Still astonished, Aquilla stood up, and coming from behind the desk, scooped up the open scroll, forcing it into the scribe's hand before traditionally tapping him on the shoulder. 'By all the unnamed gods, take the bloody thing and disappear from my sight, you stubborn idiot! Go, before I change my mind and return you to your cell, Cerialis or no bloody Cerialis!'

With Straba gone the secondus kicked over his stool in sudden frustration, giving anything to have the freedom now granted to the scribe.

The mule like most mules was at first reluctant but given a mouthful of parsnip along with a soothing word from the scribe the animal waited patiently while Straba quickly recovered his tools and precious pouch from the now vacant cell. Then, placing them lightly on the animal's back, both walked free of Lindum's barbican unchallenged, save for a few carelessly delivered jibes, launched by the men of Hispanics on guard duty.

He found the going difficult at first. Weakness brought on by prison dieting hadn't in any way prepared him for this. What meagre scraps of cheese and stale bread filched from under the nose of the cook wasn't yet taking effect and he had to cling tightly to the mule's bridle. A sudden nightmare vision of Dorona, the meeting with legate Balbilus and a subsequent flogging from Gallinus reminded him, not in a good way, that he'd featured in a very similar scenario, not so very long ago. With night setting in he decided to see in his first night of freedom, curled up by the riverbank. At sunrise he would follow in the wake of the column.

SEVENTY-SEVEN

Under their newly appointed commander, Rufus Lippa, five Hispanic cohorts and auxilia, their eyes set in one direction, encountered little sign of trouble on the first day out, save for a few mounted skirmishers who though defiant, made sure to keep a safe distance from the column. To Lippa's delight he'd advanced almost thirty miles, exceeding expectations, glad to report that Cerialis' welcome order to travel light already appeared to be paying dividends.

Yet it was a very different outlook confronting them on the following day, the beginning of the *real* challenge. Evidence arrived with the dawn when they'd entered the forest, exchanging the familiar safety of an open terrain for the unknown. Shadowing them, the first arrivals, a mixture of horse and infantry, were about to make their presence felt. Adjusting to the sudden half-light, Servilus viewed a scene dreaded by many legionaries when finding themselves in a place few of them wished to be. But the orders were explicitly simplistic, make speed, and stay together where possible, the latter command being repeatedly stressed by their centurions throughout the entire length of the winding column.

For more than an hour they travelled a slow path between the steep scarp on either side of the ravine, a perfect place for an ambush but unavoidable given the alternative of a thirty-mile diversion. One thing was certain, this section of the road had so far never been fully completed by Roman sappers. Servilus could see why. It would be a brave bunch of buggers who'd challenge nature here, in this dark place, unless protected by at least half a legion. Coming to the ears of the recruit, the low and ghostly sound of a lone cornu, accompanied by the rhythmic tap of a single drum told of the presence of war. All were tuned to the beat, the repetitive tap-tap. Iber's cohort toward the rear of the column, instinctively aware of their surroundings were aware too of the silence and mystery. Enhanced echoes filtered through the overhanging branches of trees that reached upward to an almost invisible sky. Those who knew the story told by their fathers of what had happened in a similar place as this, half a century ago, when prince Arminius of the Cherusi led the Germanic nations to bloody victory over three unsuspecting legions of Varus, perhaps now recalled the tale.

A Roman army needs space, uncluttered areas where they can see their strength laid out before them, parade fashion, to best advantage. Here the concealing valley only intensified disquiet. Close deployment would be largely impossible for many of them, meaning that gaps would inevitably appear in the column if attacked. Nervously, its soldiers probed deeper into these gloomy parts, knowing their fears would only being eased when the last unit of Rufus Lippa's force finally emerged again into the light.

Before complacency took hold, it happened! The man to the front of Servilus, staggered, fell silently, a feathered shaft protruding from his neck. Soon showers of slingshot, shafts and other missiles, joined by a thousand deafening screams, rained down from both sides of the valley, bombarding legionaries before some could raise shields. 'The bastards are using the cover!' Verra of the condominium shouted, 'ferret them out of it!'

'No, lads!' roared the voice of Iber above the din. 'Stand fast, you dumb bastards! That's what the scum want!' For once, unhearing, under assault from tartan shapes hurling themselves recklessly into the fray, commands to stand firm went unheeded, though some strove to form a ragged wall of shields, attempting to meet their attackers with some show of discipline. Others, mixed legionaries and auxilia, took the upper hand by climbing both slopes of the ravine in a scramble to fight their way to the top, where a chance to gain advantage amid the melee might be possible.

Minutes later, taking advantage of a lull in the fighting, Iber and other officers in the column hurriedly did a quick count of dead and wounded. They were lucky. Aubanus, primus pilus of Hispanics, the *real* commander of this march, whatever Rufus Lippa might think, made a rough calculation. The cost of the lightning ambush being twenty-three fatalities, the wounded just under half a score. It would be the first of many, some feared. Iber kicked the inert body of the man he'd slain. 'He probably belongs to the Coritani, prince Armet's bloody heathens,' muttered Ornio, sourly. 'One of our so called, Britannic Horse.'

'I don't understand,' the voice of Verra remarked, resting on one knee, using his scarf to stem a trickle of blood seeping from a cut to his forehead. Iber laughed, harshly, his eyes blazing like a madman as he poked at the man he'd just slain with a bloody sword, as though he was trying to make a dead man rise. 'I understand, only too well mate,' he cursed.' We're being well and truly shafted!'

Several tedious miles ahead, sliding and somersaulting down over the damp earth, men again came to grips. Shields turned outward in another attempt to stem the manic tide of Britons, in the shape of Fomah's warriors. Iber, deciding that attack was in this instance the better strategy, ordered the twin flanks to meet the foe on their own terms to gain the top of the scarp.

Servius became a part of a ragged line that advanced upward on the slippery incline. Even with his inexperience, this seemed little short of madness! The months of training undergone, the shouted orders screamed and sworn, the drills calculated to exhaust and the mantra, never but never, under any damned circumstances, break ranks! Thankfully half the cohort remembered the drill and obeyed it, remaining stiffly shield to shield, individual walls of iron fending off the mad impetus of the charge, forcing the enemy to break themselves against a wall of shields.

Conversely in Servius' sector, Iber, doing a good imitation of a goaded bull, led two hundred legionaries to stagger upwards in pursuit of an enemy now in retreat, only to discover after suffering a further shower of spears and deadly slingshot, that their opponents had melted away like so many phantoms into the screening cover of bracken and overhanging branches.

The forest hid everything. Servius heard Iber, out of reach now, bellowing like an ox. Failing to find him, the recruit, pulling himself upright through a thick clump of brushwood, suddenly saw the centurion standing beside a huge upright stone. Lying at his feet lay two mangled shapes. What made the scene doubly horrifying was Iber's frenzied state. Wielding a captured hand-axe over the inert bodies of the two corpses, like a soul possessed, he severed a limb with each stroke, like a butcher. The centurion, covered in blood, kneeling from his efforts, paused, then vacantly stared up at the dazed recruit.

At that moment Servilus felt a sharp prod in the back and instinctively swinging about, raised his sword. It was Glabas the joker. 'I think we've got 'em on the run!' he grinned mirthlessly while spitting blood. The youth staggered toward the valley floor, trying to see what he was supposed to see, what he'd been trained to see. He told himself that, as at Dorona, all was insanity. He now wanted to turn, go back the way he'd come, run to the doubtful safety of the rest of the cohort, struggling to reform below. His eyes blurring, blood and sweat hampering his vision, he wiped his brow with a shaking hand, worried he might have been hit by a sling stone, or something worse. The recent vision of a crazed Iber held him so paralysed he didn't at first sense the impacting force against his shield. He stumbled halfway down the scarp, saw the tip of an arrow shaft piercing his lower arm. Stunned, feeling the feathers that tickled his fingers, he viciously tugged forth the barb which luckily, had failed to seriously penetrate.

Every muscle in his legs, taut lumps motivated his feet to slide wildly, resembling those of a drunkard. Out of breath, he paused, tightening the strap that held the shattered shield to his arm. He then saw a lone attacker bearing down, a second before the man's heavy weight sent him pitching forward. Other shapes fought around him as he scrambled to his feet, blooded gladius poised. The Briton confronting him was formidable, tattooed, half naked and stripped for battle. He yelled in a tongue that Servilus didn't understand, though the meaning was glaringly clear. He paused, uncertain of his opponent's next move. It took only a few seconds. The man lunged, Servilus parried, and his enemy fell from a blow to the base of his neck, a blow delivered so violently it almost severed head from trunk.

When the recruit had time to look about him, he saw that his comrades had beaten off the latest ambushers and were busy reforming ranks among the dead and dying. Above them, one could still see the half visible enemy, some on horse, continuing to keep pace with the marching column, watching their painful progress. Of their own supposed accompanying auxiliary cavalry, Servius had seen little sign of any since the previous day when the troops had left Lindum. There was still no sign of them, which was worrying, even though the number given to the column in the first place was exceedingly small for the task in hand.

'We won't get away with it, that easy,' Philo remarked, falling into line beside Servius. 'As sure as the gods, they'll be at us again soon enough.'

With no sign of Iber, decurion Orneo was put in charge. Instructions to quicken the pace double time, to catch up with the main body of the column up ahead. After many fraught hours, daylight began to wane along with the enemy and by the time night fell the cohorts at last marched clear of the forest as the first stars appeared in a clear sky. All along the column, orders to set up a temporary stockade were given, small fires were kindled, and men sought whatever rest they could. Free of the forest, open country beckoned. Yet however the dice may roll, men knew the omens weren't good. The reality was that five cohorts of seasoned Roman infantry plus auxilia, already mauled, were proceeding to an unknown rendezvous with death.

Only two things presented themselves with a grasp of certainty. They'd all, one way or another, fight or die for Rome!

SEVENTY-EIGHT

TWO DAYS PRIOR to the leaving of Lindum, Rufus Lippa was serving as fourth officer in legion Hispania. Now, suddenly promoted to a new post of praefectus castrorium, or camp prefect, he had the doubtful privilege of commanding five cohorts, supported by the approximate number of auxiliary foot, one half of Cerialis' stretched command, making their way to the rendezvous. Trouble was, he now found himself cut off from most of them.

A full-time soldier down to his Spanish leather boots, Lippa never thought to question his luck, until now. Not long after vacating Lindum he was quick to realise that he was leading no ordinary march, resembling rather a moving mass of confusion, fighting the most savage resistance he'd ever encountered.

Such force had to be met with an equal ferocity, bringing into play every muscle and fibre that a trained fighting man possessed. Orders were plain, cut down all who opposed, whether man, woman or child. Any soldier not understanding this command meant a weakness that could demoralise should such a canker spread. The goal was everything. Someday others would describe the present setback as a running battle. The problem was his men weren't even walking.

Enemy archers purposely aimed high, a well-tried ploy to make men raise their shields, exposing the lower body to a variety of deadly missiles which resulted in a rising number of dead and wounded. Another day like this, Lippa thought, and he'd have no command left. He was about to order them to a crouching position, to offer a lesser target when abruptly the attack melted into the scattered woodland at the glade's edge.

Rufus Lippa wiped blood from his sword on dry grass. Glancing about, he took stock. Cut off from the rest of main command, like so many units, they were faced with two choices. Take the risk of shifting off their backsides or die where they squatted. Neither prospect appealed. A nervous junior medic he'd recruited along the way was desperately trying to assist the worst of the wounded, but Lippa saw immediately that these casualties, were the cohorts forced to leave, must out of mercy be necessarily despatched. To let them fall into the clutches of a barbaric adversary would never salve his conscience.

He heard the uneven chanting resonating around him, a wild sound that had followed him for the last ten miles after becoming separated from the bulk of the army. Calculated to unnerve, he'd heard the sound once before in another place, a decade before during a minor uprising among the Cantii, when a junior officer. It had only one meaning for him. No quarter!

Apart from the medic, one other non-combatant, his thin body partially hidden by a discarded shield, delved busily into the leather pouch at his side. How he'd arrived among them, nobody knew or cared, although most men in the cohort recognised him. It was just more bad luck that had placed Cerialis' scribe under the same cloud of bitter misfortune as the rest of them.

Lippa sheathed the gladius and knelt. 'What would you're famed Leonidas have done in these circumstances, Greek?' he muttered, familiarly.

'The Spartan king hadn't much choice, he fully expected to die,' Straba said without emotion, sweating beneath the robe he'd relieved from a dead legionary.

'Do I have a choice?'

'Why ask?' Straba replied with a grimace. 'You'll try to move on like the legate, sir, and you know it.'

'I asked because your ancestors learnt how to escape from tricky situations in the past. Xerxes, Darius, and all the rest. I thought as a budding historian you might have a few remedies tucked up your damn sleeve.'

Straba stared up at Lippa as though he were demented. 'Why do I have a gut feeling that you're about to ask something of me?'

'Shrewd of you,', Lippa grunted. 'How would you like to be part of history, rather than write about it?'

Straba squatted. 'Not one jot after Dorona, but I'm listening.'

'It's almost dark and I know these bastards. There won't be any attack tonight. I want you to get a message to our cavalry base at Durovigutum. It's not far distant. Tell them of our situation, tell them we're cut off and surrounded.'

'You *really* are serious,' Straba replied. 'Apart from the fact that the road between us and the base is crawling with the enemy.

They won't be there, anyway, I saw them with the legate yesterday at another place,' Straba emphasised. 'Looking at their condition, they're in no shape to help anyone, and I reckon they have their own problems.'

Apart from the odd rasp of weaponry, all about remained silent. A disappointed Lippa shook his bare head and looked at the scribe through bloodshot eyes. 'It won't work, then?'

'You've more chance of saving an ice-lump in a furnace,' was Straba's only reply.

SEVENTY-NINE

'**B**ROTHER YOU LOOK OLDER,' Gort remarked in greeting, casting an observant eye over the waiting Exploratores camped beneath the trees as he removed his helm. The day before, Fomah had launched the first assault upon Lippa's rear-guard, while Gort hurriedly rode from Iceni territory to a point somewhere south of Rina, receiving news of Cerialis' advancing cavalry fast closing on the Coritani capital. This now gave greater urgency to a long overdue reunion.

As for Armet, it was also the place where he'd chosen to await the first news, good or bad, of Tadoc's son, part of a plan hastily put together by the Cornovii prince and Armet after their meeting, prior to the latter positioning his forces at a suitable place further south. There, where two major roads met, a few miles south of the Roman settlement of Durobrivae, he intended to intercept and hopefully destroy, Cerialis' oncoming cavalry.

Fomah's role, Armet explained, would be akin to rolling up a carpet, pushing the Roman cohorts south where they must eventually collide with Cerialis' hard-pressed and outnumbered mounted units striving to unite with Paulinus.

Together with the new addition of Gort's retinue, an army, close to eight-thousand fighting men in strength, would be pitted against an enemy little more than half that. All Armet could do, when and if it happened, was to pray to both Epona and Astarte. Fully knowing the quality of the Hispanics he faced, his very being shuddering at the word, defeat. Perhaps he should have been less casual when regarding Venutius' earlier offer of support, he again reflected.

Not that it made any difference to the greater scheme of things. Completely out of character, his personal ambition suppressed to a surprising degree, the divorced Brigante king, despite his involvement in a draining civil war against Cartimandua, keenly recognised Armet's overall command in this struggle against Rome, such was his eagerness to help thwart a despised Paulinus.

'You look annoyingly the same, apart from the fact that you're not alone,' replied Armet, disgruntledly at last, indicating the host of dismounting riders behind Gort's back whilst suppressing the urge to lovingly embrace him.

'How did it happen, with uncle?'

Armet explained and Gort nodded concernedly. 'The bastards who did this will get what they deserve,' he swore.

'Patux risked all to save the Hud, but he'll mend.'

They walked some distance out of hearing. Gort, tactfully aware of the ambiguity surrounding their still divisive stance on the subject of Brennus, remained silent, as did Armet. 'I never wanted things to happen the way they turned out.,' Gort said instead. 'You'd better know it brother.'

'Yet you were right, Volisios and I were not.'

'You, and others like Obrig and Boudiga, were ill-used, but you did what was thought best, as did they,' Gort said, adding concernedly. 'I also know father has suffered injury during the raid on Rina.'

'He manages to thrive, thanks in no small part to Gela.' Armet gave a wry smile. 'It would appear we both come from hardy stock.'

'How is she?'

Armet raised an eyebrow. 'Didn't you see her when you rode in? Since Balbilus' cowardly attack, she's become a loyal recruit to the ranks of the Exploratores. She carries a spear now.'

Gort's glance registered surprise.

'Yes, brother, she's one of us!'

'Just like Boudiga and the Brigante she-wolf,' chuckled Gort, shaking his head. 'Looks like the land is breeding fearsome amazons.' He grinned, adding seriously, his voice lowering. 'You've been greatly insulted, what with our father's injuries, Gela's ordeal, then the loss of comrades like young Machai and all.' Gort paused. 'We speak of Cartimandua. What happened with Venutius?'

Armet shrugged. 'For answer to that, you'd best ask Cartimandua.'

Gort looked enquiringly.

Armet continued. 'Venutius and his men were intercepted along their way to us, and the she-wolf, possessing the greater force, including in their number a contingent of Cerialis' Hispanics, pushed back the king's advance. Now he's been put on the defensive, and we can't rely on any support from that quarter.'

Gort shrugged and suppressed a cough. 'No matter, it's done, though we are the weaker for it.'

'At first, I accused Cerialis. I was a damn fool to be so cleverly misled by Balbilus,' Armet cursed, changing the subject. 'Quintus, curse him, may be many things, but he's no abductor of women.'

'That doesn't tally with what I hear,' said Gort, smiling briefly before his tone became more serious. 'You know the legate well enough brother, what he's capable of, knowing his support for the Brigante queen, and other things.'

Armet rubbed a stubbled chin, 'I misjudged him mightily, as he in turn misjudged me. By having Machai and the others put to death he's now openly defied me without caring what the reaction would be. Well, he's about to find out, to his cost. I've slept too long, and there is much wrong to be righted, with or without Venutius.'

'It is a fine thing we are doing,' said Gort, agreeing with a nod. 'After all that has happened, what falls out now, win or lose, must be better than slavery under a Rome yoke. The Coritani have never yet yielded to any, Roman or Kelt.'

Armet smiled slightly at the youthful boast, then eyed his brother seriously, 'I'm reminded of the time when you chose to challenge our friend Dasal within the sacred circle, remember?'

Gort chuckled. 'If truth be told, I was petrified. My legs scarce held me.'

There were silences between their reliving of past events while filling their bellies with cheese and half-stale bread, both men at intervals falling to their own thoughts. It was true, reflected the prince, when it came to the business of cooperation with their invader, it was all there, plain to see. What Volisios had thought sensible safeguards for his people were loosely based on certain insurmountable requirements which had little chance of delivery. Now, after Boudiga's stirring of possibilities, it appeared that change, like an unstoppable avalanche, was speeding to meet them.

'Who are they?' Armet nodded towards a mixed group, mostly men herded together, squatting on the turf, their wrists bound with ropes.

'Rounded them up along the way,' replied Gort, sniffing disdain. 'Collaborators most of them.'

'What are your plans?'

'The most treacherous will die if answers to our questions don't tally with the information we possess, as sacrifice to Epona, brother mine. When we win tomorrow, the rest I may release as a good-will gesture.'

'Were I among them I wonder, would my treatment be the same?'

An uncomfortable silence then ensued between the brothers, before Gort spoke again. 'You've already answered my needs. As for an answer to your question, you'll never know it.'

Armet, despite the warm air, felt a chill course through him. Gort *had* changed. His eagerness in the past to fly into a rage

291

at the slightest provocation now seemed to have taken a more sinister tone.

'I hear tell you are much in the Iceni queen's favour,' he said, half-suppressing dark thoughts. 'What's the woman like?'

Gort grinned affably. 'Very tall, red-headed, formidable and a dedicated hater of Rome due to her humiliation.'

Armet nodded. 'Yes, we know about Decianus' veterans. Did she take prisoners?'

'Just one.'

'What happened, I suppose she had his throat cut?'

'Better than that, brother,' muttered Gort, remembering. 'She has giant mastiffs at her beck and call which she ordered to tear the bugger to shreds, like they would any unfortunate prey. Not a good way to go.'

Armet glanced to where those keeping guard on the unfortunate prisoners stood talking. Satisfying himself that none were in earshot, he reached into his leather tunic and drew forth the amulet he'd discovered at the unnamed fort and held it out. 'Remember this?'

Gort took the tell-tale bronze disc, with its image of lightning fashioned in gold, gingerly into his hands, staring for a moment in wonder at the image. 'This is Dasal's sacred emblem, 'he searched for it everywhere,' he breathed at last. 'Where did you find it?'

'It was lying in mud within the remains of a half-built fort close to Lindum. I managed to retrieve it without being seen,' Armet explained.

'This must then have been Tove's doing. Dasal could never account for its loss,' Gort muttered. 'The Hud only found out about the traitor's treachery a few days ago, otherwise I'd never have sent him on a mission to Mogonus. He'd obviously taken the disc beforehand.' Gort's voice told of obvious bitterness and disappointment. 'We should have seen the signs, recalled his birth and all. He wanted a reckoning.'

'It's been almost twenty years,' Armet sadly shook his head, recalling Tove had been born a child of the neighbouring Ordovici, just another victim of a dozen warlike sorties and tit-for-tat border raids that once took place between the two nations, during a series of bloody squabbles. Both Tove's parents never survived the attack and only much later did he learn of his birthright. 'I should have seen the connection,' the prince confessed.

'I'm equally at fault,' Gort muttered, grim-faced. 'Tove grew up with us. Over time he became like a brother. What changed him?'

Armet deliberated. 'Who really knows what lies behind a man's smile, even across many years? In some, hatred can last a lifetime, and Tove certainly covered his grievances with a heavy cloak.' Armet deeply reflected. 'Some of those attacking the fort turned out to be Ordovici. Maybe falling in with them, either accidently or with purpose, played into his hands. I doubt he could ever have planted this evidence alone.'

'Why haven't you returned the emblem to the Hud?' Gort then asked, somewhat accusingly.

'I wanted to be sure.'

Gort looked puzzled. 'Sure, sure of what?'

'That Dasal wasn't implicated too.'

'He will be either very grateful, or very angry, should you tell him that.'

'Let's trust we'll all be around to find out which,' Armet smiled. 'But Tove, of all men. What devil possessed him?'

'The demon greed perhaps, or something more,' Gort answered with a shrug. 'There have been at least two plots to kill me, and it pains me to judge that he was likely involved in both. These attempts happened in unlikely spots, places where nobody, apart from Dasal and I, knew of. Tove must have been deceiving us for a very long time, and both of us failed to notice. Other instances escaped my attention but eventually, not the Hud's. As it is......,' Gort spread his hands helplessly.

'Doesn't sound like the Tove I knew,' remarked Armet, still unconvinced.

'It's proven already, before you arrived, that Tove was acquainting Cerialis as to our recent movements, I see it now. The finding of Dasal's emblem, only too well-known to the Romans, could have meant the death of all of us, especially you, dear brother. It was all part of his strategy, how he sought to gain favour with Rome, wrongly thinking that a warrior Hud's sacred token would in some manner, buy him a way to some higher state. Instead, like many of us, he chose the wrong path and paid for his stupid treachery,' Gort muttered. He recalled the words of king Mogonus of the Parisi, not so long ago. *Choose your friends wisely, as there are those among your following that wish you much harm...........................*

'How did he die?' Armet asked, interrupting his brother's thoughts.

'I couldn't do it,' Gort confessed, unable to conceal the sadness in his voice. 'Yet Dasal was merciful. 'It was quick, a draught known only to the priest sufficed. Tove never awoke.'

Armet, popping the last piece of cheese into his mouth, nodded with understanding, feeling suddenly ashamed for his earlier suspicions having never, unlike Gort, felt at ease with the reticent Dasal. A desire to make peace with the fiery priest and return the amulet now filled his mind. But sunrise would herald a day of battle and his prime thoughts fell to dwelling on that, though not entirely. After his brother's departure, he sought out Gela amid the host, seeking solace in her presence.

That evening he felt her body move against him, warm and responsive to his touch, and when her smooth thighs parted to admit him, it seemed like the very first time. Afterwards, fully sated, she clung tightly to him, her body languid in his arms, a comforting shelter from the harsh world without. Lying contentedly beside him, she lightly kissed his bare shoulder, tracing an invisible pattern across his chest. 'Are they really dead?' she asked.

'Who?'

'Brennus' people, those at Dorona.'

'Few got away.'

'Women, children?'

'They wouldn't yield,' Said Armet, remembering. 'Most may have wished it that way.'

'Are you sorry?'

'In the long run, it makes little difference how I feel' he answered reflectively. 'They followed the Bear and chose to die under his leadership.'

'Yet you are troubled by his death,' said Gela seriously.

Armet set his lips. No, it wasn't the dying, it was the manner of it. Inwardly he shuddered, having personally been requested by legate Cerialis to attend a crucifixion of several runaway slaves, an uncomfortable lesson perhaps as to what could happen to any flouting the unfathomable will of Rome.

Gela released her hand from his, staring long and hard for an instant. 'At times I find you hard to understand,' she gently scolded. 'Brennus, sworn enemy for almost twenty years, yet you seem to have regrets? I don't think I could be capable of sharing your generosity.'

'He did what we Coritani did in return,' the prince countered with finality. For that reason, mine should have been the hand that brought him down'.

Armet well understood his own quest for revenge. After years of conflict against their several neighbours, the Coritani were only too well acquainted with it. Briganti, Dobunni, Ordovici, even king Tadoc's Cornovii, all had been foes at one instant or another, and all had learnt to fear the sight of Armet's wolf-head insignia. Not long before, the thought of those forementioned joining in opposition to the common enemy, men would have been reckoned unlikely. But now...............

When he was a child no higher than Volisios' belt, he was told of another great battle fought against Rome, many years before in the southlands. Vespasian, having defeated the Catuvellauni at their fortress at Mai Dun, proceeded thereafter to put to death all remaining defenders, men, women, children, even the dogs and livestock didn't escaped the slaughter. Volisios would oft recount the story, prompting Armet to reflect that this nightmare vision may well have contributed to his father's reluctant acceptance of a heavy Roman presence in his land.

Now, the prince wanted the coming confrontation more than he'd realised. Maybe he wished to wipe clean some of the acceptance and, he had to face it, some of the pleasures his situation had unprotestingly given him. Status and privilege when granted Roman citizenship, experiences and diverse sexual pleasures while engaging with Julia Felix and other nubile women came to mind. Then not least, legate Quintus Cerialis, a man he'd rubbed uneasy shoulders with, sharing a table at times, drinking wine from the same jug.

Or was it reconciliation with the brother he so dearly loved, which made him finally cross the line? Lapdog of Rome, that's what Gort had labelled him on their falling-out. Now he would see by results, just what kind of man he really was, for the dice were ready for one last throw.

Would there be a personal clash of weapons, a face-to-face with Cerialis in the heat of battle? Such a thought was not a sign of self-doubt. He had learnt his calling at an early age and would attempt to kill his opponent at the first opportunity offered, as he was bred to do. Rather it was something other, something he couldn't fully explain. Perhaps the reason was simple in that he'd rather not be a man who took pleasure in the slaying of another, a man who'd been an unlikely companion for several years, however casually. He wiped his chin in thought, missing his deceased uncle's company and guidance when really in need of it.

His basic plan was to meet the legate's squadrons head-on, no frills or niceties. Until the arrival of the Hispanics, at least a day further off, Cerialis would have to fight his battle without crucial infantry support.

'Let's not waste time about it, though,' muttered Gort, rising, interrupting the prince's inner fears. 'The Iceni are relying on us and Fomah to at least slow the Romans down. Simple enough I'd say, with our numbers..........................'

'Fomah will do all possible to hamper Cerialis' advance,' Armet interrupted. 'It'll largely be up to you and me, to complete the task.' The prince then asked, 'Mogonus and his chariots, any news?'

Gort gave a shrug. 'The king of the Parisi, he's like poor uncle Culchul, one of the old ones. I suspect he's keeping a wary eye on the she-wolf and won't shift from his lair, just yet. Being the crafty bugger that he is, though, he'll wait till others have done his work for him. Pity, I shall miss the chance to meet with Vixt again.'

Armet nodded, getting to his feet. 'By 'others', I take it you refer to present company? And, let's face it, you could well be right, Mogonus may be the wisest of us all, thriving when we are dead. Let's trust we won't need him, there being enough of us.'

Even so, thought the prince to himself on parting. Gaius Suetonius Paulinus, supreme governor of the province of Britannia, must never be allowed to clasp hands with Cerialis and his Hispanics.

EIGHTY

IT HAD TAKEN MANY HOURS for the newly freed slave to pass along the plodding files of Hispania's columns after their emergence from the forest, despite taking his friend the mule. Making his way alone he'd somehow escaped ambush. My survival instinct must be kicking in, he thought as he sought to regain the protection of the army. Gradually, one by one, he overtook the battered armoured cohorts and their auxiliaries. Very quickly, even surprising himself, he drew level once more with the head of the marchers, led by its captain, Rufus Lippa. From there he attached himself to a hard riding turma of Thracians, thanks to the permission of Otalus, their decurion. It was somehow in their company that the scribe once again, found himself facing Cerialis, legate of legion Hispania.

The fighting along the path of the stretching via Claudius was at first isolated and spasmodic, with little hint of what was to come. Marching confidently, as yet, they easily resisted Fomah's war-groups while continuing to advance, pressing doggedly to lessen the gap which separated them from the cavalry, still too many miles ahead.

At a now peaceful place where the attackers had again melted away, beside a swift flowing stream where corpses from both sides lay scattered, a small group of horsemen were dismounted. Their insignia instantly told Straba the riders were Pannonians. Watched over by nervous sentinels manning the perimeter, they refreshed themselves with its cool running waters. Hours before, the scribe finding himself minus the mule, which had sensibly fled during one of several minor skirmishes, claimed instead the services of a horse, riderless after one of several clashes on the road. This had enabled him, independently, to avoid anything that looked any way dangerous, relying on a disguise of a tattered old cloak and hood for protection. Thus unchallenged, making a series of calculated detours, he made reasonable progress south, where eventually, he finally caught up with what he assumed to be the rear guard of Cerialis' cavalry, telling him he'd left Rufus Lippa and the Hispanics well behind. Slipping tiredly from the horse, he knelt by the stream, there to splash its watery freshness over hands and face.

'By all that's damnable, you're the Greek, the legate's bloody scribe, damn his bollocks!' Straba turned, hand reaching for the sword Otalus had given him, before recognising the owner of the voice squatting down beside him. 'Last time I saw you, you were on your way to bleedin' Dorona!'

Straba of course remembered the fellow carrying a weighty bag of dispatches, destined for legion Augusta at Glevum. The scribe might have asked how it went, before informing him that he was no longer a slave. Instead, he lied, saying he'd been informed that the legate was somewhere nearby.

'The mad bugger's run out of luck. He took another fall earlier,' the Pannonian muttered, cursing.

'Is he dead?' Straba asked, standing.

'No such luck, scribe, but he bloody well ought to be, sod him,' the man swore while cupping water to his bearded face. 'I'm the decurion of these men you see around us, what's left of them, and it's not over yet.' The Pannonian got to his feet, his eyes scanning the first trees of a nearby wood. 'Neither he nor I seem to have your kind of luck though, running amuck among all these damn savages, like some prize idiot. Which of the gods do you pray to?'

Straba managed a weak smile. 'They called him, Tsabo of Catania.'

'What sodding type of god, is that?'

'A benevolent one, I trust.'

The Pannonian smiled back. 'If its Cerialis you seek,' he pointed a finger south. 'He might still be there, a ruined place, some sort of fortress, once. Likely you'll find him nursing his wounds.' The Pannonian sniffed his disdain. 'If you want my advice, forget the legate and fuck off, or the mad bastard may get you killed along with the rest of us!'

The Pannonian proved right. In the ruins of a long-abandoned marching camp the legate sat on a mound of damp, fallen stone slabs, his back supported by a saddle probably taken from the body of a dead horse, of which, observed Straba, there seemed to be no shortage. Expecting to be greeted by a volley of familiar invective, Straba was met with an unnerving silence all round. Certainly, looking at the many wounded occupying the site, there was little room for humour. The medic who'd finished binding the wound on Cerialis' upper left arm finally moved aside. The Greek noticed a spread of blood already seeping through the freshly applied linen, and he sensed the same feelings of nausea gripping him as in the surgeon's tent, over the incident of Petra's Horse, a time that now seemed far distant. Had nothing changed?

'I admire your timing, Greek!' Cerialis winced at a short laugh, covering the wound with the sleeve of his tunic. Bodies of the dead, both friend and foe alike lay scattered around the area, bitter evidence to recent close combat. 'I don't suppose you've brought my cohorts with you?' He wiped a trickle of blood from a cut to his forehead. 'Seen any heathens?'

Straba shook his head.

'No, you bloody wouldn't. They come then they go, but by the gods the murderous swine keep coming back!'

'You've been hurt,' Straba said pointlessly.

'Don't raise your hopes, a damn scratch is all.' Cerialis grunted as with the help of the hovering medic he got to his feet. A waiting centurion appeared and placed a russet-coloured cavalry cloak over his shoulder. 'How do you do it, scribe?' he remarked, a hint of devilment in his eye.' Is it your wit, charm or an annoying bloody persistence? Enlighten me!'

'Certainly not wit, sir,' Straba managed to stammer. 'Anyone can tell you, I've hardly a sense of humour.'

Cerialis pulled a face as he climbed slowly onto the waiting horse, the white companion to prince Armet's dark-night gift, Flavia. Straba noticed her pale flank, flecked with fresh blood. 'I surely vouch for that, Jupiter I do,' the legate remarked with another curse.

'Not the time or place I know, but thanks anyway,' stammered the scribe.

'I had to do it, Straba, didn't I?' said the legate of Hispania as the aide handed him a sheathed spatha which he then thrust forcefully into his belt. He bent low in the saddle so that Straba might hear above the sudden clatter of many horsemen riding past. 'Anyone that can do what you've managed to do and survive, is worthy of something, agreed? I won't even bother to ask how you managed to find me, *this* time.' Another eques appeared to offer a rounded shield, which he declined. 'I'll miss you, Greek,' the legate muttered. 'You've made me face myself a score of times in the past, may the gods give you pains, yet your freedom makes us quits in my book. Both of us, in differing ways, carry an equal share of lessons from the Fates. I suggest you hide yours in your pouch, you're going to need it.'

'What's *really* happening?' asked Straba, casting an eye at the scene of disorder within the ruins.

'I damn well miscalculated, that's what!' Cerialis replied, bitterly. For a moment in yet another place of death, they stared at each other vacantly. 'I underestimated their strength, that's all!' he swore in frustration. 'These bastard heathens seem to multiply like wasps The more we kill of them, the more they multiply. The way to Paulinus is barred to me, to my shame. Our cavalry can't clear the way without help from my cohorts, not against the sheer weight of the enemy. Their number includes our old friends the Coritani, Armet and the Exploratores. Ironic eh, after all the work I put in with my governor.' Cerialis laughed, a sound short and callous sounding. His brief recall of a time in Germania and the chancy business concerning the Treveri, flashed before him. What he was now faced with, would he feared, have a very different outcome.

'I suspect that prince Armet is somewhere out there, isn't he? He'd hardly miss a show like this, the traitorous swine.' He took a deep breath before confiding, 'He damn well accused me of attacking the girl Gela, when it was Balbilus...... who I should have clapped in chains. Now the prince won't be satisfied until he possesses my eagle, damn him! That's his aim!' He indicated the bronze standard carried by the signifer at his side.

'You'd risk your life and those of your men in defence of a lump of metal?' Straba challenged as Cerialis gripped the reins.

'A lump of bronze?!' he echoed. 'Remember Greek, under that emblem you were given your freedom.'

'Yes, sir, but it was the same emblem which enslaved me in the first place. Yet I served you and the Hispanics for over two years, free or not. I'll wait here in hiding for Lippa and the column, at least until I see what happens,' Straba decided, emphatically.

'Well, the buggers had better hurry up, scribe, or I'm mincemeat!' Cerialis paused. 'You're really waiting here, amid the heathens, till they come and cut your throat?'

'Like you, sir, I take my chances. Anyway, where else would I go?'

Cerialis laughed harshly. 'You've never had much trouble before, as I remember. Leastways it's your call now, even though like as not you'll suffer the same fate as the rest of us, sooner or later.'

That is exactly what the Pannonian said, recalled Straba, as he glanced again at the scattered dead and wounded. Then his eyes became distracted by a new sight, a massing of auxiliary cavalry following their individual insignia, coming into focus, crossing the ruined fort's gateless near exit. From the direction of the vital road, the bloodied via Claudius, the road north along which the scribe had recently risked both life and limb, there came sounds of a renewed clashing of arms. The attackers were coming once more.

'The rest of the army, Lippa and the cohorts, they'll soon come,' encouraged the liberated Straba, his voice rising as mounted auxiliaries continued to canter noisily past. 'For me, should I live, I'll have much to set down!'

'Venus' arse! Not that bloody history of yours?' Cerialis shouted mockingly in return, turning his nervous horse full circle.

Straba felt with his fingers the priceless passport to freedom in his pouch. 'As you wisely say, sir,' he shouted above the din, as the departing Cerialis rode to the head of his depleted squadrons. *'It's that bloody history!'*

EIGHTY-ONE

HE SAT THE ARMENIAN HORSE, FLAVIA, as they waited on the edge of open woodland, time measuring an eternity in the mind. At Armet's back, tucked into the shadows, stretched several thousand men, including the four hundred riders of what was once the brief pride of Quintus Cerialis' cavalry, Armet's' Exploratores; all part of a sworn alliance of nations set against him.

The bulk of the host, some of them Batavi, Paulinus' bane on the march to Mona, left with little to lose, continued to take up their positions on both sides of the forest-lined road that led to Verulamium. According to a bloodstained and breathless Iceni scout, Catus Decianus' seat of power was in the process of being overrun by a combined force of Iceni and Adomarus' Triinovante's, with Boudiga at the head, as the vengeful queen had earlier promised Gort. The hunt for the overweight procurator's whereabouts had so far been unsuccessful.

As for the wayward Gort, he'd ridden north, part of a strategy adopted by Boudiga, to make his peace with a newly declared enemy of Rome, his brother, prince Armet. The news that Fomah of the Cornovii would enter the scene to annoy the Roman advance as they left Lindum behind, was heartening. The Iceni queen's plan for the south and a meeting up with the forces of Paulinus, fast drawn up with determination, was now exacerbated by the many thousands of fighting men arriving daily, eager to rally behind her battle emblem, a strength more than sufficient to overcome by far, any serious opposition the embattled Paulinus might present. Concerning Cerialis, the presence of Armet and a combined alliance of several nations barring his approach, would prove to be of the greatest assistance.

'I'm relieved that you've put things right with the prince,' Boudiga said in parting, putting her suspicions of Armet behind her. 'He'll be needing you.'

'He's never listened to me before,' Gort had replied sardonically, 'until now!'

'Because of the love he bears Volisios,' said Boudiga, 'his love has long been torn, two ways.'

Gort nodded, 'My regard is as great as his, and since our recent meeting we are now as reconciled as can be. He arose to tighten his sword belt. 'It's time,' he said with finality.

'I see you drive no chariot,' the queen remarked. 'Has all your training gone to waste?'

'You know of Vixt?' Gort asked, surprised.

'I know of you and Mogonus' champion, yes.'

'I'm out of sorts, you know it takes time to work up a good team. Such luxury is denied me.'

Boudiga's lips hinted at a smile. 'Take one of mine.'

Gort shook his head, though his heart beat the faster at the offer. 'I won't know the warrior I'd be carrying,' he excused himself. 'Most of all, I'd be a stranger to the ponies.'

'Remember,' Boudiga whispered later, taking the youth aside. 'You and prince Armet must halt Cerialis. Many are relying on the Coritani cavalry to stop Lindum's cohorts ever reaching Paulinus. It's your destiny. Should the legate be allowed to pass this point,' she tapped the rudely drawn map with a beringed finger, 'it will be all the tougher. I trust neither you, nor Armet, will fail.'

Events were fast shifting. The injured Volisios and those that so wished, moved west of Rina by some miles amid thickly forested tracts of king Tadoc's land, putting a safe distance between them and the increased Roman activity which seemed to conjure itself up magically from nowhere. An obvious precaution, given the unpredictability. Leaving Venovia, Armet, accompanied by Gela, still stubbornly refusing to be left behind, plus as many horsemen as could be picked up enroute, rode fast. Sometime after dawn the two brothers first rearranged their forces into fighting order. At the spot chosen, an area of sparse woodland straddling the road on both sides of the North Way, deemed suitable for their purpose, they mentally counted the hours.

The army of Suetonius Paulinus was making better progress. Fifteen thousand seasoned troops had been moved south from a gutted Mona at unmatched speed. What terrible things had taken place at the sacred sites on Anglesey were for some still obscure, and the stories of the horror remained hard to swallow. Greater threats perhaps were to be faced, prompting watch fires to be laid, ready to signal their message to neighbouring nations and beyond.

Armet, sitting Flavia under the still silence of the trees, was deeply conscious of the tension building behind him. This was a world turned upside down, an unfamiliar feeling that made the heart beat the faster while waiting for what was sure to come, the arrival of his one-time acquaintance, Quintus Cerialis. His equites now rapidly approaching despite desperate local opposition, were edging ever closer. Narrowing the gap separating him from Rufus Lippa and the five cohorts, it was only a matter of time before both groups merged.

The waiting prince was under no illusion as to what might be the fate of the Coritani, if they were at the mercy of a now revengeful Rome with scores to settle, should they lose in the coming struggle. Would history repeat itself; would Britons suffer the same dreadful punishment meted out to the neighbouring Gaul's by Julius Caesar after his war with its legendary king, Vercingetorix?

EIGHTY-TWO

AT FIRST HAND, ARMET knew the odds that a newly formed confederacy of nations would be faced with. Could it be that these quirks of fate might help to redress an unequal balance? If Rome had taught him little else, it had certainly made him aware of its fighting capabilities. He considered what he knew of their tactics, their strengths, their weaknesses. A legion in the open had to be seriously respected, having been proved time and time again to an enemy's cost. Unrestrained, Rome would usually emerge the master. Forced to fight in enclosed spaces however, with lack of movement severely curtailed, made for a levelling of sorts, and could be Armet's ally. Yet only one thing was certain, any thought of easy victory for either contender was dealing in fantasy.

Though no man following the prince voiced his thoughts, they likely mirrored his own. All talk had diminished, along with the oat cakes and rough beer that made for a hasty breakfast, and any man's thoughts dwelling on the future would likely remain his own. Yet enforced idleness now endured by the waiting horsemen, being out of character, gave many a time to tighten a saddle-girth, here, put right a slack harness, there, anything to ease the nervousness of waiting. Beneath these spreading branches of woodland oak others made supplication to Tiranis, Astarte, Epona and other powerful deities of war.

But news from another place gave cause for much hope, and Armet received with relief the welcome tidings that Fomah continued to greatly annoy the advancing cohorts of Hispania, meaning their strength could be seriously weakened by the time any succeeded in joining Cerialis.

For Armet's massed cavalry, time seemed to crawl at a snail's pace. A bridle jingled somewhere amid the trees. In the oppressive silence it seemed almost deafening. Flavia's ears pricked up on any unnatural sound, and he fell to calming the sensitive beast with a gentle stroke of the hand. 'Whatever happens this day Flavia, keep me upright,' he whispered. At the familiar sound of his voice her nostrils flared, as if sensing the action to come, while her hooves pawed at the earth with growing impatience.

A pale morning sun shone grudgingly down on the woodland track, the recently repaired road at this point linking north to south. Armet eyed a cluster of rooks wheeling, death black against the canopy of a cloudless summer sky as they rose above him. A solitary rider then appeared from nowhere, to rein in at the prince's knee. His tousled hair fell untidily over cloaked shoulders, for he wore no helm. In his right hand he bore an insignia captured from one of Cerialis' auxiliary cavalry units, the sharp point of which the rider drove triumphantly into the earth.

'Your first Roman emblem, brother! Next, I'll bring you an 'eagle'!'

He saw the look of surprise on Armet's face as he recognised the image of an unchained mastiff gracing the standard planted in the turf. 'We caught them on the road,' Gort said, excitedly, 'maybe two hundred of the bastards!' He quickly glanced about him, searchingly. 'Did you...........?'

'Yes, Dasal has the disc, and never was a man more elated. He's gone ahead with a squadron of Exploratores.'

Gort eyed Armet, quizzingly. 'Why?'

'It's what he requested,' Armet smiled. I suspect he wants to redeem himself over Tove, and other things. I surely wouldn't wish to be in the boots of the first adversary unlucky enough to block his path.'

Gort curtly nodded approval before violently tugging the standard from the earth, delivering it proudly into Armet's free hand.

Armet knew by its emblem, the meaning of the insignia Gort had taken. Ironically, it belonged to Petra's Horse; recently reformed and reassigned to Cerialis' Hispanics! The Fates were indeed decidedly unfathomable, and the prince recalled the business of Lucidius Salva, the very first victim to fall to the now depleted Abrentii, in the days of uncertainty before Dorona.

A second rider appeared, the new bearer of the wolf-head stave, its heavy tails swinging. 'There are others on the way!' informed Cartivel, breathlessly. 'We couldn't count just how many squadrons, about five miles back,' the youth gasped, 'he's got infantry moving to join him, at least one cohort! They must have travelled at speed to catch up with the legate. Could be slingers, though, their known to be tireless runners!'

Armet knew Cerialis well enough to realise, for a fact, that the legate would never rely entirely on cavalry alone, not without infantry back-up. It wasn't his way. Another fact, the cohorts under Lippa were, at best, a further day's march away. So, from where had these unexpected foot-soldiers materialised? He must have drained half the way-forts between here and Lindum in order to enlist these ghostly reinforcements, calculated the prince. Typical of the legate, to conjure up the unexpected! Yet there was one other bit of good news to counter the bad, Fomah's cavalry were speedily moving in the prince's direction, meaning they would most likely be the first to encounter this mixture of untried garrison troops.

The day we've waited for,' Gort declared, proudly, breaking Armet's thoughts. 'There can be no turning away, not now.'

Armet agreed. 'No turning away.'

Gort closed a sweaty hand over the bronze pommel of his sword. He turned his mount, stared over the rim of the round shield, gazing up the, for now, empty road. He returned his brother's gaze.

'You are not afraid?' Armet asked.

'No,' Gort stammered. Yet the fear of his familiar curse, more frightening than any Roman army could conjure up, hovered darky, forcing him to grip the reins of the horse tightly while muttering a silent placation, throwing in an added plea, enlisting the shade of his uncle Culchul to protect him, for good measure.

This was the only way it could be, in the end, thought Armet. Nothing else mattered a bead. The sword had been too far drawn from the sheath to change the shape of things, and the elder son of Volisios, sharply aware of the price all would pay for failure, could hardly ignore such a thought.

The distant groan of a war horn carried on the air, a draconian sound coming from a growingly frustrated killing machine. Armet, with a final eye to eye glance at Gort, passed the captured banner of Petra to another then, digging his heels into Flavia's jet flanks, he moved his impatient riders, led by the remaining Exploratores, towards the might of Rome.

EIGHTY-THREE

THE MORNING OF THE THIRD DAY of Cerialis' southward progress would mark the culmination of something Rome thought would never happen, a day when men who experienced it first used the term, *death road*. Servilus, still suffering visibly from the previous day's fighting in the forest, never feeling more weary or vulnerable, thought what many others could now be thinking. The squadrons of horse the legate had promised to shadow them would have helped, had they been sufficient in strength. As it was, they were never going to add up to much, being far too widely spaced to protect little more than the lucky few.

The struggle was to gather in intensity during the following twenty-four hours as thousands from the diverse Keltic nations sought to slow the onward progress of Cerialis' five cohorts along the route dictated, forcing the overstretched units of Roman foot to struggle for every blood-soaked mile, yielding little, giving less. Under almost constant attack, with the zealous Fomah at their head, men appeared, then as quickly vanished, advancing then retreating into the cover of tangled gorse, bracken and woodland. This, despite the feverish attempt by Roman pioneers to cull back nature a distance of thirty feet either side of the imperial way, a detail which would account for suffering even more casualties than had once been anticipated. Later that afternoon others travelling from further afield, having received news of the success of Fomah and his combined force of Cornovii and Coritani, hastened to join the fray. Ordovices, Dubunni, even a warband of fanatical Silures from the west, bane of Poenius' 2nd Augusta, were continuously arriving, ready to throw themselves into the melee.

The further Hispania marched, the greater the opposition. Unlucky wayside settlements and villages within reach were now put to the torch, either ignited by legionaries or their determined foes. All livestock that may have been of use to the Romans were either driven away or slaughtered on the spot, leaving many heaps of carcasses to burn with the impartial aid of a surprisingly ferocious wind-blown conflagration destroying vital fields of their future harvest.

At certain periods, combined groups of legionaries and auxilia, brought to a standstill at point after point along the line of march, were forced to form yet another shield-square, while around them the harsh thunder of bronze, iron and bull-hide clashed unrelentingly. These enforced tactics grew heavier with every daylight hour as superiority in numbers threatened several times to overwhelm the Roman advance. Only legionary discipline, coupled with the natural urge to stay alive, kept men from yielding, knowing full well what a terrible end would be theirs if captured.

It was glaringly obvious to even the least experienced trooper under Cerialis' command, just what tactics the Briton's were using. Rather than risk all in challenging a heavily armed adversary in a risky face-to-face, they chose rather to make damaging probes in places where their foes were likely to be most encumbered by natures obstacles, bogs, dense vegetation, woodland, of which there was plenty. In so doing they put others unfamiliar with the terrain under immense pressure, enough at least to make a solid defence well-nigh impossible.

It also became abundantly clear that the encounters undertaken by Cerialis and the Hispanics could in no way be described as resembling a battle. More accurately it became a series of confusing engagements occurring at various points along the distance of one-hundred and thirty miles that separated Lindum from the prospering southern town of Verulamium.

Prominently, out of countless settlements and villages destined to suffer destruction along the bloody route, the Coritani capital seemed largely to have escaped attention. Elsewhere, settlements not put to the flame by the Britons own scorched-earth strategy, were soon being laid waste by a combination of headstrong Roman vindictiveness and determination, Yet, amid all this mayhem, king Volisios' Rina remained almost untouched.

Some might later see this as a guilty acknowledgement on Cerialis' part for imprudently ordering the deaths of the ill-used Machai five. More likely, given his anxiety to join Paulinus, he'd neither time nor inclination to slow the pace of the cavalry's advance, pausing only briefly to take down the hanging bodies of two score Thracian auxiliaries eliminated by prince Armet's men while attempting to defend the burnt-out wreckage of their fort; pitiful remains of a tiny garrison once serving as watchdog over the Coritani capital.

Thus, a deliberate and unrelenting play to wear down the alien machine was put into action by the combined powers of Armet's people and their Cornovii allies led by Fomah, plus warriors from other nations assembling along the now desperately hard-fought route. With the fighting growing increasingly savage, the closer the Hispanics approached Paulinus' rendezvous, the more notable the gaps. Legionary stragglers losing touch with their comrades, became perilously isolated, with several units, including Servilus' own, all finding themselves victim to an overwhelming tide of hostility.

His face bruised and awash with sweat, his scratched left arm from the barb fast numbing beneath the weight of his shield, the recruit struggled with his remaining comrades under bombardment from volley after volley of missiles, an irritation which only eased when close-quarter fighting resumed, and when the Keltoi renewed the assault; tactics repeated over many miles along the way, the gradual wearing down of Cerialis' troops by a fanatical enemy rarely before encountered. In all this fraught confusion, the recruit's shrinking century, failing to ward off the enemy, became separated from the rest of their cohort yet again.

Lifting his gaze, it was immediately clear to Servilus that they were stumbling blindly through yet another village of burning huts. Surrounded by a foe not short of well-aimed fire power, deadly showers of sling shot and arrows buzzing like swarms of angry hornets, striking out at anyone unlucky enough to cross their aim of fire, they stumbled on. Vague shapes retreated before them amid flame and smoke from burning thatch, wattle and daub, that together the scene resembled a wild inferno. Limping beside Servilus, Philo cursed and crumpled, swearing at the arrow that found his thigh. Without stopping, the recruit was swept ahead by the momentum and collided with a careering flash of iron, bronze and tartan that zig zagged fleetingly across his vision. A metal-ringed arm swept above his head, the force of the blow half cleaving his helm. Here the spear's iron tip made violent contact, causing the recruit to buckle instinctively. He felt the weapon's tip pierce his right leg while, with one continual flow of invective, he thrust blindly with the gladius.

A russet arc of cloaks hurried between the huts, herding both men and women, trapping them, forcing them into a defensive circle. Servilus was surprised by how few, maybe only several score, still chose to defend the ruins of their homes. Then again, he thought, there was little mercy to be found. Centurion Iber, not seen since the day before in the forest, now suddenly alive, bellowing and cursing as of old, paused only long enough to draw breath before commanding the immediate killing of any survivors. For the first time, men paused, looking to the replacement centurion, decurion Orneo. Their hesitance was unsurprising, as what Iber had been no longer existed. Instead, a madman had taken possession, a prancing, dancing maniac, leaping and gibbering before them, unarmed save for the blooded axe he'd employed in his earlier butchery.

Servilus stood by for a few seconds as he witnessed Orneo plunge the gladius deep in Iber's stomach with sustained vindictiveness. Holding the weapon firmly he violently twisted its blade several times before wrenching the blade away. Iber, bane of the recruit and hated by others of his century, screamed in agony as he fell heavily to the earth, clutching his escaping gut. 'A gift from all of us!' he shouted, grinning with obvious satisfaction, wiping the gore from the blade with the hem of an already blood-soaked scarf while he ran to regain the questionable safety of the slow-moving column. There was no knowing how many of Servilus' comrades lay dead or mutilated behind him. Despite all the mayhem though, the recruit drew satisfaction from the knowledge that he'd seen the very last of the sadistic slave-driving centurion.

There were many such scenes to come, slaughter being the name of the game. Orders of the day were the same as the day before and the day before that. Any individual seen flinching from duty was to be marked down for the severest of imperial punishments, and every serving foot slogger in the Hispanics knew what *that sodding well meant!*

The boy from Tarraco, seeing the half-conscious Philo slowly crawling, tortoise-like, on his stomach, stooped and hefted his comrade over one aching shoulder. Heedless of his own discomfort, he began carrying the wounded legionary in the vague direction taken by the contuburnium. Very soon, weighed down by his burden, with his body buckling under stress, he helplessly stumbled, then fell. Giving himself a few moments to recover, he stupidly realised that for all his efforts during the past few minutes, he'd been carrying a dead man. He should have looked more closely at Philo and seen that one half of his friend's face was nothing more than a congealing mess of blood and bone. Cursing silently, he clambered to his feet, leaving the body of the professional pessimist amid the burning huts, going in hopeful search for Glabas, Verres and others of his small group perhaps still alive amid the surrounding chaos.

Mercifully by then, almost abruptly, day gave way to night and the enemy withdrew. A makeshift semblance of order was miraculously brought to bear while Servilus's cohort carried out a roll call, attempting to count losses which, with the absence of so many faces, was abundantly clear. Almost half the century was dead or missing, the latter meaning basically the same thing under such dire circumstances. Later, heavy rain began to plague the uncomfortable survivors, penetrating cloak and armour to the skin. Thus ended the third day of the southward progress of Cerialis' trailing infantry command.

EIGHTY-FOUR

CERIALIS, GATHERING AS MANY of his scattered squadrons as could be contacted, made one last effort to break through those guarding the vital way south. At daylight, with barely twenty miles distance separating him from Paulinus, or so he mistakenly thought, the Roman cavalry broke like a wave against Armet's riders, with his four hundred Exploratores to the fore. The low southern hills around soon would be witness to the desperate clash of cavalry as both forces collided head-on.

What little order there'd been between the adversaries soon evaporated in the hand-to-hand struggle that followed, rider being pitted against rider. Cerialis, with the protection of a few trusted equites, searched in vain for the tell-tale wolf-head banner that would denote the presence of Armet. At the same time, hacking a path through the mass of wheeling horses vying to clear suitable space in which to use their weapons, the prince tugged hard on Flavia's bridle and circled the battlefield, staving off attacks from all sides as he too sought personal satisfaction. It was during these fraught moments that Tadoc's son and Gela's brother Fomah, having ridden hard with a few followers, leaving several trusted leaders to complete the roll-up of the Roman carpet, met his end, lifted bodily from the saddle after fiercely fending off the probing lances of a group of Tungrian riders, their weapons at last succeeding in skewering him to the ground. It was there that he died, only a short distance along the road from Armet, his exposed body trampled and mangled by the hooves of a turma of horse.

For several bloody hours the bitter contest raged unabated before the two commanders inevitably clashed swords, an unspoken moment of recognition for both. Yet fate intervened as a distant Roman horn blew a series of short blasts, a forlorn signal for the legate's remaining squadrons to regroup as a frustrated Armet broke away. Cerialis, bloodied and cast down, swore the oath of oaths as what he dreaded most of all, began to look inevitable.

His men had given all they had against the overwhelming weight of the enemy and the losses suffered were enough to accept a reluctant knowledge that he'd failed on all counts, especially in his arrogance when underestimating the prowess of this conglomerate of Britons. All that could be done now was retire to the fort from where he'd ridden the day before, there to await the arrival of his desperately needed cohorts and auxilia, the only force this side of Verulamium strong enough to stem the tide of rebellion.

As it was, Quintus Cerialis lived on false hopes. Of the five cohorts advancing on Verulamium, three continued to move as best they may, continuously slowed by superior numbers. The remaining two found themselves completely bogged down some twenty miles to the north, at the only junction yet built on the via Claudius, an open space which to the relief of its legionaries, allowed deployment. There they stubbornly held out behind a wall of shields, fully aware of any rations and water they carried in their near empty pouches would very soon run out.

All units battled on under sporadic assault from ever-present groups of mounted archers, who, riding back and forth, did serious damage to the ranks of the overwhelmed legionaries. This was the worst part for many, having to leave behind those suffering debilitating wounds which could no longer be treated. It meant each man was laden with a burden no soldier would want. Either to dispatch a suffering comrade or leave him facing agonising death at the hands of a merciless and vengeful enemy. All in all, the legionary force was stretched, long mile by long mile as the gap between each command became hopelessly distant.

Servilus from Tarraco, experienced the nightmare ordeal with as much stoicism as could still be mustered. The wound he'd received was not a serious one, yet it irritated the inflamed skin as if under attack from a grudging swarm of insects. Leaving behind him the body of Philo, and filching bread from the pouch of another dead comrade, he stumbled blindly on through the billowing smoke and fire rising from countless burning fields and native dwellings, a harrowing sight stretching behind him for many miles. It made the farmer in him instantly melancholy, for there'd be little harvest to be gleaned from the land this summer, meaning the future risk of starvation for those who might survive the present slaughter.

Straba the scribe unknowingly walked almost the same path having, twenty- four hours before, decided to make his escape not only from a possibly doomed unit, but also from a decidedly nervous Rufus Lippa. The moonless night had helped conceal him. Coupled with the enemy having conveniently retired from the scene, and being encouraged unexpectedly by the words of senior centurion Aubanus, the scribe crawled away under the eyes of those guarding the perimeter, pausing only to relieve a dead Briton of his blood-soiled tartan breeches and plaid shirt and slipped silently away into the welcome cover provided by the dense undergrowth.

So far, since leaving the colonia, he'd found scant time to record much that he'd been a witness to during these past few days of insanity and bloodshed, and this began to vex him constantly. After all, what was his purpose otherwise, if not to set down events as they happened? It was a question he would put to himself on an hourly basis.

EIGHTY-FIVE

LEADING THE FIRST tired squadrons of hard riding equites and other units of horse into a very much awake Portus Londinium, much later than intended, supreme legate Suetonius Paulinus, Britannia's governor, was met by a sea of hopeful faces amid a rising barrage of questions as to protection and deliverance from any possible tribulation to come. Conveyed in tongues hailing from many lands, the obviously frightened inhabitants weirdly produced an oral prediction of what would swiftly assume a sign of utter helplessness.

In an office of the newly erected basilica, so new that the painted frescoes on the walls weren't yet dry, the supreme legate took stock. Not only had Postumus' 2nd Augusta failed him, now he received information that Quintus Cerialis had apparently suffered a major set-back on his way south, so much so that he'd been obliged to organise an ignominious withdrawal with what was left of his command. Along the route he'd also received unconfirmed news from secondus Aquilla. Apparently the undermanned colonia was facing a threat from marauding Brigantes. Whether the force belonged to queen Cartimandua's faction or that of Venutius, had yet to be determined.

The situation had become nakedly clear to Paulinus. There would be no help now from any quarter within the rebellious province, especially from the one man he trusted above all others. The plan he'd arranged with Cerialis to rendezvous with him at Verulamium while on the march, now resembled a sick joke. He listened tight lipped with irritation to the few remaining dignitaries in the town. These fresh tidings couldn't have been more direct. Camulodunum, according to a reliable source, was now nothing more than a burning pyre, a place of slaughter. The supreme legate selfishly considered whether Catus Decianus was one of the slain, praying for good measure that it wasn't so, having his own particular method of torment in store for the procurator if ever the fat fool fell into his hands.

Like king Obrig's capital and other growing settlements, such was the confidence injected by the imperial powers, protective defences for the town had been discussed several times, but never finalised, a glaring oversight too lately presenting itself. From Rome's point of view, such negligence was now more than regrettable. Paulinus, having looked hard at the present situation, quickly concluded that any defence of the port was totally impossible if attacked. Evacuation was then urged but the civilian population, both Roman and cooperative Briton, was too sizable for such a possibility. And where would such a large party of poorly armed civilians proceed within a countryside fast becoming overrun by warlike bands of ferocious and revengeful hunters? Those fortunate enough to board a ship had already departed, leaving behind an almost empty quayside.

At this stage Londinium, unlike Lindum, was not a colonia, although it was fast outgrowing every other town in the province in terms of commerce and wealth, a tempting prize for anyone strong enough to take it. Unfortunately for its inhabitants, the rebels were more bent on retribution for past injustices than booty.

Paulinus' weary cavalry units, largely made up of Thracian and Tungrian auxiliaries, good as they were in combat, without strong infantry support, were not equipped to deal with the unstoppable tide threatening to engulf the port. This thought was all the more disconcerting when added to the sobering fact that many units of legions Valeria and Gemina remained at least a day's march distant.

A military man to his fingertips, Britannia's governor now made a very military decision. He'd turn the cavalry north, leaving Londinium to its fate, in order to meet with legate Roscius of Gemina and Valeria's newly promoted Arius Longa, the disgraced legate Balbilus' recent replacement, as soon as possible. Those inhabitants of fighting age in the town could choose to retreat with the equites and the rest of the cavalry, provided they had the strength, weapons and means to keep up. All others should seek any way of escape remaining open to them, which meant the majority, women, children and the elderly, would have to lie low, pray to the gods and take their chances.

The scenes of his departure from Londinium weren't pretty. Many of his riders, long bladed spatha in hand, hemmed in on all sides, fell to carving a path through the frantic mob of despairing humanity who, quickly realising they were being cast aside, attempted by any means possible to impede the governor's departure from the threatened port, many desperate souls pulling at the reins of the horses in a futile attempt to bring down both man and beast as they struggled to cut a way through the screaming mass of civilians, bloodily killing and wounding many who'd carried a hopeful thought that these seasoned troops were there to protect them.

So, in this bloody and disorderly manner Paulinus hastily retreated from Portus Londinium, at some point along the march trusting to meet up with his battered legions. Running out of options, vastly outnumbered as he was, all his strength would now be aimed at the one final goal, the only one that mattered, the defeat of an inferior enemy, decisively, upon a battlefield of *his* choosing.

Sitting in his favourite chair in the re-erected pavilion, Paulinus read these vexing stories with mixed feelings. His agile mind turned again on the hated procurator, Catus Decianus. What might be happening to him, now that the tables were turned? He fell to thinking what these savages might do with this fat lump of lard if, praise the almighty gods, he fell into heathen hands. Impalement, dismemberment, eye-gouging perhaps? Much as Paulinus relished these scenes, however unlikely, they would deprive him of his own ideas of revenge. Pulled apart by two wild beasts perhaps, or an upside-down crucifixion. One way or another he'd settle accounts, should he be so lucky.

The rebel force, growing in number, would soon focus its venom upon Londinium while, after many days of a brutal march from Mona, legions Gemina and Valeria were in no reasonable condition to engage. When finally he met with them, weighing up the situation, he was left with only one choice, a tactical withdrawal back to the threatened port he'd so hurriedly left only a short time ago. Reacting as only a clever tactician would, making the best of a dire situation, he assigned a strong rear-guard from Gemina, under command of its tough legate Marcus Roscius, giving him orders to hold off the leading elements in the rebel advance for as long as possible, screening the bulk of the task force as they fell back and regrouped. On the retreat Paulinus personally supervised a course of rigorous training, never before seen on the march, transforming his weary army into hardened automatons, honed enough to take on all adversity. Given a week, thought those who best knew him, and he'd turn the army of province Britannia into a deadly killing mechanism, feared like no other.

EIGHTY-SIX

THE ROAD OF THE DEAD. Aptly named, for the distance over many miles along the way south, offered its own personal libation of corpses, Roman and Briton alike. No quarter asked, none given, was the terrible mantra obeyed on both sides. Not since the beginning of occupation eighteen years before had such bloody scenes of open retaliation against Roman oppression been witnessed in the province, yet the days of unbridled slaughter were to be merely the prelude to bloodier events.

319

The scribe, still greatly sickened by the many brutal sights he'd witnessed since leaving Lindum, never being quite certain as to where he was heading, wisely avoided the dangerous vicinity of the death road where possible, before cautiously venturing out at intervals along a route littered with the dead and dying of a desperate and thwarted army. Somewhere ahead he hoped to contact at least one of the hard-pressed cohorts concerned with eating up the distance. Yet it was only on the following morning that he realised he wouldn't have to search further. They instead, had found him.

'Good job you're on our side, slave,' a rough voice greeted him on his waking from a restless slumber. The familiarity of the decurion instantly told Straba he was among a group of men serving under the Hispanics. Obviously, tidings of his unexpected manumission hadn't yet come to the right ears, and he was immediately brought, somewhat roughly, before a concerned Rufus Lippa. 'Damn it all, not you, again!' he cursed. 'Don't tell me you've escaped another well-earned beating from the legate?'

Straba, aware of the dire situation further south, described as much as could be recalled from his earlier meeting with Cerialis,' underlining the legate's desperate reliance on the support of his cohorts, throwing in his new status as a freed man, for good measure. Rufus Lippa listened, openly incredulous. 'You're a madman, free or no. Just how long have you been going back and forth amid this damned mess?' He indicated the unburied corpses from both sides littering the ground. To this Straba could only give a weary shrug. 'Catch a nap,' Lippa advised, resignedly. 'We'll be moving out later, at the double!'

The argument over what had gone wrong, would be long contended. Two days before, fast-moving squadrons, a mixed assortment of both equites and various auxiliaries, cut off from their regular units, devouring distance, fought their way to regain the main column. Together, the struggling Roman cavalry suffered discomfort from the start, with knots of hostile elements keeping pace at a near distance either side of the road, matching speed for speed, archers picking off targets where they chose, stinging the

Roman horse again and again with scant cost to themselves. Soon, what should have been a face- on-face contest quickly resembled a long, drawn-out rout. It was perhaps only Cerialis' well-known reputation for being lucky, that his command had retained some outward semblance of cohesion under such constant and relentless harassment.

Struggling every perilous mile along the way, enough of the legate's cavalry remained a formidable force, though men welcomed the refuge offered in the form of the battered Roman fortress of Durogrivae, sitting plumb in the centre of prince Armet's territory. Here Cerialis raged and cursed fate while waiting for his mauled and scattered units to catch up, his advance for the moment halted by the largest concentration of enemy cavalry he'd ever thought to witness.

Trounced as the legate was, he had to hand it to the Coritani prince, once his confidant, now a vengeful enemy. How had it come about so rapidly under his watch? He admitted to two big mistakes. He should have guarded the loose Balbilus more carefully. Instead, he paid small heed to a man who'd made it all too plain how much he resented the younger man's higher status and regard. As for the subject of the five executed Exploratores, he now believed that in the heat of the moment, he'd perpetrated a far greater error.

Given a wider aspect, the whole province appeared to be undergoing a serious attack of madness, at least from the Roman angle. As for Cerialis' crack cohorts, a formidable force of Hispanics, two and a half thousand strong, best of the best. How would they fare now in this bitter dance of death with little support from their cavalry arm, depleted in number as was reported? Discipline was their hope, their creed, in the knowledge that as a fighting unit, they were second to none, a group of men whose dedication was primarily identified by one word. War! Filled with confidence, thought the legate, they would reckon themselves more than adequate to trounce any ragtag rabble sent against them, whatever the damn odds were.

Yet it still appeared, if Straba's thoughts meant anything, that the rash remedy dictated by Paulinus to alleviate his perilous situation had been dumped squarely on the shoulders of the Hispanics by its hastily promoted fourth-in-command, the unfortunate, Rufus Lippa.

EIGHTY-SEVEN

'**Y**OU ARE HURTING!'
'I'm alright,' Servilus gasping, swore heavily, 'I can't feel anything!' The reason why was soon obvious to the scribe, who saw the open gash across the recruit's belly, yet another victim of three disastrous days.

The very last person Straba expected to come across in this situation was the youngster from far-off Tarraco, yet he literally stumbled across Servilus someplace along the death road. Alone, both hands pressing vainly against his gut, he appeared as disorientated as the scribe, lying for dead, hidden among the bracken, probably the reason for the boy's survival. Servilus winced as he attempted a grin, propping up his body on one elbow. 'What the gods.........!'

'Straba slid from yet another stray horse to kneel, taking some of the recruit's weight on his aching thighs. Servilus coughed, bringing up blood. 'Easy legionary, easy,' the Greek breathed.

'The murdering bastards did for all my mates. Philo, Glabas,' the recruit coughed, 'every damn one of them. They even got old Verra in the end, poor sod.'

Straba only half listened. He'd learned enough about medicine to see the youth was in a bad way, a realm from which there was no recall. Remembering advice given him by Tsabo of Catania, both a friend and place that now existed in another world, if one felt no pain then that was a time for concern. Straba took a cursory glance, The major wound was taken in the worst of places, terminal, given the circumstances. The recruit, with what remnant of strength he possessed, covered his belly, compressing the area with bloody hands, desperation showing in his eyes. Straba, reliving for a split second the day when it all began, with the debacle of Petra's Horse, mumbled, 'I have no linens to bind you.'

'Don't fool me, scribbler,' muttered the lad from Tarraco, after a painful bout of coughing. 'We both know I'm buggered.'

Straba sat on the turf and took Servilus tighter in his arms. Around them, prince Armet's jubilant riders continually circled, noisily weaving, crossing and criss-crossing, terrifyingly close to where the two sat, both potential victims. Any minute could have been their last, but unknown to the Greek, a command had been put about, issued by prince Armet on pain of death, to spare the life of the scribe.

What he knew was only what his eyes could tell. Along his line of vision, what remained of Cerialis' doomed Hispanics continued to die under the overwhelming weight of the Britons continuous assaults. In spite of faultless discipline, all possibility of anything like an orderly withdrawal seemed denied to the men of Cerialis' command, as gradually they found themselves trapped in a vice, trampled singly or in groups beneath the random hooves of foam-flecked horses as the combined force of Coritani and Cornovii, moved in for kill after kill.

The carnage during what followed took place mainly because of a major misunderstanding at the core of command, many in the isolated ranks of the legionaries having not yet been informed of the recent Coritani defection from their years of cooperation with Cerialis, a fatal error for which they were to pay a heavy price as, when their mass of Keltoi cavalry presented itself, many onlookers naturally assumed the riders to be on their side. Too late, they were callously ridden down.

With the triumphant Britons holding the advantage, the final carnage was unleashed, as years of resentment, a sense of being captive in their own lands and burdened by the yoke of Rome, came to its terrible conclusion. There was little mercy, and there would be none in the coming days as the rebellion, now under the leadership of the red-headed Iceni queen, gathered momentum further south, persuaded by the reality that the legions could be beaten, an impossible probability only days before.

The mounted circle of Coritani that swirled about Straba and the stricken Servilus now closed-in menacingly. The stricken recruit, still coughing blood, was all but oblivious to the massacre taking place around them both. The scribe uselessly wiped the youth's chin with the blood-soaked piece of rag.

Just how long the two sat clasped together, one dying, the other feeling as if he were about to, Straba couldn't recall. What he would remember to his dying day was the whirligig of riders parting the way for two triumphant horsemen, who reined in before them. On their appearance, Straba held Servilus the tighter. The first figure, flamboyant in manner, the scribe assumed from earlier overheard descriptions of the maverick, must be none other than Armet's brother, Gort. The second figure, Cartivel, held aloft the feared Coritani emblem, the wolf-head stave displaying eight tails, their added numbers denoting 'no quarter'. Nailed to its top sat the blooded head once belonging to Rufus Lippa. Both men now sat their horses menacingly, in silence, their eyes cold and piercing. Gort nudged his mount further forward. Straba, shifting Servilus, grabbed the recruit's gladius and drew his own as he stood. With two deadly weapons in hand, he prepared himself for death.

'I'm surprised your master left you unguarded, scribe,' spoke the familiar voice of Armet, suddenly reining in at Gort's side. The right hand of the prince held aloft a precious prize, a battle standard bearing the unmistakable bronze insignia of the sacred Roman eagle of legion Hispania. Straba instantly recognised the coveted emblem, having seen it many times before, lodged in pride of place within Lindum praetorium's inner sanctum. This indeed was unexpected. How the proud legate must have fought, in vain it now seemed, to retain its possession, could only be imagined. For such a person, one equipped to overcome most human adversities, the loss of the battle standard would be a humiliation not to be lived with. The question remained, when would Cerialis retrieve this sacred object? Knowing the legate as well as he did, Straba suspected it wouldn't be too long before the vengeful Roman began to scour the entire province for the stealer of his eagle, should he survive his defeat.

Accompanying the prince, the fair-haired Gela, green cloaked and blue eyed, a blood-tipped spear clutched tightly in her slim hand, sat comfortably on a rugged looking pony, its flanks still heaving while its companion, the horse Flavia, restless and blood-splattered, stood majestic, head held high, her wild eyes glaring defiance.

'Why are you hesitating over this poor wretch?' Gela's soft voice belied her now.

'Because this man is Straba, scribe to Cerialis, who lately served with our Exploratores at Dorona, now my friend.' Armet stared down at the Greek. 'I must confess, you look much tougher now.'

'How did you know where to find me?' asked Straba.

'How did I not,' Armet replied. 'Knowing your reputation, where else would Cerialis' slave be?'

'I serve the legate no longer, prince,' Straba said, rising shakily to his feet to advance, both swords gripped tightly. 'Not him, not anyone!'

At least we taught you well, scribe,' remarked Armet, half smiling while giving the nod to the pair of wavering blades. 'Cerialis was wise to release you. No more floggings, no more punishments.'

'Before you knew me, prince, I recklessly slew a small child by default,' Straba said accusingly. 'From that day, I vowed never to use weapons again. At Dorona you made me break that promise.'

'Then I trust nobody will have the courage to call you fool again.'

'I'll probably remain foolish in this maddest of worlds, prince, I find it's safer that way.'

'Then make sure you stay a live fool, scribe. Who knows, perhaps one day I might have need of you again.'

That was all. Armet, Gort, Gela, Cartivel the signifer, forever Epona's children, bearing the captured Roman eagle aloft, in an instant were gone, swallowed up by a swirl of shapes belonging to the prince's victorious horsemen, among them the Exploratores. In a few moments all noise of strife ceased, and it seemed that Straba and the recruit were the last beings left alive in the world.

'Scribbler?' Straba had momentarily forgotten the recruit lying where he'd left him, almost oblivious now as to the dread surroundings. 'When you finish your bleedin' history,' he gasped, his voice failing, 'will *I* be a part of it?'

'We'll *all* be a part, soldier,' Straba sighed, partly relieved, partly in sorrow as he threw aside his weapons to clasp tight the hand of a semi-conscious Servilus, cradling the recruit by the shoulders as he would an ailing child. 'Given half a chance I'll make damn sure of it,' he spat into the sullied earth, 'for you, for every last stupid one of us!'

FIN

LIST OF FACTUAL CHARACTERS

ROMANS

Nero Claudius Caesar Augustus Germanicus. Roman Emperor.
54-68 AD.
Took own life.

Suetonius Paulinus. Supreme governor of Britannia.
Replaced in AD 62, by the
more conciliatory, Publius Turpillanus

Quintus Cerialis. Commander of Ninth legion, Hispania,
Founder of Eboracum, later York, in AD 71.

Julius Agricola. Tribune and secretary to Paulinus.
Became governor of province in AD 77.

Catus Decianus. Roman administrator.
Fate unknown.

BRITONS

Volisios. King of the midland Coritani.
Fate unknown.

Cartimandua. Queen of Brigante.
Fate unknown.

Vellocatus. Favourite of Cartimandua,
Later husband. Fate unknown.

Venutius. Ex-husband to Cartimandua.
Fought two wars against her and
continued to fight Rome for a further 8 years,
after failure of Great Rebellion.

Boudiga. Queen of the Iceni.
Fate unknown.

MAJOR ROMAN
SETTLEMENTS
AND BRITISH
EQUIVALENTS

ROMAN	BRITISH
Camulodunum	Colchester
Crococalana	Brough
Deva	Chester
Durobrivae	Water Newton
Glevum	Gloucester
Lindum	Lincoln
Londinium	London
Ratae	Leicester
Segelocum	Littleborough
Venta Icenorum	Caistor St Edmund (site of Iceni capital)
Verulamium	St Albans

EPILOGUE

Although heavily outnumbered, Roman discipline prevailed, and in the final battle in 61 AD, the site of which is unknown, Boudiga's army was defeated.

Imperial rule was to continue until 410 AD, when their legions were withdrawn to defend Rome against invading Goths.

*

www.ingramcontent.com/pod-product-compliance
Lightning Source LLC
Chambersburg PA
CBHW021942170626
46808CB00001B/4